PEARL CITY

Tor Books by Julia Vee and Ken Bebelle

THE PHOENIX HOARD

Ebony Gate

Blood Jade

Pearl City

PEARL CITY

The Phoenix Hoard, Book 3

JULIA VEE
and
KEN BEBELLE

TOR PUBLISHING GROUP
NEW YORK

This is a work of fiction. All of the characters, organizations, and events portrayed in this novel are either products of the authors' imaginations or are used fictitiously.

PEARL CITY

A Tor Book
Published by Tom Doherty Associates / Tor Publishing Group
120 Broadway
New York, NY 10271

www.torpublishinggroup.com

EU Representative: Macmillan Publishers Ireland Ltd, 1st Floor, The Liffey Trust Centre, 117–126 Sheriff Street Upper, Dublin 1, DO1 YC43

The Library of Congress Cataloging-in-Publication Data is available upon request.

ISBN 978-1-250-83796-7 (hardcover)
ISBN 978-1-250-83795-0 (ebook)

First Edition: 2025

Printed in the United States of America

10 9 8 7 6 5 4 3 2 1

For Ken, Caleb, and JJ.
You're my favorite.
—Julia

For my family.
Thank you for coming with me to conventions
and visiting bookstores on every trip
we've taken in the last five years.
—Ken

CAST OF CHARACTERS

SOONG CLAN

Emiko Soong—elder daughter of Soong Clan, unknown talent, former Blade of Soong, also known as the Butcher of Beijing, current Sentinel of San Francisco, possibly the Empty One prophesied in the ancient poem "The Flood"

Bāo—Emiko's foo lion companion, an inanimate jade pendant that she can bring to life using a reserve of her father's talent, enjoys napping under sunny windows

Tatsuya Soong—gāo-level animator, younger son of Soong Clan, recently survived his Tourney, finishing second after his best friend, Minjae

Sara Hiroto—gāo-level dark walker, mother to Emiko and Tatsuya, member of Bā Shǒu, also known as the Walker of the Void

Soong Zhènmíng—gāo-level animator, father to Emiko and Tatsuya, member of Bā Tóu

Sugi—Zhènmíng's constant companion, an animated Hokkaido wolf constructed out of Japanese cedar tiles, eats acorns

Kaida—Emilio's and Tatsuya's cousin by their mother's brother, gāo-level dark walker, a member of the Jōkōryūkai, currently incarcerated in Mohe, Jiārén prison in the northern tundra

SOONG HOUSEHOLD

Fujita-san—Soong Zhènmíng's majordomo, píng-level beast speaker

Uncle Lau—a general of Soong House, gāo-level grasshopper limbs, leader of the Iron Fists

Kubota-san—a general of Soong House, leader of the Pearl Guard

Uncle Jake—gāo-level kinetic who uses his talent as a cook for the Soong House soldiers

Lulu Āyí—gāo-level plant master, tends the grounds of Soong Clan home

Yoko-obaachan—gāo-level dragon healer, Soong House medic

RESIDENTS OF SAN FRANCISCO

TRAN CLAN

Fiona Tran—head of house in San Francisco, gāo-level wind talent

Freddy Tran—Fiona's twin brother, gāo-level wind talent, currently not involved in clan affairs

Franklin—Fiona's personal bodyguard, deceased

Willy—Fiona's majordomo

Linh—Fiona and Freddy's cousin, head of Tran security

LOUIE CLAN

"Dai Lou" Louie—elder patriarch of the Louie Clan, not involved in clan operations due to age

Raymond "Ray Ray" Louie—píng-level charm speaker, heir to Dai Lou, lost a hand in reparation to San Francisco for his part in the taking of the Ebony Gate

"Uncle" Jimmy Louie—gāo-level charm speaker, Ray Ray's younger brother, nominal head of the Louie Clan

Leanna Louie—Ray Ray's elder daughter, Emiko's only martial arts student, illusionist of unknown caliber

Lucy Louie—Ray Ray's younger daughter

SOMAC SALVAGE

Tessa MacNeil—a Wàirén, Emiko's business partner, curator at the Tien Pacific Museum

Andie Santoso MacNeil—a Wàirén, Tessa's wife, handles IT security for SOMAC and Emiko's home

OTHERS

Adam Jørgensen—a Wàirén, eccentric collector of antique Japanese swords, donor to Tessa's museum, aggravatingly rich and attractive to Emiko, recently sworn to the Soong Hoard as a consequence of Emiko's pledge to save his life

Big Ricky Sun, Mama Sun, Baby Ricky, Sally—family that owns the Sun Emporium on Lotus Lane, purveyors of Emiko's canned magic and her favorite steamed pork buns

Grandma Chen ("Popo")—gāo-level Herbalist/purifier, owns Vitality Health Services day spa in Inner Sunset

IN ASIA

THAI TIGERS

Kamon Apichai—a tiger shifter, favored son of the Thai Tigers, Emiko's boyfriend until her crisis of conscience caused her to break both her swords and her bonds with her family

BORJIGIN CLAN

Batuhan—head of clan, claims descent from Genghis Khan, gāo-level angelic song talent, recently revealed as the General, leader of a cabal bent on leading Jiārén out of hiding and to power over Wàirén

Ariq—Batuhan's only son, failed out of Lóng Kǒu due to the uncontrollable nature of his talent, constantly wears blood jade to mitigate the debilitating effects of his talent

BYUN CLAN

Byun A-Yeong—cunning matriarch of the Byun Clan, allegedly blind in one eye, a gāo-level empathy talent who has honed her talent to become something close to mind reading

Minjae Byun—eldest grandson of A-Yeong, a rising talent in his house, a gāo-level shrieker

TANAKA CLAN

Tanaka Kenichi—head of Tanaka Clan, gāo-level weather talent

Lady Tanaka—most recent companion to Tanaka Kenichi, píng-level Dragon speed talent

Tanaka Junior—scion of the Tanaka clan, gāo-level ice talent, recently released from Mohe where he served his sentence for abusing a Talon Call

MOK CLAN

Stella Mok—gāo-level earth talent, wife of Stanley

Stanley Mok—gāo-level earth talent, husband of Stella

KOH CLAN

Sabine Koh—youngest daughter of Old Li, current head of Koh Clan by way of patricide, gāo-level water talent

Old Li—recently deceased at the hand of Emiko Soong as Sabine's cat's-paw

Nayla Koh—one of the Ice Tsunami Trio, twin sister to Nur, píng-level water talent

Nur Koh—one of the Ice Tsunami Trio, twin sister to Nayla, píng-level water talent

Awang Koh—one of the Ice Tsunami Trio, eldest son of Old Li, normally a di-level ice talent unless Nayla and Nur augment him with their water talents

JŌKŌRYŪKAI

Ogata-sensei—Emiko's sensei during her time at Jōkōryūkai, gāo-level dragon limbs

Saburo—a gāo-level fire talent from Jōkōryūkai who was temporarily contracted with the Louies

INHABITANTS OF THE SPACES BETWEEN CITIES

The Librarian—the entity who guards the secret Jiārén Library hidden under the San Francisco Public Library, she has something of a beef with Emiko

Gu Ma—the Librarian's "auntie," the guardian of the Archive, a secret repository of the totality of Jiārén knowledge, hidden under the hidden Library, loves unfiltered cigarettes and sudoku puzzles

Oda Tanaka—Sentinel of Tokyo, current holder of Crimson Cloud Splitter, ancestor of Tanaka Kenichi, poetry afficionado

SYNOPSIS OF *BLOOD JADE*

New Blade, Old Wounds

Burdened with the threat of the growing turf war between the Trans and the Louies, Emiko Soong retreats to her old habits—hiding out at home and avoiding people. Freddy Tran, twin brother to Fiona, steals Emiko away from her isolation for a rousing day of kite surfing.

As she leaves the magical boundaries of San Francisco, she is attacked by Iron Serpent, a lesser dragon who kills Sentinels to extend her own life. Emiko has no Sentinel power outside her city, and she is outmatched. Emiko survives by accidentally stealing a bit of Iron Serpent's power. The act shocks both of them and intrigues Iron Serpent. The Old One's curiosity is piqued enough that she releases Emiko and tells her to prepare, because ". . . a storm is coming."

Emiko returns to the Library to seek more knowledge about Sentinels. There, she is sidelined by Gu Ma, the Archivist. Gu Ma takes her below to the Archive, a resource Gu Ma guards for the Sentinels. Emiko fails to unlock the doors to San Francisco's Archive entrance. Gu Ma warns her that she has one more chance to open the doors and prove her power as a true Sentinel or Gu Ma will put an end to her very brief tenure.

Freddy steals Emiko away again, this time bringing her to a murder scene. Fiona Tran's aegis, Franklin, has been killed by an unknown assailant. As she searches for clues, Emiko smells ginger, the telltale scent of dark-walking, her mother's talent.

Meanwhile, Adam Jørgensen is still in possession of the legendary Jiārén sword Crimson Cloud Splitter. Despite Emiko's efforts, he and Tessa MacNeil (Emiko's business partner) remain resolute about exhibiting it at the Tien museum. Emiko struggles with obeying the First Law while also maintaining her fraying relationship with Tessa.

Emiko seeks out the assassin loose in her city, and surveils the Tran chateau. The assassin slips in and maims another of Fiona's guards. The assassin is more skilled than Emiko, and is revealed as a member of Jōkōryūkai, with a personal grudge against Emiko. The assassin escapes again.

Popo reveals the blade that killed Franklin was coated in a rare poison known as Final Breath, possibly crafted by a man named Ah Tong in Yokohama, Japan. Freddy asks Emiko to watch over his sister as a favor to him, while he stays in San Francisco to take care of the family business. Emiko realizes this is a turning point in her friendship with Freddy, in that it's not a transaction when you help out a friend.

When Emiko and the Trans step out of the train station in Tokyo, the assassin attacks again. In a harrowing battle, the assassin kills another of Fiona's security detail. Amid the chaos, they are confronted by the Sentinel of Tokyo, a great warrior who is at once incredibly powerful, and terribly confused. Emiko chases after the Sentinel, desperate to learn more about city Sentinels. She follows him to the Tokyo library. Oda, the Sentinel of Tokyo, becomes lucid within the protection of the Archive. Emiko wonders if Oda's mental state is her future. Oda offers to help Emiko as he senses her inability to access her power. After a skirmish, Emiko awakens to find her meridians unblocked, and her qì flowing through her like a springtime stream.

Emiko returns to clanhome, her thoughts heavy with the dread of facing her family and clan after abandoning them when she broke her blade. Tatsuya, her younger brother, ambushes her at the entryway. She subdues him easily, confirming his belief that she's still a formidable fighter.

Memories rush at her as Emiko returns to her old room. She

braces herself to speak with her father. His animates are everywhere in the house, ever watchful, keeping Emiko on her guard. Her father stonewalls Emiko's request for assistance with the killer and the poisoner, instead declaring that they are going to Golden Gai for a private dinner. He decks Emiko and Tatsuya in blood jade jewelry, which amplifies their talent. Her meridians freshly repaired, Emiko feels a surge of awareness from wearing it.

At dinner, Emiko and Tatsuya learn that their father has brought them there on a ruse to bring Old Li, head of the Koh Clan, in proximity with more blood jade. That proximity exacerbates Old Li's blood jade psychosis. When Old Li attacks her father, Emiko kills him. Sabine Koh, Old Li's youngest daughter, steps in to take her father's place as head of the clan.

Emiko is heartsore that she has fallen right back into her old role as the Blade. Her payment for the night's service is a vial of jade chips, imbued with her father's talent. It is the currency that she will need to gain access to the poisoner. She steps out into the rainy night and vows that she will not be an instrument of death again.

Tatsuya, used to his father's machinations, decides to blow off some steam with his classmates from Lóng Kǒu, Colin Aung and Minjae Byun. He cajoles Emiko into hanging out with him and his friends. Later that night, the assassin strikes again, this time going after Tatsuya. Emiko fights the slippery assailant but is again outmatched. The assassin nearly slays Tatsuya, but Colin intervenes and is wounded by the poisoned blade. Victorious, the assassin taunts Emiko and reveals herself. She is their cousin Kaida, and she wields the matching katana to Emiko's wakizashi, Hachi. Satisfied that Emiko is no match for her, Kaida leaves her bleeding in the rainy street, and promises to come back for Hachi once Tatsuya is dead.

Emiko gets herself patched up and resumes her search for answers. She must return to Jōkōryūkai to see her old master,

Ogata-sensei, for answers about Kaida. Returning to Jōkōryūkai should be a death sentence, but the life debt Saburo owes her earns her an audience with Ogata-sensei. In an unexpected effect of her burgeoning talent, she experiences a memory from her old teacher. Emiko learns her mother offered Kaida's talent in trade to allow Ogata-sensei to save face in the aftermath of Emiko's desertion.

Emiko goes to Yokohama to confront Ah Tong. The poisoner and his sister confess he made Final Breath for the General. Ah Tong also admits that he is about to complete a talent amplifier for the General. Emiko warns them to destroy their work and leave town.

As she leaves Yokohama, Adam phones her to announce he is in Tokyo. She rushes to prevent him from showing Crimson Cloud Splitter to anyone. Emiko offers to take Adam to clanhome where he can swear to their Hoard and learn their Jiārén secrets, in exchange for handing over the sword. A demon summoner attacks them with an army of club-wielding oni. Emiko and Adam fight them off and escape with the sword. Afterward, they share an exuberant kiss, which they both regret immediately. The heat of battle has unearthed Adam's memories of the fight at the Palace of Fine Arts. Adam agrees not to display the sword and tells Emiko he will only deal directly with her father.

An elaborate gala is held the night before Lóng Yá. All the families attend to preen and display their children and their power. Kaida makes another attempt on Tatsuya's life but Emiko is able to intercept her. Emiko has Kaida pinned, but her oath against killing stays Emiko's hand. In that hesitation, Kaida escapes again. Amidst the posturing and threats of both new and old enemies, Emiko finds Uncle Jimmy Louie as an unlikely ally. He urges her to join him, to be on the winning side of history. Emiko declines.

After the gala, Emiko wanders through the halls of clanhome, looking at old family photos. Emiko's failure to complete her training at Jōkōryūkai led to Kaida's involvement. She feels deep shame over this twist of fate at her mother's fine hand. She chops off her hair.

In the morning she fetches Adam to bring him to clanhome. Upon leaving his building, they are attacked again by the demon summoner, this time with a Japanese river demon. Adam falls in battle, so Emiko calls upon Oda for help. The Tokyo Sentinel arrives and slays the demon by using the powers of Crimson Cloud Splitter. Oda tends to Adam, and, working with Emiko, uses a few notes of Dragonsong to heal him. Oda bonds to the legendary sword and departs with it.

As Emiko trains Tatsuya for Lóng Yá, their father intervenes and reveals a family secret, a measure of Dragonsong. With her meridians repaired, her talent flows easily and Emiko steals her father's talent, which allows her to access the Dragonsong to pulverize a massive stone statue. After what feels like a lifetime of having no talent, Emiko seethes with anger to realize that her father knew what her true talent was all along. She conceals her talent from Tatsuya and knows she must continue to hide this from all Jiārén lest she be even more reviled than she already is.

On the morning of his Tourney, the family rises early to cheer Tatsuya on. Everyone is there, except for their mother, and Emiko's old resentment at her frequent absences rears its ugly head. Before they leave clanhome, she runs into Adam. He had come earlier that day to meet with her father and swear to the Hoard. Their tense confrontation makes it clear they will never return to the cautious flirtations of their past interactions.

The Soong Clan rolls into Lóng Kǒu, with all the pageantry the occasion requires.

They greet the Byun Clan, and Tatsuya must deal with the fact that from this moment forward, Minjae is not his friend but his opponent.

Emiko receives strange overtures from A-Yeong Byun, the Byun matron, and from Batuhan, leader of the Borjigin. Suddenly everyone seems to know that she was previously with Jōkōryūkai and wants her to join the General.

Tatsuya breezes through the rounds, and the field narrows to the final eight. The contestants rest and enjoy a grand feast. The judges attend the banquet as well, a panoply of Old Ones, each of them powerful and legendary figures. Iron Serpent and Kamon are among the judges.

Batuhan gives a long-winded speech, calling on Jiārén to assert their dominance. Emiko is lulled by his melodic voice until a majestic huli jing sits next to her. Most Exalted Heavenly Madam Yao guides Emiko into cycling her qì to tune out Batuhan's insidious talent. Madam Yao comments the Old Ones have come to see this tourney because they sense that events foretold of millennia ago will begin tonight, centered around Emiko.

Emiko leaves to check on the poisoner. When she arrives, Ah Tong is dead, and the amplifier has been taken. She returns to the Tourney for the next round. Batuhan uses his gift of angelic song to heal the wounded students.

The midnight matches play out, deadly in their intensity, while another fight unfolds in parallel as Emiko fends off Kaida's shadowy attacks. Minjae unleashes a vicious sonic assault that obliterates Tatsuya's defenses. Tatsuya chooses not to unleash his secret talents, and yields the match to Minjae. Emiko rushes to comfort him.

Kaida strikes. Amid the rubble of Tatsuya and Minjae's battle, Emiko and Kaida face off. Kaida is deep in blood jade psychosis, and more powerful than before, while Emiko is handicapped by her vow not to kill her cousin. Emiko rips off Kaida's anchor, to prevent her cousin from dark-walking.

When Kaida threatens Tatsuya, Emiko acts on instinct and unleashes her talent. Emiko's talent is voracious and devours Kaida's dark walker talent. Raw power overloads Emiko's body and in desperation, she sings her measure of Dragonsong and pushes her qì upward to vent it. The blast rips through space and opens a portal to the Realm. True Dragonsong drifts through the tear, and the assembly of Jiārén bears witness to the existence of their Dragon gods. The belief structure that Jiārén had based their origins on, that they had lost their Dragon gods to the Cataclysm, is proven false. Worse, all of Jiārén society has seen the extreme reach of Emiko's thieving talent. In a family of monsters, she possesses the most heinous of talents—the ability to steal another's.

She is an abomination, the Empty One foretold of.

Emiko's mother appears through the open portal, and together with Madam Yao and the qílín, builds a gate to seal the tear, forged with all the Hoard jewelry of the attendees.

Batuhan heals Kaida and she thanks him, addressing him as "the General." Emiko now has confirmation that Batuhan was the General who targeted Tatsuya and Fiona. Emiko's mother takes custody of Kaida to commit her to their prison, Mohe.

The headmaster denounces Emiko and expels her, again. Madam Yao and the qílín give Emiko a ride home, along with a token of great power to summon her in the future, a dragon's fang. Emiko returns to clanhome only to be reminded by the rest of the clan that she is no longer welcome there.

Sometimes, you can't go home.

Before she returns to San Francisco, she has a heartfelt reunion with her mother, who shares some of the reasoning behind the painful decisions of their shared past. Sara gives her Kaida's katana, Shokaku, restoring the daishō.

Back in San Francisco, Emiko is sad, but resolved. She goes to the Archive armed with new intuition. She summons the city's power and opens the doors. Oda awaits her within.

"How much do you know about prophecies?"

PEARL
CITY

PROLOGUE

Oda

Everything in the Archive looked old. The patina of years dulled the gleam of gold and silver inlays on the shelves, and dust covered many of the books in thick layers. To Oda Tanaka, the Archive had always looked like this, even when he'd first earned the right to enter, over three hundred years ago, and laid eyes on the richest vault of treasure for all Lóng Jiārén.

Only the moon gate door in front of him was new, a slab of fresh-cut granite. Sharp lines carved out the soaring lines of a majestic phoenix in flight, the creature stretched across the width of the door and aimed like an arrow into the sky.

Oda had learned over the centuries that doors in the Archive only formed with the arrival of a new Sentinel. When Jiārén gathered in enough numbers and enough strength to awaken the slumbering bones of their city, the collective power gave its city awareness. The newly formed consciousness of the city then chose its Sentinel, a living embodiment of the city's will and strength. For him, and likely the others, the mantle of Sentinel came with a vast reserve of power, and the curse of becoming intimately connected to every single resident of their city.

Emiko Soong, the world's newest Sentinel, stood in the new doorway with a complex expression on her face. Her dark eyes sparkled with a mélange of fear, defiance, and satisfaction. If Oda let his mind drift back far enough, he could recall feeling much the same way.

As the door clicked shut, Oda caught one last glimpse of a lock of Emiko's silver-streaked hair, and a faint whiff of San Francisco's damp, salty air. Emiko and her city were so young, so vital and alive.

San Francisco's door gleamed with its own internal light. Books near the new door smelled of fresh paper and glue, and the musk of newly tanned leather. Oda let his gaze drift away, past the doors he was more familiar with.

Seoul.

Bangkok.

Kuala Lumpur.

More doors, stretching into the darkness, curving out of sight.

The first time Oda had seen these doors, he'd been very much like Emiko. Young, full of ideas and energy, and ready to change the world. Oda Tanaka had not changed the world, but Emiko Soong might. Irrevocably.

He was terrified for her.

The oldest door in the Archive, the one at the very center (which was harder to find than one might think), opened with a scrape of aging metal against old wood. Oda turned away from the San Francisco door and waited patiently. In a few moments, shuffling steps approached from the darkness, accompanied by a glowing orange ember that bobbed in time to the steps.

Oda bowed low as Gu Ma emerged from the gloom. The aged woman was stooped over her walker, dressed in one of her threadbare housecoats. Many seasons ago, it might have been described as pink. A crooked unfiltered cigarette dangled from her lips, trailing fragrant blue gray smoke. Everything about her seemed soft and unfocused, except for the finely sharpened pencils tucked behind her ears, and her fathomless black eyes.

The Archivist shuffled to the table where Oda had just sat moments ago with Emiko. She moved with deliberate slowness, placing her hands and feet with care as she seated herself. Oda remained quiet, respectful of the weight Gu Ma carried wherever she went.

When she had settled herself, Gu Ma pulled a battered book of sudoku puzzles from inside her coat and laid it on the table. Instead of opening the puzzle book, her eyes slid to the open book of poems Oda had pulled from the shelves, and the scroll he'd left open. With careful movements, Gu Ma pushed aside her puzzle book and ran her fingers gently over the ancient pages of poems.

Her voice was quiet, yet filled the Archive. "You didn't show her all of it."

"I took your advice."

Gu Ma sucked on her cigarette and gave a rasp of a laugh. "For once."

He shifted his weight. "I felt like she had more than enough on her plate."

Gu Ma crushed the end of her cigarette between calloused fingers. "She's too damn young."

Oda restrained a wince as ashes drifted down to the table. "We were all young once."

Gu Ma shook her head and rolled the scroll back up, sliding it back into its hammered silver cylinder. "With this chart, she never had a chance."

It was true. With all the permutations of the Earthly Branches and Heavenly Stems, Emiko had a bazi that was one in over ten million. Oda would never want that kind of destiny but now his destiny was to watch it unfold. Or could he do more? "Maybe we should show her."

Gu Ma laughed again, without humor. "It wouldn't help and it could hurt. Everything rests on Emiko's shoulders now. A Sentinel whose Pearl is smaller than a chestnut."

Oda's hand pressed against his chest, an involuntary reflex. Behind his ribs, his own Pearl gave an extra beat that reverberated down to his toes. His Pearl was finely developed, matured over centuries, and the size of a prize pomelo. It was a deep reserve of his city's power, and an intimate connection to each and every one of Tokyo's millions of inhabitants. Many long years ago, it had engulfed his heart and taken over even those functions. Oda wondered if he'd ever get the chance to warn Emiko about that.

Emiko was young, reckless, and sorely lacking the wisdom a Sentinel required, and yet something about her inspired his faith. The Enemy would return soon, and the Empty One was either their salvation, or their doom.

Oda believed Emiko would save them. "She will find the strength."

Gu Ma thumped a finger on the book of poetry, next to the verses Oda hadn't shown Emiko. "Even if she finds the strength, will she pay the price . . . or will we?"

ONE NIGHT IN OLD CITY

The stink of corrupted tiger magic hung over the humid streets of Chiang Mai like a sweaty bedsheet. Despite my best efforts, falling back into monster cleanup was as easy as slipping on well-worn boots. Tracking a tiger through Thailand was no vacation, but it was better than being at home in my own city. I couldn't handle the way people looked at me now, after what had happened in Tokyo last month. And I had a bad habit of running away from my problems and right into someone else's.

My nose tracked the rogue tiger to Old Town, a tangled warren of narrow streets and frustrating dead-end alleys. The setting sun cast elongating shadows and the baked roads gave back the heat they'd stored all day. The humidity made my skin prickle and sticky sweat made my T-shirt cling to my arms, as if my clothing itself was holding me back. The air thickened into a soup of strong coffee, acrid diesel, and grilled squid.

I cycled my qì as Madam Yao had taught me, and the least horrific aspect of my talent led me unerringly through this heady cocktail, following the scent of cut grass undercut with the stench of old blood.

The streets were empty. No wide-eyed tourists and no grizzled hawkers competing for space with a roving army of scooters and taxis. Old Town had been deserted for two days now, as fear of a monster on a killing spree kept the locals and visitors at bay.

It felt like a lifetime ago when I'd promised myself that I

wouldn't take on any more monster cleanup. But when Kamon Apichai asked me to help hunt down his uncle, I'd packed a bag for Thailand before hanging up the phone. I tried not to dwell on how quickly I'd jumped to my ex-boyfriend's aid. This would build good rapport with the Thai Tigers, and the task fell neatly within my skill set. As my father would say, it was good business. But I would be lying if I said I came for business.

I was here for Kamon.

We may not have been together anymore, but when I stood alone and reviled at the Tourney, he had leapt from the judges' citadel to race to my side. Despite the revelation of my horrific talent, he had been there for me.

I could do no less for him now.

At the mouth of a claustrophobic alley, I found the latest victim, a young man lying on the cracked pavement, curled around a pool of blood spilling from his mangled abdomen. Like the others, his eyes were open and vacant, his face devoid of emotion.

There was a time when I could have looked at a scene like this and felt absolutely nothing. The tragedy of this death would slide off my psyche like glistening pearls of water off my blade, and I would simply catalog the details of interest. The likely weapon (claws), the technique used (downward slash), and the strength/skill of the killer (formidable). Perhaps I would admire their work.

I wasn't that person. Not anymore.

As I knelt to close the man's eyes the horror of the tableau washed over me. Writhing revulsion spawned in my gut, and I let it come, allowed it to grow until it touched the bottom of my heart and bile tickled the back of my throat. The sensation spread, a crawling dread that skittered over my skin like insects. My eyes lingered on pale, waxy skin, and the blood flies already feasting on the carnage. The feeling rolled through me like a wave and my breath caught. I bit back the tide of vomit, containing it to a hot, liquid ball at the top of my chest.

If I could feel this way, maybe I was still human.

Not an abomination.

And if I kept telling myself that, maybe I would even believe it.

Soft footsteps behind jarred me out of my navel gazing. I stood and shook off the emotions. Old habits reasserted themselves and calm detachment fell over my shoulders like icy mist. Kamon turned into the alley, low to the ground in his six-hundred-pound tiger form. In the low light his rippling stripes blurred his shape, so the first things I saw were his eyes, glowing green in the darkness. His ear twitched and he gave a low, irritated growl as he butted his head into my hip.

"Sorry, I didn't mean to leave you behind."

Kamon huffed, a blast of warm air across my legs.

No, I didn't believe me, either.

I uncurled the dead man's body. He wore the shredded remains of a gray button-down shirt, now nearly black from his blood. I pulled the soaked, tattered fabric taut, revealing an embroidered logo for a local boutique hotel. A small metal name tag read DIREK.

I cursed my stunted senses. Beyond the limits of San Francisco, beyond the boundaries of my connection to my city, I might as well have a towel wrapped around my head. The lengthening trail of bodies only reminded me of how slow this was going, how far behind I was.

Again.

I rubbed my fingers together, smearing a bit of Direk's blood. Still warm. Finally.

Kamon's head dropped to the dead man's belly and he sniffed. The growl in his chest went a note deeper. We hadn't hunted together in years, but I knew all Kamon's tells. I heard the tenor of sadness in that rumble.

I tried to reassure myself and him. "We're close."

But we were running out of time. The evil that possessed his uncle would eventually gain a foothold that not even my unholy power could reverse.

I put a hand on his neck and squeezed. "We'll find him."

He whuffed, and I filled in the words . . . would we find him before his next victim?

I lowered my eyes. We both knew the answer to that.

We made our way down the darkened alley and I sent a prayer to the Great Dragon Father that I found the strength to finish this before Kamon had to.

We got to the hotel too late. The fools had barricaded themselves inside, believing that thin walls and flimsy locks would protect them. Then Direk's chāng had convinced them to open the door and let the terror in.

The chāng was a young man with a clean cut across his neck that opened like a mouth. His cheap T-shirt had the same hotel logo. Once the spirit had cajoled the employees to open the door, it fled, leaving the lifeless body collapsed like a rag doll on the threshold.

We pushed through the hotel as fast as we could, but only found more bodies, and more unlocked doors. Each victim rose as a chāng, an undead spirit enslaved to bring the tiger his next victim.

As we searched along the top floor the smell of the tiger's power grew stronger, as well as the corruption of old blood. Deep in my core, something stirred from its restless sleep at the alluring scent of power. The sleepy feeling was my true talent, and it reached out along my meridians, seeking the power it had sensed. It felt like claws and muscles treading on my back, like an alpha predator pinning me under its jaws.

With an effort of will I grabbed the unruly beast inside me and pushed it back down. I wrestled it back, dominating it. It would not feed. Not while I had control. I held my breath until the intimate sensation of the monster backed away.

I almost jumped when Kamon bumped into the back of my leg. He tilted his head, and his left ear flicked.

"I'm fine."

The hallway suddenly seemed so small, the walls closing in on me.

His ear flicked again, harder.

"I'm fine. You wanted my help, so let's get this done."

Kamon huffed and the muscles across his shoulders rippled.

I blew out a breath. "Stop worrying."

His tail whipped back and forth.

"I can handle myself."

Kamon bowed his head, but I knew he worried about me. I focused my qì, willing my body to obey and to wrangle the darkness within.

At the end of the hall, light spilled from a door hanging at a skewed angle, torn half off its hinges. A shadow flitted across the light, bringing the sound of scuffing feet and moving furniture.

Kamon moved close, until his shoulder touched my hip and we moved forward smoothly in lockstep. I fought the instinct to reach up and instead brought my hands to my hip, where my swords hung from my belt. My left hand went to Shokaku's scabbard and my thumb loosened the katana. The environment was a little tight for the longer sword, but against a man-eating tiger, I wanted all the reach I could afford. I trailed my right hand over the pattern of silk knots on Shokaku's grip, keeping my touch light as adrenaline raced through my system and set my fingers tingling.

The scent had changed. Kamon noticed, too, as the timbre of his breathing shifted. The tiger scent was still here, heavy enough to make my eyes water, but someone else was here as well. Someone who wasn't a victim.

A survivor? Not likely.

Opportunistic thief? Also unlikely, and it didn't smell right.

I moved forward, setting the pace. Kamon and I had danced this number enough times, making it as natural as breathing. He had the raw power, but with my swords I had the advantage on reach. I'd enter first and go high. He'd come in behind me and sweep low.

My thick-soled hiking boots finished the job on the broken door, kicking it into the room ahead of me. I burst through the opening, Shokaku clearing my scabbard as soon as I had enough room to bring her to bear. My katana rang with a sweet, chilling note as her edge cut through the air. Kamon came in behind, quiet as my shadow except for the soft pad of his feet on the warped wooden flooring.

We came to a stop, my katana at high guard, Kamon's shoulders tensed, but the roar that had been building in his chest died.

A woman crouched next to the tiger's latest victim. A thin border of gold highlighted her aura. It was a faint but unmistakable sign of her status.

I knew, because I had it, too.

I sucked in a breath. I wanted to greet her, to apologize, to explain.

But the corpse on the ground was too awful for a mere apology. He had been an older man, the tatters of a suit and tie drenched in cooling blood. As the front door clattered to the floor the woman stood and turned to face us. Anger radiated from her like a furnace, from the high color on her cheeks to the tight set of her shoulders. I steadied myself but her red-rimmed eyes locked on Kamon.

"You." It was an accusation. "This is how the Apichai keep their house in order?"

Kamon lowered his head, and I did the same.

"Sentinel."

THE LAST PERSON IN THE WORLD

Eight hours earlier

Crossing into another Sentinel's territory without parlay was the height of rudeness. I'd gotten away with it once in Tokyo but I knew better now. Allegedly.

The Archive was a vast cavern that stored all the long-forgotten lore of Lóng Jiārén. It also connected to every city protected by a Sentinel. I managed to locate the door leading to Bangkok, mostly by following the bookshelves with books written in Thai.

When I pushed through Bangkok's door, I found the room empty, save for the beautifully polished teak furniture. It had a decidedly old-world feel to it and I wondered how old the Bangkok Sentinel was. Perhaps centuries old like Oda?

The clock was ticking though so I couldn't wait for the Sentinel. The urgency of Kamon's plea rang in my ears. I found a secret door behind a bookshelf and pushed until it rotated like a turnstile, revealing a neat row of wooden stairs up to the Bangkok Public Library.

I hustled up the steps and eased past a passel of children quietly reading in the sitting area to exit into Lumphini Park. The hush of the library morphed into a lush landscape of sprawling trees surrounding a tranquil lake, the air heavy with moisture and the mingled smells of nature and diesel. Noisy Asian cuckoo birds called from above, adding to the sensory overload. The park was a marvel, a hundred acres of green space smack dab in the heart of the business district. Much of Thailand felt the same, like the jungle was merely waiting to reclaim the temporarily civilized bits.

I couldn't stay to enjoy the park though. I was here to meet a certain tiger.

The locals buzzed around me, some lingering to enjoy the lake, others rushing about their day. None of them had the telltale aura that told me they were Jiārén.

The Kingdom of Thailand was over seven centuries old and Jiārén had long ago woven into this society, living side by side with their Wàirén neighbors. But the Apichais hadn't. As tigers, they gravitated to the wild spaces. They kept themselves apart, spreading through Malaysia where they were less likely to be hunted as part of the wild tiger population.

By the time I reached the Chinese clock tower in the park, the adrenaline rush of urgency had faded, and doubts drenched me like humid sweat. What was I doing here? How could I possibly help the Apichai clan? How could Kamon believe that my talent could help?

My talent was a thief of power. It was an abomination, stealing what was most sacred to Jiārén. Odds were anything I did would only make things worse. And what if the chāng took root in me? The hungry thing deep in my belly was already barely tethered—I shuddered to think what would happen if a murderous spirit took over me.

Kamon was wrong. This was a terrible idea.

I waited in the shadows of a stand of the rubber trees, the dense foliage screening me from the rest of the park. Despite the tranquility of the setting and the lush embrace of the scent of plumeria, my body vibrated with the need to move, to run, to escape. Mother had shown me by example that it wasn't wise to inflict our presence on the ones we cared about. My skin prickled from the heat and sweat was starting to make my clothes stick. I shouldn't have come.

An eternity passed until he came into sight. He seemed to float over the grass, his movements a rolling ease of loose limbs and coiled strength. In deference to the heat, he was dressed head to toe in loose linen, the sleeves of his blue striped shirt rolled up. The bright orange corona of his aura was at once familiar and shocking.

As he drew near, the sharp, crisp scent of cut grass filled my senses. I blinked at the intensity, a heady mix of nostalgia and hunger. It was as if all my senses had sharpened, to compensate for my lack of Sentinel awareness away from my home territory.

Or maybe it was just being so near to Kamon, the heightened awareness of him that I had never quite managed to suppress.

When he got close, the lines bracketing his face relaxed somewhat.

"Emiko, thank you for coming. We have a lead on Prem, and I think—"

I wiped my hands on my pant legs, cursing the heavy fabric. "This is a mistake. I should go."

He hunched over as if I'd punched him, and his voice lowered. "Please, you're the only one who can help him. My uncle . . ."

I studied the waves of his hair, the line of his strong neck and shoulders. "You're asking me to do something that . . ." I choked. "Once I start, I might not be able to stop."

He looked up, his eyes fierce and bright. "You can."

You have to.

The words were unspoken between us. But I had never had the control that Kamon had. That all the tigers had, taming the beast within.

If I failed, Prem would die by my hand.

I couldn't do it. My throat tightened and fear left a sour tang in my mouth. I was afraid, and I hated it. All I wanted to do now was flee this place with all its color and heat and demands, and return to the cool gray sanctuary of my city. As much as it hurt to admit, my mother was right. My talent posed a danger to those I cared about. I steeled myself to say what I had to and leave.

"It's too risky." I pivoted to head back to the library.

He reached out in a flash, his hand shaped in a distinctive curve. Eagle Claw! I dipped on instinct, evading his grasp. As fast as I was, Kamon was faster, turning down into a butterfly kick and finishing on the other side of me.

We had sparred like this countless times. Eagle spreads its wings met with Eagle preys on its food.

Muscle memory took hold and we grappled, hands and forearms locking and unlocking as we struck one another. Our motions flowed like water, interspersed by a flurry of strikes. He was bigger, faster, and stronger than me and I had never beat him fair and square.

Instead, I had always cheated.

But we weren't together anymore and I couldn't end this match with a heated kiss.

His eyebrows drew together in firm, slashing lines, uncompromising. He wanted this fight to prove something, and I was afraid of what that meant.

Like a cobra, he struck at my neck. I grabbed his forearm with both hands, and fell backward, letting the momentum carry us both to the ground, and I tossed him over me. I scrambled backward, but I was too slow and he shifted into his tiger form.

Skies! I couldn't outrun a tiger.

He rumbled low in his throat and twisted, and then he was on me, hundreds of pounds of apex predator. My brain stuttered in primal fear as his jaws opened over my face. Horror supplanted reason as a fang scraped across my jaw, drawing blood.

The thing, the hunger, inside me vaulted to the forefront, a white-hot rush of power surging through my meridians. I threw my hands up and grabbed his fur.

My talent rushed out of me. It howled with glee as it latched on to Kamon's talent and gobbled up huge chunks of his power. The scent of cut grass flooded my nostrils as flashes of memory danced past my eyes.

The two of us walking on a beach.

Standing on the prow of a rocking boat.

Drenched in rain outside of Beijing.

Kamon faded, like color leached from a photo. His black and orange stripes blurred together and his fur receded. Six hundred pounds of tiger muscle melted and shifted as Kamon's bones danced under his steaming skin, rearranging themselves into his human form. The massive jaws hanging open over my face retracted. The fangs pulled back as Kamon's form stuttered somewhere between tiger and human.

When Kamon shifted, it was a smooth, organic transition, as natural as water flowing downstream. Whatever was happening now . . . it wasn't that. Kamon maintained his position over me, even as his tiger form slipped away from his control. If the process caused him pain, he didn't show it. He kept his eyes steady on mine as my thieving talent drained his power.

More memories rushed through me, along with more of his tiger magic. His pain when I fled after Pearl Market. When I fled from him. My core sang like an overcharged battery.

No. I didn't want this!

I screamed and forced my hands to unclench. Kamon's shape stuttered again, pushing back toward his tiger form. My talent roared in anger. It wanted more.

It wanted everything.

But I'd broken the connection, and that was the crack I needed. I wedged my will into the gap and beat my talent back into its cage. Sweat prickled over my skin as I wrestled my talent down. I vented the pent-up energy inside me as a blast of qì flattened the grass around us. Nausea swept through me as the power in my core dropped precipitously. I sensed that if I wanted to in this very moment, I could shift, taking a form that my body was never meant to.

Kamon returned to his tiger form, still looming over me. I panted for breath, trying to regain my composure. As Kamon's power had peaked within me, it had been . . . intoxicating. And despite what his physical proximity might be doing to my hormones, it definitely wasn't the stirring of old feelings. This was more . . . primal. It was hunger. It was a need to consume that could only be sated by consuming more and more.

It was my worst fear. If I ever let my talent loose, really let it loose, would I be able to stop it? Would I even want to?

They were right to call me abomination. Tears rolled out of my eyes, streaming down my hot cheeks and stinging the cut on my jaw. I swallowed hard, letting the waves of shame and relief roll through me. My body shuddered as the adrenaline faded. Long moments passed in silence between us until my heartbeat settled back into some semblance of normal.

If Kamon noted my turmoil he brushed it off with a twitch of his right ear.

I scowled at him. "What if I hadn't pulled it back?"

He twitched his ear again.

I levered myself up to sit. "Well, I'm glad you have such confidence in me, but I still say this is a bad idea."

Kamon growled softly in his chest and nuzzled against my shoulder. My arms came up of their own accord, but this time I simply wrapped my arms around his warm body and clutched him close to me. The heat from his body and the steady beat of his heart soothed the warring emotions in me, and we hashed out the rest of our argument without words, ending up right where I'd known we would finish.

I dropped my arms and Kamon backed up to let me stand. I knuckled away the tears in my eyes.

“Terrible choices are still better than no choices, right?” My voice was hoarse from crying.

A ripple went across Kamon’s shoulders.

I couldn’t have said it better myself.

THE SENTINEL OF BANGKOK

I couldn't look away from the Sentinel of Bangkok. She was lean and brown, her eyes deep and hard like polished jet. I sheathed my katana slowly and bowed low to convey my respect and acknowledgement of being near her territory.

But I didn't apologize because we weren't in her territory. Like me, she'd been selected by her city to act on behalf of her Jiārén community. She embodied her people and the power of her city, and she wielded that combined might to protect her city.

She was far from home, though, and I wondered why.

"I looked for you in the Archive . . ." I began.

She made a chopping motion with her hand. "Gu Ma may indulge you, but you're not welcome here."

The Sentinel turned her focus to Kamon. "Did you think I wouldn't notice?" Her tone was sharp enough to cut stone.

He dipped his head and his tail thrashed once, but I knew his body language. If you know anything about cats, they lack contrition.

I tried again. "You're beyond your territory, I noticed."

She stood, leaving the corpse on the ground. She wasn't as tall as I was, but her body radiated an indomitable will. I knew if I needed to confront her, she would be like an immovable object. I'd already categorized all the jewelry she was wearing, the piercings of ruby along her ears and the bracelet of beaten gold and ruby cuffed on her bicep. I cast a wary eye on the curved swords she brandished on each hip. They were slender and medium-length, good for cutting and keeping attackers at a distance. It gave me a slight clue as to what I'd be dealing with, but her scent told me more. Her talent had a nutty fragrance, with an undertone of char. She smelled like Stella Mok.

"A chāng loose around Wàirén is a problem," she replied. "A chāng loose around Jiārén is a catastrophe." All at once, every hesitation I had earlier at the clock tower came back in full force. Her words confirmed my fear that a chāng taking possession of a powerful Jiārén could cut through a population like a tsunami.

Kamon leaned heavily against my side, as if reminding me of what he'd proven at the clock tower. He believed I could control my talent.

I tried to muster some conviction into my voice. "We have a plan."

The Sentinel raised an eyebrow and sneered. "Does it involve your thieving talent?" she asked. "I can't think why else you would be here."

I nodded, the distaste in her voice sliding off my back. If anything, it was mild compared to what I'd experienced, even in my own city.

"Yes."

"And how will you catch this chāng?"

I tipped my head toward Kamon. "Pack bonds."

Her lips parted in surprise. "The bonds survived the chāng's possession?"

Kamon flicked an ear and gave a grudging nod.

It was not something they wanted generally known but as their clan head, Prem had the ability to broadcast to all their clan. Even now, under the sway of the chāng, Prem's thoughts leaked out when the bloodlust slipped.

While it wasn't exactly GPS, it was a good compass and Kamon sensed when we were close. Sadly, the trail of dead bodies was a strong indication we were on the right track—after all, that had likely been how this Sentinel had made it here. Or did she have some other means of learning where Prem was?

Was it because she was a Sentinel?

No.

Like mine, her power ended at the city's boundaries, of that I was certain. Beyond Bangkok, her powers were as blunted as mine when I left San Francisco. Judging by her aura, she was some kind of earth talent, with a powerful connection with the land. Perhaps her skills let her sense where powerful talents intersected with her connection with the earth.

Her interest in Kamon's pack bonds was clear. Together they would be able to pinpoint Prem's location.

But why did she want to? I didn't buy her earlier statement. It was true that a chāng was a danger. But that didn't mean a Sentinel would leave her territory to hunt an out-of-area threat. No, her red-rimmed eyes told me her interest was personal.

I nodded at the body on the ground. "Who is he to you?"

She didn't answer me, but she shifted her weight. The walls swayed and the rafters above us groaned. The warped wooden floorboards rippled slightly as if she was calling the very earth to her feet. And maybe she was, despite being three floors up. She was a rare talent indeed, if she could do so from this height.

A moment later, the tables and chairs around us stopped wobbling.

Rather than respond to my question, she'd chosen to give us a demonstration of her power.

Arrogant. I could appreciate that. But I didn't like it.

She needed Kamon but not me. I wasn't going to let her leave me behind. He and I had fought together countless times. He knew all my moves. I didn't even need to signal.

The thing about earth movers was that they were tied to the ground. They never looked up. Or sideways.

I screamed, mainly for the distraction, and I dove right, somersaulting over the table while Kamon leapt straight at her. Rather than biting her or slashing her, he merely pinned her while I flanked her.

"We don't have to do it like this!" I yelled and snapped a steel wind tile between my fingers.

The floor rocked beneath us and hardened spears of earth ripped through the thin wooden flooring like it was tofu. The heaving motion threw Kamon to the side and the Sentinel rolled to her feet, arms outstretched. A low drumbeat hit my chest, right over my Pearl, vibrating in the small space within where I carried a tiny fraction of my city's burgeoning power. I threw the tile at the Sentinel's feet along with a good shot of my qì. The energy flowed down my arm like water falling downhill.

Gods, the little things were so much easier now.

The tile disintegrated at the Sentinel's feet and a solid pearlescent sphere of hardened wind sprang up around her, shutting her away and rendering her into a blurry outline. The sphere rocked from an impact but stayed together. The drumbeat hit my chest again, harder. This time when the Sentinel hit the steel wind the surface cracked.

She was drawing on her Pearl, pulling up her reserves to batter her way out. Her Pearl had to be more potent than mine. Bangkok was old, and had been a safe harbor for Jiārén for centuries since it had barely been a brief oasis on the Chao Phraya River. The collective power of the area had grown with each passing year, and this Sentinel had clearly nurtured her Pearl for many years. With that kind of juice at her disposal, she'd be out of there in moments. When the third drumbeat hit I ran up to the edge of the sphere with my hands up, yelling into the cracked surface.

"Wait! Wait! We both want the same thing! Give us a chance to make it right!"

The pulse in my Pearl faded out as the Sentinel drew her power down. Her voice was muted through the steel wind. "The Apichai already had their chance."

"Then give me a chance. I will make it right."

A snort. "As if I value the word of a thief."

Kamon prowled up behind me, his warm weight a familiar comfort behind my knees. I needed to make this work. We couldn't afford a fight right now, not with Prem getting farther away every moment.

In the space of my hesitation the drumbeat hit my chest again. The Sentinel was not going to be patient about this, either. I took a chance and put my hand over my Pearl.

"You should value the word of a Sentinel."

I felt another beat through my chest, but this one originated from me. And by the way the power faded from inside the steel wind, I knew the other Sentinel felt it, too.

Her voice was hesitant. Was she surprised? "You fool. You'd swear? On your Pearl?"

I only had the barest idea of what she was asking of me. Oda had explained that the longer I nurtured the Pearl, the stronger it would become, and the harder it would be to separate myself from my city. I'd seen for myself how his own sanity had worn thin after centuries in service to Tokyo. A promise made on my Pearl risked that connection. Even as immature as my Pearl was, I was putting a lot of power on the line. No Jiārén wanted to do that.

But I wasn't most Jiārén.

"Yes. I swear, on my Pearl. Let Kamon and me do what we came to do. We'll subdue Prem and destroy the amulet. That will eliminate the danger of the chāng to your people."

If she noted my careful wording, she didn't comment. Maybe swearing on my Pearl was shocking enough to make her miss it. The steel wind cracked again and through the widening gap I caught the Sentinel's eye, a gleaming black gem staring at me.

The Sentinel moved close, until her narrowed brown eye was

inches from me. "Do you realize what you're swearing to? Didn't Iron Serpent visit you?"

That rocked me back, but it also confirmed that this might be the only way to secure her cooperation. I hadn't considered that another Sentinel might be able to use my Pearl, but that was going to be a problem for future me. In the present, all I could do was nod quickly.

Kamon pulled away from us, his tail swishing with agitation. He prowled to the window, his nose high. I knew that look. He had Prem's scent.

Kamon growled. My eyes flicked to him and back to the Sentinel.

"Do we have an agreement?"

"If you fail, you won't like the consequences."

"Do we. Have. An agreement."

"Witnessed."

Kamon growled, a low rumble so ominous that my teeth ground together as he witnessed my dangerous bargain with the Sentinel of Bangkok.

Another rippling pulse hit my chest, and I knew in my bones that I had just signed an inviolable contract, guaranteed with my power. There was no backing out now.

The Sentinel hammered on the steel wind with her fist. "Now, get me out—"

Silent as death in the darkness, Kamon leapt out the window. I took off after him and yelled over my shoulder.

"Sorry!"

TIGER, TIGER

Kamon threw his head back and roared, the sound lifting the tiny hairs on my body. In a flash he raced off, leaving me to follow. The Bangkok Sentinel's cry of anger faded as I leapt off the rickety fire escape and caught the railing on the next level down. The whole structure groaned under the impact of my weight and I had a sickening moment of free fall as the stairs pulled away from the building.

It was silent for one tense second before corroded metal began to scream and buckle under the stress. Rust and metal shavings rained down on me as the fire escape began its collapse into the alley. I kicked my body back and on the forward swing launched myself down the alley, following Kamon.

My qì flowed smoothly, running through the patterns Madam Yao had taught me at the Tourney. I landed on the cobblestones without a sound, cushioned on a pillow of dissipating qì, my legs already pumping to run. As I bolted forward, I held up one hand, raising a roof of energy over me that deflected falling debris away from my head. When the fire escape landed with a shuddering crash behind me, I jumped again and rode the blast of air to throw myself forward another fifty feet and pull up even with Kamon.

Gods but the power felt good. I still couldn't believe that Freddy, Fiona, or my brother just lived like this all the time and took it for granted.

I'd been robbed of this, and even worse, suppressing my power meant I'd never had a chance to train it. My peers were expert wielders of their talents with over a decade of specialized training. Me, I had unleashed it by accident a handful of times.

But maybe today would be different.

Kamon didn't spare me a look as I pulled even, his eyes focused beyond the end of the alley and on his uncle's coming fate. I ran at his side and the narrow streets of Old Town whipped by in a blur.

It took all I had to keep up with a full-grown tiger running flat-out. Kamon bounded off buildings and cars to take tight corners at top speed. I managed to keep pace by cycling my qì and supplementing my speed with little boosts of power.

I usually didn't keep my qì cycling for long periods like this. It wasn't something I ever needed to do, much less had the opportunity to try. Now I found that the more I kept my qì moving, the more insistently my hungry talent tried to push to the fore. The pull urged me to close in on Kamon and sink my talons into his power again. My first instinct was to squash the sensation but to suppress it I would need to pull back my qì flow and I couldn't afford to fall behind.

Kamon had proven that I could pull my talent back when I needed to. Maybe I needed to stop thinking about it like I had to hold it back—maybe I had to use a little of it all the time, like releasing pressure from a steam valve in small increments instead of a geyser.

I watched my spacing with Kamon and maintained my qì flow. The hungry growls of my talent leveled out to a dangerous rumble behind my eyes. It certainly wasn't gone, but at least now it wasn't spinning out of control.

Kamon's eyes met mine. Did he sense my talent, and how it was locked onto him? Would one predator recognize another?

Kamon's eyes slid off of me and he put on a fresh burst of speed. I tried to ignore the monster riding behind my eyeballs and did my best to keep up.

We left Old Town through the Chiang Mai gate. It should have been crammed with tourists, but like the rest of the town it was eerily deserted. We veered right and ran down Wua Lai Road, the usually bustling street populated only with abandoned vendor booths and food carts. Kamon slowed and lifted his head, scenting again. Up ahead, something banged with a metallic screech. Fresh blood marked the pavement leading to a narrow alley.

I pushed past Kamon and drew Shokaku. The stink of the corrupted tiger's power filled my nostrils. Prem and the chāng were close. The clanging ahead continued, and as we rounded an upended cart the blood trail thickened.

At the end of the alley the shops were all closed, their metal shutters drawn down tight. The blood trail led to a slender figure standing with her back to us. The latest chāng was a young woman in her twenties, dressed in a dirty nightgown and wailing piteously, crying for her mother while slamming her fist on the shutter. Half of her body was drenched in blood from a killing wound at the neck. Every time she brought down her fist she left a crimson half-moon on the metal.

Kamon and I drifted apart, looking for the angles Prem would take. The poor girl reduced to a chāng wasn't our target here. But somewhere close, Prem was waiting for the right moment to strike and claim another victim.

Bang. Bang. Bang.

I tuned out the girl's shrill cries. As much as they grated on my nerves, they must have been absolute torture to the girl's loved ones locked inside the store. To be tormented with a gruesome facsimile of your love, even knowing that it means to lead you to your death. How long could someone resist before the voices drove you insane with the need to open the door? How long had the people at the hotel held out?

My usual nose for sniffing out talents wasn't helpful here. The tiger had clearly been all over this alley before we arrived, and his scent was everywhere.

My eyes roamed across the rooftops as Kamon prowled through the shadowy corners. The darkness above us was almost oppressive, but I couldn't spot any dangers other than my jangling instincts. Maybe my own monster could find something. I let my talent loose a little more and it swelled in response, taking the slack I gave it. It went after Kamon the moment I gave it some leeway but I wrenched it back and tied it down. After a moment of calm I released my hold again.

Bang. Bang. Bang.

This time my talent didn't lunge forward. I took a step and it stayed in my shadow, senses questing out toward the dark corners. My will unclenched, but I left it hovering over my talent, like a hand above a wary animal.

The alley was silent except for the sounds of our breathing and the ceaseless rattling of the closed shutter. The chāng's pitiful cries had diminished to quiet whimpers. Every few seconds the chāng's fist beat wetly on the metal.

Bang. Bang. Bang.

A cry of utter anguish from inside the store, followed by the sounds of a fight and moving furniture.

No!

Another scream. It was the sound of sanity and resolve crumbling to bitter self-destruction.

The rolling shutter rattled as someone threw open the locks on the inside. The chāng's cries grew in volume as she crouched and wormed her bloody fingers into the gap at the bottom. Hysterical crying drifted out from under the shutter as it opened. The chāng drove the empty shell of its victim onward and strained to lift the gate.

Kamon and I leapt forward. Too late, I sensed the darkness along the rooftop transform into several hundred pounds of muscle, fur, and killing claws and teeth. Prem melted out of the shadows, his haunted eyes locked on the chāng. I caught a flash of a circular pattern on Prem's chest. The aberration in his stripe pattern marked where the amulet had cursed him.

I dodged for the chāng and drove my shoulder into her, throwing her to the side. My momentum carried me into the shutter and I crashed into it, forcing back whoever was inside.

A mass of black and orange stripes crashed into Prem and Kamon rolled his uncle to the center of the alley, fangs and claws slashing. Their throaty roars ripped open the night's silence, filling Chiang Mai with the sounds of terror.

I kicked at the shutter's track until the metal bent, to keep it locked down. When I crouched to check on the chāng, I found her quiet and still, the young woman's face gone to the blank expression I'd seen on the other victims. I closed her eyes. When Prem had come out the vengeful ghost's task had been completed.

I vowed there would be no more chāngs. I stood and turned to the battling tigers.

Kamon and his uncle tumbled back and forth in a blur of thrashing limbs and raking claws. As deadly as it looked, I could tell Kamon was holding back, unable to bring himself to harm his favorite uncle, despite all that had happened.

I put my sword away and looked for an opening. At the pace they were going at each other, I was just as likely to hurt Kamon if I waded in with my blade. No, like Kamon had suggested, there was only one reason he needed me here.

On the far side of the alley another figure dropped down from the roof and landed without a sound. The Sentinel of Bangkok stood quietly and watched the tigers maul each other. Her eyes found me over the melee and one sculpted eyebrow went up. She tapped her chest with one finger, the exact spot where my own Pearl was buried.

My time was up. If I was going to save Kamon from this thankless task, I had to do it now. I wasn't just going to tackle a six-hundred-pound tiger, though. As usual, I was going to cheat.

I pulled a Might of the Mountain tile from my other pocket. I fed a bit of qì into the tile and took position just at the border of the fight, looking for my opening.

Despite the years since our last hunt, Kamon and I still moved well together. I saw the moment coming with stark clarity as Kamon put together a sequence of moves I knew well. Two strikes to Prem's nose brought him rearing up on his hind legs, roaring in pain and anger. Prem lunged down, but Kamon had baited him into it, going low and trapping Prem.

Kamon roared and twisted like a fish, flipping Prem onto his back. I threw my tile, jumped, and yelled.

"Now!"

Kamon let go, letting Prem land squarely on the tile, crushing it beneath his weight. A small zone of increased gravity under Prem's back nailed him to the street like a pinned butterfly. The old tiger roared, the sound echoing off the buildings. The increased gravity grabbed me in midair and brought me down on Prem's chest like a falling piano. I hit him with something like three times my normal weight and blasted the air from his lungs.

I fell forward, catching both of Prem's forelegs in my hands. When my skin made contact the tiger's eyes widened and underneath the predator's gaze I saw the look of an animal that has just realized it is now the hunted, not the hunter.

My talent stretched and purred like a primordial jungle cat and sank its fangs into Prem's power, his tiger talent, and the corruption brought onto him by the cursed amulet. My talent didn't care. All it wanted was power.

Prem roared again, the sound blasting my hair back. My talent tore into the old tiger, shredding through his power like wet tissue. Power flowed into me in huge, dripping gobbets, each serving thick with the cloying taste of stale blood, sour fear, and greed. I maintained my grip on Prem's legs, even as the power made me gag and heave.

Like Kamon's before, Prem's pelt melted under my assault, his stripes blurring, the color fading. He twisted and writhed, trapped between my talent and the increased gravity. My talent tore at him, ripping out bigger and bigger chunks as it went.

This time, without the distraction of an active fight, I saw in horrifying detail how my talent stole power from Prem. The Thai Tigers all had glowing auras of solid orange that marked them. That aura crumbled under my talent's assault as tendrils of black crept in from the edges. The more I drained, the more the blackness spread, fracturing Prem's aura until it was only a few isolated pools of dimming color.

Power thundered through my veins. Stars danced across my vision as my being filled up with the scent of spring grasses, the taste of blood, and a tiger's growl built in my chest.

Prem shrank under my assault. His limbs melted away, revealing the middle-aged man beneath, still in good shape, but showing the softness of his age. Showing his weakness. He was naked, except for a length of hemp around his neck, and a nondescript amulet of corroded wood, carved with runes made illegible by years of moss and decay. My arms swelled and brilliant orange and black stripes swirled to life on my skin.

I threw my head back and my jaw hinged open, fangs ripping through my gums. Any tiger who let his power get taken like this didn't deserve to live. There was no place for weakness here. A roar ripped out of me, the deafening war cry of an alpha predator marking its kill. I slammed my weight back down, my arms now bulging with ropy muscle and covered in a thick black and orange pelt.

I brought my muzzle down, inspecting the worm underneath me. I sniffed in disgust. The weak little man smelled of piss and cowardice. I opened my jaws. My fangs would make quick work of him, a fine death for the lowly insect. The pale little man squirmed under me, whimpering as my fangs closed on him.

"Emiko."

A hand landed on my nape. A strong hand, but it did not grab, did not attempt to make me submit. It dug deep into my pelt, massaging the back of my neck. The voice was strong. Sure. Familiar.

"Emiko. It's over."

Someone appeared at my side. My kill was here, in front of me, but something about this other drew my attention, like a more delicious meal.

I twitched my ear and bent back to my kill. First things first.

The hand tightened. "Emiko."

My head swiveled and I locked with a pair of dark eyes glittering with unknown depth. Steam wafted off Kamon's bare shoulders. My nose twitched at the fine traces of his blood that followed the shallow scratches along his neck. This was blood that I could respect. I leaned forward, nostrils flaring.

"Emiko."

Kamon's hand grabbed my ear, turning my head to look at him. His eyes held me steady as his other hand reached out with Shokaku.

My sword. I must have dropped it during the change.

An awkward, clumsy weapon. A poor excuse for sharp fangs and claws.

Kamon slid the sword carefully along Prem's chest and the dirty hemp rope parted. The amulet fell to the ground with a hollow sound and did not bounce or move. Kamon carefully kept his eyes away from the amulet. Prem's breathing slowed and the tension in his spine melted away. Kamon put the sword down and brought our foreheads together with both hands, his smooth skin to my thick fur.

"Emi, come back."

The smell of his talent was clean and bright, fresh-cut grass and crisp, summer air. It was the sense memory of being content and happy at his side. I gasped as the power drained away, as my limbs shrank, and my perceptions shifted from tiger to human. Kamon held me up, kept me from collapsing on top of Prem, who curled up on his side and sobbed quietly.

From the other side of the alley, the Bangkok Sentinel took in the scene with widened eyes. I hoped it was simply shock on her face, and not horror and revulsion. It was hard to tell from a distance, and I didn't really know her. I got to my feet with a groan and tried to project as much dignity as I could, while ignoring the fact that Kamon and I were naked as jaybirds.

I held out my hand and Kamon put Shokaku's hilt into my palm. As I wrapped my fingers around her familiar knots I gave her a silent apology for my disrespect. I brought Shokaku down in a short, brutal arc and cut the amulet in half. A high, tinny sound like a distant scream came from the wood, along with a burst of greenish mist.

Before I could understand what was happening, my talent pushed to the fore again, clamping down on the energy released from the amulet. In one quick bite, the energy that had empowered the amulet vanished, and the remains of the amulet withered to colorless dust.

Had the Sentinel seen that? Maybe not, since we weren't in her city of power. I covered my disquiet with a look of mild disinterest. Like something my father would do.

"Has the issue been resolved to your satisfaction?"

The Sentinel blinked and her eyes traveled down to Prem, who was trying to curl himself into a ball. "The tiger is—"

I steamrolled over whatever was about to come out of her mouth. “The tiger is no longer a threat to your people.”

Whatever happened to Prem next, the Thai Tigers would take care of him.

The Sentinel sighed, clearly unhappy. “Witness.”

Kamon put his hand on my shoulder. “So witnessed.”

SENTINEL'S HALL

Asking the Bangkok Sentinel for passage through her side of the Archive was out of the question, so the Apichais chartered a plane for me instead. I slept for most of the car ride to the airstrip. I had expended wild amounts of power and I didn't have my city's deep reserves to level me out. As I napped, the Pearl nestled within me rippled beneath my skin, waves of soothing coolness easing the ache in my bones. I missed my city but a part of me didn't want to leave Thailand. Or more specifically, one certain tiger.

Kamon handed me a small duffel bag on the tarmac. "Thank you for coming to aid my clan."

I took the bag, my thoughts clear now on what I had to say. How I had to clear the air between us. "I owed you."

His body language changed in an instant, going from loose and easy to very still. I caught only the barest movement of his jaw as if he clenched his teeth. His words were low and precise. "What did you think you owed me, Emiko?"

There wasn't enough air to fill my lungs. "An apology."

"For what, exactly?" His tone was curt.

I swallowed hard, my throat closing up. "I shouldn't have walked away without telling you why. I'm sorry."

There it was. The thing we'd never talked about ever since he'd helped me recover the Ebony Gate.

His eyes went hard and flat. "No, you shouldn't have."

The lack of emotion in his voice flayed me, but now that I had started this, I had to finish it. I forged ahead, old hurts cutting their way out of me like a rusty blade. “I’m sorry. I . . . I don’t have a good excuse except that I was so ashamed after what happened in Beijing . . . I . . . couldn’t talk to anyone. I ran, and I kept running for a long time.”

He looked away, his gaze going distant. “Did you know how many times I went to your house to look for you? That I checked the safe house in Shinjuku, too?”

I shook my head. My chest tightened at the look on his face and shame flushed my cheeks. I wanted to close my eyes, as if that would stop the tears that were threatening to fall.

Kamon’s toneless recitation was relentless. “I didn’t know if you were alive. Your father said only that he felt the loss of the Clan Blade and I thought you had died.”

Tears streamed down my face now as I relived those dark days, when I had lost all time and reason after breaking Truth. How my soul had shattered along with my blade. In a way, I had died.

His flat delivery continued. “I didn’t eat for two weeks. Then Fujita-san sent me a note, that he believed you had gone to California. So I waited for you to call me.”

I never did.

“Finally my clan intervened. Prem sent me to the monks so that I could grieve properly and put my memories of us to rest.”

I fell to my knees, my body shuddering as I finally admitted to myself the pain I had caused him. “I’m sorry I hurt you.”

“You hurt me because I loved you so much and I had to see that it wasn’t the same for you. It hurt because I needed you, but you didn’t need me back.” His big shoulders hunched as he went on. “It hurt because I had to learn that in your darkest time, you didn’t turn to me. That I wasn’t enough for you.”

The words tore out of me and I stared up at him. “No! Never. I always needed you.”

My eyes stung from the salt of tears and regret. I should have said all these things years ago, but foolishly I had assumed he knew how I felt. So I stumbled forward, each word scoring another hit on my battered heart. "Kamon, I needed you too much. Don't you see that's exactly what's wrong with me? That I'm always empty inside without others?"

He put a hand on my shoulder and knelt to face me. We were so close and it was all I could do not to collapse onto the hot asphalt. "Do you still feel that way? Empty inside?"

The Pearl thumped in my chest, reminding me that I was never alone. I reached for Bāo, my fingers clenching the pendant too hard. "I'm afraid all the time. And now I know some of that feeling comes from my talent, locked up for so long."

He shook his head. "Even now, after proving you are more than your father's pet killer, you are afraid of who you are?"

I was a coward, and Kamon was the only one I had ever admitted it to. The only one who I trusted enough to reveal this shameful truth to. I hung my head, wishing I didn't have to admit this part, too. "I had no other place in my clan. I was the Blade, the only thing I knew how to be."

"You know that's not true." His words were gentle, but firm.

Agony speared my insides in reliving all I had lost. I tried to focus on why I had started this at all, ripping off all that scar tissue and bleeding anew.

"I'm still afraid. But I'm trying. Can you forgive me for the pain I caused you?"

"I forgave you long ago." He paused. "I forgave myself, too."

The pressure in my chest drained away, and my world tilted. "Why?"

"Because we did our best." His words got softer and I strained to hear him. "If we could have done better, we would have."

That was exactly what I wished—that I could turn back time and do better.

But all we had was now. Tears slid down my hot cheeks and

down my neck, leaving my skin feeling as raw on the outside as my soul did within.

He stood up and pulled me with him. My knees were soft, almost unable to hold up my weight. Our foreheads touched, and this was perhaps the real goodbye I'd robbed us of before. I let his forgiveness wash over me and something inside settled. We each drew a few slow breaths, foregoing words for this quiet connection. The broken parts of my soul knitted, and for the first time in two years, I let myself miss what we had.

I grasped his forearm. "Thank you for standing by me at the Tourney. It meant everything to me."

He nodded and returned my grip. "I wanted to be there for you."

I gave him a watery smile.

The past was truly past, and maybe what we had now was better. Friendship and honesty.

When we hugged before I got on the plane, my heart said goodbye to the regrets of all that had gone before and gratitude filled me for this time for us.

"Goodbye, Kamon. Take care of Prem."

"Thank you, Emi. I'm only a call away."

My chartered flight back from Thailand gave me plenty of time to replay all the events in my head. The heat, the colors, the surge of power that had coursed through every meridian in my body. Had I really transformed into a tiger? Iron Serpent's face flashed across my mind, the shock in her shiny black eyes when I stole her shape, her scales, and strength a few weeks ago. Kamon had been right—a tiger wasn't a stretch for my talent.

I couldn't stop thinking about it. For once I had intentionally used my talent. Without Kamon there to bring me back from the brink would I have lost myself to it? Would I have let my talent keep consuming until there was nothing left? What would be left of me? Was there really any difference between me and the chāng?

I rubbed my fingers together, marveling at the difference between my smooth skin and the memory of thick fur and claws. After years of hunting with Kamon, we'd established a rhythm and instinct of each other's moves, but this experience brought things to a different level. The empty seat next to me reminded me how few people knew me, truly. Now that we had mended our bridges, I wished he were here, but his place was with his family right now. His uncle had a long road to recovery and while they would never be able to make amends to the families of the victims, they had to try.

The looming shadow of Kamon's relationship with Fiona didn't help, but I hoped he was happy. I didn't pry and he didn't volunteer. He had moved on, and with someone whom I saw often given that she was a major power within my city. Kamon had spared me a chat about his new love, but I couldn't help but notice that when his clan needed help, he hadn't called the Trans.

Maybe the truth was simpler, they'd needed my talent. It was the first time someone had needed me for something other than my sword arm. I was treading uncomfortable waters, and if I wasn't careful, I'd get yanked below and drown. I grabbed a blanket and pulled it tight around me. For a few more hours, I would be among the clouds, like our dragons. I could pretend for a little while and ignore the problems so far below me.

My rideshare dropped me off at the edge of Lotus Lane. I stepped out of the car and breathed in the cool, damp air, and luxuriated in the heavy pulse of my city's power below my feet. The last vestiges of my tension drained away. I was home.

Even the sight before me did little to dampen my good mood. The building in front of me had a wide facade half covered with scaffolding and translucent tarps. Through the tarps it was easy to see that the face of the building was undergoing a dramatic remodel. The scaffold towered high above the building, showing off the bones of the distinctive curve of the resting hill roof. I could imagine the roofline with artful slopes and curves covered in blue-gray tiles supported by bright red timbers under the eaves.

Crows lined the rails of the scaffolding, seemingly oblivious to the workers. The closest one swiveled its head and peered down at me with one large eye. One by one, the rest of them turned to look at me as well. The city watched me through all its denizens, even the winged ones. I could always count on a few crows to trail me around the city. They seemed to have taken an outsized interest in the new construction project. I gave the birds a half-hearted wave.

A painted sheet of plywood nailed high on the building announced the imminent opening of the Sentinel's Hall of the Golden Phoenix, a new community building to honor the Sentinel of San Francisco.

All for me. Imagine my joy. As if acknowledging me, the crows began to caw loudly. I winced as several workers jumped in surprise. Were they *managing* the workers? Was Freddy feeding the crows again? Just how much had changed in a couple of days?

As I paid for my ride, my phone pinged. The Legacy app helpfully informed me that my dear friend, Fiona Tran, was currently enjoying a beautiful salad for lunch. Or, at least, someone had taken a picture of a salad for her.

Fiona had been unusually quiet since the events of Lóng Yá. Although I was in touch with Freddy, his sister had retreated. Fiona's distance chafed, the gnawing sensation that I had done something wrong. I didn't know yet if her behavior had anything to do with her relationship with Kamon, or if, like most Jiārén, she was simply avoiding me after the unfortunate reveal of my talent after the tournament. Both reasons stung.

I scrolled farther through the app and frowned at the lack of crying/squealing heart emojis. It had been two weeks since my last message from Leanna. It wasn't like the little squirt to let more than a day go by without lighting up my phone with her latest internet discovery.

In a short amount of time, I'd become completely invested in Leanna's progress in the martial arts. Even her little sister, Lucy, had joined our lessons. It still felt strange when they called me Sifu, so I diligently planned their lessons, eager to live up to the title.

Shepherding my brother through his Lóng Yá had been both gratifying and shocking. Teaching him helped us make a connection we'd been missing our whole lives. That connection tied me closer than ever to my family, reminding me that they were always there for me. Then watching him run his Tourney made me wonder what kind of monsters we were raising our children to be.

Lóng Kǒu Academy, the Dragon's Maw where Jiārén elite sent their children to learn and train. Only the toughest endured all six years and ran the final gauntlet. What were we forcing our children to sacrifice, in order to survive? I'd been kicked out long before that milestone but the haunted look in my brother's eyes and the bitterness in Freddy's voice were clear reminders that no one came through the Tourney unchanged. Was this why I wanted to train Leanna? For the Tourney?

I wished she didn't have to go at all, but there were surprisingly few choices available to scions of powerful clans. Fewer still led to different outcomes. In the end it all came down to the struggle for power, and clan treachery.

I couldn't care less what Uncle Jimmy thought of me, but the prospect of being cut off from Leanna hurt more than I expected. I resolved to find Jimmy later today or the next day. As the head of the Louie Clan, I needed to stay in touch with him as much as I needed to reestablish communication with Fiona.

As Sentinel, I was basically a public servant, which meant any of the Jiārén could call upon me to enforce the city's peace. Given that Fiona Tran was the head of the Trans, who controlled all magical exports and imports through my city, and that Uncle Jimmy was the de facto operating head of his clan, which controlled all the banking and political outreach and lobbying of Wàirén, they were two of the largest constituents in my city. All these considerations made me feel like a politician, something I'd never had any desire to be.

"Sentinel!" The voice came from up the street and I cursed for letting myself dither here, of all places.

I plastered on a smile and turned to face Samuel Chen, the Lotus Lane Merchant's Association's Sentinel Relations Liaison. I tried not to choke on his title. Why did I need to liaise with anyone?

Samuel jogged up the sidewalk to me, a thick clipboard tucked under one arm. His orange safety vest nearly blinded me. Samuel had the kind of build that hinted at an adolescence in martial arts that was now going soft around the belly in middle age. But his face was open and inviting, with clear eyes behind wire-rimmed glasses. Like every other time I'd seen him, he was wearing his bright blue hard hat, which he removed to mop the sweat off his bald head.

He bowed at the waist and eyed my duffel bag. "Good morning, Sentinel, did you just get back?"

"Sam, please, just Emiko."

He laughed and nodded, clearly intent on ignoring my request. Did people listen to me less now that I was the Sentinel?

Sam looked up at the burgeoning construction and beamed with pride. "Just so you know, we're ahead of schedule, and everything looks great."

Samuel opened his clipboard and leafed through some pages.

"Actually, since we've earned a few extra days with the crew, I asked them about possibly adding a second set of eaves to the roof. You know, to make the building even more grand. I've got the drawings somewhere—"

I held up a hand. "That's fine, really, Sam. It's beautiful, and much more than I think we need already."

His eyes widened. "You're the first Sentinel of San Francisco! We have to show the other cities that we hold you in the highest regard! I was just talking with Julie, your new media coordinator, and she read that in Beijing they—"

"Sam, no."

Wait, did he say *media coordinator*? I had to stop this train before it picked up too much speed. This kind of . . . adulation was not something I'd ever sought.

"The building is more than enough, really. And I'm sure you have more than enough projects that could use your talents."

He blinked and I knew I had him. Lotus Lane wasn't big, and the construction was a massive use of their resources. Before I'd left for Tokyo, all of this Sentinel's Hall planning had stunned me and I'd done my best to avoid dealing with it, hoping it would wither during the planning phase. To my dismay, the Louies had generously donated the underlying plot of land, and paid the initial deposit to the architects and engineers. Fiona, not wanting to be outdone, had then established a generous beautification fund. Any remaining funds could be applied to additional Lotus Lane projects. Like new basketball courts for the youth center. New paving and benches for the park.

I put an arm around his shoulders and steered us back up the road. "Why don't we see if there aren't any improvement projects that would help Lotus Lane, alongside the Sentinel's Hall?"

Samuel perked up. "Yes! I could draw up a list of items for your approval."

"Perfect. And you know that if you ever can't find me, you can always bring your projects to Freddy, right?"

Samuel nodded. "Oh, yes. Mr. Tran has been very helpful. You're lucky to have him on your staff. It's just, he's been so busy with everything else, I don't feel right putting more on his plate."

My smile turned a little brittle. That . . . didn't sound ominous. What had Freddy been doing? "Everything else?"

"Oh! You shouldn't worry. Really. Mr. Tran has it all under control."

I found Freddy ensconced in his office, a tidy room on the corner of the second floor that would have a sweeping view of Lotus Lane when the construction tarps finally came down. His head popped up from behind a wall of monitors when I knocked on the doorframe.

The Freddy Tran I knew usually dressed in board shorts and tank tops to show off his surfer's physique to good effect. I could rely on him to have a ready supply of CBD gummies in his pocket at all times, which he had been known to feed to my crows for fun and sport. The Freddy behind the desk today was about as far from *normal* Freddy as I had ever seen.

Instead of his usual surf attire he wore a crisp lavender dress shirt with the sleeves rolled up to his elbows, exposing a wide bracelet of hammered silver on his wrist. And pants. I blinked. At least the lack of a tie and the open collar assured me that this was, in fact, my . . . assistant, and not some alien impostor. The crisp line of royal blue that outlined his head helped, as well as the slight tang of sea spray in the air despite the windows being closed. Freddy waved a hand and a miniature version of his signature wind tunnels appeared, sucking away a pile of papers to clear one of the chairs.

I dropped my bag onto the floor and took the clean chair, which gave me a clear line of sight to Freddy through his protective wall of computer monitors. Other than me, Freddy was the most powerful Jiārén in the building. I knew this in my head. And judging by the hollow urgency in my belly, my talent knew it as well.

For most of my life, I had viewed my ability to smell other talents as a useful and often lifesaving gift. Now I wondered if it was a more insidious facet of the hunger within. I could smell my prey.

Was this my life now? Was I going to have to recalibrate every time I got near another strong talent? Sitting this close to Freddy felt like leaning over the edge of a massive pit of swirling, sucking wind, with eager feelers reaching out to pull me in. All I had to do was let go and fall into the pit, and I could gorge until it was sated. If it ever could be sated . . .

I closed my eyes and pushed back on the growl in my belly that had nothing to do with my missed breakfast. Only when it was safely in the back of my mind did I open my eyes. Freddy had waited patiently for me, his hands folded in front of him.

"Welcome home, Sentinel."

I scowled at the title. Freddy responded with an easy grin. That was the problem with making friends. They stopped being afraid of you, and then they did ridiculous things like smile back at you.

"I was only gone a couple days, Tran. What did you do?"

He held up his hands like he was warding me off. "In my defense, you weren't available, so I had to make an executive decision."

The Freddy I knew also didn't use phrases like *executive decision.* It was jarring enough to make me forget my hunger for a moment. Who was this guy? Before I could press him there was another light knock at the door.

"Mr. Tran? I have that write-up you asked for."

Freddy looked up. "Hey, Stacie. Thanks for doing that so quickly."

The soft voice belonged to a young woman in business-casual attire. Her soft pink blouse with its loose bow tucked into black wide leg trousers made her look like she had been plucked out of a financial office in the city, but for some reason she was working here. Her aura was the palest pink. Maybe a bit of persuasion or charm.

My talent sniffed like a great cat and promptly determined that Stacie's talent wouldn't make much of an appetizer. Someone in the hallway behind her, however, was powerful enough to spark my talent's interest.

When Freddy's attention shifted to her, Stacie stepped into the room to hand over a stack of printouts. As Freddy leafed through the papers her eyes finally landed on me. She gasped and stepped back, clasping her hands and dropping into a bow. I barely registered the shocked look on her face before it disappeared behind a curtain of her dark hair.

Oh no.

"Sentinel! Oh my goodness, I'm so sorry, I didn't even—I didn't mean—"

Freddy intervened to save the poor woman. "Stacie, this is our Sentinel, Emiko Soong. She really prefers to be called Emiko. Emiko, this is Stacie, my new assistant."

What was my life turning into, that my assistant needed an assistant?

At the mention of my name the person in the hallway poked his head into the room and I bit back on my surprise at the sight of his peach-tinted hair. Despite being dosed with Final Breath, Colin Aung looked no worse for wear. Colin's eyes sparkled when he spotted me. Before I could say anything, he smiled, gave me a wink, and ducked out of sight.

Colin was here.

In San Francisco.

My brother's friend had been a promising student at Lóng Yá, poised to finish in the top eight in the Tourney. But one rainy night in Tokyo he'd taken a strike from a poisoned blade meant for my brother. Our clan owed him. I'd advocated for him with Father, but he'd been firm that while we could gift the Aung family generously to show our gratitude, we weren't bringing Colin into the Soong fold.

So what had brought Colin here? My expression and prolonged silence must have been obvious as Stacie cleared her throat, clearly more uncomfortable with each passing second, as if she were waiting for me.

I was not used to having people looking to me for direction. My life had been one of lurking in the shadows while others like my father and Tatsuya received all the attention. I thought about how my brother was poised to take the reins of the Soong Clan someday. How much everyone loved Tatsuya at home. How kind he was. He was different from our father in every way possible and I admired that. I tried to channel Tatsuya's demeanor. It took a bit of effort to wipe the scowl off my face and replace it with a lift of my lips. Stacie came up from her bow and my smile must have looked right because her shoulders relaxed considerably.

I gave her a little nod. "It's nice to meet you, Stacie. How long have you been working for Freddy?"

She perked up considerably when I uttered her name. "Oh, I've been here a month, but only with Mr. Tran for a few days, since Nikki left."

Freddy had more than one assistant? What in all the shattered skies was going on? When I turned to him with an incredulous look on my face, Stacie interrupted, her words pouring out in a rush.

"You shouldn't listen to what they're saying, Sentinel. What happened at Lóng Yá doesn't change anything. Nikki was one of the worst and—"

Freddy cut in. "Stacie."

Apparently Stacie could find her voice when her opinions were strong enough. Her cheeks flushed with heat. "I'm not wrong, sir. Anyone who doesn't trust our Sentinel shouldn't be working here."

Wow. That was both reassuring and disappointing, all rolled into one convenient carry-out package. If I'd wanted this kind of abuse I would have just stayed in Tokyo.

Freddy turned back to the papers in his hand and did his best to ignore the awkward silence after Stacie's outburst. He scribbled some notes in the margins and handed the stack back to her.

"This looks great. Please make these changes and send it out."

When she hesitated to take the papers back, I reached out and touched her hand. Stacie startled at the contact, but this time I could see it was surprise, rather than fear.

Stacie's wide eyes met mine and I reached for the appropriate response and settled on "Thank you. I appreciate your trust."

As I said it I realized that I meant it. I'd spent years leaning on people's fear, using it as a lever to get things done. Having someone's trust was a newer experience for me. I'd felt a little of that trust with my family during Tatsuya's Lóng Yá. It was a different sensation, and it was growing on me.

Stacie dropped into an even deeper wai than before. "I know you'll protect us, Sentinel, whatever happens. I promise I'll do my best for you, too."

I didn't miss the tension tightening the corners of her eyes. Whatever was going on, it was clearly weighing on her. But before I could ask, she scooped up her papers and swept out of the room.

When the door clicked shut, I gave Freddy the eye, although this one was far less lethal than when I first sat down. "You want to tell me what's going on?"

MONSTER

Freddy shuffled through the papers on his desk. "You know, I had a feeling about what I was giving up when I stepped aside for Fi . . . and I was right. You couldn't pay me enough to do this job."

I let the shock at his statement sit for a moment before I smiled. "Then it's a good thing I'm not paying you."

Freddy flashed a huge grin and pointed a finger at me. "See? There it is! I knew you could crack a joke."

"Who said I was joking? At least if I was paying you, I could fire you."

Freddy snickered.

Despite my mood I smiled. Freddy had a way of doing that. It was one of the reasons I enjoyed being around him. He stood and moved to the back of the office where he had a small tea station set up on a bookshelf.

"How did Colin end up here?"

Freddy's eyebrows drew down in concentration as he measured out the oolong. "Your father sponsored him. Very generous of your clan to support the Sentinel's Hall."

Yes . . . generous. I sensed Tatsuya's hand in this latest maneuver. This felt like one of Father's moves, tinged with my brother's gentler sensibilities. Tatsuya was learning quickly. Maybe Colin couldn't work for the Soong Clan but they could sponsor him to work for the Sentinel of San Francisco. After my showing in Tokyo, though, I didn't feel like this was an upward career for young Colin and said as much to Freddy.

He shrugged as he turned on the electric kettle. "Working for a Sentinel is a rare opportunity. Colin knows that."

"And what work is he going to do exactly?"

I had been gone for two days and this role of the Sentinel was spiraling out of control, into a realm that I couldn't fathom.

Freddy flashed me a mischievous grin before he poured the water over the leaves. "I thought you could use a driver. I can't always tunnel you everywhere."

I threw a tissue at him. "I am perfectly capable of driving myself."

He raised his eyebrows. "Have you seen his aura? He's going to be good to have around."

It was precisely that talent that had enabled Colin to throw himself in front of Tatsuya during Kaida's attack. I frowned. His talent was useful in moments of danger, but that was exactly what I was afraid of—that it would be dangerous for him and I would have one more person at risk. I didn't exactly lead the life of safe seclusion that I had once imagined for myself.

Colin had done our clan a tremendous service. It would be a grave insult to his family to send him home. Tatsuya had outmaneuvered me. I sighed in resignation and let Freddy catch me up on the time I'd missed during my adventure in Thailand.

The more he talked, the more my mood soured. Even Freddy's potent oolong didn't help. The Jiārén gossip network had been working overtime and news of my abominable talent had reached its saturation point. Despite a possible clan war between the Trans and the Louies, people from all walks of Jiārén life found the energy to pick a side about just how much of a monster I'd become.

It was a lot to take in, but nothing earth-shattering. I'd been reviled for a large part of my adult life. The shame of my newfound talent wasn't terribly different from that. If I had even one supporter like Stacie for every ten like Nikki I'd call it progress.

Freddy drained his tea and poured another. "Actually, it's much better than one in ten. I'd say more like fifty-fifty."

Progress, but still disheartening. "So only half the city hates me."

"Well . . . *hate* is a strong word."

"I eat talents, Tran."

He rolled his eyes. "Okay, when you say it like that . . ."

I'd known this was coming, but saying it out loud still hurt.

He continued, blithely ignoring the fact that we were in the Sentinel's Hall, a place dedicated to the protection of the city's Jiārén—many of whom were currently terrified of its Sentinel. "They just need time to see you doing the very thing they need you for."

Freddy's aura rippled, the rich blue fanning out as he pantomimed someone, ostensibly me, running around and . . . swashbuckling?

The salty tang of his talent swirled around me as he moved, and apparently not satisfied with its recent feast of tiger magic, my talent stirred again. Sour panic spiked in my throat as I shoved down the gnawing hunger that threatened to hollow out my gut. I placed a hand on my chest, just over my Pearl, and let the waves of the city run through me, up through the soles of my feet and along my spine. The cool reassurance of my city comforted me and the hunger dissipated. I exhaled slowly, and my jaw relaxed.

There. Almost normal. As if anything in my life was normal.

I picked up the thread of our conversation. "They're right, Tran. I'm a threat to every gāo talent in the city."

"I don't think Stacie sees it that way."

"Because she's not a gāo talent. Aren't you listening? I've made an enemy of every powerful Jiārén in existence, just by . . . existing!"

Freddy leaned forward, his expression stern. "You're not my enemy."

"I may not be your enemy but I'm still a danger to you."

Now he sat back, his expression thoughtful. After a moment he seemed to come to a decision and he opened a drawer in his desk, pulling out a ring of keys.

"Have you seen the renovations to the courtyard yet? It's still in demo but you can already see how it's going to come together."

"What? Tran, I'm—"

He cut me off by standing and making for the door. "Come on, I'll show you."

And then he was out the door and I had no choice but to chase after him. I found him in the next office, speaking quietly with Stacie. Her office was about half the size of Freddy's with only a small window onto the street. Her eyes widened and she nodded as she listened.

The adjoining office was the mirror of Stacie's, and Colin sat at his desk behind a stack of colorful flyers that announced, loudly, the opening celebration for the Sentinel's Hall. Colin meticulously folded each sheet into thirds and stuffed it into an envelope. His aura was a silvery blue outline around him. Most Jiārén from powerful families learned very early how to hold in their auras to avoid announcing their strength. In Colin's case I suspected he wasn't holding it back very much. Dragon Sight, a form of limited foresight, was a useful talent, but he had no reason to keep it locked down the way combat talents did.

I knocked lightly on the door and Colin looked up from his work. His face lit up again.

"Hey, I was wondering when I would run into you."

I rolled my eyes. At his talent level, he'd probably seen me coming a few hours ago. "My name's on the building. It wouldn't take long. What are you even doing here?" I pointed at the pile of busywork. "Is Freddy punishing you?"

Colin chuckled, his hands moving smoothly through the motions as he talked. "Oh, it's fine. I told Mr. Tran I was happy to help out however I can."

Mr. Tran. If he called me Ms. Soong next, I was going to go buy denture tablets.

He nodded his head toward a stack of journals in the corner. "The flyers are just something Stacie needed a hand with. Mr. Tran asked me to get caught up on things here in San Francisco, so I've been reading the archives kept by the Librarian."

Impressive. "She let you leave with them?"

"It took some convincing. She seemed a little concerned when I told her I was working for you."

Ouch.

The Librarian was a god in her domain, the secret Jiārén library hidden beneath the San Francisco main library. She had a . . . less than optimal opinion of me, and only barely tolerated my presence because of my status as the Sentinel. In my defense, the ghosts had totally not been my fault.

He dropped his voice lower. "'You will return these volumes in the condition in which I have given them to you.'"

It was a passable imitation and got a laugh out of me. I looked around the little office. My father had said any help from our family would look too much like a handout to allow Colin's father to save face. I hoped Colin didn't feel that way.

I promised myself I wouldn't pass up the chance to do right by Colin. Not after what he'd done for Tatsuya. "So, you got me to take you under my wing after all."

He made eyes at me. "Thank you for showing me the way."

"Don't thank me yet. I'll be asking Freddy to make sure you're kept very busy."

He stood and dropped into a wai. "I look forward to it."

At least he didn't wink at me this time.

Freddy popped into the doorframe beside me. "You guys all caught up?"

Ah yes, my assistant who was still mysteriously avoiding my questions. "Yes, now—"

Freddy clapped me on the shoulder. "Perfect! Let's go!" He actually winked at me as he waltzed down the hallway, jingling his keys.

I followed him downstairs and out a back door where we emerged into a central atrium that opened to the sky. More scaffolding and plastic tarps screened off the inner walls of the building but the central space had been cleared out.

Freddy pointed out a few things but I barely heard him. His avoidance of this topic was starting to annoy me. When he started describing the water feature that would be installed in the center I grabbed his shoulder and spun him around.

"Tran! Stop ignoring me!"

"You didn't want a tour?"

I gritted my teeth and took a shuddering breath. My annoyance escalated the rumbling hunger in my belly, making it louder, more insistent. I could almost taste Freddy's talent. I tried to bring everything back under control, both my talent and this meeting that seemed to be veering wildly off course. Above all else, I had to get away from Freddy before I did something I would regret.

"Is there anything else? Anything important before I leave?"

Freddy seemed oblivious to my internal struggle. "Oh yes, I scheduled a private meeting with you and Uncle Jimmy."

Gods, the hits just kept on coming. "What? Why? I'm not—"

"He called to ask for it and we can't afford to alienate either of the clans, much less both of them."

The smell of Freddy's talent tickled at my senses but I shook it off. "No. Jimmy's iced me out from Leanna. If he wants to be like that, I don't need to engage."

"Emiko, he just wants to talk."

"Sure. Whatever." I grumbled. "Your sister isn't talking to me, either."

That bothered me a lot more than Uncle Jimmy. Him, I expected to pull a stunt like this, using my connection to Leanna to manipulate me. But with Fiona, it was the uncomfortable feeling that it was my fault that she wasn't talking to me. Kamon and I had put some unfinished business to rest. But we hadn't done anything inappropriate. And yet her silence felt like a rebuke.

He shrugged. "On that front, I don't have any help for you."

Frustration rose in me, flushing my cheeks. I'd only been home from Japan a couple of weeks and already the city was fraying apart. With no word from either Jimmy or Fiona, their feud seemed ripe to burst into open war. All this as I struggled to control my talent, fumbling with it like a novice.

Freddy had stepped close during my pity party. His voice was quiet and steady. "My father used to do this. He came up with so many ways to set my nerves on edge."

What?

"You're all over the place, Emiko. Your aura is spilling out. Your qì is a mess. It's no wonder you feel like your talent is uncontrollable. You barely have control over yourself."

"My talent is a monster, Tran. It wants to eat you. It would be so easy. If I let go, it will take everything it can."

He patted my forearm and even that contact made my talent go wild. "Emiko. Your talent is not some animal living inside you. It *is* you."

I managed to meet his eyes. For once, they held no humor in them. "That doesn't make me feel any better."

He made a face. "If you only knew how many times Fiona and I blew up our house when we were kids."

Something in his demeanor shifted, and his easy smile dropped away. The change was subtle, but he suddenly seemed *right* in his crisp shirt and slacks. Instead of the Lazy Tran, I was now standing in front of the man who could have led his clan if he hadn't chosen to step aside.

"Emiko, you're never going to learn to use your talent by keeping it locked up. There's only one way to learn."

No.

"Unacceptable." I wouldn't subject anyone to that.

Freddy lifted his right hand and a small whirlwind blossomed in his palm, the whipping winds pulling at my hair. "You say you're dangerous? A threat? You've always been dangerous. Did anyone ever have the luxury to think the Blade of Soong wasn't a threat?"

It was a little shocking hearing something that Father might say, coming out of Freddy's mouth.

He brought the tiny vortex of air closer and the wind whistled past me. "We're dangerous people. And we all learned to control it. Now it's your turn."

The look on his face was at once commanding and open, free of fear or judgment. His wind tore tears from my eyes as I struggled to bring some order to my talent. With Iron Serpent, Kamon, Prem, and . . . Kaida, my talent had simply leapt out of me, a weapon gone wild and out of control. Even with Prem when I'd tried to ready myself in advance, it had taken everything I had to rein it back in, to pull it—

To pull *myself* back.

Freddy edged closer and my talent strained against my will. He nodded to me, and brought the whirlwind up to my face.

His voice was quiet and calm but managed to cut through the wind. "Do you know what Stacie and her friends say about you?"

I shook my head.

"They say even if you are a monster, you're *our* monster. They trust you."

He smiled and a piece of the easygoing Freddy I knew shone through. "I trust you."

He grabbed my wrist. My hunger responded in an instant and broke free.

The only hint I got when my talent struck home was a slight widening of Freddy's eyes. It felt like leaning back, dragging on a chain tied to a massive truck. Even as I pulled back the truck advanced, scraping my shoes across the floor. The sea salt tang of Freddy's talent filled my nostrils and my meridians came alive with his power.

Freddy shook off the initial shock and released my wrist to place the edges of our palms together, forming a cup between us. "There it is. Ease up. I believe in you, Emiko."

A whisper came from the city's Pearl, cooling my skin, a trickle of the city's own magic bolstering me. Leveling me out. My hunger eased, the need to devour reduced to a sip.

In the small space between our hands, a tiny vortex appeared. It was miniscule but steady. I inhaled the bracing scent of his talent, the aftertaste of brine hitting my palate. With a slow exhale, I pushed.

"Tui," I commanded softly and Freddy's eyes danced with excitement as my vortex grew in size.

Images of Freddy flashed across my mind. Surfing. Partying. Fighting. I grunted as he took a punch in one memory and the impact hit me in the stomach.

The flicker of air slowed, sputtering.

He grabbed my arm to hold me up. "Breathe, Emiko. Cycle. You can do this." He used his other hand to raise a small cyclone between his palm and the ground.

I marveled at the flow of power rushing through him, my steady consumption of his talent feeding the thing inside me, feeding me. And yet, Freddy still had enough to spare.

I closed my eyes and pushed my qì through the pattern Madam Yao had taught me. The salty bite of Freddy's energy coursed through my system and blended with my own, turning into something . . . different. On instinct, I also turned my palm downward, directing my qì to the ground.

Before I could examine it closely Freddy crowed, the sound of his voice echoing off the building. I opened my eyes and my stomach flipped. We hovered in the air near the second-story windows, our hands locked together. The two miniature whirlwinds had merged into one larger one beneath us, pumping out a steady blast of air that kept us afloat. All around the atrium, construction tarps whipped and snapped in the swirling chaos. A scaffold groaned and tipped over with a crash.

I screamed over the ripping winds. "What are you doing?!"

Freddy laughed and laughed. "It's you, Emiko! You're doing it!"

And just to prove his point he pulled his hands back and laced his fingers behind his neck. He leaned back into the wind like he was lying on a recliner. The sea salt of his talent faded, leaving me with something that smelled similar to his talent, but subtly changed somehow.

This new flavor of power coursed through my meridians, seemingly of its own accord. I certainly didn't remember forming the funnel under us.

And just like that, my unconscious mastery slipped away like a shadow through my fingers. My stomach flipped again as gravity reasserted itself from twenty feet up. Freddy and I yelped as we plummeted.

A new cushion of air bloomed under us and we touched down with some semblance of grace. I dry heaved once but managed to keep from actually throwing up.

Progress.

Freddy's grin stretched his face. "Might need to work on the dismount but that was awesome!"

My knees wobbled as I readjusted to solid ground. The thrill of using my talent was a fading glow in my senses but I didn't miss the lingering tinge of fear and revulsion in the sensation.

"I could have hurt you, Freddy."

He waved a dismissive hand. "Never in a dragon's age."

The courtyard was in shambles, scaffolding and tarps thrown to every corner. Some of the windows had blown out as well, and broken glass glittered across the stone tiles. Guilt stabbed at me. I hadn't hurt Freddy, but what about the people in the temple? The people who worked here? For me.

Freddy put a hand on my shoulder. "It's okay, Emiko. I had Stacie clear out the building. I had a feeling things might get . . . exciting."

Laughter danced in his eyes.

I batted his hand away. "That was reckless! You can't just—"

His eyes went serious again. "No, I can, and I did. You needed to hear it and you needed to do it."

I shook my head, still in the grips of the fear that I couldn't control the hunger gnawing within. Even now, when it should have been sated.

Freddy grabbed my shoulders. "Emiko, you can't hide from your talent."

I froze because that's exactly what I wanted to do. It's what I had learned to do my entire life, without even realizing it. And the time for hiding was in the past.

Freddy was right but learning control meant stealing someone's talent. Over and over again. How long before I stole too much?

A slow clap broke the silence, followed by the crunch of boots on broken glass. I turned to the sound and my world stretched like mochi dough. From outside my body, I watched with detached amazement and shock as my mother strode into the courtyard.

There was something surreal about seeing Sara Hiroto here in the courtyard, her padded tanzen a concession to our crisp late-spring weather. Her kimono was so deep gray it was nearly black, lined with a blushing silk and embroidered in pinks and reds. Her symbol, a crane in flight, stretched across the left lapel and shoulder. Black pearls were expertly tied into the embroidery for the crane's eyes.

Like the kimono, my mother was a lesson in contrasts. Clothing made as finely as Mother's spoke to a life of wealth and luxury. The tight line of emerald green that surrounded her spoke to the rigid hold she kept over her aura, a lifetime holding the secret of her terrible talent as closely as possible.

While her attire was feminine and classical, the hulking naginata at her back made a clear statement about the true depth of her strength. Her skin was pale and her eyes, inky dark, pierced through me.

They were my eyes and it was uncanny to look into them. The last time I'd met her eyes had been in clanhome after she'd put Shokaku in my hands. Mother had given me the katana to protect me, to give me balance. Somehow my parents never saw the irony of their interactions with me.

Colin appeared behind my mother, his eyes as wide as saucers. His head swiveled between me, my mother, and the tableau of debris my training had left in the courtyard.

Freddy recovered first, lowering himself into a deep wai. "Hiroto-san, it is an honor."

Mother turned to Freddy and I saw the mask go on, the polite fiction Asian parents presented to the public. She gave him a small smile, the merest stretch of her lips.

"The honor is mine, Freddy. Your parents are well?"

"Yes, thank you. You've traveled far to visit, can I offer you some tea?"

My mother was certainly no stranger to long-distance travel but she demurred. "Thank you, but I need to speak with Emiko. If I might borrow her for a moment?"

This was surely one of the strangest conversations I'd witnessed.

Freddy danced somewhere between his slacker persona and the CEO he occasionally unearthed. He turned back to me, as they finally deigned to include me in the discussion about me. "Of course, of course."

Before she turned to me she put a hand on Freddy's arm. I

recognized it, a version of Father's power moves. "Thank you, Freddy, for being such a good friend to Emiko. Your sister as well. Emiko is lucky to have you both."

Freddy beamed. "It's our pleasure."

He slung an arm around Colin, squeezing his shoulder. "And thank you for adding to our staff by sponsoring Colin to join our team here at the Sentinel's Hall."

Mother's polite smile warmed a notch. "Colin is Tatsuya's dear friend and we are happy that he has chosen to train with Emiko here in San Francisco."

Train with me? It was like everyone in my family knew about this plan except me.

I turned to Freddy. "Could you let Fiona know I asked about her?"

He regarded me with a critical eye. If I didn't know any better I would have said it was his version of my scowl. Less threatening, but just as judgmental. "I'm your friend, Emiko, and I'm telling you as a friend—go talk to her yourself."

I was right. Being the Sentinel really did mean that no one listened to me anymore.

Then Mother was at my side. Sara Hiroto bestowed one more warm smile on Freddy and Colin before we turned for the exit.

When it was just the two of us in the courtyard, her mask dropped away. Sara Hiroto's face returned to the expression I'd known my entire life and the glint in her eye said it was time for business.

A SIMPLE TASK

I had endured years without seeing my mother and now in the span of mere weeks we were face-to-face twice. Except for Tatsuya, we were not a hugging kind of family, but I wanted us to be. Despite the awkwardness of it, I gave it a try.

"Mother." I leaned forward, clasping her in my arms and giving her a squeeze. It took her half a beat, but she returned the hug with startling intensity.

"Emi-chan. I don't have much time." Her eyes traveled over my face slowly and she smiled as her gaze drifted to Shokaku's pommel. Though nothing could replace Truth, having Mother's katana meant a lot to me. The weight of her in my palm was just right and she struck true. Carrying her on my hip together with Hachi felt complete. And if the sharp memories of who had carried this sword before me chilled the warmth of my pleasure in holding her, then that was only right, too. Kaida had paid too much and I too little for the right to hold Shokaku.

I gestured to the Hall. "Would you like to come inside?"

It was strange playing host to my mother.

She shook her head. "It's best if we keep this visit short."

I bit back the first response that came to mind. The second wasn't much better. "It's easier that way, isn't it?"

My mother believed her fearsome talent, and therefore her presence, made her a constant danger to our family. Her absence from our lives was a consequence of her commitment to keeping us safe. How my parents could dole out lifesaving sacrifice right along with lasting emotional trauma was one of the unexplained mysteries of my universe.

Her pained expression colored my spite with a tinge of guilt. At least with her I could gauge her emotions. I could do this all day with Father and never once know if I'd landed anything.

I lowered my eyes. "Forgive me. It's been a long day. The Zhao Clan blacklisted me, so I had to fly back from—"

Mother clutched my shoulders, her grip painfully tight. She held me until I brought my eyes back up to hers. Her voice trembled.

"It's not easier. It never is."

I tamped down the swell of emotion in my throat. Dealing with either of my parents wasn't easy, but for different reasons. And I had very little time with my mother to use as a baseline. With a shrug, I shook her hands off.

"What did you come here for?"

Because she certainly wasn't here for a social visit. Her eyes tightened at the corners, another tell I wouldn't have gotten from my father. After a moment her expression softened.

"Actually, it has been some time since I've eaten. Is there someplace . . . ?"

How were they both so good at keeping me off-balance? But I couldn't refuse the olive branch. Not if I was serious about starting fresh with her.

"Of course. How do dumplings sound?"

If playing host to my mother was strange, walking into Golden Dragon Potstickers with her was absolutely surreal. The bell over the door tinkled cheerily as we entered the restaurant's crowded, bright green interior. A wave of tantalizing aroma washed over us, thick with pork broth and five spice, along with the jumbled sounds of a dozen conversations and clattering dishes.

By the time the door shut behind us every conversation stopped, leaving the bell to tinkle again into the dead quiet. While most of the eyes fixed on me, more than a few slid over to my mother. Some eyes widened with fear, but many crinkled above proud smiles.

The silence lingered for a few painful seconds until the doors to the kitchen burst open and Chef Kelly barreled into the dining room. Her chef jacket was immaculately white, buttoned to her neck, the crisp lines accentuating the breadth of her shoulders. Kelly commanded attention the way a planet commanded gravity, and she took in the stunned silence for a moment before barking at her diners.

"What, you've never seen our Sentinel before? Stop staring, you're making her uncomfortable!"

A tiny smile stretched my lips before I hid it. Had I managed to win Chef Kelly over?

The restaurant patrons slowly resumed their eating and Kelly lumbered over to us, setting down a platter of twenty piping hot potstickers, the slurry fried to a wafer-thin crisp that held them together. She glanced at my mother, then back to me, and her lips flattened in clear annoyance. "Maybe you need another order?"

My lips twitched in amusement. She knew I could easily wolf down an order of twenty on my own. "Yes, please."

Kelly grunted. "Only this time, since you have a guest."

Clearly I had maxed out my weekly potsticker allotment with this visit. Mother tilted her head, her expression quizzical. She was used to more deference, but I appreciated that she let me take the lead with Kelly.

We sat and broke our wooden chopsticks with quick snaps, striking them against each other in identical motions to sand off the splintered bits. I poured black vinegar into a plate, forming a lake of tangy goodness to soak my potstickers in. Mother accepted the plate from me with a nod and I made another for myself. As we finished the quiet ritual of preparing for our meal, Kelly returned with a second plate of dumplings.

We dug into our meal and the din of the restaurant rose around us, broken only by the sounds of our chewing. It was strangely companionable, and I couldn't remember the last time I had eaten a meal with my mother. The tables were so small that we had to sit close, our knees practically touching. Only now that we were seated could I draw a breath and let my spirit settle. Freddy had spun me up, ripping away my control over the ever-gnawing hunger deep in my belly. But he'd done something and for once my talent lay quiescent. Sated. The mélange of gifts around me didn't rouse it. Gratitude for Freddy's high-handedness settled on my shoulders like a warm blanket. For this brief time with my mother, I could have ease from the slavering beast within. And I didn't examine too closely the possibility that I could have this ease if I fed it more often.

I focused on Mother. What had brought her to seek me out? She had never done that before. I smelled the faint ginger scent that always clung to her clothes and now I wondered how much of that was her talent. Could it also be from her dark-walking? Did the Void have a smell like taking the subway? I'd never asked her anything about her talent before.

But now I wanted to.

San Francisco's hazy weather had cleared away and afternoon sun streamed in through the restaurant windows, painting us in soft warmth. Mother's skin glowed pearl bright and smooth. With a start, I realized that she looked much younger than she should have. I did the math and reeled. She had been younger than I was now when she'd become a mother. And now we looked like sisters. Was her Void walking suspending her in time?

A busboy brought out a curved white pot of tea with two small cups. I poured the tea, a hearty oolong that paired perfectly with the pork filling.

Finally, I asked, "What does it feel like when you're in the Void?"

Mother looked up from her plate and set down her chopsticks.

Her eyes took on a faraway gaze, as if she'd already stepped into the Void just by me asking.

When she answered, her voice was soft.

"It's like sliding into a lake. Everything is quiet, and I lose my sense of time and place. My body doesn't have any weight." She paused and took a sip of tea.

"Sometimes I just want to close my eyes and sleep, but that's dangerous. If I drift I could lose myself." Her fingers touched her anchor, a quick tracing of the delicate embroidery.

I was too nervous to breathe, afraid she would stop talking and we would lose this tenuous connection.

"The first time I started dark-walking, I feared that there were other things there. Things I couldn't see, things I couldn't hear. I always sensed other presences around me."

She gave a small laugh, her cheeks rounding. "Later, I didn't worry so much about what I couldn't see or hear because I realized they probably couldn't see me or hear me, either."

Despite her casual tone, I shivered at this admission. My clothes were suddenly too rough, as if my skin had grown thin. I shoved the last potsticker into my mouth and chewed vigorously. I let the taste of Shaoxing wine and ginger wash over my tongue before I asked another question.

"How long have you known about the dragons?" I asked. Her lips turned down, her expression sad.

"I didn't at first, but then I began to search around the seams. There are no hard edges in the Void. But there are places where other Realms peek through. It's as if smell, color, and light can't be contained too long, and they spill over in places. It took years, but I eventually found my way into Lóng Jiā."

I tensed, my body going from hot to cold and back. This was what I had done at the Tourney—inadvertently torn a seam in the Void space and allowed the sound and power of our ancient homeworld to spill forth. The echo of Dragonsong ricocheted around my chest as if I was hearing it anew. It had been beautiful and terrifying—a legend made reality. If Madam Yao and my mother hadn't sealed it, who knew what would have happened?

But sealing it couldn't unring that bell. We'd thought we were alone here, that we had found refuge from the Cataclysm. I had ripped away that feeling of safety. Because if we could find them . . . they could find us. Because of me.

Fear dried my mouth and throat, and even sipping the perfectly brewed tea didn't take the edge off. I didn't know what to say to my mother, how to express the magnitude of shame I'd felt at that moment in the mud. The noise of the busy restaurant gave me cover as I struggled to regain my composure. I wanted my mother to keep talking to me.

"How did you learn about the seams?"

She pursed her lips and exhaled a slow breath. When she spoke, her voice took on a familiar cadence. From the edges of memory I could feel my legs bumping against my small stool, struggling to stay still as Mother brushed my hair and told me a story.

It had been a long time since I had thought about those moments with her.

I was practicing for Lóng Yá. The headmaster came to inform me of the good news. Because my talent was so rare, I would be instructed by an Old One. Me, a nobody. I wasn't from some Custodian family. She told me to wait in front of Tiger House. I stood in the courtyard at the appointed time, nervous because there is nothing that can prepare you for meeting an Old One.

Your father had graduated already. I didn't have the protection of the Soong Clan yet. And though the professors always fulfilled their obligations to me as a pupil, it was clear they had nothing left to teach me about the practice of being a dark walker. I'd had years of theory and forays—short trips, little hops—things that made it clear to me that I had only scratched the surface.

I needed more.

A swirl of wind rustled the leaves in the courtyard, whistling through the crevices and cracks of Tiger Pavilion. I gripped my kimono and hunched, bracing against the now chilly wind. My eyes searched the skies, but there were no storm clouds in the pocket Realm of Lóng Kǒu.

Instinctively, I cycled my qì, letting it gather at the base of my spine, pulling it lightly until I could feel it at the very top of my skull. If this was a test, I had to prepare to step out of this Realm fragment.

I craned my neck, left and right, searching for the threat. The air grew heavy around me, and my ears started to feel like I was ascending, though I hadn't taken a single step.

With a pop, a swirl of iridescent color appeared in front of me, as beautiful as abalone shell. I took a step back, my hands gathering into a fighting stance, ready to pull my tantō.

Back then, my dark-walking let me make short trips. My talent gave me just enough to reappear behind my opponent. I always took small steps, making short falls into the dark. Never farther. Never longer.

My heart raced like a rabbit, but curiosity made me stay. I had never seen anyone materialize in the Realm like this before. I didn't know what it looked like when I appeared in front of others. As far as I knew, there were no telltale signs. No change of color, no bracing wind to herald my arrival. In fact, that's what made me so dangerous—the fact that I could appear anywhere, at any time, without alerting anyone.

In the faint haze of color, a muted gold outline appeared. I blinked, unsure of what I was seeing. First, there was nothing but a cascade of shimmering color, and then it dissipated in a fall of golden sand, leaving behind a towering qílín with another majestic being perched on the qílín's back. My hands relaxed, not because these beings weren't dangerous, but because these were

Old Ones. The weight of their power pressed in on me. Attacking them was folly. I had to flee.

It is one thing to see a small illustration of the qílín in the student scrolls, and quite another to have one standing before you.

The qílín stood tall, my head reaching only to its wide chest. The wind had stopped but the qílín appeared to have its own atmosphere as light dappled across its golden coat, and its silver mane and fetlocks rippled in unseen wind. It stretched its eagle wings, wider than I thought possible, and the rush of movement made me jump. The qílín's eyes, deep set and black as night, glittered with amusement. Was it smiling at me?

Before I could regain my composure, the other being, a huli jing, leapt off the qílín, her nine tails fanning out behind her in a glow of silver luminescence. When she landed, not one blade of grass dared to move.

When she spoke, her voice was low and rich, echoing throughout my skull as if she was talking to me from the inside out. "So you're Sara, the unparalleled dark walker of your generation."

I was taken aback. I knew I was alone, but I guess I had not considered the fact that it meant I had no peers. I bowed respectfully. "Yes, most exalted one. I am Sara."

She laughed, and her fangs flashed, their sheer size triggering a mild spike of alarm. "There is no need to be modest. Surely you realize that very few can do what you can do, what your bloodline can do."

I had never known what my bloodline could do. Even with my access to the vast libraries that Lóng Kǒu offered, there wasn't much written about the dark walkers. I hadn't ever met another one. Even my brothers could only do a fraction of what I could do. My parents weren't alive to teach me, and my obāchan was not a dark walker.

A hot rush of anticipation rose in my body, and I rocked forward, my body weight shifting. I finally had the perfect instructor, a being so powerful and rare that her presence rarely graced this campus unless it was for the Tourney. Was she also going to be one of my judges?

"I am the most beloved, benevolent Madam Yao. You may call me Madam Yao."

"Thank you for coming to instruct me."

"Oh, no, no, dear. I am not your instructor. I am to be your guide, to take you somewhere you've always known you could go." She held out a delicate paw, her bones slimmer than my own wrist.

I stepped forward and placed my hand in her paw. Deep power thrummed through even that small contact. With little effort, she vaulted onto the qílín's back and pulled me with her.

Madam Yao snuggled in close behind me and her voice was soft against my ear. "Fall back, Sara."

My first test. I always thought my talent could only transport me. I had never tried to bring anyone else with me into the Void.

I touched my anchor pin, a crane in flight on my lapel, and I fell back.

As Mother had told me her story, her words wove a spell over me. By the time she finished, most of the patrons of the Golden Dragon Potstickers had left and the mealtime rush was over. The busboy started stacking dishes at the table next to us, the noise bringing me back to the present.

I picked up my cold tea and hastily downed it, then placed a hundred-dollar bill on the table. Mother stood up and picked up her naginata. I pulled on my haori.

Kelly bustled over and frowned. She shoved the money back at me. "Your money is no good here, Sentinel."

We did this song and dance every time I came in. I'd helped out the Lotus Lane Merchant Association once and now none of the vendors let me pay them. Except for the Suns. I had to get my weapons and supplies from somewhere and Sally Sun was happy to take my money, which kept things blessedly normal between us.

I sighed and turned to hand the money to the busboy. "Please share with the rest of the staff."

Kelly sniffed but I had found her weakness and I wasn't above using it to get my way. "Thank you for the meal, Kelly."

My mother bowed. "It was wonderful."

Kelly's frown disappeared. Mother's effect on her was obvious. There was something about her quiet deadliness that made everyone wary. Mother was a reminder of the old ways, and people were either terrified or dazzled by her presence. Kelly blinked a few times in rapid succession before muttering, "Thank you for coming in."

Once outside in the hustle and bustle of Lotus Lane, I turned to face her. "Why are you here, Mother?"

She held out her hand and her aura unfurled, an emerald-green corona of light. The sharp spice of ginger filled my world.

I stared at Mother's hand, the inherent promise and threat of going with her to the dark spaces she'd long walked. I took her hand.

"Fall back, Emi-chan."

Sound and light muted. I smelled only the pungent sting of ginger. The scent of Mother's talent was so intense my nose itched. I welcomed it because it meant she was close. I clung to her hand, my lifeline in the Void. She was my anchor and I ignored the other sensations of this place, the insidious quiet and the disturbing buoyancy. I lost track of time as we moved through the Void. We could have been here seconds, or hours.

While I had spent much of my time learning to await my prey in the shadows, this was my mother's world. Kaida's world. I was a stranger here and if my mother let go of me, I would wander, lost forever.

As if she heard my thoughts, she squeezed my hand, her touch cool and strong.

She had me.

Light seared my brain as we emerged from shadow and I sagged to the ground as Mother let go of my hand. The city welcomed me, the air heavy with salt and moisture bathing my skin. I sucked in deep gulps of air. Had I been holding my breath in the Void? Probably inadvisable. Walking in the shadows was terrifying and if I never did it again, it would be too soon.

The city's Pearl beat steady and strong, a deep thrum assuring me that I was safe in my territory. Cool, noontime sun shone down on us. Our location had a stunning view of the Bay Bridge as the last of the morning fog burned off the water. I turned around and Coit Tower rose above me, an art deco concrete structure atop Telegraph Hill.

Despite what must have been our sudden appearance here, the bustling crowd of Wàirén tourists flowed around us, a rushing stream divided by the unforgiving rock of my mother's steady presence. I hid in her lee until the crowd passed.

Although I had lived in the city for a few years now, I'd never come here. My mother didn't strike me as a sightseer, either.

She held out her hand again and I let her hoist me up. "I've never given you a task that I didn't think you were ready for, Emi-chan."

That was an ominous opening.

Mother led me to the parking lot, a small cul-de-sac next to Coit Tower. Without bothering to pause, she stepped out into the stream of cars cruising around the little loop. I didn't know if it was the Wàirén habit of not seeing us for what we truly were, or my mother's imposing looks, but traffic paused just enough to let her through. I hurried to keep up with her and followed her over the lip of the circular planter in the center of the turnaround.

Mother threaded through the succulents and stopped at a small concrete monument in the middle of the planter.

She pulled me forward and placed my hand on the monument. "Tell me what you feel."

The concrete was cold and damp. I concentrated for a moment before I understood what she was showing me. San Francisco was alive under my feet, a gentle pulse of vibrant life that fed a thrill of energy up my legs. The monument under my hand was cold and dead. It was a disturbing black spot of numbness in the middle of my city.

When I turned to look at her, my mother simply pressed my hand down. "What do you feel?"

Like my father, she was testing me. She knew I couldn't feel the city here. There was something else. Something I was missing. I closed my eyes and cycled, tuning out the world around me.

As my qì spun up my talent rumbled and began sniffing around. Even though we spent so little time together, the scent of Mother's talent was familiar and laced with nostalgia. Now that I had a quiet moment to study it, I realized the ginger aroma did not smell exactly the same as my memory of Kaida's. Mother's talent was more spice and heat, while Kaida's was more herbaceous. Once I recognized that, the faint trace of Kaida's talent was painfully obvious. In fact, it pervaded the entire parking lot, as if Kaida's talent had saturated the ground.

Mother squeezed my hand. "You found it."

It wasn't a question. I opened my eyes and looked down. The strongest source of Kaida's talent was under my feet. And now that I was looking right at it, my mother's talent was here, too.

Dread pooled in my gut at the discovery.

"Why here?" I looked at Mother and her eyes tightened at the corners.

"It seems I can't stop placing challenges along your path," she whispered.

The Gate my mother and Madam Yao had fashioned from all the Hoard items at Lóng Yá was under my hand. Covering a portal to the Realm. Here in my city. The enormity of it all swelled inside me until I felt like my head would explode.

I had a barely contained clan war here. Jiārén everywhere reviled me, more than any other time in my notorious career. Our whole family, our clan, edged closer to the precipice, and my mother saw fit to put her Gate here, of all places? Tears of frustration pricked at my eyes but I shoved them down and buried the feeling under many layers of anger. I would not cry in front of my mother.

It all came out in one agonized growl. "Why?"

Mother's eyes softened, but only a little. "There was nowhere else."

Before I could protest, she went on. "A Gate is a delicate construct."

She swept her hand toward the bay. "Like a bridge. Many forces must be considered in the construction of both, then weighed against the materials to be used. Building a Gate takes time and consideration, both of which I had none of last month."

"I hope you're not fishing for an apology." I'd had little time or consideration of my own as I tried to not kill my cousin at the end of Tacchan's Lóng Yá.

"Not at all. You did what you had to do, as did I. But we are left with the consequences."

Mother held her hands over the monument and the spicy ginger scent of her talent beckoned. Deep, gentle power flowed from her and the planter faded from underneath us. The Wàirén milling about paid no attention as the center of the parking lot seemed to vanish from sight, leaving us hovering in space over a massive gate of Hoard gold and gems.

The Gate was an ugly slab of ill-formed metal, scorched and studded with shattered bits of gems and jewelry. Ugly as it was, it had prevented my disastrous actions at Lóng Yá from spiraling out of control. Gates controlled openings to the Void, places where the daring or the foolish could venture to other worlds. Like Yomi. Or the Realm.

Only, no one had ever opened a path to the Realm, until I'd stolen my cousin's talent last month, in the most horrifying society debut ever. My split-second decision cost me any vestiges of sympathy I might have had among our people, and shredded the fable that our Dragon lords had perished millennia ago. Before more Dragonsong, or worse, could emerge from the portal, Mother had formed a Gate to close it, using the combined Hoard gems of countless Jiārén, stolen on the spot. We really weren't winning any popularity contests these days.

This much Hoard would always feel imposing. Knowing that Most Exalted Heavenly Madam Yao had a hand in its making made it a near religious artifact. Standing above it even for a few moments felt like I was getting the start of a sunburn.

Mother gave a heavy sigh and grimaced. "Madam Yao called it more of a wine cork, and less of a Gate. I tend to agree with her."

A rippling pulse of power rolled through the ground at my feet. A flash of brilliant purple light appeared at the edge of the Gate and I lifted my hand to shield my eyes. As the light faded I caught the faintest sound of crystalline Dragonsong. When the brief euphoria of hearing it again faded, I had a terrifying vision of the chaos of an open portal to the Realm in the middle of San Francisco.

I steadied myself before I trusted myself to speak. "It's not closed all the way, is it?"

Mother made a sound of disgust. "Correct."

"Please tell me you're here to fix it."

She gave a frustrated huff and crossed her arms. "There's no fixing this. If I couldn't close it with all the Hoard I had at my disposal and Madam Yao's help, then there's nothing else to be done."

"What am I supposed to do? I don't suppose you're planning to stay?"

Mother shook her head. "You know the answer to that. I've already stayed too long."

Her answer rubbed me the wrong way, as usual, but that's what calluses were for. "You still haven't told me why it's here."

"All Gates are connected to their creators. Both the one who makes the Gate, and the one who opens the portal."

I sucked in a breath. "I didn't open it! It was Kaida's talent that I . . ."

Mother put a hand on my arm. "You know it wasn't just Kaida's. Kaida is a strong dark walker, but she would never have been able to open a passage to the Realm. You did that, my daughter. Your talent, combined with Kaida's."

Kaida, the cousin who looked more like my mother than I did. The cousin who had wielded Shokaku before me, who despised me, and who had tried to kill Tacchan under the General's command. Monstrosity seemed to run in our genes.

My vision started to darken at the edges. I might have been hyperventilating a little. "This is *my* Gate?"

That got a little smile out of her. "Well, why don't we call it *our* Gate."

Sure. That sounded so much better.

"Emiko, Gates are always hidden because they attract the wrong kinds of attention. The risk is great, but there is always something to be gained when crossing the Void. This one even more so because of how unstable it is . . . how it can still be manipulated. The lure of this Gate will prove irresistible for . . . certain people."

I narrowed my eyes at her, remembering her brief interaction with Batuhan at the end of Tatsuya's Lóng Yá. My mother huffed a breath. "Yes, Batuhan. I suppose the time for such secrets is over now."

"Do you really have more secrets that are worse than what I've already learned?"

She made a moue. "Worse? No."

I noted that wasn't a denial of further secrets, but decided against pursuing that line for now. "Why is Batuhan so interested?"

"He's only ever been interested in one thing. Power."

"You seem to know a lot about him."

She made an impatient sound. "Focus. Batuhan and possibly others like him are looking for this Gate as we speak. If the Gate continues to destabilize, it will be like hanging a sign at the Glorious Emerald Pagoda, inviting everyone to your city."

Now that I looked for it, there was a subtle wrongness to it. Like a blade forged with the balance slightly off, or a grip just a hair too large for your hand.

"What happens if the Gate opens?"

"Nothing good."

How did I keep getting backed into these impossible corners? "I'm sure you'd be much better suited to this task."

My mother didn't bat an eye. "Most times, I would. But not this time."

"You close portals all the time. Why can't we just close this one and be done with it?"

She looked away from me, the kind of tell I'd never see with Father. "That's different. When I'm dark-walking, it's my portal, and mine alone. I step through and close it behind me. Madam Yao showed me how to do it, something about balancing the power expended on both sides of the opening. She has a number of spirited theories on the subject, should you choose to discuss it with her."

None of this sounded promising. "If even Madam Yao can't close this, what hope do I have?"

"You opened the portal, and you're a Sentinel. Within your city, you can keep the Gate stable."

"How do you know that? It's not like being Sentinel came with a user's manual! And I don't know anything about Gates—"

"I think you know a thing or two about Gates."

I closed my eyes and took a breath while pushing away some very un-filial thoughts. My mother took my hand in hers. "And you know about the poem."

That turned my stomach to ice. "What does the poem have to do with any of this?"

"Your father and I believe your fate is tied to this Gate."

I'd never fallen out of an airplane before, but I imagined that the feeling of all-encompassing helplessness would be similar. Certainly the rushing sound in my ears had to be close.

It took me a moment to find my voice again, and when I spoke, my voice cracked a little. "And yet, you still brought it here."

"I tried for years to steer you away from it, and look where my efforts got you."

I wanted to curl up into a ball. "So I'm doomed."

Mother grabbed my shoulders and turned me to face her. "No. Certain doom would be putting the Gate anywhere else. Bringing it here, to you, is the best chance we have. Because of you, and your connection to this city."

I pinched the bridge of my nose. The sharp point of pain between my eyes felt like it was going to be with me for a while. "I appreciate the vote of confidence, but I still don't know how I'm supposed to secure it."

"Have you considered asking the city to do what you need?"

"Mother. The city isn't a—"

"Have. You. Asked?"

Why was it always like this with her? With Father? Always the student called before the teacher. I reached for the city again and found her waiting for me. My interactions with the city had always been emotional, primal. I knew the city had emotions and needs as well, but it had never spoken to me, so I'd never tried speaking to it. The city flowed up through my legs and her calming presence soothed the jagged edges around my heart.

How would I even ask? How would someone ask the ocean to move? I knew the city responded to me sometimes, but it was . . . primal. Maybe that was the key. The Gate was a dead spot in the undulating fabric of San Francisco's magic, a place where the normal flow of life and power stopped. As the city melded with me, I considered the Gate and let my fears come to the surface.

What would happen if the Gate opened? What havoc would it wreak on my city? On my people? To Tessa, Leanna, Popo? The feeling became a sick, sour sensation at the back of my throat and my breathing went quick and shallow. Cold sweat prickled my skin and I broke out in gooseflesh. San Francisco surged within me again, and the sick feeling subsided. I focused on the Gate, forcing myself to imagine even more terrible outcomes should it open.

The city pulsed again, and this time the feeling reverberated up my spine and an echoing pulse came from the Pearl in my chest. The pulse went back and forth a few more times, and on each pass, the fabric of the city's magic under my feet grew.

Layer by layer the city's power washed over the Gate like a tide rolling over the beach. Each time the ginger scents of the Gate dulled a little more. The wrongness of the Gate, the crack in the seal that exposed the chaos of the Void, quieted, buried under many protective layers of the city's magic.

Like a Pearl.

From the way her shoulders relaxed, Mother must have felt it, too. Her eyes shone with unshed tears. "I'm very proud of you."

I blinked. Praise was rarer than dragon feathers in our home, doubly so from my frequently absent mother. But acknowledging that praise would only make the situation more uncomfortable for both of us. So I knuckled away my own tears before they could fall, nodded, and mumbled something incomprehensible. After a moment, we found our footing again.

San Francisco eased down. The pulse in my Pearl slowed, but a new sensation appeared in my chest. Much like scar tissue, the presence of the Gate in my city felt like a bump under my ribs. I resisted the urge to scratch at it. “Is that it? Is it fixed?”

“For now.”

“Until when?”

“That’s why I can’t stay. I need to return to your brother, and find you a better solution.”

I’d spent more time with my mother in the last two months than in the last two years and it still felt too soon for her to leave. And I wasn’t too proud to admit I felt a stab of jealousy that she was going back home, to Tatsuya, and leaving me here with the Gate.

She must have seen something of that on my face because she pulled me close for another unexpected hug. Her voice was a fierce whisper in my ear. “Guard it well, Emi-chan.”

I tightened my arms around her, as if I could hold her in place. But of course, she was Sara Hiroto, the Walker of the Void. Nothing could hold her down. The scent of ginger bloomed around us, thick like warm soup and nostalgia.

Mother leaned away from me and cupped her hand along my cheek. “I will return.”

Liquid darkness spilled out from under her tanzen and flowed around us like ink curling through water. She took a half step back into the black and vanished, leaving my arms empty and colder.

BLACK TIE

How did she manage to do this to me? Or maybe I had done it to myself. From the moment my talent had rent our family to near death and forced Mother to trade a Talon to the Shinigami, I had been marked for this. My destiny had spooled out from there and now I was firmly on the twisted path—a tangled prison that I couldn't escape.

Whatever gravitas my mother had that lent her so much freedom of movement in large crowds of tourists had not been passed down to me. I wove through the parking lot, dodging cars, tour buses, and throngs of gawking sightseers. With every step, my emotions roiled, a hot flush of resentment alternating with a cold spike of fear. My city responded in kind, bathing me with heavy fog and a bit of warmth from the ground as I stalked to a find a spot where I could reasonably hail a rideshare.

Maybe the saving grace was that no one knew the Gate was here. And my city had showed me how to hide it, to mask its uncanny signature. I latched onto that like a drowning man, hoping I had time to work out something with my city, some way to bury my mistakes. I exhaled and jogged down the hill.

At the base of the hill, a brilliant white armored personnel carrier masquerading as a car was parked at the curb. Colin leaned against it, with his head down and his eyes fixed on his phone.

His head popped up when he heard my footsteps and he stowed his phone into his pocket. "Hey, need a lift?"

"Sure . . . what are you doing here?"

Colin looked up. I followed his gaze and squinted until I saw the microdrone hovering over the intersection. It was nearly silent, and painted to blend in with the sky, the best tech Tran money could find.

"Freddy's keeping tabs on me?"

Colin shrugged. "Mr. Tran told me to hang out and see if you needed a ride." He held up his phone and waved it. "This app shows me where you are."

I narrowed my eyes at the drone in annoyance. I didn't like being so easy to find. But I couldn't refute that I did need a ride. "Huh. Yeah, I need a ride. Let's ditch the drone."

Colin's eyes lit up and he patted the car door. "Cool. Let's see what the company car can do."

Sometimes Jiārén found truly unique and modern applications for their talents. Colin could *drive.* Dragon Sight had limited practical applications, but Colin had found a good one. The earthy, leather tone of his talent's scent even matched the car's interior. He piloted the Tran tank through San Francisco's maze of one-way streets with the kind of casual aplomb I only saw with natives born and bred here. Even with my two years in the city, Colin had me turned around in moments, taking turns seemingly at random. His route took us through an unbroken string of green lights as surely as if the city herself was guiding us. He swung the massive SUV into blind corners with abandon that made me cringe, picturing little grandmas pulling their groceries behind them being squashed under our tires.

As we neared my place in Dogpatch, Colin kept up a steady stream of chatter and I asked him the occasional question. When he mentioned his two younger sisters, a pang of sadness went through me. Would I ever see Leanna and Lucy again?

Maybe it was better if I didn't think about it for now. The terrible thing inside me was untrained and unrelenting. Though I didn't appreciate how Kamon and Freddy had forced my hand, they were right—I had to learn how to wrangle my talent into some semblance of controlled force. Until then I was a boiling pot with the lid about to blow.

Colin's easy expression turned to confusion as he pulled up to my house.

The battalion of crows guarding my house was certainly unusual. They stood in unblinking sentry duty across my drought-tolerant front yard, along my roofline, and scattered through the backyard that led to my rear house. Or maybe it was disappointment, because my whole double lot could fit in the front drive leading to the Tran château.

"Here?"

"Yes."

He shook his head. "I never would have guessed the Blade of Soong would be living in a place like this."

"I'm not the Blade anymore," I said quietly.

He cleared his throat. "I didn't mean any insult."

Colin had only seen what Tatsuya's life was like as the scion of a Hoard Custodian family with the luxury flats, palatial estates, and all the trappings befitting a Soong. I had none of those things here and I didn't miss them. They had never belonged to me anyway. But this city did.

I was about to open the door when I stopped. "I know this isn't what you were expecting, after Lóng Kǒu."

He gave a little shrug of his shoulders, seemingly at ease. "It's not so bad, and the change of scenery has been nice."

It was easy to see why he and my brother had gotten along. "I haven't had the chance to thank you, personally, and on behalf of my family, for protecting Tatsuya. You—"

Colin put up a hand to stop me. "Tatsuya's my friend. I had to step in."

"It cost you so much."

His brave facade cracked and he gave a little humorless laugh.

"Me, not so much. My sisters are more than a little mad at me, though."

"I'm sorry."

Colin's performance in the Tourney should have been a leg up for his family, especially his younger sisters. Hosting Colin here was poor payment for what he had done for my brother. Helping his clan, his sisters, was beyond my reach.

There was nothing more I could say, so I opened the door and got out. Colin gave me a wave as he drove off, which only sharpened the guilt twisting through me. What could I do for him? Was he really better off here in my city? I shook off the feeling that, thousands of miles away, my father was still arranging my life.

The crows turned to look at me in unison as I stepped onto the porch, then took flight in a flurry of wings as I approached my front door. Between the crows and the fresh lemon scent of the water running around my yard, I was confident my house had been secure during my absence. I keyed open the locks on my door, mechanical and magical, and went inside.

I put away my things on autopilot, busying my hands with mindless tasks while I tried to sort out everything that had unfolded the last few hours. I needed help.

I wanted to talk to Oda. Or Gu Ma.

But a visit to the Archive would have to wait. For now the Gate was hidden, and I had an engagement this evening I couldn't get out of—Tessa's long-awaited museum gala.

This was her big night, and the Asian sword exhibit was going to draw crowds. It was also going to mean a certain patron would be there, someone I hadn't seen in weeks. Adam. We had parted badly in Tokyo and my eyes closed in regret. I had accomplished my objective, but the sacrifice had been our once growing ease. It hadn't been a relationship exactly, but it had held the promise of one. Now there was an uncomfortable tension between us and we would have to navigate the new status Adam held within my clan.

I gritted my teeth and told myself I'd been through much worse. I could survive one lousy party.

The key to surviving a battle was in the preparation. In the secured rooms of my cottage on the rear of my property, I had the varied tools I needed to arm myself for any kind of conflict. My swords hung on the wall in places of honor. My shelves held neat, pull-out drawers holding my supplies of canned magic from the Sun Emporium. Behind secret panels in the walls, I had a growing Hoard of gold and gems that burned with Dragon power like radioactive ore.

None of it would be enough tonight.

Instead, I had three dresses laid out on my bed, and my little brother on a video call. Because I wasn't so proud that I wouldn't consult an expert when I knew my own skills were lacking.

Tatsuya's lip curled in dismay. "Are these all you have?"

"What? I'm not a party person."

"That is no excuse for such a poor selection of clothing."

My little brother didn't bother to hide his scorn. Once he'd been a toddler running after me while eating custard buns. Now he wasn't so little and he could eat me under the table. Certainly, having survived his Lóng Yá had instilled a little more confidence in him. Enough even to talk back to his elder sister.

"Yes, these are all my formal clothes. It's not like I do this very often." I'd ruined too many nice outfits with bloodshed and my meager selection was the result of natural attrition.

The newest outfit was the vintage Yohji Yamamoto I'd brought back from my visit to Tokyo. Fujita-san had impeccable taste and didn't try to wrap me up in too much color or fluff. The two-piece outfit had clean lines and soft pleats of charcoal wool, and the cowl-neck blouse covered enough of my city's markings so as to not draw undue attention to my scars and ink. It was flanked by two black dresses. One was a short black mesh sheath dress that I loved for the cool slide of the fabric against my skin. Almost like chain mail. The coils caught the light but didn't shimmer in a way that I found unseemly. The other was an unrelenting black Armani dress that Fujita-san had stocked my closet with when I'd first moved here. The gown had a high slit above the right leg and made me look ten feet tall. Also it had nice room for movement if I had to chase something or someone down. Not that I was planning to do that tonight.

Tacchan scratched at his chin. The bruises around his face were gone, courtesy of a fortune in herbal medicine, but I still saw his battered features when I closed my eyes. His Lóng Yá had taken a toll, but he'd been able to step back from the brink before it had taken everything. Including his good heart.

Tacchan sighed. "I don't think this will work."

"I'll make it work. Sometimes you go into battle with the tools you have, not the tools you want."

"Nee-san. You're going to a museum exhibit. Not a fight."

I scowled. "Everything's a fight."

I'd managed to avoid meeting Tessa in person since coming back. My unexpected Thailand detour had at least bought me an extra day.

My brother sighed. "Just wear the one in the middle and your double strand. Nee-san?"

"Yes?"

"Try to have fun, please?"

I thought he was going to tell me to put on some of the Korean lip oil he'd sent. I turned the phone around and waited until he was looking at me. "How's Minjae?"

It was my brother's turn to scowl. "You know he hasn't called me. I don't think he's even been out of his house since the Tourney. No one's seen him."

"I'm sure his grandmother is keeping him close." She was up to something. The way she'd stared daggers at me at the end of the Tourney had been a clear enough threat.

Tatsuya didn't bother to keep the bitterness out of his voice. "Six years of friendship apparently isn't enough to merit a call."

"I'm sorry, Tacchan."

And I was. Freddy had warned me that this was the inevitable consequence of the Tourney. Friendship meant nothing. Family meant *everything.*

"Tacchan, it isn't just about you and Minjae. There are bigger things in motion. You know that. You saw it yourself at Lóng Yá."

Tacchan gave a short bark of laughter. "It's not like I know what I'm supposed to do about that. I doubt Minjae does, either."

I wasn't so sure. My brother had an innocence to him, a shell that had protected him during his years at the academy. On the other hand, Minjae had the ruthless streak that all Custodian families tried to encourage in their offspring. That ruthlessness had cracked Tacchan's shell of innocence during the boys' last fight in the Tourney finals. My brother was learning, the hard way, and I grieved for him and hoped this new edge didn't turn out to be too brittle for what was coming.

"I'm sure Father has a plan for all of us," I responded.

"Of course he does, but he hasn't told me anything about it."

My laugh was devoid of humor. "Why would he? You'll know when he decides you should know."

Tatsuya dropped his eyes. "I hate being in the dark."

"So do something about it."

"How? Father—"

"The last thing Father wants is for you to seek him out for answers. When you're leading the clan, you won't have him as a resource. You need to build your own power because Father won't let you borrow his."

"It feels like I'm back in school again. But worse."

"Little brother, you have no idea."

Tatsuya smiled as if he knew a secret. "Speaking of going back to school . . . how's your training going?"

"Training?"

He waggled his eyebrows. "You know . . ."

Dragon Father, save me from teenagers. "I'm not training. I can't, Tacchan. What my talent does . . . if things go wrong . . . what if I stole someone's talent, forever?"

I'd managed to keep it in check with Freddy, but I didn't trust myself to be able to do that all the time. He'd played me, and I couldn't let him do it again. At least until I understood it better. All the families already thought I was an abomination. I was terrified they were right.

My brother had an odd look on his face. "You're . . . kidding, right? No, you're not. You weren't here."

"Look, Tacchan, I'm sorry that—"

"No, no, it was while you were still the Blade. It's not your fault. But you didn't see Father training me before Lóng Kǒu."

Skies. A sinking feeling deepened in my belly. "What happened?"

"He pushed me. Like he does everything. Like he probably did with you."

Tatsuya's gaze unfocused. "I got the whole story about you out of Fujita-san, after you left. I convinced him that with all that had happened, I needed to know the truth about . . . everything."

Regret worsened the queasiness in my gut. I'd left clanhome so fast. In my defense, my welcome had worn thin with our soldiers, and Mother had advised me to leave. But I should have told Tatsuya the story myself.

His eyes found mine again and his mouth curled into a sad smile. "So we have two things in common, Nee-san, because they both thought we were animators when we were young."

That knocked me back. "Tacchan. You are an animator. Like Father."

Tatsuya's look took on an intensity I wasn't used to seeing from him. "Nee-san. I'm not. My talent is puppetry. Only when I restrain it, can I use it like animation."

His eyes tightened at the corners. "I still remember that day. Something flipped inside me, and my talent changed. Father says it happened when my meridians matured. All I know is that I suddenly had control of Fujita-san instead of my toys."

My brother's voice dropped low, turning hoarse with fear. "Emiko, it was as if I'd set the house on fire. When my talent changed, it felt like my world turned upside down. I couldn't control it."

I knew what that felt like. Painfully.

Tatsuya's whisper was almost too low to hear. "I didn't know what to do. I didn't know how to let go of him. I . . . hurt him, Emi."

"Gods." I'd always assumed Father had trained Tatsuya to stretch his talent to puppetry. All these years, and I kept making stupid assumptions where my father was concerned.

Tatsuya's voice steadied. "Yoko-obaachan and Uncle Lau got me under control and knocked me out. The next day, Father took over my training, and for a year, I only trained with him."

My eyes widened when I realized what he'd said. "Wait, even though—"

He nodded. "I learned to puppet Father. Over and over again. Each time thinking I would hurt him. Or worse."

My estimation of my brother had changed drastically during this phone call. "Why didn't you tell me?"

He looked away and shrugged. My brother wasn't the little boy he'd been when I'd become the Blade, but now he seemed very young again.

Why hadn't I told him the truth before I left? Was it fear, or did I just have some genetic need to hold back information? It seemed everyone in our family harbored awful secrets. Tacchan's revelation now made the horror of my talent diminish. We were a family of monsters, bound by blood and secrets.

The flash of youth and innocence across Tatsuya's face was there and gone in a moment. With a visible effort he put his game face back on. "It doesn't matter. What matters is that I'm telling you now."

If he was trying to channel Father, he was doing a pretty good job of it. "And why are you telling me this now?"

To his credit, he gathered his thoughts before answering. "Like Father's been saying, things are about to get shaken up. Your unveiling has upset the status quo. I think it's best if you know what I'm capable of."

"So you're telling me that during all of our training, and all of Lóng Yá, you were holding back? You could have smacked me around any time you wanted." The idea was hard to wrap my mind around.

He ducked his head. "I've been practicing a long time, Nee-san. It's second nature now. Father made sure of that."

Of course he did.

"Now it's your turn. If I can do it, so can you. You can't run away from your talent."

I watched in fascination as my brother's face hardened. His eyes took on a steely glimmer of my father's gaze. "As the future leader of our clan, I need to know that I can count on you. You will master your gift. If you're constantly worrying about it getting away from you, you'll be a vulnerability, to yourself and the clan."

My brother's words were a punch to the throat. When had he gotten so ruthless? The worst part was I knew he was right. I arched an eyebrow at him. "Is that an order?"

He blinked, his jaw relaxing, and then he was my little brother again. "No, but I'm asking my big sister to do the smart thing. You didn't kill Kaida, so I know you can control your talent. You just need practice."

Freddy's words echoed through my head. If I didn't know any better, I might guess that they had planned this, coming at me on two fronts. But my brother didn't run in Freddy's circles. No, this was just the universe's way of getting me off my butt.

Between Kaida, Prem, and Freddy, I was putting a good record together of not killing people with my talent. Tendrils of shame licked at me when I realized the one person I'd come closest to ending with my talent was my father. But I'd been so young. And knowing my father, he'd probably viewed the whole experience as a unique opportunity.

I was going to regret this but, "Actually, I practiced a bit with Freddy today."

Tatsuya pushed the phone up against his nose, his eyes bright with excitement. "And?"

"Fine. You're right. I didn't hurt him."

I couldn't believe I was listening to advice from my little brother. Truly not so little anymore. But I wasn't so stubborn as to not admit to myself when he was right. I might not like my options, but doing nothing was clearly the worst choice.

Tacchan's face was wreathed in a smile, his eyes crinkling. "See? Oh and I meant to tell you that we worked something out for Colin to join your Sentinel's Hall."

"I could have used a little warning." I sensed my father's fine hand in that but perhaps my brother had been a greater influence than I'd realized.

"Colin was thrilled, and his family was relieved."

I heard all the things my brother didn't say. That Colin's family didn't have the funds or status to turn down an offer like that. That our clan had found a tactful way to show our gratitude for Colin's bravery in getting between Tatsuya and an assassin's blade that fateful night in Golden Gai.

They'd pinned their dreams on his top-eight finish landing Colin a high position with a Hoard Custodian family, but his wound had prevented him from running the Tourney and winning some of the Winner's Pot. Yet another reminder of how unfair our system was.

Suddenly, going to a cocktail party with bunch of Wàirén for a sword exhibit didn't seem so daunting anymore.

MUSEUM NIGHT

As I approached the halfway point on the Bay Bridge, I braced myself for the tearing sensation of leaving my city. It didn't work. It still slammed into me with the force of a hammer in the gut. I panted and gripped the steering wheel tighter. Leaving never got easier, and maybe it felt worse today knowing my city had the unwelcome addition of the Gate loitering there, too. I put my foot on the gas and sped the rest of the way to Berkeley.

One of the things I sorely missed whenever I left San Francisco was the way the city made parking a breeze for me. I shoved my irritation to the back of my mind as I circled the blocks around the Tien Pacific Museum for the third time. My anxiety was high enough, I didn't need this pointless frustration fraying my nerves any further. I cycled my qì as I drove slowly along the block. My eyes searched for parking while my mind searched for serenity.

Popo would be proud of me.

On the fourth circuit I found a spot toward the rear of the building, where the blocky steel exterior glowed in the harsh light of the streetlamps. Honestly, this was better. The loading ramps were open and a parade of caterers marched in and out of the rear of the museum. I was late already, and the idea of coming in quietly through the back eased my nerves a little.

The fact that I would have picked this entrance for a lethal mission was mere coincidence.

A bright flare of light caught my eye as I parked my Jeep. A sprawling video screen at least fifteen feet high dominated the rear wall of the museum. Adam's face looked out on the street and his self-assured eyes seemed to find me through the glare of my windshield. The video panned out, showing an array of swords behind him.

As if I needed another reminder of why tonight was a bad idea.

But tonight was Tessa's big night and I owed it to her to be here. More than that, I wanted to be here for her, even though I dreaded another encounter with Adam. This exhibit was a major event for Tessa's sleepy museum, and this success was bound to lead to more. Tonight was about Tessa and the museum, not me.

I got out of the Jeep and scoped out the loading dock. It was a hive of activity and the workers were all too busy to concern themselves with what looked like a lost party guest. With the quiet luxury of my designer dress, I cut through the waves of caterers and slipped into the main gallery, trailing behind a waiter with a tray of champagne flutes. I grabbed a glass for camouflage and tried to blend in to my surroundings.

I was much more familiar with the backstage areas of the museum, the dim and deserted hallways where Tessa's office was located. The main gallery was a large open space with high ceilings and exposed ductwork. Partygoers mixed and mingled, the press of bodies moving through the museum like the ebb and flow of mysterious tides.

Being around this many people made my hands itch. There were too many shadows, too many hidden faces, too many angles to keep track of. I'd become too accustomed to my enhanced Sentinel senses. Here in Berkeley, lights and sounds came to me as if muffled through wet cotton.

I fell back on the tried-and-true strategies of reluctant partygoers everywhere. I put my back against the reassuring bulk of a support pillar and pretended to sip my bubbly. From this vantage point I could at least keep most of the gallery in view.

The widest interior wall was a stark expanse of brilliant white. Tessa and her crew had used this as their canvas to hang Adam's weapon collection. In the open space, two complete sets of samurai armor stood in glass encasements under spotlights. Smaller collections from other donors played supporting roles on the other walls and in rooms that branched away from the gallery.

To my relief, I didn't see Adam anywhere. I knew he was here, for sure. And even without Crimson Cloud Splitter, he was proud of this collection. Maybe he was in one of the smaller exhibits? Like Tessa, Adam had a lot of hands to shake tonight. I swirled my glass, taking these extra seconds to gather my thoughts.

What would I even say to him if I saw him tonight? I'd done the right thing, getting Crimson Cloud Splitter into Oda-sensei's hands. But doing the right thing was rarely neat and easy, and any apologies that threatened to cross my lips felt empty and hollow before I even uttered the words. I'd obeyed the First Law. That was all that had mattered.

Unfortunately, the First Law couldn't repair what I'd broken.

For a short period of time, I'd pretended that we were normal. That we could go to a casual dinner at Tessa's, enjoy easy moments of laughter, and hang out at the gym. But I'd never been normal, and Adam had been too close to the fringes of Jiārén society, especially with Crimson Cloud Splitter in his possession.

I told myself it was only right that someone like the Sentinel of Tokyo wield that weapon. That Adam was safer for it being out of his possession. But the memory of his hunched form, the crushing despair in his eyes after losing the sword wouldn't leave me. And that was the price I paid for being foolish enough to think I could avoid First Law, or pretend I wasn't bound by it.

I would obey the law and protect the Hoard.

As I strolled through the gallery, I finally spotted Tessa. She looked radiant in a royal-blue satin sheath, her blond hair caught up in an artful twist. She'd swapped out her usual Converse for sparkly gold platform sandals. I hardly recognized her, but she was clearly in her element, glad-handing a pair of sedately dressed silver-haired patrons. Andie stood at her side, elegant in a black satin vest over wide-legged tuxedo trousers. She'd styled her black hair into sleek pin curls, glamorous as always. She caught my eye and tilted her head.

I smiled and held up my glass in a silent toast.

Since my return from Tokyo, I hadn't been back to their house for dinner. It didn't stop them from continuing to invite me. I hadn't wanted to explain about Adam, and the smallest and worst part of me admitted that seeing Tessa and Andie together gave me a pang of envy. They were so in sync with one another, their moves and emotions born of years of trust and intimacy. Would I ever have that with anyone? Could anyone want me like that after knowing what I was really like?

I sucked in a breath at the sharp twinge in my heart. It almost made me want to down the alcohol in my glass, but that had never been my way.

I pulled out a smile and moved over to Tessa once I saw a lull in the traffic of patrons.

"Emiko!" Tessa beamed at me, her dimples flashing before her arms pulled me close. I drew in the smell of her strawberry-scented shampoo and a rush of affection washed over me. She was a dynamo and I was lucky she'd befriended me.

"Congratulations, Madame Director." I winked at her.

"Couldn't have done it without you and Adam."

I shook my head. "This was all your vision and Adam's connections. I was just here to provide a little context."

Andie made quotation gestures with fingers and mouthed the word *context*.

I flushed at Andie's gentle mockery. In truth, I had been a major roadblock, pushing hard to get Adam to pull Crimson Cloud Splitter from the exhibit.

Tessa's blue eyes danced with amusement. "I'm grateful nonetheless."

Andie slid an arm around Tessa's shoulders. "You should come for dinner next week and we can celebrate a job well done."

The two of them shared a look, a wealth of emotion and tenderness between them that was almost tangible. My fingers instinctively reached for my pendant, the comfort of the cool jade. Should I tell them Adam and I'd had a falling out? I bit my lip, uncertain. When Tessa turned her gaze to me, I capitulated. Being with them in person, I couldn't find it in me to deny them. "I'd love that. Please let me know what I can bring."

A portly gentleman in a too snug red cummerbund cleared his throat and Tessa's eyes widened at his approach. "Mr. Heinrich, how lovely you could make it."

I recognized that name. A member of the board of trustees for the museum. I stepped back and Andie hid a smile as I ducked into the crowd, leaving Tessa to her duties.

I held my champagne like a shield, raising it to my lips whenever I saw someone who looked like they might be about to engage. This let me make a complete circuit of the museum and all the rooms without suffering any unwanted conversation. The other exhibits were impressive in their own rights. I got close enough to each piece to confirm that the pieces here were simply Wàirén artifacts. No more unexpected Hoard pieces.

When I made it back to the main gallery, I set my flute on the tray of a passing server. Unsurprisingly, my steps found their way to the main wall of swords. Aggravating as he was, Adam had impeccable taste in swords.

I quickly settled on a Tokugawa period wakizashi as my favorite. Despite dating from the sixteenth century, it was in pristine condition, the lacquer sleek and black, embellished with hammered copper. My fingers itched to trace the pebbly rayskin and test the weight of the blade. It was a very fine sword and on par with the rest of the collection. Truly, the patrons were missing nothing without Crimson Cloud Splitter here. I leaned forward to read the display card when I caught a flash of movement to my left.

Adam was easily a head taller than any other guest, and the breadth of his shoulders commanded a wide space around him as he strode toward me. He paused when the caterer stopped him and handed him a tumbler of whiskey. Our eyes met as he took a sip, his lips hovering over the crystal.

His normally messy curls had been tamed by pomade into a restrained wave tonight. The display lighting managed to flatter him as much as sunlight, the soft glow casting his skin to unreal perfection. The fit of his tuxedo was a testament to precision tailoring, and the beautifully fine black wool of his Brioni draped artfully over every steely inch of his physique. It was all just civilized veneer, because I'd seen the man fight off a pack of club-wielding oni. A warrior lurked within him, ready to emerge at any moment. *Handsome* was too tame a word for how he looked. Adam was a descendant of Vikings, set loose among the lambs here in the gallery.

Had our mad dash through the streets of Akasaka only been a few weeks ago? That man had fought beside me, wooed me, and in the giddy aftermath of our escape from the oni, I'd given in to the attraction that had plagued me since our first meeting. But the handsome man I'd kissed in the Tokyo moonlight was nowhere to be found tonight.

After what I'd stolen from him, I didn't expect to see that tenderness again. I hadn't merely stolen a sword—I'd made him break a promise to people he considered family. People didn't forgive things like that.

But we were grown-ups. We could be cordial. I could paste on a polite smile even if a part of me mourned what had never had a chance to blossom. Whatever the state of our relationship, he was part of Soong Clan now, and my responsibility.

As if reading my thoughts, Adam's lips pulled into a smile that didn't quite reach his eyes. His cool blue eyes watched me as if I were someone dangerous. A threat. And I was, but never to him. Now that his attentiveness had morphed to wariness, I recognized what I had been avoiding all along. That one day he would see the true me, and that he wouldn't like it.

You knew this would happen, I told myself.

I straightened my shoulders, and if his eyes softened a moment, I let myself enjoy it. I'd taken care with my appearance today, rubbing the ends of my hair with rose oil and coating my lips with a velvety red stain. I'd told Tacchan it was for Tessa's big night but knowing Adam would be here, my pride wouldn't let me do any less than my best.

Everything else faded into the background. Our little drama played out in just a few seconds of silence, and then it was over. He took another sip of his whiskey and set it down before three long strides placed him directly in front of me. My senses recovered and I took in more details than just Adam.

Like the young man at his side. He looked to be in his mid-twenties and stood in sharp contrast to Adam. Where Adam wore his slim tailored attire, the young man was fresh out of a Harajuku streetwear shop, his modern haori excessively oversized. The black folds of fabric were trimmed with pink sakura and could easily fit someone fifty kilos heavier. He was taller than I was, but the younger man affected a deep slouch that allowed his clothing to swallow him even further. Muddy, sullen eyes looked out from under dark bangs long enough to brush the bridge of his nose.

Adam either didn't notice or didn't mind the attitude. He pushed the young man toward me with a big hand. "Emiko, this is Kenji Yamamoto."

Kenji. My hackles went up as I made the connection back to the framed photo hanging in Adam's condo. Why would he bring the last son of an Outclan family here tonight? What was Adam angling for?

Cordial. We could be cordial. I stuck out my hand. "Nice to meet you, Kenji."

Kenji's eyes widened a fraction, then narrowed, as if he just now realized who I was. We shook hands and his gaze swept over me in a familiar fashion. I was used to this, being assessed by men larger than me. I was also used to them seeing something in my expression that alarmed them, a whisper in that section of the hindbrain that told them I was dangerous.

What I wasn't used to was the jagged burst of qì that stabbed me in the hand. Kenji snatched his hand away and turned to Adam.

"Ani, I told you I don't want anything to do with them."

As Kenji spoke, his aura flickered and deepened, until a streaky red glow surrounded him.

My eyes flew to Adam's. He held my gaze, his expression implacable.

Our Dragon gods could be cruel, and with dawning horror, I realized why Adam had brought Kenji here. Tonight.

It was to see me, specifically.

And not for some mundane reason like burying the hatchet. Oh no. Adam's agenda became clear in an instant. My hand shot out, grabbing Adam by the wrist. If we hadn't been at Tessa's party I would have squeezed down on the nerve and brought him to his knees. Instead I settled for dragging him to a quiet corner and a fierce whisper of disbelief.

"Adam! You told him?"

He had taken an oath of secrecy mere weeks ago. He didn't even have the decency to look guilty about it.

Adam shook free of my grip and his other hand covered the circular scar on his palm. His eyes flicked to a space above my head. "After . . . Sugi, I started to see things. I saw it with you, first, that last night. Then here, when I took a walk through Chinatown."

Sugi was my father's constant companion, a wooden wolf that his talent animated. To seal Adam's vow to protect the Hoard, Sugi had bit his palm, drawing blood. He was now bound by the First Law to protect our secrets from Wàirén. What he was talking about now felt dangerously close to breaking it.

He turned to look at Kenji. "It helped me confirm some things I'd suspected."

His tone was accusatory and I looked away, frustration and guilt making me feel small. Our paths had crossed with his quest to find out about my people and my own duty to fulfill the Talon Call. Adam would have gotten himself killed eventually but it didn't change the fact that he'd helped me and my clan.

And now he could see our auras.

"Adam, you swore an oath. You can't break the First Law."

"I only told him what was his right to know. It's his family's legacy. I won't keep that from him."

"That's not for you to decide."

Adam flung out an arm. "Look at him! I know you can see it. He's a bigger risk to the First Law than I'll ever be."

For his part, Kenji seemed remarkably relaxed about the whole encounter. Kenji snagged a flute of champagne from a passing waiter. Adam rolled his eyes and took the glass out of his hand.

"Hey! I'm legal!"

Adam returned the glass to another waiter. "And I told your mother I'd keep you out of trouble."

I jabbed Adam in his chest with my finger. "And you think spilling clan secrets to him is the best way to keep him out of trouble?"

Kenji rolled his eyes. "I'm not going to tell anyone. You can keep your secrets."

I hit him with my maximum death glare, which at least got him to shut up for a moment. His eyes widened as his hindbrain probably told him to run as fast as he could. He might have Jiārén ancestors, but he was clearly Wàirén, born with thin blood and soft hands into an even softer world. The closest he'd come to danger was crossing a busy street against the light.

Adam threw Kenji a dark look as well. "I told you to listen and learn."

The young man laughed but there was no amusement in it. "Ani, they don't want me and I don't want them. This drove Father insane and I don't need to be a part of it."

I found myself in the odd position of agreeing with Kenji.

Adam turned to me. He remained smiling but his eyes were hard. "You owe me."

Despite his calm demeanor, his voice strained with emotion.

That was the problem with hotshot investor entrepreneurs—they had the unerring ability to find your weak spot and press on it. He'd had the money, time, and contacts to get the fan to the auction for the Lost Heart of Yázì and I'd used it. I'd let him save me from a lightning strike, invoked the protection of the clan rather than let him get cleaned by Fiona's people, and I was still paying for it. Then I'd appropriated Kenji's family heirloom and turned it over to Tokyo's Sentinel. And we were never going to get over this.

But maybe we could get through this. I looked back and forth between Adam and his unhappy party guest. Maybe we would be square after.

Ever intuitive, Adam nodded. "I'm cashing in my chips. All of them. Kenji needs you."

Adam had a point. I couldn't let some rogue Jiārén talent blunder out into Wàirén life and expose us. But Kenji was not Leanna. Leanna wanted my training. I shook my head slowly. "I'm not sure I can do this."

Adam leaned in, his voice raspy in my ear, the heat of his breath warming my skin. "You owe him."

I didn't back away, and his sudden closeness brought the heady scent of whiskey mingled with soap. It didn't help my thought processes.

My indecision only galvanized Adam. He grabbed Kenji's arm and pulled him over so the young man stood between us. "This is Kenji. I've divulged Jiārén secrets to him. You know what the First Law demands."

Kenji's wide eyes jumped between Adam and me as we stared daggers at each other. Our intense argument must have finally gotten through to him because his voice cracked. "What? What does it demand?"

Adam's gaze traveled up and down my body. "How many blades are you carrying right now, Emiko? You have to protect the Hoard. You know what you need to do."

He was calling my bluff. I did have a pair of knives strapped to my thighs. My old habits were right there at my fingertips. The easy solution to breaking First Law would mean I simply subdue them with nerve strikes and march them into an unused part of the museum. My knife point under Adam's chin. Two moves and they would never tell Jiārén secrets again.

Prune every branch, my old self whispered.

I took a deep breath and let it out. That was a different person. I'd made a promise on Golden Gai. I had managed to solve the Kaida problem without ending her life, and she had been trying to kill me. I could handle Adam without resorting to violence.

"Don't push me, Adam."

I gave Kenji another glare that told him to stay, then grabbed Adam by the arm and pulled him away so we could at least talk without the boy hearing everything.

Adam sensed the shift in my attitude and at least had the decency not to gloat. His face softened, reminding me of easier moments with him. Before. "I just want him to know about his family."

"If his family had wanted him to know they wouldn't have gone Outclan." My tone was sour.

"Maybe they didn't have a choice, and I want to give that choice back to Kenji."

"Only a clan head can make that decision, and we don't even know what clan his family came from."

Adam smiled, a shark in an Italian designer tux. "Maybe your father could decide, then."

I was not equipped to bargain with him.

My father had soldiers younger than Kenji in the Pearl Guard. Even the ones who weren't battle-seasoned had earned more self-assurance. Any one of them would tear Kenji to pieces, with both their hands tied. Adam had no idea what he was asking for. I thought about how I'd been unable to get Colin a position with the clan. How Father had neatly twisted my ask such that Colin would be shamed by coming to the Soong Clan.

"My father would say no. You're asking me to throw him into the dragon's jaws, Adam. This isn't the favor you think it is."

"I want Kenji to know what it means to be Jiārén. I don't care how we get there. Make it happen, Emiko."

I didn't like his tone. But I admitted to myself that going toe to toe with Adam always had the wrong effect on me because when he was stern like this, I worried less about hurting him. These glints of ruthlessness only made him more like us. More like me.

I stole a glance at Kenji. He was nodding to those who passed by him, and pretending to be interested in the suit of Edo-era armor. But I caught him stealing nervous glances at us when he thought we weren't looking.

"Adam, he wouldn't surv—"

Glass crashed behind us and I spun toward the sound, my hands hovering over my blades. Kenji lay on the floor in a spray of broken glass and wine, his legs tangled with one of the waiters. Every set of eyes locked onto the tableau and Kenji's cheeks reddened with embarrassment.

The sharp, acidic scent of vinegar hit me and Adam's priceless samurai armor tipped over, crashing into the interior of the glass. People yelped and crouched, imagining an earthquake. I was already halfway across the room to Kenji.

When I got to him I grabbed him by the arm and pulled him to his feet. "Calm down."

The boy whirled on me, his eyes wide with panic. "I'm not doing anything!"

Right. Given the crowd of onlookers I tried for a little discretion and felt along his bicep, looking for his meridian with my finger.

A jagged red aura pulsed around Kenji's head and he jerked away. "Hey, what gives?" The suit of armor shook itself to pieces and a crack appeared in the display case.

Someone screamed. Kenji flinched again and the case shattered, spilling glittering shards of glass and pieces of antique armor. I backed away and pulled Kenji with me as my careful arguments with Adam burned up like so much tissue-thin joss paper.

Kenji wriggled under my grip. "Let me go! I didn't do anything!"

Skies, could this night get any worse? I held him still long enough to jab a finger into the meridian in his armpit. He yelped but the stinging scent of his talent faded and the gallery pieces stopped rattling. I dragged Kenji to the rear of the gallery and out a set of double doors. In the maintenance hallway I threw him to the floor so that he was sitting with his back to the wall. The doors opened behind me and I turned to find Adam following me.

I held up a hand to stop him. "Go out there and fix things. Please make sure Tessa doesn't freak out. I'll handle this."

"And by handling this, you mean . . ."

I sighed. "I'm not going to kill him, Adam."

Kenji found his voice again when Adam turned to leave. "You're leaving me with her?"

Adam was frustrated. He'd given me the same look many times. "Kenji, this is your family's legacy. It's your right—"

Kenji threw up his hands. "I can't believe you're still on this! It was just a freak accident!"

There was real fear in his voice now. I got the sense that this was not Kenji's first *accident,* and Adam knew it. The look Adam gave Kenji now was equal parts relief and regret. Adam was finally starting to understand just how much poor Kenji's life was going to be turned upside down, only now it was too late to back out.

Once we were alone again I knelt in front of Kenji and took a moment to look the boy over and give him a full assessment. He held up fairly well under my stare other than backing up until his head hit the wall.

His aura flickered, then dimmed. He had no control over his talent but who was I to judge? Without exposure to Hoard pieces, his talent would be stunted, like a plant grown in the dark.

My father wouldn't take him, but maybe there was another way.

The double doors creaked open again and I spoke without taking my eyes off Kenji. "Adam, I told you I would handle this."

The boy's eyes widened and focused past me. His talent stirred again.

I turned and found "Uncle" Jimmy Louie standing at the door, in a dressy version of his usual crisp slacks and sweater. In his hand he carried his signature cane, made out of what had to be a kilo of buttery yellow Hoard gold shaped like a dragon's fang.

Well, there was my answer to the Kenji question. Of course Kenji's talent would react to Uncle Jimmy's cane. And Kenji didn't have the benefit of a lifetime around Hoard gold to control his reaction.

Jimmy Louie was well near the top of my least favorite persons list right now. On a good day our relationship could be generously described as civil. Jimmy's nephew, Ray Ray, had tried to kill me. Twice.

Despite our history, I doubted Jimmy had come here tonight specifically to send Kenji over the edge and ruin my night. No, that was just Kenji's terrible luck. And mine.

Whatever Jimmy might want from me seemed like a low priority. And I wasn't above being petty with him since he'd cut Leanna off from me. "Find me later, Jimmy. I don't have time for you right now."

"Sentinel."

It was the title, and the way he said it. He'd never called me that unless there were other people around to hear it. And his voice sounded . . . broken. I stood and noted the hollows under his eyes, and the whitened knuckles gripping his cane. He was usually so self-assured, but right now he looked like he might fall over from a stiff breeze.

His voice was raspy, like he'd taken a punch to the neck. "Dai Lou . . . my brother."

Oh. Oh no. I had the sudden sensation of being pushed toward a cliff.

Jimmy closed his eyes and his voice steadied. "My brother is dead. And I need your help, Sentinel."

And here was the answer to my first question. Yes, my night could get worse.

ATTACK

I had to put Kenji on the back burner.

The subtle black sesame scent of Jimmy's talent emerged and my hackles went up. My ability to smell talents was a closely guarded secret so I forced myself to stay still as Jimmy's power bloomed around me. I wasn't in San Francisco, so I didn't have an excuse to call him out for using his talent.

The scent of black sesame floated past me and Jimmy fixed his eyes on Kenji.

Uncle Jimmy cleared his throat. "Young man, you look like you could use some fresh air. Why don't you head outside? That should make you feel better."

Kenji's eyes went wide and soft. He nodded slowly and got to his feet. "Yeah, that sounds like a good idea."

He sounded like he was talking in his sleep. Without another look at either of us he turned and shuffled down the hallway toward the loading dock.

I turned and gave Uncle Jimmy a glare. He'd done the same to me when we'd first met, used his charm speak on me after he'd invited me into his home and hospitality. It was incredibly rude and I had yet to settle the score with him on that count.

Jimmy didn't need to be a mind reader to know what was going through my head. My eyebrows crawled up into my hair as he did the other thing that he never did around me unless someone was watching. He clasped his hands together and bowed. Deeply.

Skies. Whatever this was, it was serious.

"My condolences on your loss, Uncle Jimmy. Dai Lou was a stron—"

Jimmy cut me off. "We can skip the pleasantries this time, Sentinel. I'm here about Leanna."

The sickening cold that gripped my heart was exactly the reason I'd held myself apart since I'd broken my blade. When I allowed myself to be connected to too many people, there were far too many levers to use against me, too many ways to be hurt. The rolling sensation of anger, nausea, and fear boiled through me all at once and destroyed my ability to think. Before I drew another ragged breath I had two fistfuls of Jimmy's fine wool sweater and I slammed him against the wall. His breath exploded from him and his shocked face swam in my vision, colored black and red.

"What did you do?"

Jimmy pawed at my fists. "Not me! Not—"

I growled and pressed him into the wall. If I had to, I would squeeze the answers out of him one drop at a time. "Where is she?!"

Jimmy sucked in a breath. "PUT. ME. DOWN."

Without the mantle of the Sentinel to bolster me, the black sesame of his charm speak spiked through my head and my hands unclenched like a lock popping open. I stumbled back a step, shaking my head to get Jimmy out of it. Uncle Jimmy landed back on his feet and held his cane up like a shield.

His gaze skewered me like a blade. "You fool. Do you really think I would harm Leanna?"

The fog of Jimmy's charm speak fell away as quickly as it had landed on me. But the shock had been as effective as a slap across my cheek. No, of course he wouldn't harm his great-niece. She was his only hope for the clan since Ray Ray was . . .

I groaned. Why couldn't my enemies just stay down? "Ray Ray?"

Jimmy nodded. He'd already regained his stoic composure.

"My little nephew was busy while we were all in Tokyo. Staged a coup. He had a welcoming party ready for me when I returned."

This was disappointing, but not totally surprising. I'd had my doubts about the loyalties of Jimmy's soldiers. When Ray Ray had imprisoned me in the vault of their family bank, he had demonstrated a surprising number of the Louie henchmen would follow his lead. It wasn't that Ray Ray was a brilliant mastermind—far from it. He was a follower of the Cult of the Ninth Dragon, the Realmseekers. These cultists believed Jiārén should return to the Realm. And apparently Ray Ray had swayed enough of his clan to his unhinged belief system.

"The girls?"

"I don't know where they are. But Ray Ray won't harm his own daughters."

Maybe not intentionally but that didn't mean they wouldn't get hurt. I would trust a bagful of angry weasels before I trusted Ray Ray.

My mind flashed to the worst dinner party of my life just a few weeks ago. "And Dai Lou?"

Jimmy's expression cracked a little and his eyes flicked away from me. "I don't know what happened to my brother. But it doesn't matter. Ray Ray had more spine than I gave him credit for."

My arms prickled like they were electrified. Adrenaline surged through my system but I had nowhere to vent my energy, my anger, my frustration. "Why didn't you come to me sooner?"

Jimmy looked frustrated as well, and angry. "I've been a prisoner in my own home. I've been trying to contact you. Tonight was the first chance I had to get away. If my nephew has the girls somewhere in the city, you should be able to find them, right?"

I threw my hands up in the air. "But I'm not in the city!"

Our eyes met as we came to the same chilling realization in that moment. I'd been beyond the border of San Francisco for several hours now. For those hours, Ray Ray Louie had complete control of his clan and no need to worry about me. How much damage could he do in those hours?

My phone's ringtone shocked me so much I bobbled the phone as I pulled it out. I stabbed at the screen when I saw who it was. "How bad is it?"

Freddy's voice came quick and choppy. He was panicking. "It's bad, I'm—"

"I need a lift. I'll meet you in front of the museum in five."

"Got it." The phone went dead.

I only had a minute, maybe two. My breath quickened and the lights in the hallway seemed both too bright and too dim. Unspent anger and power crackled at my fingertips. My talent growled within, eager to spring free. Uncle Jimmy must have seen something on my face because he backed up a step. Maybe he was just anticipating Freddy's arrival.

I doubted it.

I nodded toward the exit Kenji had taken. "Walk with me."

Uncle Jimmy wasn't the kind of person to respond to my tone of voice, which just emphasized how far off his game was, when he followed me down the empty hallway.

"You're sure the girls are okay?"

He grunted. "I spoke with Leanna on the phone yesterday. She's confused, but she sounded all right. Lucy is more upset, but Leanna is managing her."

I felt a little spark of pride to hear Leanna had stepped up to take care of her sister. "What's Ray Ray planning?"

It was like watching a door swing shut as Jimmy's expression changed. We weren't talking about the girls anymore. Now we were talking business. I came to a dead stop so fast Jimmy almost tripped over me. "Your girls are out there somewhere!"

Jimmy regained his balance. "You think I don't know that?

Leanna is the future of my clan and I will ensure that she has a clan to come home to!"

"Your clan? It's not yours anymore, your nephew saw to that. Who knows how much is even going to be left at the end of all this."

Internal clan warfare wasn't pretty. I'd seen it a few times, and even instigated one skirmish when I was the Blade. When someone drew a line and people started picking sides, it was all downhill from there. All you could do at that point was get out of the blast radius and prepare to sort through the wreckage.

Jimmy's eyes hardened. "I can still salvage—"

I stepped into Jimmy's personal space and backed him up against the wall. "Jimmy. Whatever's left of your clan after this is over . . . It won't be the same. Leanna and Lucy are what matters. Family first. We need to get them to safety."

Jimmy put his cane up between us and pushed me back. "The clan is the family—"

"Tell me what Ray Ray is planning!"

"I'm not going to speculate."

"Don't give me that. You know. Spit it out."

Jimmy stared back at me, his eyes hard as obsidian.

I spun away from him and hit the exit door a lot harder than I needed to. Just getting outside seemed to take half the weight from my shoulders. Freddy would be here any moment. I paced a tight circle and pointedly ignored when Jimmy followed me out.

There was no way to win this argument. Jimmy was right in one respect. Without the legacy and strength of the Louie Clan behind her, Leanna and her sister would be a target for anyone with a grudge against them. He was wrong, however, in his assessment of his situation. Fractured as it was, the Louie Clan I'd known as late as a few weeks ago was already gone. Jimmy was still living in the very recent past.

However much I wanted to find Leanna and her sister, this was exactly as much help as Jimmy was going to give me. Jimmy was cast in the same mold as my father, and people like them only respected one thing.

Oda had warned me against doing this, but I didn't see another way to change Jimmy's mind. I cycled my qì and reached inside myself, sending my energy to meet the quietly pulsing orb of energy in my chest. Oda said it was a reserve of my Sentinel power, a stored bit of San Francisco that I had with me at all times.

I'd never had a reason to try this . . . before now.

When my qì touched my Pearl the tingling energy in my arms ignited like flames. Light and sound sharpened as my Sentinel senses returned to me as if I'd returned to my city. The first thing I noticed were the pale pink wisps of charm speak Jimmy had extended toward me.

He knew I was beyond my city. Had he chosen specifically to find me here, away from my power? I didn't know, but the possibility burned away my empathy. The fear I held for Leanna and Lucy's safety sharpened until it became anger, a jagged ball of fury in my belly. I didn't know how long my Pearl would last, so I decided to hit him fast.

I grabbed the earth beneath us and cracked open the concrete. Jimmy yelled and his power disappeared as his concentration broke. "What is the meaning of this?"

His arms flailed as he dropped knee-deep into the ground. I didn't seal him in, but I closed the opening enough to make him work for his freedom. And he'd lose his fine leather loafers in the process.

I leaned in close and jabbed him in the chest with a finger. "Let's not mince words, Jimmy. You're hardly in a position to make demands when you come asking for my help to clean up your mess."

Jimmy opened his mouth but I pulled on my Pearl again and let my Sentinel aura go big and bright. For once in my life, I got him to shut up and listen to me.

"You let this happen. You let Ray Ray fall down the rabbit hole with the Realmseekers. You allowed this disease to fester inside your house and it almost killed me. And you have the nerve to come to me for help and then make demands about my methods?"

Jimmy leaned away from me as I got closer, but the defiant glint in his eye didn't falter. "I serve my clan. Leanna knows that."

Who in their right mind wanted this kind of life for their children? Tacchan's physical wounds from Lóng Yá were healed, but the mental and emotional beating he'd endured was still fresh. And he'd finished second. What madness did Uncle Jimmy envision for Leanna?

"What happens when she finds out you let her father go insane?"

"Ray Ray doesn't matter. I raised her, she's mine more than his!"

"And what makes you think she'll want anything to do with you after I bring her back?"

Jimmy shook his head. "She'll do what her clan needs of her."

He was giving a lot of credit to a traumatized eleven-year-old girl. Maybe Uncle Jimmy didn't have a lot of experience with teenagers. "She's just a kid, Jimmy."

Uncle Jimmy huffed a laugh. "Were you much older when your father sent you to your fancy Swiss boarding school?"

I narrowed my eyes. "That was different."

"You were twelve. Were you so eager to learn from . . . the Swiss?"

My anger faded to sadness. Would we ever stop destroying our children? "Fine. But that doesn't mean it shouldn't be different. Leanna deserves better."

Jimmy's voice softened a little. "On that much, we can agree."

He was too much like my father. Arguing with him was like screaming at a hurricane. If change was going to happen, it wouldn't happen with him. It would happen with Leanna. Which made ensuring her safety that much more important.

I relaxed my grip on the earth and let Jimmy crawl out. His shoes somehow remained stuck below. A tragedy.

Jimmy brushed the dirt from his slacks. "You'll find her?"

It took a great deal of effort to keep my voice measured.

"Don't mistake my fondness for your nieces as an opportunity to exploit my goodwill."

He gave a quick nod.

"As your Sentinel, I will help you find the girls. And as your Sentinel I will not tolerate being taken advantage of."

I pointed back to the doors to the gallery. "Adam Jørgensen is in there. He's one of mine. Make sure the boy gets back to him."

He nodded. I caught the barest hint of the seawater scent of Freddy's power. Any second now.

I held Jimmy's gaze. We'd never be friends, but in this we were allies. "I'll find the girls."

Jimmy nodded back. Even in his stocking feet he managed to look dignified.

Freddy's power appeared out of nowhere and swallowed me like a rogue wave at the beach. The lights of the museum winked out and I tumbled into darkness.

I tumbled out of Freddy's funnel of air and went down on one knee. Freddy landed beside me in a neat crouch. He scanned around us while I got my stomach under control again. I'd kept my qì moving during the whole trip, which had the benefit of saving me from my legendary undignified landings.

Coming back to San Francisco helped. As soon as my feet touched down a wave of soothing energy ran through me and washed away the sour nausea. My senses realigned as well, and the city came alive to my eyes and ears. I didn't really know how I could use my powers to find Leanna and Lucy, but I knew in my bones that I could do it. Freddy and I would take care of whatever nonsense Ray Ray had attempted, and then I'd find the girls.

Then I looked around.

The Tran château had seen better days.

Fiona's groundskeepers kept meticulous hedges along the perimeter of the property. The hedges broke open for a set of ornate wrought-iron gates that closed off the sweeping driveway. All that greenery was a burning shambles now, and the gates had been ripped from their moorings, left on the driveway in a tangle of twisted metal. The jarring melody of pitched combat reached us from the house, a discordant song drifting through broken windows and shattered doors.

Freddy was famously laid back and good-natured, but the wreckage of his home swept all that off the table. His power swirled around him dangerously as we approached the broken gates and found a trail of bodies. The Trans had given as good as they'd taken; at least two Louies in black suits lay sprawled out for every Tran in dove gray. I knelt next to a slender figure in gray and turned the body over.

Relief flooded through me when I saw it wasn't Linh or Fiona, followed immediately by anger and guilt. Fiona's soldier wasn't my friend, but she was a resident of my city. I pressed my hand to her neck and found a thready pulse. My fingers found her meridian and I gently pushed my qì into her. Her eyes popped open and drifted for a moment before clearing with recognition.

Freddy held his finger to his lips and whispered. "Liz, who did this?"

She swallowed and winced. "Ray Ray. The Louies. They came out of nowhere."

It was good to have the confirmation. Deep in my belly the seething fire of my anger ticked up a notch.

Liz had a streak of drying blood running from her hairline past her left ear and that made me worry she wouldn't survive the night without a healer.

But there wasn't a healer in sight. Given the number of bodies I'd already seen, more awaited us within. No healer could care for all of the injured.

Ray Ray had taken the girls and lined this walkway in blood. Any thought of a measured response had long vanished. I would take retribution because that was all my anger would accept. I would meet this declaration of war in my city with the full might of the city's magic, and my own talent.

Ours.

I didn't know if that whisper was mine or from within my chest, but it didn't matter. We were one in this. The dark thing I contained slithered and jostled, eager to be unleashed. My nostrils twitched, the hot mélange of so many talent scents stinging my skin.

My city's magic surged, rolling up from the soles of my feet and along my spine, strengthening my resolve.

I pointed to ruined double doors on the front of the château. "I'm going in."

Freddy nodded. "I'll go around the back, we'll meet in the middle."

"No, I need you to—"

"Emiko." His tone of voice was low and hard, something I wasn't used to from him. "We're not arguing about this. I'm going in there and I'm going to find whoever did this to us."

Freddy was strong, but he wasn't ready for what we might find inside his house. His eyes glittered, all but daring me to cross him. I saw I wasn't going to win on this, no matter how much I wanted to protect him. "Fine. I'll go upstairs, you clear the ground floor. We'll meet in the middle."

He gave me a quick nod and ran off to the other side of the house.

Liz seemed to have a bit of a stubborn streak in her because she tried to get up. Her words jumbled together as she spoke, probably from a concussion. ". . . want to help."

The Louies had broken the simmering tension in my city into all-out war, and they'd done it when I'd been beyond the city limits. They were cowards who knew they could not face my wrath, who had put someone like Liz in these dire circumstances.

The heat in my gut roared, becoming an inferno at my core. San Francisco responded to my anger with a groundswell of energy like a geyser of jet fuel dumped onto my rage. I pushed Liz down as gently as I could.

"Stay here. We'll handle this."

The city's power coursed through me like fresh blood, filling my veins. My emotions pulsed like a heartbeat and the city matched my rhythm. In that ebb and flow, my qì surged with the city's power. My talent awoke and curled itself around San Francisco's energy like an old lover. Power radiated off my skin as light and heat, and I stood to face the château.

My voice blasted out of me and blew the shattered windows out of their frames. "Louies! Your Sentinel is coming for you!"

INVASION

The interior of Fiona's house was a ruin. Huge chunks had been gouged out of the floor, walls, and ceiling wherever I looked. Dark cracks spread along the once-pristine marble flooring. Qì blasts had smashed Fiona's antique furniture to shreds of fabric and splinters. A marble column at the corner of the foyer had shattered into pieces that sprayed into the house. The aftermath of the Louie intrusion told me Ray Ray had attacked like a sledgehammer, pummeling his way past the Tran defenses with a barrage of kinetics.

The foyer was quiet but the sounds of pitched battle reached me. I ran up the sweeping staircase. Huge fissures ran up the marble stairs and the stone cracked ominously around me.

I drew my blades, twin folding karambits with polished wood handles I'd worn strapped under my formal attire. With a flick of my wrists, both blades snapped out and I slid my fingers into the loops. The curved blades would work well in the tight hallway, especially when I closed in. Until then, my talent was itching to get into the fight.

Power swelled within me as I cycled my qì, blending my own energy with San Francisco's, then cresting like a wave ready to crash. The city's energy thrummed inside me like a drumbeat. I took a breath and San Francisco rushed in to fill the space. My body crackled with trembling potential.

The scent of smoke led me farther into the house. I followed the trail to a beefy fire talent who clearly wasn't expecting me. When he turned to look at me I jabbed him in the solar plexus. The ring of my karambit connected with his sternum with a crack, turning him into a wet noodle. I grabbed him by the lapels and a quick leg sweep took him down. He yelped again as he slammed into the floor. As he twisted, trying to get away from me, he exposed the left side of his neck and the intricate tattoo that emerged from his collar.

A black, circular pattern of entwined dragons. At the center of the design I caught a glimpse of a pair of red eyes.

Realmseekers.

Jimmy had really slipped, thinking he had Ray Ray's crazy beliefs under control. This exact group of zealots had upended my life once already when they'd stolen the Ebony Gate and put San Francsico in the path of the ravenous ghosts of Yomi. The anger in my chest tightened to a razor-sharp point.

I let him catch his breath and waited patiently for him to take stock of his situation. The rage in my chest strained against its chains. I leaned in close and let my aura go big. The fear in his eyes as recognition dawned was deeply satisfying.

No Jiārén ever saw their own aura. I knew my Sentinel aura was gold, but I didn't know what my true talent did to that color. When my talent latched on to the Louie thug and began draining his qì, the way his eyes went big and round let me know he definitely saw something he really didn't like.

Maybe my talent wasn't as much of a burden as I had thought.

I clenched my fist and jerked the fire talent closer. My voice was a low rumble. "You know who I am."

The baked bread smell was almost gone from him now and the foreign energy coursed through me, skewing my senses, making the room seem stretched and overly bright. I clenched my teeth against a surge of nausea. The fire-less talent nodded his head and started making a thin, high-pitched whining noise.

I twisted my fists into his lapels. As I did the fire talent leaked out of me, like water slipping through my fingers. His jacket smoldered. My world spun as the stolen qì bled away. I slammed him into the floor. With each word I picked him up and slammed him down. Smoke drifted up from my fists.

"Where. Is. Ray Ray?"

The man cracked like a rotten egg. "He wants their Hoard!"

Skies. My stomach froze into a block of ice. Taking another clan's Hoard was like ripping out someone's heart. A clan that lost their Hoard lost status and power, both figuratively and literally. If Ray Ray succeeded, Fiona would be disgraced. The Trans would lose their seat on Bā Tóu. The alliance she had forged with my father would be meaningless and the entire status quo of Jiārén power would be upended.

No wonder Ray Ray had ousted his uncle.

The wall to my left clicked and a hidden door pushed open. Linh Tran stepped out at the head of a small army. Most of her soldiers looked like they were in rough shape.

I stood, dragging the weeping Louie up with me. As always, Fiona's most trusted lieutenant was all business, from her no-nonsense pageboy haircut to the tactical vest strapped over her gray silk charmeuse blouse. She looked like she'd taken a few hits but the glitter in her eyes said she had plenty of fight left in her.

Linh got right in my face. "Who else did you bring?"

I would have hugged her if the situation wasn't so dire. I shook my prisoner like a rag doll. "Just me and Freddy. This one said Ray Ray is after your Hoard."

Linh gave him a look of disgust then turned to her less injured soldiers. "Take care of this trash and search for any more survivors."

As her soldiers got to work Linh pushed past me. "Follow me."

A clan's Hoard was the most valuable thing they held, both in terms of monetary value and Dragon power. Every piece in existence had been brought to this world when our people had fled the Cataclysm, when our Dragon gods had gone mad and tried to destroy each other.

Things of such value were best kept in secure locations. For Jiārén that meant a Realm Fragment, an unmoored piece of our old world, anchored to this world with ancient magic and a Door. Access to these fragments was limited to those of the clan's bloodline, or those who had taken an oath to the clan.

Freddy met us at the bottom of the stairs, his eyes wide and very white, his tanned skin slick with sweat. When I looked a question at him he waved it away. Judging by his jittering aura and the pulsing scent of seawater, he was barely holding it together.

Linh snapped a quick bow when she saw Freddy.

Some of the tension melted from Freddy's eyes. "Thank the Dragon Father. How bad is it?"

"Bad. They hit us out of the blue, with far more manpower than our intelligence gave them credit for."

It was the closest I'd ever seen her come to cracking. Linh's face crumpled for a fraction of a second before she regained command of her emotions. "Fi and I got split up. I took a group of our wounded to hole up in the safe room."

I cut in. "Freddy. We need to get to Fiona. They're here for your Hoard."

In another life, Freddy would have been the head of his family, instead of a well-tanned surfing aficionado. Another glimpse of that man came through in the hard expression on his face as he did the same calculus I'd already done. It only took him a second.

He nodded to me. "Let's go find Fi."

Linh led the way to a large dining room. One of the interior walls had been smashed to pieces, revealing a descending staircase. More Trans and Louies littered the entrance to the stairs, their bodies prone. Best-case scenario, they were unconscious. My lips thinned. More likely than not, many were dead.

I edged closer to Freddy as Linh peered down into the basement. "You okay?"

He shook his head, his red-rimmed eyes staring through the bodies on the floor. "No. But there's nothing I can do except find Fi."

I put a hand on his shoulder and his hand covered mine. "Whatever we find down there, you stick next to me."

He managed a crooked smile. "The big gun, right?"

The memory of our first big dustup made me grimace. "Just don't go off showboating again."

Freddy's jaw hardened. "Oh, none of it will be just for show."

I pulled Freddy behind me and drew Shokaku. Its longer reach would let me maintain a perimeter around Freddy.

Then, because four extra paws would be even better than two extra hands, I pulled off my necklace and whistled the little tune that spun Bāo out of my pendant. The little jade figurine dissolved and my two-hundred-pound foo lion appeared in a cloud of peppery mist.

Bāo shook out his curly crimson mane and butted me in the hip, nearly sending me to the floor. It was half greeting and half indignation. Typical cat. I ran a hand through his golden fur and grabbed him by the ruff.

"We've got work to do, boy, you ready?"

The rumbling purr in his chest vibrated my hand and conveyed both disdain and readiness.

Again, typical cat.

Bāo sensed what I'd called him up for and he immediately went to Freddy's side and stayed on his hip. Having an extra set of eyes to cover Freddy would free me up to devote my full concentration to Ray Ray.

Linh led the way down to the Door. The unspoken question hung in the air between the three of us. Fiona was powerful by any measure, and deadly in combat. I sent a prayer to the Dragon Father anyway.

With a slow inhale, I concentrated on cycling my qì and relaxing my limbs. The anticipation of a big fight was always harder than the fight itself. The hungry thing inside me was impatient. It had fed just enough to whet its appetite for another meal. That was almost worse than knowing a fight was coming.

REALM

The Tran Door had been obliterated.

Where a massive set of double doors of beaten silver and polished steel should have stood, there was instead a glowing portal of crackling energy. The errant flows of chaos from the open portal licked along my skin like electricity. The scent of smoke was even stronger here. More fire talents. Did Ray Ray have that many on his payroll?

The remains of the door lay scattered across the floor like detritus from an earthquake. More bodies lay buried amid the rubble, with more blasted into the opposite wall from the force of the Door's destruction.

It shouldn't have been possible. The Louies didn't have the raw power to do this. Especially if Ray Ray had split away from Dai Lou.

After a long moment Freddy remembered to close his mouth. I closed mine, too.

His eyes narrowed. "Fi's on the other side."

Linh squinted into the glare of the exposed portal. "Perhaps it would be best if I—"

Freddy shook his head. "No, I'm going through."

There weren't a lot of good possibilities awaiting us on the other side. But I understood Freddy's decision. If it were me, I'd want to go, too. Bāo shook out his mane and growled, already tired of waiting for the humans.

I spun up my qì as we moved to the portal. Crossing to the Realm used to turn my guts upside down. Now my qì moved smoothly around me and created a buffer of energy to soften the impact of the raw chaos of the Void. Mother navigated the Void as easily as crossing the street. Was she in there now? Would she feel it when I Crossed?

Freddy grabbed my elbow and we stepped through. Blazing light forced my eyes shut as we moved forward, pushing against the swirling chaos that tugged at my hair and clothes. I raised a hand, trying to block the endless light hammering in from all directions.

"Just a little farther." Freddy's voice was close, yet distant, a trick of how the portal folded space through the Void and allowed us to walk to another world.

The light of the Void vanished as quickly as it had appeared and new sensations bombarded us. I staggered as we came out of the Void and my senses struggled to recalibrate. I'd lost my sense of San Francisco, at the same instant as emerging into another world.

A dizzying rush of loss punched me in the chest from the broken connection with my city, followed by the slow pulse of Dragon power that came from being in the Realm. My limbs went from numb to warm as the ambient power of this Fragment rippled through my meridians. The thing that was me, but so much more ravenous, flexed within, as if stretching itself. Reaching.

There was so much power here. Maybe enough to fill me up. I tried to ignore the sensation and the feeling of satisfaction it promised.

I blinked away the sunspots and stepped forward, Shokaku held across my body. Cries of pain and exertion appeared as abruptly as turning on a television, along with crushing stone and splintering wood. Behind me and to my left, Bāo's rumbling growl went up again, hitting a pitch meant to reach directly into his prey's primitive hindbrain.

My vision unblurred and I found myself at the end of a long, narrow courtyard. A low-slung building with a timber and thatched roof closed three sides of the space. Beyond the roofline, a lush tropical forest reached for the violet night sky. Much like the Door, the courtyard was in shambles, with shattered stones and fractured beams strewn across the packed dirt.

I'd never been in another Hoard family's Realm Fragment before. It had the surreal quality of feeling oddly familiar, a tangible feeling that the Soong bamboo forest should be just to my left, under hazy purple skies.

Freddy broke through his shock the fastest, bolting for the far end of the courtyard, with Bāo hot on his heels.

I blinked.

Freddy's aura was a storm of royal blue streaking around him. Even Bāo seemed to be bigger and bursts of glowing green energy exploded around his paws when they made contact with the ground.

But none of that compared with Fiona.

Alone at the far end of the courtyard, Fiona was a one-woman hurricane of destruction. With her gāo-level wind talent, she fought for her life and her clan in her Realm Fragment, where she was strongest.

I ran, a step behind Freddy, with Linh beside me. The buffeting winds around Fiona veered us all to the right and we leaned into the gale to make headway. A nimbus of royal blue surrounded Fiona. She floated a meter off the ground with her arms held out, her shredded clothes and hair whipping in the wind. Blades of hardened air formed behind her and plowed into the swarming knot of Louies.

The three of us took cover from the weather behind a cluster of broken trees. Lucky for us, the Louies missed our entrance, with all their attention on Fiona.

All on her own Fiona had beaten the Louies to a standstill. Toward the end of the courtyard the building had been reduced to a pile of rubble ten feet high, penning the Louies in. Fiona rained wind blades down on them and it was all the Louies could do to launch kinetic strikes to break up the hardened air. Behind a protective line of his enforcers, Ray Ray Louie cowered under a crumbling section of the house, screaming orders at his men.

Freddy's eyes were wide and white as he took in the destruction around us. "It's gone!"

I could barely hear him over the howling winds. "What?"

He pointed to a wall that had been reduced to dust. "Our Hoard!"

Oh, skies.

The shattered wall opened onto a large space ringed by a series of empty pedestals, some of which had been tipped over and smashed. Other than the ruined furniture, the space was empty.

We were too late. Ray Ray Louie, perennial screwup and disappointment, had managed to pull off the nearly impossible. "Has Ray Ray claimed it?"

Freddy closed his eyes for a moment, then shook his head.

Almost. Ray Ray had almost pulled it off.

Freddy grabbed my arm. "He can't leave."

I nodded, my talent unfurling in my gut like a stretching jungle cat. "Agreed."

Linh pointed to the fight. "We have to get Fiona out of there!"

Fiona was holding her own, but she couldn't move any more than the Louies could. I'd never seen her aura glowing so brightly, but I didn't miss the way the color stuttered whenever she unleashed another wind blade.

Freddy narrowed his eyes. "Linh, you're getting Fi out of here. Emiko and I will give you some space to move."

Linh nodded. "Okay, what's the plan?"

Freddy's expression hardened. "I'm not sure yet, but Ray Ray is mine."

I peeked around our cover. "Leaving me with, what, the thirty to forty heavies he has with him?"

He raised an eyebrow. "Too many?"

Freddy's question bounced off me as I stared at the cluster of Louies defending their clan head. The men and women moved with quiet efficiency, shifting smoothly in and out of position. Those in the front let loose with their talents, a mix of kinetics and fire, then rotated to the back to cycle their qì for another shot. As they moved away, someone else stepped up to throw another barrage at Fiona. It was an effective strategy, guaranteed to wear down a gāo-class talent, even if the attacking soldiers weren't of the same caliber.

It was nothing I'd seen the Louies do. And it looked a lot like Jōkōryūkai tactics. My blood went cold.

Now that I had the thought, I spotted them, mixed in with the Louies, wearing black and gold over their usual nondescript combat wear. At least a dozen Jōkōryūkai acting as little generals, whipping the remains of Ray Ray's soldiers into a semblance of order to keep Fiona from routing them. Bad enough that Ray Ray had the Realmseekers, why was Jōkōryūkai fighting with him as well?

The sounds of battle faded and my vision tunneled as my talent found a familiar scent. Like a predator scenting prey, my talent reached out across the courtyard and wove sinuously between Ray Ray's soldiers, ignoring the bland buffet of uninteresting talents. In the space of a breath, it found its target, and when I inhaled the bright scent of cut green apples filled my nose.

My knuckles cracked as I clenched at the tree branch in front of me. Ray Ray had brought Leanna here, of all places? Was he insane? My eyes caught up with my talent and I found a smear of faded color, like paint that had been washed from a canvas. Only this smear moved, ducking in and around the Louie guards, making steady progress toward Fiona. Even a month ago, her talent couldn't reach this far. The little squirt was getting stronger.

But not strong enough.

I pulled back, my heart hammering in my chest.

Freddy patted my shoulder, his brows creased. "What's wrong?"

I took a breath and unclenched my fists, willing my hands to stop shaking. "Leanna's out there. And Ray Ray has Jōkōryūkai with him."

Freddy's gaze went from me, to Linh, to his sister, and back to me. The silence between us was sharp, and heavy. He only had one priority today. "I'm going after Ray Ray."

"I know."

I had come in here ready to decimate the Louie foot soldiers. I couldn't let Ray Ray claim the Tran Hoard and tip the balance of power in my city. I wanted to help Freddy save his clan.

But Leanna was there.

How was I going to save her from being hurt?

This was not my kind of fight. With enough numbers, ants could swarm a serpent. But with Leanna lost in the thick of battle, and Fiona faltering, this was no time for half measures. To Freddy's credit, his eyes only widened a little when I told him my idea. He peered around the tree and gauged the distance to the target.

"You're sure?"

I limbered up my shoulders and neck, then drew Hachi in my left hand. The time for words was over.

Freddy gave me a worried look then nodded to Linh. He knew what my talent would do. The sharp tang of seawater bloomed in the air as Freddy's talent sparked to life between his hands. "On three. One, two, th—"

Before he finished the last word, I closed my eyes and Freddy's funnel opened beneath me. My stomach lurched as gravity quickly disappeared and then reappeared. I opened my eyes inside the seething winds of Fiona's hurricane. Freddy's aim was nearly perfect. I spotted my landing and tucked my arms to my chest. Fiona's winds carried me the rest of the distance and

I slammed into the biggest Louie enforcer from behind like a cannonball.

The guy was built like a brick wall and might have weighed the same. It certainly hurt like hitting a brick wall. To my relief the big man went down like a felled tree. I uncurled on the way down and whipped my arms out, Shokaku and Hachi finding a wealth of easy targets on both sides. Blood sprayed in all directions and I stomped on my landing pad's face to knock him out for good measure.

I threw back my head and let loose a bloodcurdling howl as the coiled tension and anger in my chest broke loose.

At this moment the Louies realized that something was seriously wrong with their strategy. My talent jumped onto the man at my feet and began draining him. Bright green dragon scales rippled down my arms and legs as the stolen talent coursed through me. Scattered images of a life of pain flashed through my mind. I knew all about pain. Every pair of eyes turned on me as the Louies realized I was standing amidst them, with both my swords bloodied, and their drained comrade whimpering at my feet. So no one saw when Linh leapt through the air on feather-light feet and snatched Fiona away. Fiona collapsed into Linh's arms and the maelstrom died away, leaving the courtyard strangely quiet.

Which made it even more perfect when Freddy popped out of one of his funnels, directly behind Ray Ray.

Raymond "Ray Ray" Louie, one-handed, half-brained shame of the Louie Clan, panicked and screamed. His talent reached out with clutching tendrils of rancid black sesame, compelling his men to come to his aid. Even the Jōkō weren't immune to Ray Ray's compulsion. The Louie ranks bolted to his side in droves and left themselves completely open to my blades.

I waded into them. Alone among so many enemies, it was like harvesting wheat. Thrashing, chaotic, bloody, screaming wheat. My swords flashed left and right as quickly as I could move them.

Blood ran crimson bright down my blades. As I tore through my enemies I scanned around me, looking for the telltale blur of color. Where was Leanna? My vision hazed red as the Louies closed in on me.

Most of Ray Ray's soldiers were kinetics, and their powerful qì blasts slammed into me from all directions. Some glanced off my dragon limbs. One caught me in the belly and sent me to my knees, dry heaving. More kinetic strikes pummeled me. A rib, two, maybe three cracked, sending a spike of pain through my chest. The stolen qì in my system petered out, leaving me woozy again. I fell forward and landed on my fists. Only years of training saved me from the indignity of losing my swords.

The Louies surged, sensing the shift in momentum. There were too many of them.

Far in the distance, Freddy yelled.

Bāo roared, the sound very far away. Blood slicked my hands and turned my skin into a roadmap to ruin. I traced the crooked paths and despaired. How could we stop Ray Ray from leaving with the Hoard?

My concentration slipped. In that split-second lapse, my talent lashed out and grabbed the nearest victim. The acidic scent of his kinetic talent flooded my senses. Someone landed a kick to my ribs that lifted me off the ground. My breath exploded from me, along with a burst of my stolen kinetics. A half-dozen men in dark suits fell back as a wall of invisible force slammed into them.

In the middle of those falling bodies, someone gave a high-pitched squeak of pain.

I scrambled toward that sound, slashing left and right with my swords, cutting down the men in front of me. There it was, like dripping watercolors, a blur in the air. I sheathed Hachi as I got to my feet.

What did I look like, running at her with my sword, my arms

covered in blood? Did I look like death come to collect her? Was this what I'd looked like at Pearl Market?

Leanna lost her nerve and screamed, her illusion talent falling apart like cotton candy in water. She was pinned under one of her father's soldiers. The man looked unconscious, maybe dead. Leanna's eyes widened with horror as I reached her. I grabbed her by the collar with my left hand and wrenched her free.

Ray Ray had dressed his daughter in miniature tactical gear, a lightweight vest fitted with knives. She screamed when I pulled her out. Ray Ray's soldiers backed away as I turned in place, my katana clearing a wide circle around me. Leanna pounded on my arm with her fists.

"Let me go!"

I kept my eyes on the Louies. "You shouldn't be here!"

Leanna jumped, and the sudden weight shift threw me off. She came down with both her hands laced together, slamming down on the inside of my elbow. Skies, I'd taught her that move. My hand popped open and Leanna vanished into a blur of pastel colors again.

The Louies closed in once more and I drew Hachi, whirling both swords to keep them back. My talent followed the tart scent of Leanna's talent to my right in a zigzag path that angled to her father.

I followed, searching for her while slashing and elbowing Ray Ray's goons out of my way. "Leanna! Get back here!"

Her voice rang out from ahead of me. "Leave me alone! My family needs me!"

I cursed Ray Ray to the ninth level of hell for choosing today, of all days, to involve his daughter. But who was I to judge? I had followed my father's directives for years, killing and maiming countless victims. Maybe men like Ray Ray and my father were no different, using their offspring as mere weapons to carry out their will. The only difference was their level of competence.

My heart squeezed.

I didn't want that for Leanna.

My nose found her scent. Ahead of me, Freddy and Bāo had Ray Ray backed into a corner. The big man gibbered with fear, but his enforcers were kept away by a wall of Freddy's funnels. He needed to finish this, and soon. There was no way he could keep up this kind of effort for very long.

Some still tried to go to Ray Ray's aid. One leapt over the funnels on a burst of Dragon Wings. Jōkōryūkai! Bāo met her in midair with his jaws wide open. Curved fangs as thick as my wrist clamped down and made short work of the woman's rescue mission.

Freddy eschewed the tricks and showmanship today. Here, fighting for his clan, Freddy left nothing to chance. Brutally efficient funnels popped into existence around him, sucking away flames and projectiles and sending them back at his attackers.

I lowered my shoulder into the man on my left and pushed him into the path of a gout of flame that would have roasted Leanna. The man screamed and went down in a smoking pile of limbs.

Freddy advanced on Ray Ray with the finality of an executioner's blade. He raised his hands, as calm and easy as taking a walk in the park. A funnel appeared and Ray Ray winked out of sight only to reappear, moving sideways like he'd been shot out of a cannon. Ray Ray slammed into the wall, his head hitting the stone with a nauseating crack I heard over the riot of sound around me. Blood splattered across the stone and ran down his scalp.

Leanna unveiled from her illusion, a dozen paces in front of me, right at the lip of one of Freddy's funnels. She tried to force her way through the crowd, but the Louie soldiers were too far in disarray to do anything but hinder her.

Ray Ray slumped off the wall and landed on wobbling knees. Before he found his balance Freddy sucked him away again and Ray Ray reappeared, moving in the other direction, slamming into the opposite wall.

Another sickening crack. Ray Ray slumped to the floor with a pained groan.

Leanna cried out, her voice all but drowned in the chaos. I finally wormed my way through the crowd and got my hand on the back of her collar. She pawed at my hands as I pulled her out of the scrum.

Freddy spoke, his voice deep and rich with the unshakable tone of a clan head.

"We will no longer treat with your clan."

Oh, gods. I knew what was coming next.

"We will war with your house until it lies in ash.

"Your clan will die.

"Your Hoard will scatter.

"Your talent will wither."

A hush fell over the courtyard. Freddy's funnels kept himself and what was left of Ray Ray isolated from everyone else. The Louie soldiers could do nothing except witness their head's fall. Even the Jōkōryūkai backed off.

Freddy stood over Ray Ray's broken body and continued his recitation. "The dragons will forsake you, and no one shall know your name."

Leanna writhed in my arms like a fish. I pulled us down behind the broken stump of a tree. Leanna continued to struggle but her panicky energy had dwindled to sobbing. I covered her ears as best I could and peeked over our cover as Freddy continued his pitiless recitation.

"Witness me,

"Witness my hand,

"Witness my oath."

He slashed his palm with a remnant of marble and blood welled, deep and red. He placed his palm on his forehead and the bloody print glared at me like an eye.

I shivered and even my talent quieted. Leanna whimpered.

Bāo roared, witnessing.

This was it. After weeks of dancing around it, the gloves were finally off between the Louies and the Trans. All our carefully constructed rules, the way Jiārén pretended to be civilized as we slashed and tore at each other, Freddy had just thrown it all out the window.

Freddy brought his arms down in a swift, fatal motion. Ray Ray Louie dropped out of sight. More funnels appeared and sucked away huge chunks of rubble. A high-pitched, keening scream turned everyone's eyes up to the horror of Ray Ray plummeting through the air. I pulled Leanna close and the force of her sobs and her fists beat through my chest.

The head of the Louie Clan crashed to the earth with a wet, bone-crushing thud. A section of the house as big as a car landed on Ray Ray's body like a bomb, followed by chunk after chunk of rubble, each piece shattering the one below it.

The courtyard fell silent except for the shifting rubble over Ray Ray's makeshift tomb, and Freddy's panting breaths. One by one, his funnels disappeared, exposing the grisly ruin of Ray Ray's end. Freddy turned in place, his aura blazing around him like thunderclouds, his eyes fever bright. His voice boomed like a drum.

"Your head has fallen! Submit!"

A big man in a tattered suit jacket gave a choked sob and went to his knees. More followed behind him, a wave of men and women collapsing to the ground. I'd seen it before, a cathartic mix of battle-weary exhaustion and obeisance. The knowledge that you'd fought your hardest, but the decision was now out of your hands.

If it had ever been in your hands to begin with.

I exhaled, and my shoulders sagged. It was over. Freddy could retake their Hoard and set his clan back to rights. Ray Ray was gone, but I had Leanna safe with me. And without Ray Ray, I suspected the Jōkōryūkai would withdraw. Both clans could go on, even if it took some time to heal these fresh wounds. I closed my eyes and hugged Leanna tight as she cried.

Only when her sobs quieted did I hear the haunting, angelic melody floating in from the lush forest beyond the house.

A CHANGE IN FORTUNE

All over the courtyard, the Louie enforcers went still as stone, their eyes glazing over. While most of them became statues, several rose. As one, these soldiers shed their black and gold suit jackets, revealing the utilitarian garb of the Jōkōryūkai beneath. More than one pair of eyes stared hard at me. The scent of jasmine floated in with the music and I hung my head. Of course Ray Ray wouldn't have the support of the Jōkōryūkai. All this effort, just to discover we'd been fighting the wrong man.

A massive set of double doors dominated the inner wall of the house on the other side of the courtyard. Those doors slid open and Batuhan strode through, his arms spread wide and his chin held high. His long hair flowed free at his back except for two small braids at his temples. Tall and broad-chested, he wore a fitted cream jacket with green embroidery winding down each sleeve and deep green tactical pants tucked into riding boots. The jacket hung open over his bare chest, where he wore a pair of broad bandoliers encrusted with rows of glowing blood jade beads. Behind Batuhan, at least fifty Borjigin marched in tight formation, each soldier outfitted in pale fighting leathers over leather boots. Each one wore a blood jade pendant hanging at their necks.

At the head of the column, Ariq, Batuhan's son, rolled along in a wheelchair, his skinny arms pumping at the wheels. He was dressed identically to his father, except unlike everyone else in his clan, he wasn't wearing any blood jade.

Batuhan walked through the courtyard like a force of nature, angelic song blazing, his blood jade putting out a palpable energy like a bonfire. The scent of his talent curled around us, tantalizing and delicious. My talent forgot it had eaten and the hungry part of myself wondered how it would taste to absorb the soothing balm of the Borjigin's talent.

I shoved down my fatigue and made eye contact with Batuhan. "You make a wrong turn somewhere?"

"Not at all, Emiko. We came to see you." He smiled and his gaze dropped to Leanna. "And her."

Batuhan was as affable as ever, but after our encounter at Lóng Yá, I had a better sense of him. His charm was his camouflage, as much as my father's stoicism. He stopped in the middle of the courtyard and his soldiers fanned out around him, each one of them crackling with power from their blood jade.

Freddy's face was pale and covered with a sheen of sweat. Taking down Ray Ray had cost him, but he spun up his talent, digging into his last reserves. Bāo bounded to his side, knocking down a dozen Louies to clear a space around them. I shook my head at them. This wasn't a fight we could win.

A squad of Batuhan's tribesmen broke off, moving through the immobile Louies with practiced efficiency and surrounding Freddy and Bāo with a picket line of curved sabers. The Jōkōryūkai dispersed among the Batuhan, blending into their ranks. As they moved, I found a familiar face staring at me.

Saburo. I'd fought the old Jōkō twice, balancing our scales. What would happen now if our blades crossed? When our eyes met, Saburo's eyes darted to Batuhan, and then back to me. The old man held my gaze for another half a breath before disappearing into the crowd.

I turned back to Batuhan. "You brought all your friends with you."

"Consider it a show of respect." He smiled affably.

I gave him a nod. “I’m honored, but you shouldn’t have.”

“It’s not just for you.”

He pitched his voice to a gentler tone. “Leanna? Do you want to stay with Emiko?”

Cold fingers curled around my heart as I looked down. I forced my arms to relax and Leanna pushed away from me. Her red-rimmed eyes trembled with anger. The fist in my chest clenched down, squeezing black, rotten anguish from me.

“Leanna, I—”

She vanished into a wash of blurry color and slipped out from under my arms. A cold spike of pain flared in my side and my hand flew there. I grabbed at the blurry space and felt Leanna’s small hand wrapped around the hilt of a knife.

Leanna’s illusion disappeared and her eyes bored into me, tears of rage running down her cheeks. The icy hand around my heart crushed down. Skies, I thought breaking my sword had been difficult. I squeezed my own hand around Leanna’s, holding her to the knife in my belly.

“Leanna . . .” What could I say that didn’t sound condescending or inane? My heart cracked again as I pulled the knife from my flesh. Leanna’s arm trembled, but I overpowered her easily, wrenching the blade from her fingers.

The dagger was a Husa of exquisite make, sized perfectly for Leanna’s slender hand, with a handle of lovingly polished horn. It had to be a gift from her father, or from her uncle. A dangerous, and deadly, gift.

I was a fool. I’d let my time in San Francisco make me soft, let it change my view of Leanna. I was deluding myself, seeing her as a carefree child with some burgeoning martial arts skills. Leanna had only ever been Jiārén.

Like me.

And now, with her father crushed to death under thousands of pounds of rock, she was also nominally the head of her clan. But she was also my student, and an eleven-year-old girl.

I flipped the Husa around and offered the blade back to her. Her eyes widened as surprise pushed past her anger, and a storm of emotions flashed across her face. I knelt, keeping my movement slow. The moment spun out like glass, exquisitely fragile. I pitched my voice low, just for her.

"Leanna, you fought well today. Regardless of our differences, you are my Jiārén. Do you understand?"

The young, innocent girl I'd been training returned. She was beyond her depth, and thrashing as hard as she could to stay afloat. As much as I wanted to help her retain that innocence, that wasn't what she needed. Her world had become very complicated, and I would do what I could to help her navigate her future.

Leanna nodded. I slid my eyes a fraction toward Batuhan, to make sure she knew what I was talking about.

"I can't protect you here. Go with him and find your sister. Remember your lessons, and look for your chances. Your uncle is looking for you. Bǎohù Jiārén."

Fear crept around the corners of her eyes as I spoke, but they hardened when I reminded her that she was Lucy's guardian. Our friendship would suffer the same fate as her innocence, but maybe we could be allies. It hurt, but it was the best I could hope for. Leanna took the Husa from me and I closed my hand around hers until her fingers stopped trembling. I held her gaze, mentally willing her to understand me.

"When all this is over, you may call for me. I will always show up for you."

She gave me the slightest nod of her head. Barely any movement at all. Leanna straightened and her chin lifted. On another day, I might have laughed. It was a near-perfect imitation of her uncle's mannerism. The bands around my chest eased a little. Despite the blood and grime on her face and clothes, she looked every inch the clan princess. Whatever Leanna needed to survive the next challenge, she would find the will to persevere. She turned from me without another word and walked toward the Borjigin line.

My breath caught when she reached Batuhan, but he only put a fatherly hand on her head. I resisted the urge to lunge at him for touching her. Leanna stared stoically back at him.

Batuhan said, “After Ariq, you are the first, Leanna. The start of a new world, a new generation.”

Two of Batuhan’s soldiers stepped forward to escort Leanna out of the courtyard. She didn’t look back as she disappeared through the doors. It wasn’t the outcome I’d been hoping for, but at least she was out of immediate danger.

Batuhan returned his attention to me and looked over the frozen Louies. He looked like a diner who was unhappy with his meal and getting ready to send it back. “I didn’t have to come, you know. I could have left you to the Louies.”

I made a show of examining the dead and injured Louies at my feet. “I think you mean you left them to us.”

He shrugged. “It was only a matter of time. Their numbers would have overwhelmed you. But before you died, you would have eliminated a significant portion of them, leaving the remaining men eager to pledge to me.”

In his sly smile, I saw the beauty of his play. In one move he crippled two houses and added their Hoards and men to his, all without lifting a finger. He sounded exactly like Father, playing his calculus of life and death from afar.

“And yet here you are before it could come to pass.”

“I wanted to give you another chance. You surprised me, at Lóng Yá. That hasn’t happened in a long time.”

I stiffened. “That wasn’t for your benefit.”

Batuhan’s lips quirked in amusement. “Your father tried so

hard to keep your talent a secret. Yet there you were, blasting it on our biggest stage."

I squeezed my fists so hard my knuckles cracked.

He waved a careless hand. "I already knew about your talent, but your display helped prove my case to my allies."

"Your case?"

Batuhan's eyes glittered as he gave me a shallow wai. "Yes. For years, I tried to convince your mother. To use her talent as intended, to reclaim our birthright, and her rightful place amongst Jiārén. Your mother is powerful enough to stand up to our gods, Emiko, but she wouldn't work with me, so it is strangely fitting that her daughter finally proved that our Dragon gods are alive."

NEGOTIATIONS

Batuhan had approached my mother? He'd known about the dragons?

My understanding of my world was being tossed around like a small boat in treacherous seas. One wrong move, and the cold, dark unknown would swamp me and pull me under. I looked over to Freddy but he seemed as confused as me.

Batuhan took a step toward me and opened his hands. "It's a shame, really, how little you know about your own mother. About her family. And how everyone has been hiding it from you."

Batuhan was right, I didn't really know my mother. All I had were a few memories from my childhood, and as an adult, I knew how deceptive those memories could be. For that matter, how deceptive both my parents could be. My mother gave me very little and my father told me only what he deemed necessary. That thin, sharp icicle of truth pierced my core and stilled my hand.

Freddy's voice broke the silence. "Emiko, don't . . ."

His voice trailed off when I turned to him. My face must have been grim, but I had to know what Batuhan knew. I needed it like I needed air or water.

I turned back to Batuhan. "You knew?"

He gave me a pitying look. "My tribe traces an unbroken path to the first Jiārén who crossed the Void." His eyes flicked to Freddy, and back to me. "All the Custodian families can. It's how we maintain power."

A flash of anger passed over his face. "But my tribe preserved the truth of our journey, instead of draping our story in shame and cowardice."

Scorn dripped off his words as he walked slowly toward me. "Doesn't it strike you as odd? Lóng Jiārén, so strong, so brave, running in fear during the Cataclysm? Does that sound like the act of a dragon?"

The story had been ingrained into me from childhood. "The dragons had gone mad, they were killing each other. There was no choice but to flee. The Realm was—"

Batuhan ripped a staff from the hands of an immobile Louie and snapped it across his knee. The sound echoed around the courtyard like a gunshot. "Lies! You heard their song! You know now that your ancestors robbed you of the truth! Every family who propagates that story does nothing but weaken us, making us cowards!"

He brandished the broken haft. "We were conquerors! At the height of our power, we stood together and found ourselves stronger than our very gods! After countless generations, the dragons finally produced Jiārén who rivaled them in power, able to do things no dragon had ever dreamed of.

"Your mother's family, Emiko. A clan of dark walkers, able to open doors to new worlds with a thought. The Hiroto were our people's salvation, to free ourselves from the dragons."

Freddy cut in between panting breaths. "Lies."

Batuhan sneered. "You think everyone enjoyed living under the dragons' rule? Look at our lives now. What makes you think our lives were some paradise, simply because we were in the Realm? The dragons were our keepers as much as they were our gods."

"What did my mother's family do?"

"Other families allied with my ancestors, in all, nine families who chafed under the dragons. We decided we would leave. Rather than go to war, your mother's family brokered a deal with the families who wished to stay. We would bring what Hoard we needed to start anew, and the Hirotos would open a portal to bring us to a new world, where we would rule."

Anger lit his eyes again. "But they were betrayed. Someone told the dragons, and they came to collect their playthings, bringing all their might to bear."

His face fell. "One dragon, two even, our ancestors would have triumphed. But all nine united to crush them? It would have been a massacre. Your mother's family were heroes, Emiko. They held the portals open, allowing as many as possible to escape. Most of the Hirotos died that day, closing the portals to keep the dragons from following."

His voice dropped to a somber rumble. "But . . . it was chaos. Instead of migration, it was panic, and death. Our ancestors should have come to this world as conquerors, but they lost so much Hoard in the chaos, their talents were stunted. They were reduced to refugees, forced to eke out a life on the margins, hiding from Wàirén, waiting for the day when they found enough of their Hoard to restore their power.

"Some families turned on the dark walkers, blaming them for the disaster. Others wanted to go back, and beg forgiveness from the dragons. Instead the first Bā Tóu decreed that dark walkers would instead be . . . controlled. Bā Tóu didn't want a dark walker going back and leading the dragons to this world. Your mother's family was systematically crippled for generations."

Batuhan looked up at me. "Can you imagine it, Emiko? A world where your mother is revered for her talent, instead of reviled? Where *your* talent is revered?"

My head swam with the implications of Batuhan's story. As far as I knew, my mother and Kaida were the only dark walker talents.

It was intriguing, but intrigue had never been my strong suit. And we still needed to get out of here. "What does any of this have to do with me?"

"Join us, Emiko."

Batuhan waved a hand across the courtyard. "I would spend hundreds of lives like these to save one such as yours."

Well, he certainly knew how to make a girl feel special. In the creepiest way possible.

"I gave you my answer in Tokyo. Nothing has changed."

He shook his head. "On the contrary, Emiko. Everything has changed. You are the catalyst for change we need."

Batuhan took a step toward me. "We are dying, Emiko, and it is the most sinister of deaths. Slow, painless, and unnoticeable until it is too late."

Something wasn't adding up here. "You don't strike me as a Realmseeker."

The look he gave the Louies spoke volumes. "Don't lump me in with these fanatics. We share a few objectives, but I'm not a fool. Submitting ourselves to the dragons would be our doom."

Batuhan tossed aside the broken staff. "I didn't need the Realmseekers. I needed another Hoard. Why eight Hoard Custodian families? Are we such sentimental fools? No, because Bā Tóu can't help but lie to us, about our history, about our power. Their rules keep our strength fractured, so we can never regain our true greatness."

He pulled aside one of the bandoliers, exposing the left side of his chest, where a jagged red line had formed over his heart. "I'm dying, Emiko. And when I'm gone, Ariq will die as well."

Through all of this, Ariq had remained silent in his wheelchair, a neutral expression on his face. His eyes were half lidded, and he seemed to be meditating. He didn't look like he was about to die. In fact, he didn't look much different than the last time I'd seen him. His aura remained crumpled and distorted, something I'd once had in common with him. The color looked more vibrant here in the Realm though.

At the sound of his name, Ariq's eyes opened and found me.

Was Batuhan hoping to gain pity points, by parading his son before me? All I knew about Ariq was that he'd suffered the same ignominy of being expelled from Lóng Kǒu. While I'd been hard-pressed to show I possessed even the basic skills of any Jiārén, Ariq seemed to have the opposite problem, a talent he couldn't turn off.

And while I couldn't help but feel sympathy for another outsider to our rigid society, I also wasn't about to let Batuhan rampage through my city.

Ariq let out a long breath and spoke slowly. His voice was a papery whisper. "My father only wants what's best for all Jiārén, Emiko."

"And maybe I wouldn't have a problem with it, except he keeps putting me and mine in danger to do it."

Ariq opened his mouth but seemed to run out of energy. His head dropped to his chest.

Batuhan grunted. "You see? We were never meant to live like this, surviving on scraps. We are gods in our Realm Fragments. We should be gods here."

"This isn't the Realm."

The big man's eyes glimmered. "You're right. It isn't the Realm. Yet."

In the corner of my vision, Freddy and Bāo edged closer to me. I took a step to the side, angling myself to join up with them. What was Batuhan planning?

Batuhan's talent spun to life, pushing a wave of rotting jasmine scent over me. "I won't let Ariq die because Bā Tóu are too fearful of our own power. Because so many of our own people are unwilling to take hold of our birthright. Blood jade was a temporary solution for Ariq. But thanks to you, I can finally take the next step."

A hard ball of ice dropped into the pit of my stomach. "What do you mean?"

"I'm going to save him, and this is your last chance to take part. I will return Lóng Jiārén to our rightful place. I know the path to save all our families."

His arrogance made me want to vomit. "You brainwashed my cousin and sent her to kill my brother. So you'll forgive me if your arguments about family fall a little flat."

Batuhan sighed. "I expected Zhènmíng to have taught you broader vision. Change is inevitable, and painful. You were the Blade of Soong, the Butcher of Beijing. I would not have imagined you so fearful of doing what is necessary."

Freddy sucked in a breath at Batuhan's words.

I rippled my fingers over the grips of my swords as my heart rate ticked up again. "I think you lack imagination about what exactly I am willing to do."

Batuhan narrowed his eyes. "I would gladly burn all these lives to bring you to my side, Emiko. How many do you imagine I would destroy to save my son?"

One of Batuhan's men stepped up behind him with an object swathed in gray silk. Batuhan unwrapped it. The silk poured off the item like water and exposed an edge covered in silver filigree that sparkled in the light. Another half-dozen men entered the courtyard, each of them hauling a bulging bag over their shoulder. They upended the bags and a mountain of priceless silver mounded at Batuhan's feet.

At the sight of their looted Hoard, Freddy moaned deep in his chest, a sound of raw agony. I sucked in a breath.

Batuhan pulled a gently curved sword from the silk. It was somewhere between Shokaku and Hachi in length, with less curve, and sheathed in dark wood decorated with more elaborate silver filigree. That blade was Thuận Thiên, a sword at least as legendary as my Sword of Truth. It had to be the Trans' crown jewel. With one quick motion, Batuhan unsheathed the blade, flinging the scabbard aside.

Dragon power radiated off the sword, thick and choking as heavy smoke. Batuhan raised the sword in his right arm and the weapon gleamed with menace. The wide bell of his sleeve fell back, his forearm a wash of interlaced ink. In a slow gesture he closed his left hand over the open blade so firmly blood dripped from his hand, the iron scent hitting my senses like a hammer.

Something that could never be sated stirred within me and my eyes lasered in on the ever-growing puddle of blood near his boots. He swept out his arm and an arc of blood sprayed the Hoard, dark red splatters, black against the silver. Batuhan bellowed a war cry powered with his talent, his aura flaring incredibly wide, big enough I thought it would touch me. The color of it was a corona of flowers, pink as a peony then misting to a shade so fine and light it read golden. As his voice rang out in undulating cries, the wound on his hand sealed. The scent of jasmine, heavy and lush as a garden in bloom, swirled around me and my body vibrated with the need to consume it.

The sound shook the flagstones beneath our feet. In that instant I moved, my feet a blur as I covered the last twenty feet between us. I let my talent rise to the fore, the hunger guiding me.

Batuhan thought he could come after me and my city. If he wanted to poke the monster that badly, then I would give it to him. I locked eyes with one of Batuhan's guards, a rat-faced kinetic, his arms raised to deliver a strike. My knuckles ached to punch his face, smash his teeth. I bared my own teeth and my enemy faltered, his eyes going wide.

My talent slipped its leash and a primal sound burst forth from my lips. The Borjigin screamed and knocked down two of his mates trying to run away.

My talent was faster. It plunged its fangs into the kinetic and drank down the man's qì like a cool glass of water. Disjointed images of the man's life flashed before my eyes. The acidic sting of vinegar flooded my senses followed immediately by the earthy, sweaty tang of unbridled fear. The aroma grabbed something in my hindbrain and hit me like a shot of concentrated espresso.

Batuhan didn't deign to look at me. His face glowed with feverish light as his lips formed the words, no longer singing now. "MINE!"

I dove for his forearm, his rosy aura a beacon to my senses, the scent of his blood a siren call to my talent. Before my palm could even touch his skin, the power of the stolen Hoard surged like an ocean wave, rushing over us. My talent gobbled it all up, the Tran silver, and Batuhan's talent, fat and swollen from his blood jade and the stolen Hoard. Cool jasmine coursed through my system like a fragrant stream. The power of Batuhan's talent rippled through my chest and filled me with the surety of his single-minded purpose. Finally, my talent luxuriated in simple contentment as power filled me up.

The sensation lasted only a moment as Batuhan clubbed me across the cheek with a massive fist. The impact threw me across the courtyard. He opened his mouth wide, a blast of sound emanating from him in an unearthly tenor. Dragonsong. His aura soaked up the power of the Hoard gems and the force of his song knocked me back several more steps.

"Witness!" he roared.

In one resounding voice, Batuhan's soldiers called out, "Witness!"

Freddy's face crumpled and he fell to his knees, his hands clutching at his chest. A similar pain stabbed me behind my ribs, as a massive amount of Hoard changed hands.

Powered by lethal amounts of blood jade and boosted by the legendary artifact in his hands, Batuhan's angelic song talent exploded like a bomb. The scent of jasmine, thick as fresh blood, blanketed the courtyard like fog.

His voice rang out, singing his words in two rising notes. "One Tribe!"

A cleansing wave of energy barreled through the crowd of paralyzed Louie soldiers like a tsunami. All over the courtyard men and women fell to their knees, their eyes wide with rapturous joy, tears streaming down their cheeks. Everywhere I looked, wounds healed and bruises faded. Everywhere except me and Freddy.

Bāo roared and slammed his paws down. The blast wave flattened the foot soldiers around him and Freddy and threw a cloud of dust into the air.

I ran toward Batuhan, who seemed to be ignoring the melee, instead directing his guards to gather up the Hoard. I shoved my way through men and women still coming to terms with their new belief system.

Before I'd covered ten feet something slammed into my side and I rolled to the ground. I looked up to a pudgy Louie staring down on me, his face glowing with renewed health and religious zeal.

He raised his arms for a kinetic strike and screamed, "One Tribe!"

The monster in my belly roared and came out again. The kinetic's strike died on his fingertips as my talent drained his energy off in one gulp. He had a fraction of a second for the ecstatic light in his eyes to dim a little before I threw the kinetic energy back in his face. A wall of invisible force blasted out of me and slammed him and another three soldiers back at least ten feet.

The Louies around me screamed as I rolled up and brandished my swords. They threw themselves at me and my swords flashed left and right. Bright, arterial blood sprayed in the air. Time slowed and my talent parsed the scents of all this fresh prey, eager for its next meal.

While I swung my swords, my talent struck, feasting on easy targets. As Shokaku and Hachi stole their limbs, my talent stole their talents. The stink of fear swirled around me, thick as porridge, a heady cocktail of primitive pheromones.

It just made me want more.

New snatches of memory sizzled across my mind like a movie on frenetic fast-forward. Energy from half a dozen talents poured into me, along with the emotions of the same terrified Louies. A wave of nausea roiled in my gut as images of disparate lives strobed through my eyes.

I spun through the crowd with Dragon speed. Bāo's crimson mane flashed between the moving bodies and I inched my way toward him. My hands ached, fingers and forearms screaming in pain. Jewel steel sang through the air, biting into meat and bone. I kicked, using my boot to dislodge a body off my sword.

More. I needed more. My left arm morphed from green to blue dragon scales, my fingers stretching into frost-covered talons.

Someone ran at me with a pair of machetes, screaming her love for Batuhan. I met her charge on my right arm, now pebbly granite, and her blades shattered. I jerked my fist up and crumpled her face.

Batuhan must have left, because the scent of his talent was fading. The Louie fervor slowly morphed into panic as they found themselves trapped between my horrifying talent and a ring of Borjigin guards.

More.

I feasted on their fear as easily as their qì, and the monster inside me swelled until I felt it would burst from my chest. My vision blurred into a parade of unfamiliar faces.

They came at me. Dragon fire leapt from my hand and took one of the enforcers full in the face. The flames stuttered and the color shifted from red to blue, before turning into a shower of ice shards. Kinetic force erupted from my hands, blasting in wild directions as I tried to make sense of all the different talents I'd consumed.

Blinded by fear and driven by Batuhan, the Louie soldiers dogpiled me, paying no heed to my swords or my powers. I swung wildly, hacking off limbs, and still they came. My talent gorged, draining qì from everyone around me. As the Louies crushed me under the weight of their bodies, my mind buckled under the onslaught of unfamiliar faces, names, and memories.

I heard screaming.

It was me.

RETURN

I stalk through Pearl Market.

Screams of pain and terror surround me, an enveloping wall of emotion made tangible.

Fists pound impotently on doors and windows. I locked them all before I entered. The Blade of Soong is here, and all those who crossed our family will suffer my punishment. No one will forget.

My orders drive me forward as surely as my father's hand at my back. The next one cowers behind a flimsy stack of chairs. I sweep the chairs away and grab the scrawny little mouse by the wrist.

The mouse shrieks as Sword of Truth collects her grisly dues, then collapses, fetal and gasping. I drop the price of her transgression and it lands with a heavy, wet sound on the blood-slicked floor. The air is rich with the earthy scent of bile, blood, and thick, unctuous fear.

Scents blend with sounds and together the symphony of anguish trickles past my defenses.

I move away, in search of the next mouse. More screams echo through the market.

It will be days before I realize that much of the screaming was my own.

* * *

My throat was raw, my body battered, my mind shredded.

Deprived of their talents, the Louie enforcers set upon me with fists and feet.

I curled, fetal, on the ground, and endured the beating. My limbs trembled, out of control as if I'd grabbed a live wire. It was all I could do to hold onto my swords. A dozen different talents coursed through my system, swamping my senses with a vomit-inducing mélange of scents and colors. Power surged through me and my arms shifted, rapid-fire, from dragon scales, to granite, to fire and ice. Pulsing waves of kinetic energy burst from me and kept the foot soldiers from completely swamping me. I struggled to stay conscious as my mind drowned under a flood of names, faces, and memories that were not my own.

The first talent I remembered smelling was my father's. His peppery scent was an indelible sense memory that always took me back to clanhome. I associated the scent with a young girl's naive sense of safety, and my father's office and statues.

And Bāo.

The sharp pepper scent of my father's animation talent exploded around me as Bāo roared and bowled into the Louies, tossing them left and right like matchsticks. The physical weight of their bodies vanished in an instant as Bāo appeared at my side, a vision of glowing golden fur with his burnished crimson mane. A nimbus of luminous green energy surrounded his dinner-plate paws and dripped from his fangs.

With the Louies already bereft of their qì, my foo lion was a huge, inviting target. Battered as I was, I put all my will into pulling my talent back, to keep it from draining Bāo.

It wasn't nearly enough. My talent leapt out of me and plunged into Bāo, seeking the reserve of my father's animation talent at my lion's heart. I cried out in horror, but the sound was only a hoarse whisper.

The monster bellowed as it sank into my friend.

My talent purred and curled through Bāo, luxuriating in my father's energy like a dragon swimming through an onsen. Bāo's jaws opened wide and he caught a too-slow Louie by the leg. The bone snapped like a tree branch and my foo lion whipped his head to the side, flinging his victim to the other side of the courtyard.

Bāo turned to me and ruffled his mane, his gesture of impatience.

Confusion and blood loss made my movements slow. I staggered to my feet. It felt like every bone in my body was moving in directions they weren't supposed to. Bāo hovered close and got his shoulder under my arm.

"Maybe this wasn't such a great idea, boy."

That got me his I told you so huff. Why was the ground moving so much?

Freddy's talent bloomed around me in a rush of tangy seawater. A dizzying tunnel of color opened in front of me and Freddy popped out. His shirt was shredded and bloody, shallow cuts crisscrossing his arms and chest. His eyes were wide, white, and sunken.

"Can she walk?"

That was rude. Why was he talking to Bāo? I tried to say something but the words turned to mush.

Bāo huffed.

Freddy reached for my other arm. "Right, stupid question. Let's go."

The world tilted and spun. I smelled seawater, heard rushing winds, and then I saw only blackness.

The smells returned first.

Menthol.

Ginger.

Star anise.

Ginseng.

Pu-erh tea.

Water burbled happily nearby and I caught the soft murmur of voices punctuated by the soft click of ceramic teacups on a tabletop.

Unfortunately, waking up meant returning to the myriad injuries I'd suffered. I tried to take a breath, only to be cut short by sharp pain on one side of my chest, and what felt like a thick bandage on the other.

A heavy weight moved off my legs and quiet feet padded away from me. The voices changed in tone and someone approached me. A cool hand brushed over my forehead, accompanied by the calming scent of clean water.

I opened my eyes. It took longer than expected for my vision to focus, and when it did, I stared for a long moment at the elderly woman hovering anxiously over me. She wore a pale pink cardigan over a white blouse and her hair was cut in a sensible bob. Her eyes and smile spoke of familiarity, but the creases across her brow indicated concern.

Names and faces spun through my mind, becoming a blur that set my heart racing.

The woman took my hand in hers. "Shh . . . breathe, Emiko." Gentle fingers applied pressure along my wrist and my mind quieted.

This place was familiar, but I couldn't place it. I looked down at myself and found the sleeves of my dress had been cut away, and a neat row of acupuncture needles marched down both arms. I realized there were needles in my face, along my ears, and I resisted the urge to yank them all out.

Someone was going to be very mad that my dress had been ruined. Who?

The woman holding my hand remained quiet. When I tried to speak, I coughed with the effort and she smoothly brought up a mug of warm tea with a straw. The scent of the tea tickled my nose and memories as the warm liquid soothed my throat.

I looked to my right and was somewhat surprised to find my other hand buried in the blazing mane of a very large cat. My hand moved of its own accord, scratching behind the cat's ears. The cat purred, the sound a deep rumble like an engine that set my hand vibrating.

My mind crashed back into place.

I stared in horror. How could I have forgotten? "Bāo? Popo?"

Popo smiled and a tear ran down her cheek. "You're back."

"What happened? Where's—"

"Shh. You're safe, that's all that's important for now. You need to rest."

"But—"

"Rest." Popo put her fingers behind both my ears and pressed in gently. Drowsiness pulled at me, and the last thing I remembered was Bāo flopping his big head back down on my legs.

The next time I opened my eyes my mind finally felt like it fit in my head again. The familiar lines of Popo's ceiling stretched above me. She'd stashed me in one of the lesser used rooms of her spa. Had Freddy carried me here? The comforting weight and warmth of Bāo's head rested on my thigh. The nightmare of forgetting both Bāo and Popo was distant but still disturbing.

Bāo felt me stirring and he moved closer to my hand. I obliged him with scratches for being a good friend and watching over me. He acknowledged that and padded away to lie down on a sunny patch of floor. By the angle of the sun coming through the window, I guessed it was late afternoon, which meant I'd lost most of a day.

I was behind the game again, and I needed to get caught up

quickly. A few moments to prepare wouldn't hurt, though. I sat up and closed my eyes, turning my focus inward until my world was only darkness, my breathing, and the subtle thrum of the city's energy. My qì spun through my meridians and I reached for the city.

It was like missing a step at the bottom of the stairs. The place I expected to feel the city was strangely distant, and the city's power was muted somehow. I strained and found it, but the sensation was clumsy. Faint wisps of San Francisco's power came back to me and flowed into my meridians. Weak. Thready.

My city's connection had sustained me through so much, and I was used to having to wrestle with it, lest it overwhelm me. This trickle was manageable, but troubling. Why was it so weak now?

I let the cool threads of the city's power wind around me, the pulse of my body seeking to find equilibrium with the city's power. The exercise calmed me and cleared my mind. Alert now, I ran through all the problems I was dealing with:

Batuhan in my city;

The Trans, wiped out and bereft of their Hoard;

Leanna and Lucy, held hostage; and

My mother having left behind a Gate to the Realm.

Not to mention Batuhan's revelation that maybe our dragon history wasn't as I had believed.

That maybe we were all thieves of the highest order, stealing from our gods.

I scrunched my eyes closed, wishing I could block it all out. But that had never worked for me. My life's decisions consisted of me barreling forward and through my problems, like a wrecking ball. Why should now be any different?

I would start with the easiest problem first—was Batuhan right about our ignominious origins? Did my father know?

I had to ask. When I had my strategy laid out in my head I picked up my phone.

Father answered on the first ring. "Bāobei, it's good to hear from you."

All the noise in the background threw me off a little. "Ba, what's happening there?"

There was an infinitesimal pause. "I'm sorry, Mimi, I'm busy right now, do you have a real question for me?"

Skies, a terrible opening on my part. I bit back a sound of frustration. There were no easy paths with him, he insisted on making everything a test. I had a limited span of his attention, so I had to make it count.

My father had a mind like a primordial spider god, weaving traps and plans that extended far beyond the vision and imagination of most everyone, including me. But I was learning. I could safely assume that he knew everything I did, or had at least considered the possibilities. Father had to know Batuhan was in San Francisco, and he would plan on me acting against him. But in order to counter the General, I had to know why he was here.

"Why is Ariq dying?"

Father grunted, a sign it was a good question. "His talent is an anomaly. As far as I can determine, it has no outward action, and only consumes the young man's energy."

He paused, then went on. "It may be an inward-facing version of your talent. In any case, he is unable to control it. Batuhan's shortsightedness led him to blood jade. I'm sure you've noted that the viability of that solution is rapidly reaching its end."

Ariq needed more dragon magic than his own body could produce to stay alive. Without someone close to him able to withstand the effects of blood jade, he would die. Batuhan was looking for a way to provide more dragon magic for his son, without the blood jade. Several dots connected to each other in distressing order.

"Is Batuhan planning something involving Mother's Gate?"

Father's grunt was different this time, irritated. "That is his most probable course of action now. If he opens it, there are few paths that do not lead to chaos."

My father's pragmatism sometimes lent him a decided flair for understatement. When I'd inadvertently opened a portal to the Realm at the conclusion of Tatsuya's Tourney, real Dragonsong had come through, terrifying in its power. The old stories said our gods used Dragonsong to create worlds out of the nothingness of the Void. What would it do to this world? To the people who lived here?

"Ba, the Trans—"

"Do I need to know this?"

Irritation made my words quick. "Batuhan claimed the Tran Hoard."

"I felt it." He paused and Sugi's paws clicked in the background, wood on tile. "We all did."

Maybe my mind was still getting up to speed, but I couldn't come up with a question that didn't feel like a waste of his time. Finally I settled on something Batuhan had mentioned. Something involving Bā Tóu, and therefore my father. "Is Batuhan's story true?"

That got me a long moment of silence. I thought the line had gone dead when Father spoke again. "The stories of the Cataclysm were written by those who crossed over from the Realm. Those with the desire to write stories about themselves rarely paint themselves in a bad light."

"Wait, do you mea—"

"I'm sure you have work to do as well, Mimi. It was good to hear your voice."

With that pronouncement, my father hung up, leaving me questioning the very fabric of Jiārén history I'd been taught as a child. Bāo looked up from his sunny patch of floor and gave me a shrug of his massive shoulders. His version of *What did you expect?*

* * *

I cradled the hot cup of tea in my hand and imagined the heat from the liquid entering my body and warming my limbs. When I showed up at Popo's doorstep, I usually got some kind of herbal remedy. If I was lucky, sometimes I got soup. Today we were starting things off with a strong cup of bitter tea.

The spa was half lit and quiet, all of the day's patrons satisfied and sent home. The two of us sat at the table in her consultation room. Bāo lounged on the floor at my feet, his belly providing comforting warmth for my bare feet.

Popo held my other hand, her nimble fingers poking and prodding along my wrist, turning my hand over and back while she muttered to herself. "You're as healthy as I've ever seen you, Emiko."

She looked me up and down. "Normally you would have needed a liter of soup, the way you looked when Freddy dragged you in last night. What did the Sentinel do to unblock your meridians again?"

I shrugged. "I was a little unconscious for that part."

Popo gave me a dirty look and muttered something about people ignoring important details. She finally settled on patting my wrist. "There's nothing wrong with your meridians or your talent."

"Then why can't I feel the city? I need to find Leanna but I can't even sense what's across the street."

It was Popo's turn to shrug. "It's not like there are any books on this. If I'm guessing, overloading your talent has interfered with your connection to the city."

I wanted to scream. "Another reason this talent is a curse."

Popo's demeanor shifted. "Emiko. Our talents are neither good nor bad. They simply are. What is good or bad is what we choose to do with them."

"It felt pretty bad to me last night."

Popo patted my hand. "That's not your talent being inherently bad. That's you being bad at using your talent."

Ouch.

She tsked. "Also, it can't have been fun to have all those Louie idiots in your head. Have you tried using your talent with someone who isn't trying to hurt you?"

"Once . . ." Actually that wasn't true. I'd been instinctively using it with Father all through my childhood. And in a flash of insight, I realized that perhaps my talent was part of the reason Mother stayed away from home. After all, look what I had done at the Tourney.

"And . . . ?"

"Yeah, it wasn't bad. Or at least, it wasn't as bad as last night." I certainly hadn't lost my sense of self after my experiment with Freddy.

"You see? Borrowing talents from your friends probably won't hurt either of you."

I didn't miss her deliberate word choice. "Probably?"

She smiled. "It's not like there are any books about this, either."

Still, I saw what she was trying to do. "Thank you, Popo." I gave her a deep wai.

Popo stood and swatted my hand before gathering up the teacups. "Aiya, what are you doing, bowing to me?"

I grinned. Between the two of us we got the tea service cleaned and put away. Since she hadn't liked the bow, I pulled her in for a hug.

"Thank you again, Popo. For everything."

She patted my back. "Do you know how you're going to find the girls?"

I let her go. "I think so. I need to get right with the city, first, and I think I know exactly where to do it."

LABYRINTH

I walked out of Popo's spa into the dull gray of San Francisco twilight. To conserve his energy, I whistled Bāo back into his pendant form, a comforting weight against my skin. The neighborhood of Lower Sunset was winding down for the night, and the sounds of traffic all seemed very far away. This made the shiny white Escalade parked on the street stand out even more, along with the peach-haired driver at the wheel. I scowled and looked up to the microdrone buzzing above the spa.

Colin hopped out of the driver's seat when he spotted me. "I'm sorry, but Mr. Tran hasn't been answering my calls and—"

"It's okay, he's got a lot on his plate right now."

Colin visibly relaxed. "Cool. Can I take you anywhere?"

Once again, Colin's talent didn't steer us wrong and in record time he pulled neatly into a parking spot just down the street from my house in Dogpatch. I unclenched my hand from the door handle. "Great, I'll be right back."

I dashed into my house to strip off my ruined party clothes and change into something a little less blood-spattered. I stood in the shower and let my senses seek out the city. It was like the city felt smaller than before. Even so, I felt the waves of the sea within my Pearl, the sound of the breeze on the shore, and my battered body started to knit itself back together. When I tugged on my charcoal tactical pants, and a black tank top, my ribs still twinged but no longer felt broken. I shrugged on a cropped black haori, feeling almost normal. But starving.

All I'd had to eat in the last twenty-some hours were a few cups of tea, so I raided the meager contents of my kitchen. Luckily I had two of Mama Sun's famous steamed pork buns left in the refrigerator, sitting next to my plastic dish of hot sauce packets. I wrapped the buns in a wet towel and threw them into the microwave. While I waited, I rounded out my balanced meal with two handfuls of my remaining sakura Kit Kats from Tokyo.

The chocolate had a little dairy. Did that count as protein? Probably. I was pretty sure Mama Sun put onions in the pork mix. So yeah, all five food groups. I'd eat on the way. I stuffed everything into a go bag with the rest of my Sun Emporium goodies, grabbed my swords, and bolted out the door. I got back into my bespoke rideshare and gave Colin my destination and one of the buns.

The Sentinel Archive was buried under the San Francisco Public Library, behind a door hidden in plain sight, attended by a demon Librarian, down a locked secret elevator, guarded by a creature I was pretty sure was a dragon, and finally behind an impenetrable door only a Sentinel could access. It was a library beyond imagination, filled with the lore and knowledge of countless generations of Lóng Jiārén.

I was not going there.

However, the underground chamber that led to the Archive had given me a hint about what was important to my city. At the northwestern corner of the city, Land's End beach stretched to the west with spectacular views of the blustery Pacific Ocean. One of the key features of Land's End used to be a labyrinth.

As we pulled into the parking lot of the Legion of Honor my Pearl pulsed like a faint heartbeat, the first sign that I was on the right track. Colin parked and amiably nodded when I asked him to wait. I made my way down the trail, dodging overgrown poison oak and blackberry brambles. The salt tang of the air grew stronger as I drew closer to the ocean. Crows stood watch in the trees as I passed. A side trail branched off before reaching the beach, cutting through the woods. I took the side trail and broke out onto a narrow cliff that ascended directly to the Land's End Labyrinth.

A wide, flat plain of rock opened before me, facing the ocean. On a good day, the Golden Gate Bridge would be glorious and blazing red across the bay. But for now, the bridge was a faded specter, shrouded in darkness and fog.

With the darkness, the beach was devoid of tourists and locals alike. The only sounds were the crash of surf below me and the plaintive cawing of the crows. The Labyrinth was something of a well-known secret in San Francisco. It also wasn't much of a labyrinth anymore. There used to be a maze laid out on the ground, an impromptu art installation made of smooth beach rocks. Like so many nice things, bad people had decided that we couldn't have it. Some enterprising citizen had arranged stones in the shape of a heart where the maze used to be. It wasn't as eye-catching as the maze, but at least the heart seemed to be less attractive to vandals.

My mind flashed to the crude circular maze carved into the floor at the entrance to the Archive. Even if they weren't the same, I was sure the maze was meant to evoke the Labyrinth. Regardless of the maze's presence, I was sure that this location was important to the city.

I closed my eyes and gasped.

Glowing blue lines of energy blazed in the darkness behind my eyelids. The lines started at my feet and stretched out before me, ending in the center of a maze with a shape that looked disturbingly like an eye. The design overlaid the cliff where the Labyrinth used to be.

I opened my eyes again and the blue lines of light disappeared. The path melted from my mind like water through my fingers. Walking a maze with my eyes closed on top of a cliff wasn't my idea of acceptable risk. I looked around and found the crows still to be my only company.

A particularly large one stared at me. I stared back.

"You better say something if I'm about to walk off the cliff."

It cawed, setting off the others into a cacophony. I told myself it didn't sound like laughter.

I closed my eyes and the hidden maze blossomed again. I stretched out my senses, feeling for the cliff and the stones around me. It was aggravating, doing this with my connection to the city so hampered. It felt like sword fighting with oven mitts. Keeping my eyes shut I took the first step into the maze.

The path snaked back and forth through the Labyrinth, leaving nearly no unused paths. Before long I found myself at the center, and the unblinking eye. I stepped into it.

Whatever had been separating me from the city evaporated as my foot touched down. My mind plunged into a bottomless pit and the magic of my city swallowed me whole.

I thought I'd had a sense of San Francisco's power when I came home with my repaired meridians. With my improved ability to cycle and trade energy with the city, I'd felt as powerful as ever in my life.

It was barely the tip of the iceberg.

San Francisco drenched me with the strength of a waterfall. Tingling power flooded my veins, set my nerves on fire, and made my skin itch with unspent potential. I opened my mouth to scream and power flowed into my throat, the greedy energy coursing into every fiber of my being.

Images, sounds, and scents flashed by like a speeding BART train, momentary visions flickering through my mind. I tried to hold on to the images. Golden Gate Park shrouded in fog, the bells of a cable car, seagulls gliding on thermals and calling above windblown surf. And there, in the heart of my city, an ominous dark star like an ink blot on an otherwise pristine canvas. The visions sped up, blurring into a nauseating swirl of color and chaotic noise. My mind slipped into the torrent, sucked out into an endless sea by an undertow of madness.

I flailed, scrambling for purchase even as I was pulled further into the magic of San Francisco. The power swelled to a fever pitch, swamping me under an avalanche of sensations. Before the light and sound broke me, the storm ended as if a switch had been thrown and I found myself in an eye of calm.

The space around me glowed, setting every hair on my body on end. I stopped moving and let my mind drift, the sudden quiet punctuated only by the hammering of my heart. I luxuriated in the lazy pulse and flow of the city's energy. As I relaxed, a thrilling clarity rushed through me and my mind expanded, filled by the city's eye. My consciousness spilled out and stretched into every nook and cranny in the city, extending even to where the land disappeared under the surf.

Salt wind filled my lungs, the bedrock beneath the city was my bones, and the life of all the people and animals moving through the city was the blood coursing in my veins. My eyes looked out on the city from a million perspectives, all different, and yet all as one. I inhaled, and my breath whistled over the Golden Gate and tickled the curling bangs of a little girl in her stroller near the wharf.

Little girls. Maybe I could use whatever this place was to find Leanna and Lucy.

More than ever, I felt as one with the city. The feeling of where my body ended, and where the city began, blurred in my mind. My limbs seemed to change with each blink, now my hands, now a tree, now a crash of foaming white water. San Francisco was a literal ocean of magic, emotion, and raw energy. The inexorable tides of power pulled at the fabric of my mind and threatened to dilute me into nothingness.

No! I clawed at my mind, pulling the ethereal bits of me back together.

It was like trying to keep sand on the beach. Another wave of San Francisco washed over me and pulled away a little more of me.

I would not be subsumed by the city. The city was mine, not the other way around. The Sentinel was a role I had taken on, a mantle of power. The city wasn't me. I pushed back with my own energy and my Pearl pulsed again, creating a small bubble of me-ness in the swirling maelstrom of the city. A few moments more and my bubble expanded. It acted like a buffer, holding the city's consciousness at arm's length. The longer I stayed in my bubble, the more solid I felt, the more my mind felt like me again.

Time to take control.

I cycled my qì. Here in the heart of the city, San Francisco's energy blended readily with mine. I sent the combined result out into the storm and nudged the city.

It was like trying to move an elephant, but some experimentation showed me that a light touch was best. Gentle coaxing moved my view of the city toward the Louie mansion on the Gold Coast. Uncle Jimmy stalked through his home, angrily giving orders to those who would still listen. With his nephew gone he was in charge again but I had serious doubts about the Louies returning to their original power in San Francisco.

The image tore away like a scrap of paper in the wind. I tried to bring it back but the city overpowered me with barely a thought. The pictures broadened, showing me other people within the city, an endless flow of faces and emotions. The sensation was similar to when I'd drained the Louie soldiers, but this time it was muted, like the emotions came to me through a filter.

More faces raced past. It took a moment, but I realized what the city was showing me. I didn't recognize the faces, but I could identify the item they all had in common, the blood jade pendant I'd seen Batuhan's soldiers wearing.

"Where? Where are they?"

Maybe the city responded to my voice, or simply my intentions. My view of the city zoomed out but my sense of the Borjigin stayed with me, like some kind of radar. I sucked in a metaphysical breath. They were everywhere.

Batuhan wasn't just here for the Tran Hoard. He knew Mother's Gate was here and he had his soldiers out looking for it. From what I could tell he had hundreds of people on the ground. It was only a matter of time.

"Okay, I'll make sure they don't get to the Gate. Now show me Leanna."

San Francisco pressed in. Under the crushing force of a literal ocean, my bubble stuttered and shrank. My ears popped and I doubled over as pressure spiked in my head. The parade of Borjigin faces paraded past my eyes again, this time at dizzying speed.

I tried to block out the vision and yelled, "I get it! But I need to find Leanna, too!"

The city clamped down on me, squishing me like a bug under a boot. My protective bubble imploded and the city's sentient force swamped over me. I tried to shut it out, but colors, sounds, and scents blasted through my mind, the sensations too fast to discern, blurring into a river of noise that pulled me down. I fought, clawing with my hands and my mind, straining to keep my face above the chaos, to keep my mind from dissolving into the city.

I kicked my legs, visualizing like I was swimming against sucking currents. My consciousness crept back from the edges of the city, pooling around me. My legs and arms gained heft and weight as my mind coalesced around me again. I almost heard it when my mind sprang back into place, like a rubber band snapping back to its unstretched length. Whatever I had done to commune with the city was gone. I was again an intruder within the city's eye.

Relief bubbled up, a fizzy lightness rising up my spine. I was me again, just a piece of flotsam in the swirling eddy of my city's power.

Unseen force pushed at my back like a speeding truck. I punched through the eye wall and I was again in the swirling vortex of the city's power. Blinding light dazzled my eyes and I raised my arms up in futile defense. My mouth opened in a silent scream.

I hit the damp sand face-first, tasting salt and grit on my lips. My head throbbed like a bad shōchū hangover, and my eyes were rusted steel bearings grinding in their sockets. I was on the beach below the cliff, surrounded by an unbroken ring of burly crows, their shining eyes all fixed on me.

The sensation of the city pulsed under me like a heartbeat under the sand. It resonated up my arms and into my skull, pounding away at me. The image of the blood jade pendant flashed in my mind again.

I rolled over and lay on my back, my body wracked with pain. Behind my eyelids, images of the city ran at impossible speeds, and I groaned from the strain of trying to process it all. At last it slowed, and I debated opening my eyes. In the end, I kept them closed and just ran my tongue over my teeth, feeling the ridges and smooth planes. The salt burned my lips and crumbly cool sand ran down my neck and into my shirt. The pulse of the city thumped in my chest, the Pearl almost quivering within me. I ran my fingertips over that part of me, the small scars and ridges of my skin giving way to the smooth hard shape of the city's Pearl.

As I did so, my fingertips tingled with strange power. It wasn't electricity, but the sensation crawled up my arm and blurry images flashed across my vision. A yawning sensation opened in my gut, like standing over a towering drop.

Or a bottomless ocean.

My hand flinched back and the vision faded. I didn't need to use the Labyrinth. My Pearl connected me to the city. I could use it to see with the city's eye.

This is how I could find Batuhan. How it could lead me to

Leanna and Lucy. If I was willing to risk losing myself entirely to the city.

A ringing sound echoed around me, not from my ears but inside my jacket.

Right.

I reached into my pocket and pulled out my phone. It was Fiona. She started up right as I accepted the call.

"I need you to track the Borjigin so I can get our Hoard back."

Of course she did. I squinted up into the gray skies, looking for the microdrone she probably had tailing me.

Could I do it again? Immerse myself in the city and make it out with my mind intact? In a perfect world, I would have days or weeks to study this in the Archive, consult Oda, even Gu Ma. But when had my life ever been perfect?

"I . . . think . . . I can do that."

"Come to One Bayhill hotel."

Click.

I stared at my phone. Trust Fiona to summon me like a lackey when she was the one who needed my help. I sighed and pushed up into a seated position. The crows hopped around me, as if waiting for something.

"You're out of luck. Freddy's the one with the snacks."

ONE BAYHILL

The One Bayhill had been a boutique hotel, one of the last in San Francisco. I had no idea that the Trans had purchased it until Colin rolled us up to the front drive and the newly installed eight-foot-tall black wrought-iron gates slid open to admit us.

Where there had once been smooth asphalt to allow for ease of entry and valet access to cars, there was now bumpy cobblestone, lending old-world charm fitting to the turn-of-the-century building. The Trans probably held the building through a series of shell corporations to obfuscate their ownership. There was no sense owning a safe house if anyone else knew where it was. The rubble that Ray Ray Louie and his henchmen had left behind was no place to gather a family or convene a war room, both of which I had no doubt Fiona and Linh were already doing here.

As I stepped out of the SUV, crows circled in the gray skies and their caws echoed in my ears. The comforting hum of my city's power rippled through the soles of my boots. Before I even approached the lush rosebushes framing the doorway fluttered before unfurling dozens of new pink blooms. In a thousand little ways, the city always told me that it knew where I was. And if I was willing to tap into the unfathomable power beneath me I could be aware of everyone else. I shivered.

One person I was acutely aware of, was Colin, since I felt doubly responsible for him now. He'd been unnaturally quiet during the drive from Land's End. I worried he was second-guessing his choice to come here, considering the clan war about to consume San Francisco.

I ducked down into the car. The kid was putting up a good front but I didn't miss his white-knuckled grip on the steering wheel. It took him a moment to school his expression to something neutral when he looked at me. Gods, he reminded me of Tacchan.

"Is there anything else I can do for you, Sentinel?"

He could get himself to safety. "Nothing right now. I want you to take the rest of the night off. I'll call if I need you."

Worry lines crept in around his eyes. "If you—"

"Take the night off, Colin. I mean it."

Colin's gaze flicked to the hotel. "That bad?"

"Make sure you're behind wards tonight."

His eyes widened at that, but he gave me a firm nod before pulling away. I watched him disappear around the corner before turning back to the hotel.

The doors opened and a burly man in a sharkskin suit stepped out. His skin was brown and unlined, his black hair gelled back in a smooth wave with no part. Fresh bandages covered the knuckles on his left hand and his aura rippled with the faint red of dragon limbs. I thought of the stalwart Franklin, and my lips pulled down. His absence was a stinging reminder of how Kaida had carved through our lives, like a killing scythe.

Franklin's replacement bowed low, and I nodded in return.

"Sentinel, she's waiting for you in the Golden Gate ballroom." He held open one side of the big double doors, and I stepped through.

My boots sank into the plush blue carpets. The faint scent of jasmine tea greeted me from a beautiful spread on a Louis Quatorze console set against a burled walnut paneled wall. Two elegant white ceramic teapots held court over plates of shortbread biscuits and a crystal bowl mounded high with tangerines. One would never know this family had just come out of a battle that had devastated their residence and decimated their numbers.

Men and women dressed identically to the guard who had escorted me in milled about the hotel's front desk. My eyebrows rose in approval as I saw what they were doing. They were cleaning their weapons.

For a moment, I watched the soothing motions as they dipped linen cloths into camellia oil and small pots of wax. Their deft movements were rhythmic, long ingrained muscle memory. Even if today was probably the first time these weapons had tasted blood in a long time.

Caring for your weapons was very meditative. It gave you time to think about your next moves or gain some space from the violence that you just experienced. Fiona's people needed that right now. The woman closest to me looked up from her work and bowed, her shoulders hunching slightly over a curved blade.

"Sentinel, down that hall, on your left," she said, gesturing to the east hallway.

Was Freddy in there with her? After being separated during the battle, I hoped they could give each other some measure of support. Or stoke the fires of vengeance.

The aspirationally named Golden Gate ballroom did have a view of the bay, although not the Golden Gate itself. Fiona perched on a chair at the head of a long conference table, gazing out at the bay. Even bereft of her home and her Hoard, Fiona somehow maintained her signature cool demeanor. She swiveled around to face me and stood.

Whatever catastrophic damage had been done to the Tran château two nights ago had apparently not affected the depth or quality of her wardrobe. Perhaps in light of their current situation, her clothing was more understated than usual. That didn't stop the creases on her slacks from being razor sharp, or the fabric from her sleeveless silk blouse from glittering in the light. She wore a new Hoard piece on her left arm, a chain of chunky, hammered sliver links wound around her bicep. Each link was inscribed with tiny glyphs, and while the power of the piece was undeniable, it seemed a little outside of her style.

Maybe Fiona was down to her emergency wardrobe. Not that I could throw stones. All I had stashed in my safe houses were extra boots, Kit Kats, and weapons. I needed to take a page out of Fiona's book.

"Sentinel." She greeted me with a small bow.

So it was going to be one of those meetings.

I suppressed a sigh and bowed in return, matching the depth of hers.

Freddy slumped at a portable wet bar in the center of the room. He hadn't even changed out of his tattered clothes but at least his wounds were bandaged. From the droop of his shoulders and the bloody gauze, he was still reeling from Batuhan claiming their Hoard. He sat on a barstool with his elbows on the bar, his head hung low over an empty teacup.

Linh stood on the far side of the counter, playing bartender. Her blazer hung over a chair, and she had found time to change into a crisp white shirt under a loose shoulder holster. Instead of polishing glassware, she methodically ran a short blade over a series of whetstones.

To my relief, despite the three gāo-level talents around me, the hunger inside me lay quiet, as if it were full for once. I ran two fingers quickly over the Pearl in my chest, and it vibrated softly, a cool wave of sensation washing across me. My connection with the city was the strongest it had ever been, and my talent lay a ready pool within me, undisturbed. A rush of gratitude bolstered my emotions because my city had done what I thought was impossible—curbed the insatiable hunger.

Freddy lifted his head, his eyes dull with pain. His aura, normally a vibrant blue, seemed faded and small here in this vast ballroom. I wanted to rush over to him, to put my hand on his shoulder and tell him that I would do everything in my power to help him, but something about Fiona's stance kept me where I was.

"Do you know where he is?" she asked.

I gestured around us. "As long as they're still in the city, I can track them down. I can't make any promises once they leave the city boundaries."

Fiona lifted a brow, unimpressed. "I'm going to need you to do better than that."

She tilted her head toward the bar. Linh pulled a black wooden box out from under the bar and brought it to the conference table. With practiced motions, Fiona unlocked and lifted the lid, spinning the box to face me.

The interior was lined with burgundy velvet, cradling the shiny gold Talon that I had traded to her family when I needed their assistance in tracking down the Ebony Gate. Fiona withdrew the Talon and set it upright on the table. The Hoard gold gleamed with faint red light. The cylindrical base was engraved with my family name and finished with a pattern of dragon scales. The piece narrowed at the top to a needle-sharp Talon. Fiona pricked her finger on the tip of the Talon and wiped a smear of blood across the hanzi.

A sickening pull in my gut was the only warning I had before pain twisted through me, winding up my spine and demanding in no uncertain terms that I was to respond to this Talon Call. The sensation was ripping through my parents and Tatsuya, too.

I gritted my teeth. "Terms?"

"Soong Clan will offer me and my agents extraordinary physical aid and use of all available talent for the next seventy-two hours to effect recovery of the Tran Hoard, and support me with a show of force in repelling the General during that time."

It was an exact mirror of what I had asked from her to recover the Ebony Gate. Fiona was pushing all her chips in. As the Sentinel I was limited to what I could do within the city's boundary, but certainly that wasn't true with my father. He would be bound to bring all his resources to bear, which were considerably greater than mine.

Assuming I could find Batuhan, Father had ample manpower to face the Borjigin in the field. And between himself and Tatsuya, the Pearl Guard would have the support of a squad of nearly indestructible animates. This was the right move for Fiona, it gave her the best chance to put her clan back to rights in San Francisco.

It just might cost me my sanity to tap into the city's vast awareness to locate Batuhan. Is this what had brought Oda so low? Living alone for centuries had to take a toll on your mind. How much harder would it be to hold on to your sanity as a city's worth of minds pressed in around you?

Fiona cleared her throat, then deliberately removed the beaten silver links from her arm and held them out to me.

I stared at them.

The last time I'd answered a Talon Call, the Shinigami had seared a deathmark onto my palm. The chain Fiona held out wasn't just a piece of Hoard jewelry—it would be a proxy for the very clan itself. It would enforce my vow with dire consequences.

I removed my haori and took the chain from her. She gestured at my right arm and I complied, winding it over my bicep. On my sword arm. The snug weight of the silver throbbed as it locked in place.

Fiona handed me the bloodied Talon.

My hand stopped within an inch of the Talon, hovering. A small part of me imagined heat coming off the gold, ready to burn my hand when I grabbed it. Talon Calls were dicey affairs. I'd survived two of them by the skin of my teeth. What were the chances I'd be so lucky a third time?

Freddy came to my rescue. "Emiko? You okay?"

The sound of his voice pulled me back from my spiraling

thoughts. Despite the wounds on his body, and his obvious fatigue, sincere lines of worry creased his brow. From the start of our wild adventures, Freddy had been a steady presence, keeping me tethered to what was truly important.

It didn't matter that I might lose myself in the city. It mattered that I wouldn't be able to live with myself if I didn't try to help my friends, and my city. Fiona was all in. So was I.

I nodded to Freddy, then to Fiona. "Witness."

Linh pushed up from her chair. "So witnessed."

I pressed my thumb to the sharp claw of the Talon and my blood sealed the contract. The pain in my neck subsided, and I drew in a long breath and exhaled slowly as the tension left my shoulders in a rush. I needed to call Father and Tatsuya.

Linh opened a drawer and tossed over a packet of sanitary wipes. The sting of the alcohol on my wound reminded me of what was real, and that much greater pain awaited me. There was no way that fulfilling this Talon or carrying out my duties as the Sentinel would leave me or my city unscathed. I took a step back, uneasy about what I was about to do next to search for Batuhan.

Fiona speared me with a look. "One more thing."

Now it was my turn to lift my eyebrows. "Yes?"

She waved a hand at Linh. "Gather everyone. Freddy, I want a head count and an inventory of all our assets. We'll join you shortly but first our dear Sentinel and I will have a toast."

Freddy's eyes widened and he perked up, suddenly interested now that his sister was excluding him from the conversation. Linh dragged him out of the room as she veered toward the exit.

Fiona sauntered over to the bar. I waited as she set out glasses, plopped an enormous single artisan ice cube into each one, and then a splash of Hennessy X.O cognac into hers. She poured a measure of soda water into mine and added a lemon wheel. At least she remembered.

"To our success."

It felt like a mockery of the last time this Talon had changed hands, but I gamely returned her toast. Fiona wanted something, and she didn't want Linh and Freddy to know about it. "To our success."

We clinked our glasses and I took a perfunctory sip. Tension burned away my patience. When she finished tossing back her cognac, I gave her a hard stare. "What do you want, Fiona?"

She set down her glass. "I'd like to ask you for a personal favor, as a friend."

I blinked. "A friend might have returned my calls or texts."

"I think our friendship can withstand a few weeks of ghosting, Mimi."

Confusion washed over me and I wished Freddy had stayed. I needed a translator, someone who spoke Fiona. "Spit it out, already."

"Kamon called me after the attack. He offered to bring a contingent of Apichais to San Francisco."

I went still, as if anticipating a blow. My instincts went on red alert and I considered a few options before saying something safe. "That's good."

"I told him no."

"Wait, what?" Who looks a gift tiger in the mouth?

Fiona gave me a wide smile, her pearly teeth glinting under the soft glow of the chandeliers. "Well it wouldn't be appropriate since I broke up with him weeks ago."

"You did?" How many surprises was she hiding?

Her lips pulled down. "Yes. I know it's hard to believe since he was such a devoted beau, but he was all wrong for me and I couldn't lead him on once I realized that."

My head swam as a riot of emotions crawled out of my chest and tightened my throat. I had thought they were perfect for each other, and I wanted Kamon to be happy. No matter how much I missed him. Now I desperately wanted to sink into the plush rug and hide from this onslaught of conflicting emotion.

"I don't know what to say."

"Well, Mimi. It wasn't easy turning down the help of the Thai Tigers. And certainly we could use them. But since I didn't want to send mixed signals, I figured out how you could help me."

I struggled to keep up with her. "How?"

"You're going to ask Kamon to come to San Francisco and bring the Tigers with him."

"I am?"

Now her smile turned arch. "Yes, Mimi. You are. Because we both know that if there is one person he is even more devoted to than me, it's you."

And there it was, out in the open between us at last. But she didn't sound angry. She expressed as much emotion as one might display reciting an old news headline. I had been sadly mistaken to think that my emotions had been confused before. My heart whipsawed between the unexpected relief that Fiona had called it off, and a prickly tangle of feelings about Kamon that I couldn't afford to examine right now.

My voice went low. "Is that why you ghosted me? Because you think he's still devoted to me?"

Fiona gave me a pitying look.

"Not everything is about your sad love life, Mimi."

I bristled. "Then why?"

Her face grew hard, her jaw working as if she fought for some internal control. She took a step closer to me and pointed to the door. "Because they are all counting on me. Maybe that's something you wouldn't understand since you ran away from your clan."

The strain on her face was real, and despite the sting of her words, there was no venom in them. Still, I wanted to defend myself.

"I serve my clan."

She laughed, but it held no mirth. "I'll grant you that. But you aren't going to lead your clan someday. You don't have everyone in your clan waiting for you to step one foot wrong so that your brother can resume his place."

Ah. So that's what this was about. I wanted to put my hand over hers, to offer some small gesture of comfort, but now that we were talking, I didn't want to risk stopping the flow of her words.

Fiona waved her hand up and down at me. "You made such a spectacle of yourself at Lóng Yá that I had to think twice about how we would engage in the future."

I couldn't argue with that.

She shook her head. "You couldn't just keep your horrifying talent under wraps? And then you ripped open a portal, all the way to the Realm." When she laughed again, it held a high note of distress. "And Kamon had to rush down to stand at your side after all that."

It all sounded awful as she said it, but her tone was even, practical. She might have been reading me her grocery list. Fiona wasn't complaining, she was telling me about the optics. How it looked to her clan.

Her voice finally took on a ragged edge. "I had to spend the last few weeks proving to the rest of my clan that I was not second place, that our continued alliance with your clan was beneficial, while also letting down Kamon easy. So no, Emiko, I didn't have a lot of time to return your calls and texts."

She had called me Emiko.

I reached out and hugged her. It took her half a moment, but Fiona's arms came up as well and rested lightly on my back.

She snorted, a sound of disbelief. "How will my brother cope, knowing I got a hug out of you first?"

I shrugged. "He'll survive."

We stayed like that for another breath. Fiona's perfume held notes of citrus and vetiver, not quite masking the saltwater scent of her talent. I was struck by how small she was, something that was easy to forget with the might of her will. She was under enormous strain and no matter how much she tried to show everyone that she had it under control, it was a rickety bridge over a raging ocean of despair. I didn't want her to drown.

"I will do everything in my power to get your Hoard back," I vowed. The silver on my arm pulsed in response.

The expansive flagstone courtyard and artfully designed gazebo had probably seen many picturesque wedding ceremonies. I certainly didn't need a beautiful location for what I was about to do, but it felt appropriate to do it somewhere I could see the sky and touch my city.

And I didn't want to risk wrecking another of Fiona's houses.

Fiona and Freddy hung back at the rear exit doors as I walked out to the center of the courtyard. The hotel was old, and like a gnarled tree it had roots deep in my city. When I stepped onto the flagstones San Francisco came to life. Like the breath of a giant beast, the magic of my city ebbed and flowed beneath me.

At the first step, my Pearl responded, lighting up with a subtle frisson of energy. By the third step, my breathing synchronized with San Francisco, and the scent of the sea washed over me.

I paced a large circle around the courtyard, letting my breathing ease, until it felt like the city and I were two sides of the same coin. The city's energy flowed in and out of me as I cycled, but like at the Labyrinth, I sensed the ephemeral membrane that separated us. Whatever it was, this was the thing that kept the city from overwhelming me.

It was what kept me, me.

And I was about to poke another hole in it.

Fiona made an impatient noise, which Freddy cut off with a shushing sound. I smiled. Freddy always had my back.

I closed my eyes and sped up my cycling. This time I pulled

on the store of energy inside my Pearl. The odd sensation I'd felt before started again, and the feeling spread across my body. A wave of vertigo swept through me and I went down to my knees.

Freddy made it two steps toward me before Fiona caught his arm and pulled him back.

Wait, how was I seeing this?

I drifted up and looked down on my bowed back, kneeling on the flagstones, my arms splayed out like wings.

A waterfall of sensations fell on me with the crushing weight of centuries. As the city poured into me, the power to crack mountains brushed across my fingertips. If I reached out, the power would nestle into my palm.

In the next microsecond, my mind started trying to process everything. Instead of opening my eyes, it was like cracking open my skull and shunting the images right into my brain. I was dimly aware that my mouth was open, possibly screaming.

Fiona wrestled Freddy back toward the hotel.

Inside the building, Linh made call after call, bringing in all of Fiona's remote assets.

Across the street, a family of tourists stopped for a photo with the city lights in the background.

In Golden Gate Park, a moody teen lurked in the darkness of a broken streetlight. He hefted a tire iron and considered which car to break into tonight.

More faces rushed into me, an entire city of lives, each of them calling for my attention. Their combined voices merged into a wall of sound that filled my world. This was it. This is what drove Oda to madness. Who could live with this?

I cycled faster, bypassing my Pearl now. The connection was there, I could take what I needed, and keep my mind intact. As it had at the Labyrinth, my qì formed a buffer between me and the city. The pressure on my mind eased and the sensations separated, becoming more distinct.

Through millions of viewpoints, I searched across the expanse of my city. Faces flashed across my mind. Here and there I spotted them, the blood jade pendants Batuhan's soldiers wore. I leafed through the images like the world's biggest book and looked for more of them.

Concentrating on finding the Borjigin took my eye off the ball. San Francisco found the crack in my armor and flooded back into me. The images blurred together again, swirling around me like a storm.

San Francisco's power picked me up like a feather and threw me into the gale. I screamed. Or, I tried to scream. My body dissolved away to nothing. Here, within the city, my mind and body were no longer mine. The city's presence suffused me, permeated me, and obliterated the barrier between us.

I curled into myself, drawing around my core, the light at the center of my being. If I protected it, maybe I would remain myself. I visualized my arms and legs and cycled my qì, trying to create both physical and metaphysical barriers.

San Francisco let go of me slowly, like a greedy child unwilling to give up a toy. I built my defenses back a layer at a time, until I was again a foreign object. When my body re-formed around me I had a half-second warning before the city lights returned and I crashed to the flagstones in a heap.

My head felt like it was stuffed with cotton balls, all the light and sound around me was so dull and muted. I massaged behind my ear, where a whining buzz at the edge of my hearing threatened to cut through my neck.

I was staring back at the glass doors leading to the hotel. Behind them, Fiona stood with her arms crossed, a stoic expression on her face. Two of her heavies had Freddy restrained by his arms, even as he leaned toward me. When I levered myself up to sit, Freddy visibly relaxed and Fiona opened the doors.

Fiona's heels clicked across the flagstones like a metronome until she stopped to crouch next to me.

"You're back. Did you find him?"

"I'm fine, Fiona, thanks for asking. Wait, was I gone?"

"You vanished for a moment. Don't scare me like that again."

The high of riding on the city's power faded slowly from my system. I bit back a curse when I focused on Fiona and saw her through the dissipating lens of San Francisco.

Fiona looked terrible.

Not really. Even on her worst day, she looked like she had walked off a Milan runway. What was clear to my Sentinel eyes, however, was the dull finish that clung to her skin and hair, as if one of the spotlights that followed her around was set just a little too dim.

She remained a powerful talent, but she just glittered a little less now. My eyes went to the silver at her neck, her wrists, pinned in her hair. She was likely wearing every last bit of Hoard silver she had in the world now, and it didn't even come close to what they'd had just yesterday. Without her Hoard, every member of the Tran family was that much weaker now, and in the coming fight every bit of power was going to matter.

Fiona caught my look. "What?"

I waved her off. It wasn't anything she didn't already know, and it wouldn't make her feel any better to know that I could see it. "It's nothing. Just getting my bearings again."

"Did you find him?"

Before I could say anything, I winced as the silver chain on my arm clamped down. If Fiona had something cutting to say to me, it died on her lips and her eyes widened. I caught it a moment after, when the buzz in my ear crystallized into a faint melody of painful beauty.

The world swayed and warbled. Fiona went down to one knee,

her hands clutching at her head. Behind her, Freddy bent over and put his hands on his knees, his breathing quick and shallow.

I locked eyes with Fiona. Freddy hadn't been there, but we had. We'd both heard it.

She nodded, her eyes teary with emotion. "Dragonsong."

As quickly as it had arrived, the Dragonsong cut off, leaving the three of us gasping for breath. I let myself back down to the ground and rolled onto my back, staring up at the sky. I was in that hated position again, playing catch-up.

Fiona got herself under control, but the waver in her voice was there. "What's going on, Emiko?"

I scrubbed at my face and cursed the twisted path of my life. Before the self-pity could take root I stood and looked out into the city. "I know where he is. Batuhan found my mother's Gate. Get your people ready, Fiona, and meet me at Coit Tower."

COIT TOWER

The Dragonsong was getting louder.

I knew a tiny fragment of Dragonsong, the short sequence of notes Father had taught me and Tatsuya before the Tourney. When combined with Kaida's and my talents, even those few notes had been powerful enough to open a portal to the Realm. True Dragonsong that came through my portal, from the throats of the hallowed dragons we had thought long dead, had been both glorious and terrible to hear. Something about the alluring tones made me want to drown myself in the music.

It had terrified me, and I never wanted to hear it again. And certainly not in my city.

From my position at the bottom of Telegraph Hill, Coit Tower rose above the trees. Spotlights lit the structure from underneath, casting the fluted concrete brightly against the night sky.

When I closed my eyes, the Dragonsong pulled at me like an undertow, drawing me up the winding road that led to the top of the hill. The little bump of metaphysical scar tissue in my chest was on fire now. San Francisco's power clashed with the leaking Dragonsong, and the result was a constant sharp burning sensation. Batuhan had managed to open it enough to destabilize it again, putting my whole city at risk for his plans.

With my eyes closed I scanned the area. My city was a tapestry of light that extended in all directions. The intensity of the light waxed and waned by the strength of the dragon magic in that area.

Between me and the top of the hill, at least a hundred sparks of light clustered along the roadway and hid among the trees that dotted the hillside. Batuhan had brought his army to my city. Invaded my city. Anger spiked in my gut, hot and sour.

At the base of Coit Tower, a flare went off every minute or so, like a geyser of energy. Someone was using a lot of power up there, right next to the dark blot that marked Mother's Gate. Another cluster of bright points surrounded the Gate. And there, in the middle of that tight ring of light, two tiny pinpoints, one just a little brighter than the other.

I opened my eyes and San Francisco returned. My hands and arms itched to move, to strike out at these interlopers, these invaders to my city. But I didn't care to underestimate Batuhan, not when the girls were so close. Not when the Gate was so close. He was likely wearing all his blood jade, and who knew what he'd concocted to open Mother's Gate, a task I would have said was impossible before tonight.

No, the smart thing to do was to wait, and stew, until my allies arrived.

The Tran contingent arrived at Coit Tower in a caravan of a half-dozen SUVs, a downgrade from their usual procession of a dozen or more. Fiona's pearlescent Range Rover stopped at the base of Telegraph Hill. Her entourage of white Escalades followed and fanned out to block the intersection from incoming traffic. Linh hopped out from the driver's seat and it struck me as wrong that anyone other than the ever-stoic Franklin would open the door for Fiona.

"Hey, Fifi."

She arched an eyebrow. "Mimi."

"You ready?"

She turned to the hill behind me, her gaze calculating. "Batuhan's up there. With all his soldiers."

"Yes."

"He's forcing open a Gate. Your mother's Gate."

"I think so."

"And he knows we're coming."

"Undoubtedly."

Fiona's smile was predatory. "Good. Let's see if he's ready for us."

Behind her, Freddy and Linh gave orders to their soldiers, perhaps three dozen men and women in dove-gray suits. While Fiona's people were usually attired with an impeccable eye and taste, tonight I noted more than a few wrinkled jackets and torn seams. The tightly cinched tactical vests were another concession that we were in a different kind of fight.

As the Trans sorted themselves out, a small fleet of blacked-out Mercedes sedans pulled up behind the barricade of SUVs. An army of black-clad Louie soldiers disgorged from the cars, dressed in suit jackets with gold trim at the cuffs and lapels.

Uncle Jimmy got out of the lead car. He carried his trademark cane, but his usual kindly-uncle dress code had been tossed out tonight. Gone were the roomy wool cardigan and sensible shoes. Instead, Uncle Jimmy sported a silky black quilted windbreaker, embroidered with gold dragons. I wouldn't be surprised if the zip-up concealed a myriad of fun surprises underneath. His younger clan members wore the same zip-ups, a reminder to Lotus Lane that they belonged to one of the big players in town.

Like Fiona, he wore all his Hoard gold tonight. Chunky rings sparkled on his fingers and a heavy gold watch hung on his left wrist. This was Jimmy's true face, not the congenial smile he usually showed. The stark lines around his eyes and mouth radiated menace like a shark. A predator. Jimmy had come up like the rest of us, the hard way, and tonight he meant to show he still knew how to deliver a strike.

I raised an eyebrow to Fiona.

She waved away my unasked question. "I invited him. It turns out Leanna and Lucy are much more important to Jimmy than a feud with me."

Before Jimmy got within earshot she lowered her voice to a whisper. "And I found myself in need of some cannon fodder."

Uncle Jimmy pulled even with us and put his cane down. Despite the deep circles of fatigue under his eyes, the metal-shod end of the cane hit the pavement like a gunshot. "Where are my girls?"

I pointed to the tower. "The Borjigin have them."

Jimmy's eyes hardened as he scanned up the hill. "Curse his eyes. And curse the day I ever met the man."

With that, Jimmy turned on his heel and returned to his men. He huddled with a tight knot of them at the back of one of their sedans. My gut twisted whenever I thought about how Leanna and I had parted. But my feelings weren't nearly as important as getting the two girls out of the line of fire. "Fiona, where are we on Wàirén containment?"

Fiona turned to wave Linh over when a rending screech of ripping metal cut through the night air. One of the Louies had rammed his sedan into the back of one of the Tran SUVs, lifting the rear of the bigger car off the pavement. He gunned the engine and pushed the SUV off to the side. A caravan of black sedans rolled slowly through the opening, with Uncle Jimmy walking briskly ahead of the lead car.

His cane hit the pavement with each step. In addition to his gold rings he'd donned a necklace of blood jade beads and a pair of leather bracers on his arms studded with gold and gems. Power oozed off him like smoke from a smoldering fire.

Fiona and I backed up as his cars approached.

Jimmy never broke stride. "You coming? I'm getting my girls."

The first wave of Borjigin tribesmen bore down on us from up the hill, screaming like berserkers. Even without their famed horses, the sight was still daunting. Dozens of soldiers sweeping down on us with their curved swords raised high. Behind them, dozens more launched arrows and dragon magic over the heads of the vanguard to hammer us from above. The strategy should have landed like a solid one-two punch on the leading edge of the Louies. Against most, the initial onslaught would have crushed the line.

Whatever soldiers Ray Ray had recruited to attack the Tran château, Jimmy had clearly kept some good ones in reserve. As the Borjigin descended the road and came through the trees, the sedans behind Jimmy roared to life, threading around him on the narrow road. With marching band efficiency Jimmy's team formed a defensive blockade around him. Black-suited men popped out of the car windows and began throwing talents back at the Borjigin like there was no tomorrow.

Kinetic strikes screamed through the air, ripping trenches in the hill and knocking over trees. Fire and ice flew in equal measure, to be met with responding blasts of energy. Metal screamed as the bulky Mercedes sedans took a pounding, but Jimmy must have sprung for some armored version of his cars because despite the beating, the cars continued to move at a steady pace.

More Borjigin poured out of the trees behind the Louie caravan. The scent of seawater appeared, sharp and stinging as Fiona and her family let loose. The winding road became ground zero for hurricane-force winds and Fiona's cutting scythes of hardened air.

The pulse of the city thundered below my feet and fed me what felt like a limitless supply of energy. I kept my talent chained, I wasn't going near it if I didn't have to, and the city helped me make up for it. The trees came alive at my thoughts, whipping left and right to knock down our enemies. At my side, Bāo roared and covered my back, using claws and fangs to turn my attackers aside. I tracked the Borjigin as they swarmed down on us, calling out as they popped up on both sides of the road. Roots pulled free from the earth, clutching for feet and legs before pulling them into the dirt.

Through the fight, the presence of the Gate never left my mind. Every pulse of energy that swept over Telegraph Hill landed in my chest like crawling fingers of ice.

And still, the Borjigin came, throwing themselves into us with seemingly unstoppable zeal. I had never seen this many Jiārén in combat at the same time, going all-out like this. A tribesman broke through the Tran line and came at me, his stone limbs hurtling at my head. His gut wasn't stone though, and I went low, pulling Shokaku across his midsection. Leather, skin, and viscera parted like tissue paper. Right behind me, Freddy opened a funnel at my back and caught another interloper, throwing her fifty feet into the night sky. She disappeared into the darkness.

It was my fight with Kaida all over again, multiplied a dozen times over. I blocked out the thick scent of blood, the piercing screams, and cycled my qì as I swung my sword. The power of my city flowed through me like cool water, keeping me centered. Keeping the monster in my belly at bay. Another pulse of Dragon power rocked the hill, and I looked up again, dread thick in my veins.

How many more until Batuhan cracked the Gate open?

In the middle of it all, Jimmy continued to walk at an even clip, his cane coming down in measured beats. Even from twenty feet back I could feel him cycling his qì. What was he up to? His talent wasn't particularly useful in a pitched battle like this. He'd always been skilled at the subtle touch, but he was clearly winding up for something big.

While Fiona and Jimmy had brought their best soldiers, there were simply too many tribesmen. As the Trans and Louies tired, the Borjigin had men to spare, rotating in from the rear of their formations, bringing fresh energy to the fight with crushing regularity.

We put up a good effort but it was impossible to track them all.

One of them broke through, his Dragon speed talent weaving him through the Louie onslaught. The man's swords looked like twin smears of silver aimed at Jimmy's throat.

Uncle Jimmy finally entered the fight. The distinct, black sesame scent of his magic filled the night air in an instant, at an intensity that staggered me. Jimmy barely twitched, just a slight movement of his head. Negligent. Disdainful.

Dragon.

He cracked the lid on all the power he was spinning up and his voice boomed like he'd struck Heaven's own taiko drum.

"Blind."

The Borjigin speedster screamed and stumbled, his swords clattering to the pavement. He rolled over and over, his hands clawing at his face, until he rolled off the side of the road and down the hill.

Shattered skies. A slimy tentacle of real fear slithered through my belly. Jimmy had used his talent on me before, but with his trademark deftness. I'd always assumed his light touch was the hallmark of his gāo-level power. He'd hidden his ability to wield his talent like a sledgehammer until he had no choice but to unveil it.

Jimmy's move must have been some signal to his men because the sedans shifted strategy. Instead of fighting the Borjigin, they pulled in tight and formed an attack wedge. Jimmy stepped nimbly onto the hood of the center car. With Jimmy protected in the middle, the formation picked up speed and plowed up the hill, running over any Borjigin in their path. Bāo and I ran to stay abreast of them, and the Trans followed suit.

From his perch on the center car, Jimmy wielded his cane like a scepter, the buttery Hoard gold of the handle glowing like a torch. The phalanx of cars rounded the last hairpin turn to the top of the hill. Coit Tower rose out of the trees to our left. Up ahead, the road topped out at the small roundabout at the base of the tower. Brilliant flashes of energy backlit the tight formation of fresh Borjigin soldiers blocking the road.

The Louie cars didn't slow, and Jimmy let loose the punch he'd been saving up.

Jimmy raised his cane like a pennant. The gold blazed like a miniature star. He whistled one high, pure note of Dragonsong, the sound aching in its clarity. Several Trans went to their knees, hands clasped over their ears. The Borjigin formation rocked back on their heels. Jimmy brought his cane down in an overhead swing aimed up the hill, right at the center of the Borjigin.

"Sleep!"

Uncle Jimmy, friendly, ever-smiling, cardigan-wearing patriarch of the Louie Clan, erupted with Dragon power like a bomb. The scent of black sesame covered Telegraph Hill like pea soup fog. Even though he'd directed his attack forward, the Tran soldier next to me fell to his knees, his eyes rolling up. I caught him just before his head bashed into the pavement.

Ahead of us, the force of Jimmy's charm speak spread out in a wave. The formation of Borjigin fell backward like bowling pins. The Louie caravan trampled over them without losing a beat. I nearly tripped over all the bodies as we rushed along the suddenly clear road.

Our group crested the top of the road. In the parking cul-de-sac, Batuhan stood on top of the monument in the center planter, dressed in lamellar armor, hundreds of sections of studded leather protecting him from neck to ankles. Instead of metal studs, each segment of his armor glowed red from a bead of blood jade the size of my thumb. More blood jade draped off his shoulders and hips. Belts and bandoliers, strings of beads, bangles, and pendants glittered and clicked up and down his body as he moved. Piles and piles of silver weapons, jewelry, and ingots were strewn around the planter. Power baked off of Batuhan in nauseating waves, like standing before an open furnace. He had his eyes closed and his legs spread wide, like a warrior king atop the world.

Next to him, Ariq sat in his wheelchair, again free of any blood jade, and looking more sallow than our last encounter. Batuhan hadn't been lying, his son was dying. Ariq sat with his eyes closed and his brows drawn down, his hands held rigidly at midline before his chest. He was cycling like his life depended on it.

Maybe it did.

The rest of the Borjigin tribe spread out around their chief in a loose ring, swords drawn, and qì spinning up. Like their leader, they all wore hardened leather armor, a surcoat that hung past the hips and covered the shoulders. Their arms were left free and mobile as half of them readied bows, and the other half readied their talents. Toward the middle of their formation, a lone tribesman had stripped to his waist. Sweat slicked his arms and shoulders, and ropy muscles danced across his back as he pounded out a steady beat on a massive drum.

More importantly, these tribesmen were clearly fresh and rested, while all of Jimmy's and Fiona's soldiers were running on empty. Armor and weapons clattered behind us as the remains of Batuhan's forces regrouped and came up the road to block our escape.

Batuhan seemed to not have yet noticed our arrival. His head bobbed gently to the beat of the drum until his eyes flew open and he sang a complex series of notes and thrust his hands down. The music jerked me to my knees, demanding my obeisance. In fact, everyone in the parking lot fell to their knees except for Jimmy, up on the hood of the car, who seemed to be holding himself up by sheer force of will and the support of his cane.

The concrete monument at Batuhan's feet flashed with brilliant light. In my mind, the protective layers of San Francisco's magic wobbled as the Gate inched open. The Dragonsong that had been tickling at my mind all night went up another notch in volume. Batuhan opened his eyes and swept his gaze over us.

"Excellent. You're all just in time."

OPEN

Batuhan's drummer continued to beat out his steady rhythm.

Uncle Jimmy hopped down from the hood of the car and nearly stumbled as he landed. His right hand maintained a death grip on his cane but his left was tucked against his chest now, as if he'd broken a bone. He walked stiffly to stand in front of his men, smacking them with his cane as he went, getting them back to their feet.

I got up as well. Fiona and Freddy looked like they'd both taken a direct hit to the face. They were really missing the support from their Hoard. Bāo shook out his mane and reattached himself to my hip. I shouldered my way past the Trans until I was even with Jimmy. Although Batuhan stood directly before us, Jimmy's eyes were locked to the left.

Behind a screen of a dozen men armed with swords, Leanna and Lucy sat on the asphalt. Leanna was still dressed in the tactical vest, but all her knives had been taken from her. Lucy's eyes were red, her dirty cheeks streaked with tears. Leanna had one arm draped protectively over her sister's shoulders, and while her eyes were red, too, they still had a defiant gleam in them as she glared daggers at the backs of her guards.

The light in her eyes dimmed a little when she saw me, and she looked away quickly. My heart squeezed. How had Leanna's life become so hard so quickly?

San Francisco rumbled in my chest like a thunderclap when I

laid eyes on the two girls. Batuhan would pay for threatening innocents in my city. On my next intake of breath, the city's power rushed into me like water plunging into an empty vessel. Pins and needles danced along my arms as power crackled across my skin. Every hair on my neck stood on end. I felt that if I moved, the world would tremble.

Uncle Jimmy stepped forward, his eyes grim. "Release the girls, Batuhan. This is a clan fight. You could at least do it honorably."

Batuhan sneered. "You would condemn these girls to a life of mediocrity! I'm giving them, and all our children, the world they deserve, the world they were meant to have!"

He pointed an accusing finger, waving it from Jimmy, to Fiona, and me. "The legacy you and your kind stole from them!"

Jimmy knew a lost cause when he saw one. He raised his cane and the black sesame scent of his charm speak descended on us again. **"Sleep!"**

His aura flared, a blaze of bright pink, and I caught the edge of damp, rotting wood underneath the sesame as Jimmy's talent rolled out. The soldiers guarding Leanna and Lucy rocked back on their heels and two of them dropped to their knees, senseless. At the same time, Jimmy cried out and fell to the ground in a heap, his left arm clutching spastically, his neck arched back to a painful angle. His guards rushed to his aid and the girls cried out in dismay as their uncle groaned in agony.

Batuhan shook his head. "Blood jade is not meant for the weak."

With all eyes on Jimmy, no one noticed as I stepped off to the side, lining myself up. San Francisco's power thrummed inside me, threatening to pop out my eyeballs. Whatever else happened tonight, however much Leanna might hate me, the girls were coming home safe.

Batuhan was just opening his mouth, about to spout off about something else when I absolutely could not hold in the city's magic anymore.

My arms crackled with energy as I thrust them forward. I clenched my hands into fists and grabbed the fabric of my city's power. A rumbling growl shook Telegraph Hill and Batuhan whirled to face me, his eyes wide. Behind their guards, Leanna grabbed her sister and covered Lucy's face with her body.

The ground at my feet split with a crack like thunder. Chips of shattered concrete sprayed up and peppered the tribesmen in front of me. Two of them went down, clutching at their eyes. I pulled my arms in and the cracks spread out, rippling away from me and spreading out under the feet of Batuhan's guards. A dozen talents flared to life, all of them at least a second too late.

My city's power soared through my system in an exultation. I threw my arms apart and the roadway bucked up and rolled out in two waves, peeling the tribesmen apart. Men screamed as the very ground betrayed them, throwing them aside like so much trash.

Jimmy's men wasted no time and ran into the opening. Sure hands grabbed the two girls and rushed them back to Jimmy's side. Borjigin soldiers gave chase, only to be cut down as Bāo bowled into them. Two hundred pounds of pouncing fur and claws sliced through the soldiers, leaving the girls free to make their escape.

Their uncle stood supported between two of his soldiers. A new squad of Jimmy's men, ones I hadn't seen before, circled the group and linked arms.

From inside the circle, Jimmy made eye contact with me. His eyes were sunken and red, bloody tears running down his cheeks. The girls ran to him, crying, arms clutching at their uncle. Jimmy brought an arm down to stroke Leanna's head and he gave me a nod.

And that was all I got from him before the scent of green apples bloomed and the ring of illusionists made all traces of the Louie

Clan vanish in the blink of an eye. The last thing I saw was tears of relief running down Leanna's cheek. She didn't look back at me.

Fiona appeared at my side. I'd never seen her this disheveled before, but her eyes focused on her stolen Hoard, and then to Batuhan. "Finally, we can get down to business."

With the girls safely away the urgency of the city's magic ebbed. The parking lot was a wreck and the Borjigin scrambled back over the distorted concrete to rejoin their leader. While everyone else had been thrown off their feet, Batuhan remained unmoved from his perch on top of the concrete monument. Mother's Gate was a dead spot, untouched by San Francisco's power.

Several of Batuhan's men searched the parking lot, but Louie illusionists were the stuff of legend. One of them had once made a moving semi-truck disappear completely before my eyes. It would be child's play for a team of them to make a small group of people invisible. Batuhan sighed.

"They'll come back, eventually. They'll all have to."

He turned to me. "Have you changed your mind?"

Fiona stepped in front of me before I could answer. Her voice rang out across the hilltop. "We will no longer treat with your clan. We will war with your house . . ."

Freddy and Linh lined up behind Fiona, and the rest of her foot soldiers spread out around us, some of them facing downhill to take on the Borjigin who had come up behind us. Bão took his place at my back again, his hackles rising.

Batuhan laughed and the sound drowned out Fiona's words. "You've already lost, Tran. Every family knows it. Your seat on Bā Tóu is forfeit. This feud was over before it began."

Fiona hadn't been saying the words out of any need for decorum. She just wanted to distract him. Now she wound up and took her shot. From this close, her wind blades were devastating. With none of her usual showmanship, she brought both her arms forward, clapping her palms together.

In unison, Freddy, Linh, and several other family members mimicked Fiona's movement. With a wedge of focused wind talents behind her, Fiona scooped up their collective power and threw it in one giant wind blade aimed at Batuhan's face. Thunder cracked and echoed across the parking lot, only to be whipped away by the sudden appearance of hurricane-force winds.

Batuhan never moved, other than to keep nodding his head along with the drumbeat.

His outer line of guards stepped forward as a synchronized unit and slammed their feet down. As one, the guards bellowed and put their arms up, wrists crossed. The combined might of a dozen gāo kinetics unleashed a countering wave of invisible force that scattered the Trans' wind blade, turning Fiona's hardened air into a meandering breeze.

Fiona dropped to one knee, panting for breath. Behind her, the rest of her family didn't look much better.

Batuhan lifted an eyebrow. "Do you see now how weak we have become? Dependent on gold and silver for what was once our natural state of being? When I'm done, we'll all be as strong as we were always meant to be. As we all once were."

The drumbeat hit a crescendo and Batuhan lifted his voice. Again, he sang the strange melody, this music that was somehow connected to the very core of my being. When had I gone down to my knees? When had Batuhan's talent become Dragonsong? Tears streamed down my cheeks as Batuhan's haunting song melded with the whisper of true Dragonsong leaking through the cracked Gate.

I wanted to stop him, but I also wanted to submit myself to the music of our gods. My head slowly dropped until my forehead hit the asphalt. Bāo growled, butting me with his head, but I couldn't move. The drumbeats surged again and Batuhan's music changed. When had he become so powerful? How much Dragonsong did he know?

Behind me, Freddy was prostrate on the ground, sobbing quietly. To my side, Fiona knelt with her head down, her knuckles on the pavement, her shoulders quivering with tension. All over the parking lot, men and women wept before the majesty of Batuhan's talent. My limbs refused to move. It was all I could do to move my eyes to look around.

No. I couldn't move my body, but I could move my qì. I closed my eyes and cycled. The pattern Madam Yao had taught me was second nature now. As my qì flowed through me, the smothering effect of Batuhan's Dragonsong dimmed. Feeling returned to my body, and my head cleared. The true Dragonsong was getting stronger now. Whatever Batuhan was doing to open the Gate was working.

I cycled faster, and my qì seemed to take on a life of its own, moving through my meridians of its own accord, barely needing my guidance. I got my elbows under me, and pushed up until my head lifted off the ground.

Batuhan was the only one standing in the parking lot. Even his own men were either on their knees, or completely debasing themselves on the ground. No one saw me lift one leg and slowly plant my foot. I got my hand in Bāo's ruff and held on for dear life. It was the hardest thing I'd ever done, just forcing myself to stand up.

By the time I was upright, Batuhan's song changed again, into an undulating melody that felt like it was going to shake my bones to pieces. My qì swirled through my meridians now, faster than I'd ever been able to cycle before. Sweat prickled my skin as I reached for the city and found her answer right where I expected her, a comforting swell of quiet power under my feet. San Francisco rolled through my limbs like a morning marine layer and settled over my mind, reducing the Dragonsong to a murmur.

It still took all my concentration to move one foot in front of the other. Bāo matched my pace, his low rumble of a growl sending vibrations through my arm. Batuhan had his eyes focused on the

Gate. The only guard still moving was the drummer, and he had his eyes closed as he pounded out the frenetic beat.

Shokaku slid out of her sheath with the lightest whisper and her jewel steel glimmered in the glow of the starlight. I closed the distance and tightened my hand on my katana's grip, the silk knots fitting into the gaps between my fingers like gears meshing together. The Dragonsong grew louder as I approached, and a small part of me yearned to look through the door. These were our dragons of legend. What would it be like to see them in the flesh, to stand before the staggering power of their mere existence?

Mother's words rang through my head. The danger was too great, no matter if Batuhan's story was true. I wasn't going to let him risk my city this way. San Francisco's magic contained the Gate, but it was holding on by only the thinnest of margins.

Another step closer. I was practically using Bāo as a crutch. One more and Shokaku's reach would be enough. His leather armor was no match for my blade. His height and position on the pedestal made a head strike difficult. I would go for the gut and eviscerate him, incapacitate him long enough to finish him off.

I dragged my feet forward, leaning into the Dragonsong like it was a headwind. I drew back my sword.

Batuhan's head popped up, his eyes fiery bright and fixed on me. "Yes, of course. You are the answer. Come to me."

He sang the last three words and his angelic song slammed me between the eyes, running straight into my brain. My qì field barely blunted it, and a dim memory of Madam Yao reminded me that I was much too close to him, right at the apex of his power. I faltered and stumbled forward. Bāo's roar cut off as he vanished from sight. Batuhan grabbed my hand and hauled me up. His massive hand enclosed mine, trapping my sword.

"Your talent is part of this Gate. The portal and the Gate are tied to you, cousin to Kaida, and daughter to Sara. You are the key."

My qì was moving too fast to stop. When Batuhan's hand touched my skin, the memory of his talent, of the satisfaction, was too great to ignore and the hunger in my belly roared to life. My arm electrified, the sensation pulsing from his hand in waves. I tried to pull back the monster, but cool, jasmine-scented power flowed through me again as I drank in Batuhan's talent.

It was like drinking from a firehose. Augmented with his blood jade, and standing atop the stolen Hoard, Batuhan was a geyser of energy I could never hope to consume. Two warring tides of energy churned inside me, Batuhan from one side, San Francisco from the other. I battered his fist with my left hand, while his talent shredded my senses.

I drew back my arm to spike him in the eyes when a vision flitted across my mind. The woman was unmistakable, with her delicate, straight nose and slashing brows over piercing eyes. My mother, but not as I knew her. She wore an elegant dress of vivid blue. Her eyes sparkled with mischief and a smile tugged at the corners of her mouth.

She was young. Vibrant. Reckless.

The sight of her was more than enough to throw me off. My cycling stuttered and Batuhan's power overwhelmed me from within and without. The city's presence in my mind faded and my vision blackened at the edges. The magic around the Gate cracked like an eggshell.

Batuhan hauled me close. His hand was an iron band around mine, and his eyes glittered with religious fervor.

"Let go of your old fears, Emiko. When Dragonsong changes this world, we will return to our rightful place. My son will live. Jiārén will no longer cower like rabbits. The world will be as it should be."

His talent combined with the Dragonsong, bending my will and my knees. Batuhan followed me down. He grabbed my other arm and placed both my hands on the concrete monument. Batuhan lifted his head to the night sky and sang with aching clarity.

"She calls the pain,

"She takes the pain."

No! I screamed, but nothing came out of my mouth. The word was trapped inside my head, like I was trapped, powerless, inside my body.

Beneath our hands, the concrete monument cracked open, revealing the golden Door my mother had fabricated with the help of two Old Ones. The protective layers I'd laid over it with San Francisco buckled. The unstable energy of the portal swelled like bloated, rotting fruit. Batuhan's fingers crushed down on my hands. I watched in impotent horror as Batuhan sang the poem that dictated my doom.

"She finds the way."

The Gate glowed, sparkling light refracting through the embedded gems. Bright fissure lines appeared, crawling across the surface of the metal. A fresh wave of Dragonsong poured through, and an immense wave of pressure built under us. We were kneeling on a time bomb of dragon magic, and we'd just flipped the switch.

Batuhan barreled ahead, his body and aura incandescent with power. He reached inside his vest and pulled out a glass vial. I tried to move my free arm, but the weight of worlds held me down. It took all I had to keep my head up and watch Batuhan crush the vial in his hand.

Blood poured from his lacerated fingers and a new scent, sweet and cloyingly floral, bloomed around us. Batuhan's power, already at dizzying heights, redoubled again with the addition of the amplifier he'd acquired in Tokyo. Batuhan's voice rose to inhuman heights and became true Dragonsong.

"They forge the world anew!"

The sound that came from my throat was not mine. My qì boiled like a storm, funneling a churning mix of San Francisco, my hungry talent, and Batuhan's strange Dragonsong. I was too full of everything—containing it was impossible. The potent blend of power rushed down my arms and poured into the Gate.

The jeweled construct shone like a star and light blotted out my vision. Caught between our combined power and the dragon magic beyond, my mother's Gate to the Realm cracked in half. The sound was the breaking of worlds, the rending of cities.

Rippling peals of thunder tore across the top of Telegraph Hill and threw me away from the Gate. Everyone around the Gate was blown back like dead leaves. Ariq's wheelchair toppled and he sprawled on the ground. Batuhan was also flung away and landed a dozen feet from me. He got up instantly, his eyes fever bright with joy, his face cast in strange, ethereal light.

For a moment I saw what his followers saw, a leader and a visionary. One blessed by fortune and fueled with conviction. He was the General, here to bring chaos and war to my city, to Jiārén. In a flash of fear I realized what he had wrought.

In the center of the cul-de-sac, a brilliant pillar of violet fire burst from the ground and lanced straight up like a beacon. Dragon power, as palpable as a raging furnace, pushed me back. I raised an arm to shield my face. When the Dragonsong hit, it drove me to my knees, an unfiltered chorus of the gods that demanded my submission.

From his knees Batuhan raised his arms and cried out in triumph.

Beyond the glare of power, Coit Tower stood in the strange light. I watched in horror as the surface of the tower morphed. The fluted design of the walls flowed like water. An undulating pattern of waves traveled up and down the tower before forming into a pattern of dragon scales.

As suddenly as it had appeared, the Dragonsong vanished, leaving my ears yearning for the music in the empty quiet. Without the pressure of the Dragonsong on me I collapsed to the ground. The city reached for me, and in that fraction of a second, I had enough warning to cover my head as the portal twisted in on itself like a serpent devouring its tail.

The violet pillar of light exploded, casting everything in a flickering instant in the light of the Realm. Something huge, ageless, and terrifying surged under my city, claws and fangs tearing a hole through the fabric of San Francisco. The portal collapsed with another ripping thunderclap that threw me across the parking lot. I slammed against a tree and the world switched off.

DRAGON

Sound returned first. A high-pitched, aching whine that cut through the wet cotton stuffed in my ears. The sound bored into my brain like a hot stiletto.

Pain, my oldest, dearest friend, brought me back. Pain woke me up, with the ringing howl of my tortured eardrums. Pain let me know I was still alive, acutely aware of the sharp sting of dozens of lacerations across my arms and hands.

Anger, my next oldest friend, reared its ugly head next to my pain and demanded that I get to my feet. Anger reminded me that someone had done this to me. Someone who needed my immediate and irrevocable attention.

Adrenaline poured into my veins and set my arms and legs tingling. My muscles quivered with the need for violence. I unclenched my hands and found Bāo's pendant cutting into the flesh of my left palm. The pattern of Shokaku's knots were dented into my right. The need for vengeance brought everything back and I rolled over and up to my feet. I stowed my pendant and drew Hachi.

The anger in my chest died with a whimper. The pillar of light was gone. In fact, San Francisco was almost completely dark as far as I could see. The only light came from the dragon atop the mound of shattered concrete that used to be Coit Tower. On either side of me, Freddy and Fiona sprawled on the pavement. I hoped they were only unconscious.

My limbs froze as I considered the jarring physical reality of what I had only ever considered as the idea of our gods. The dragon was beautiful. Terrifyingly beautiful. His sinuous body was nearly fifty feet long and as thick as a car. The shifting light came from luminous blue scales that covered him from eyes to tail. As he moved, his scales shimmered like mother of pearl, dazzling to my eyes. A massive foot with hooked talons the size of my forearm wrapped around a crumbling chunk of concrete.

Brilliant white whiskers sprouted from the dragon's elongated muzzle and bracketed a wide jaw filled with sharp, shining teeth, large enough to swallow me whole. Glowing feathers of white streaked with yellow and orange framed his head and obscured his antlers as they rippled in the light breeze. His aura was as wide as the sky itself, a never-ending aurora of color and light.

Part of me wanted nothing more than to drink in the dragon's majesty. The other part screamed to close my eyes against the brilliance of this creature.

We liked to tell ourselves we were descended from dragons, but confronting one showed me just how small we were.

Whatever Batuhan had done to force open the Gate hadn't lasted. My city moaned in pain, the sensation like cold fingers worming through my guts. The layers of power we'd placed over the Gate re-formed themselves until Mother's Gate closed again over the portal. After all the Dragonsong that had ripped through my city, the relative quiet now was frightening.

I cycled my qì and forced open my hindbrain's panicked grip on my limbs. As my arms unlocked, I slid my swords back into their sheaths. They closed with a click.

The dragon's eyes opened.

I'd handled plenty of Pearls in my life, but none like the dragon's eyes, lustrous black orbs the size of a breadfruit. They shone with a strange inner light, glimmering and without flaw. With no iris or pupil, they should have looked like dead stones. I took a step back because somehow, they conveyed power, and menace, and I knew they were looking right at me.

The dragon's head lifted from the rubble, muscles rippling under shining scales. He huffed out a breath and warm air blasted over me, nearly knocking me back again. The dragon loomed in close, his pale whiskers flicking back and forth, until one perfect, black eye hovered a mere foot from me.

His nostrils flared and I went down to one knee when the dragon spoke to me.

He didn't speak through his mouth. An overwhelming presence, a force like the universe pressing down on me, appeared in my head and words formed in my mind. The dragon was a god, a literal force of nature, the breath and spirit of the seas and clouds, and his words seared through me.

"So, this is where my wayward rabbits have been cowering."

Tears streamed down my cheeks. It took all my willpower to keep my forehead off the ground. Every cell in my body screamed out to debase myself in the dragon's presence. The dragon lifted his head and the pressure on me lessened. The dragon looked around us, then lifted his head to the sky and scented the wind. His head swung down to me again until his glassy eye speared me. His voice dripped with contempt.

"In this . . . squalor. Perhaps I should end your misery."

He moved closer and his whiskers flicked across my face. Waves of moist heat baked off his scales. I forced myself to hold my next breath, then let it out slowly as I wrestled my qì back into a semblance of order. Showing weakness before the dragon was a sure path to my doom. And if he hadn't killed me yet, maybe he had some reason not to.

The dragon's nostrils flared again, and this time his lips pulled back into a gruesome, wolfish smile. From this distance I saw every minute detail of the deadly row of fangs in his mouth.

"Mmm . . . delicious."

Whiskers continued to paw at my face and a ripple of sinuous movement danced across the dragon's flank.

"Pepper, sawdust, and . . . ginger."

At the last word the dragon moved closer, and my heart froze. I'd never met another Jiārén with the ability to smell talents. And the dragon seemed to be able to smell—

"Dark walker. Not all dead then, after all these years."

The dragon's featureless black eye locked on me. Fathomless power seemed to swirl within the dark depths of that eye. His voice hammered me down from inside my mind.

"You will be a fine addition to my collection. You and all of your brood."

He lumbered up from the pile of rubble that used to be Coit Tower, his taloned feet slipping as his fearsome weight crushed the concrete chunks to powder. In the ethereal light given off by his scales, the dragon's belly was shrouded in shadow. The high sheen of his dorsal scales faded until they became drab and muted across his entire underside. In some places the scales seemed to be missing completely, exposing raw patches of leathery flesh the color of turbulent seas. Thick blood wept from his hide where it looked like his scales had been torn off.

"I am Cháofēng, and you will bow to me."

The words thundered through my blood, compelling me to act. Cháofēng's power was old, with a sense of massive inertia, like a crusting rime of stinking sea salt, deposited on a rocky cliff over the course of centuries. His will crushed mine, blasting my qì and emptying my meridians. The burning, acid scent of salt and brine suffused my senses, blotting out the world. My mind lifted away, and with a strange detachment I watched my body kneel on the concrete. I screamed inside my own head as my back bent and kowtowed to Cháofēng.

Lush, cool air, thick with moisture and a tinge of crisp ocean salt, filled my lungs as San Francisco surged into me through my arms and legs. Fog rolled off my shoulders and crept across the concrete, spreading out from me in a circle of hazy gray light. I cycled San Francisco's power through my meridians and Cháofēng's grip on my will faded. My mind locked back into my body like a rubber band snapping back into position.

I gasped as life and control returned to my arms and legs. The Pearl in my chest beat in a steady, thumping rhythm in counterpoint to my heart. I got one leg under me and pushed up, straightening my back until I looked the dragon in the eye.

Cháofēng's grin widened. **"Impertinent. Crushing you will be the finest amusement I've had in an age."**

Twenty feet away, Batuhan struggled up from his knees as well. Blood trailed from his ear, painting a grisly track down the side of his neck. Like me, lacerations covered his chest and arms. Unlike me, he had the entirety of the Tran Hoard at his feet, amplifying his power.

The piles of silver and gems glowed with the faint red hue of Dragon power. Batuhan's back straightened and the various wounds across his arms sealed in an eyeblink. When he spoke, he lacked the timbre of his prior majesty, but he managed to keep his voice steady

"Begone, dragon. I have no need for you here."

The aching tension in my shoulders melted away as Cháofēng's attention slid from me to the leader of the Borjigin. Cháofēng's tufted, feathered brows crouched low over his eyes and his whiskers whipped back and forth.

"The little rabbit believes it can speak. How . . . quaint."

Batuhan's eyes flashed. "This world is not yours. Begone!"

Cháofēng arched his neck, impossibly high until he towered over us. **"I am your lord. Bow."**

Batuhan's aura flared as he cycled, and his voice rose to a thunderous pitch. "You are not my god!"

Lightning crackled around Cháofēng's head. His fangs flashed in the sudden light, and his voice was a low, deadly croon. **"Not just your god, rabbit. I am your world."**

The hair on my arms stood up as electricity crackled in the air like a thunderstorm about to break. Cháofēng rose even higher and the pitch of his magic soared. Across the top of Telegraph Hill, trees exploded into strange shapes and brilliant colors, and the remnants of Coit Tower morphed into serpentine shapes. The fabric of San Francisco's magic sagged under the growing metaphysical weight of Cháofēng's power.

Dragon power exploded out of Cháofēng like a dam bursting. The wave of energy bowled me back and I came up in a crouch. Hot, stinging wind blew my hair back and forced me to squint. Batuhan had stayed upright, his arm held up against the wind, his power surging around him in a corona of blazing light.

I reached for my city and San Francisco responded with a subtle frisson of energy that dragged along my spine like broken glass. As I pulled more of the city's power into me, it blended with my qì and the dissonance faded until it was only a dim distraction in the background. If I hadn't been facing down a literal dragon, I might have worried more.

Once again the landscape of the city's magic unfurled before my eyes, a flexible plane of metaphysical energy. The dragon was massive, but not as big as I would have guessed. Batuhan appeared as an enormous black bear, almost the same size as the dragon.

Something about my connection to the city must have alerted Cháofēng because his head shifted in my direction. Another blast of the dragon's will slammed into me, compelling me to submit. I threw my arms forward and San Francisco's power blossomed from the ground at my feet, forming a thick layer around me. Cháofēng's will shredded through my protective barrier but I retained my own mind.

"Bow!"

The dragon's power pushed me back and my boots scraped across the pavement. I spread my arms and San Francisco's buffer zone widened like a surf break, softening the blow as Cháofēng's attack rolled over Freddy's and Fiona's unconscious forms.

Batuhan took advantage of Cháofēng's distraction to sing a deep bass note that plucked at my soul. The fragment of Dragonsong seared across my sight as a lance of bright pink. It landed in Cháofēng's side, where his wounds were unprotected by scales. The dragon roared, and the sound filled the night.

Cháofēng reared, his body twisting back and forth as he clawed at his side. Batuhan raised his voice and his Dragonsong changed. The spear glowed even brighter and set the dragon's flesh on fire.

Batuhan bellowed into the night sky. For the first time tonight, I caught a tinge of fear in his voice. "I will not serve you!"

In my city senses, a pulse of dull red power swelled Batuhan's form until he looked to be twelve feet tall. Cháofēng screeched as the spear in his side seemed to leech power from him. The dragon slammed a foot down and cracked the parking lot in half, the fissure running right under Batuhan's feet. The big man jumped to one side to avoid being swallowed, and as he did he stepped away from the Tran Hoard.

Cháofēng's eyes flashed like twin stars and he pounced forward, driving two taloned feet deep into the pile of Hoard silver.

"Mine."

Pain stabbed me in the chest and sent me to my knees.

Batuhan stumbled as well even as he threw his arms in the dragon's direction. "No!"

The pain dragged across my ribs like a dull blade as man and dragon fought for control of the Hoard. Cháofēng curled around the mound of silver and twisted until his jaws rested next to his flank. In a flash, he tore a chunk of flesh from his side and thick, dark blood gushed over the silver.

"Mind your place, insect, this Hoard is mine."

The pain redoubled as the Tran Hoard switched allegiance. Cháofēng's image in my mind swelled, the dragon growing to towering size, tall enough to stand above Coit Tower were it still up. Power from the Hoard flowed into him and the fresh wound healed over. Some of the missing patches of scales reformed. His hide and feathers brightened until they shone with inner light. Cháofēng's body thickened until it seemed his weight would crush all of Telegraph Hill.

As Cháofēng grew, Batuhan shrank to normal size. He raged and sang another sequence of notes, but without the Hoard behind him, the new melody was a pitiful imitation of Dragonsong. His new onslaught splashed harmlessly against the dragon's refreshed scales.

The dragon loomed close to Batuhan and blew one discordant note through his nose. Batuhan's attempt at Dragonsong vanished, like the sound had been sucked out of the air. He went down to his knees, his chest heaving as he tried to catch his breath.

I inched away from the dragon. If he was so interested in Batuhan I was not above using the distraction to get away. I dragged myself over the shattered asphalt until I reached Fiona and put my fingers against her neck. Relief coursed through me when I felt her pulse beating steadily. I pressed one hand over her mouth, then dug my fingertips deep into her neck and jolted her with my qì.

Fiona's eyes flew open and I clamped down on her to keep her quiet. Her eyes rolled back as she tried to look around. I pulled my hand away and she turned over onto her stomach.

I got close enough to whisper. "We have to get off this hill."

She shook her head and shut her eyes. Pain lines bracketed her mouth. A concussion, probably. "I'm not leaving without my Hoard."

The chain on my arm pulsed in response to Fiona's statement. I pointed at Cháofēng and for the first time, Fiona Tran seemed at a loss for words. "I think our priorities have changed."

The dragon hovered over Batuhan, humming a low tune that made my teeth itch. It seemed to be a lot worse for Batuhan, as he seemed unable to even blink, lying spread out for Cháofēng's inspection. Cháofēng inhaled deeply and his whiskers played over Batuhan's face and neck, probing at his meridians.

Cháofēng's voice was an ominous rumble in the back of my head, like a building collapsing on top of me. **"Fascinating."**

The dragon's whiskers pried open Batuhan's eyes. **"Who trained you, little rabbit?"**

Batuhan's voice was the creak of a rusting hinge. "My father, who was—"

Cháofēng made a disgusted noise. **"Pity. You stand at the precipice of true power, and still your world is so painfully . . . small. How do you stand it?"**

"Not . . . your . . . servant."

The dragon leaned in closer, an amused glint in his eyes. **"Who said you would be a servant? Your kind were never servants, you fool."**

Cháofēng lifted his eyes to the night sky. **"You exiled yourselves to this . . . wasteland. The very air here offends me. And you play at being kings of your garbage pile. Pathetic."**

A voice broke out of the darkness beyond the dragon. "Let him go!"

Cháofēng turned and the glowing light on his scales rippled down his body. When the light reached the far side of the parking lot, Ariq crawled out of the shadows, his arms torn and bloody from the splintered pavement.

The dragon smiled. **"Ah, the whelp."**

And for the first time since I'd met Ariq, I saw his aura. Even

Fiona sucked in a breath. Most Jiārén had auras that extended about a foot from their bodies. Stronger talents, and active use of that talent, increased the size and intensity of it. And everyone of any significant talent learned early to suppress their aura.

Ariq's aura was a swirl of color that spun around him like a storm. It was not a sky-filling expanse like Cháofēng, but it put all other auras I'd ever seen to shame. Like his father, his talent smelled floral, and even across the parking lot it was potent enough to overpower my senses.

It seemed Ariq's talent was a branch of his father's, because his lacerated skin sealed over his wounds as fast as he could tear it open on the jagged rocks. The dragon waited patiently for Ariq to crawl to his father's side, leaving a trail of blood behind him. Fiona took advantage of the lull, and raised her hand. A gentle platform of her hardened air lifted Freddy off the ground and brought him to our side.

Ariq seemed to get stronger the closer he got to the dragon. At the halfway mark he came to his feet. Another ten feet, and his eyes cleared and his aura steadied. He reached his father and stood over his still form. For all his prior frailty, he had enough spine to face off against the dragon. "You are not our lord!"

Batuhan had been right. The increased magic of Dragonsong had healed his son.

Cháofēng snorted, another mind-rasping note of music that froze Ariq in place. His whiskers moved to play over Ariq's face and neck. **"Excellent. Just as unique as your sire. It's always better to collect the set."**

Fiona roused Freddy and I was about to pull them both back with me when Cháofēng raised his head to the night sky and began to sing. My hands flew to my ears to block out the terrifying beauty of the music. It was useless. Fiona and Freddy both curled into themselves, their mouths open in silent screams.

Skies, we thought we knew what Dragonsong was. This was probably only the tip of the iceberg. How much power did the dragon have at his disposal?

Cháofēng's Dragonsong ripped across the top of Telegraph Hill and completed the transformation of the trees and rubble. Flowing arches of delicate stone sprang from the ground and met majestic towers of translucent jade that thrust up from the earth. Trees erupted with new growth and strange flowers in alien shapes and colors burst from their limbs. A fountain of clear water tumbled from the tallest tower, the flow sparkling with inner light like diamonds in firelight.

But none of that compared to what happened to Batuhan and Ariq. Both men cried out in pain the moment the Dragonsong hit. Their backs arched and lines of pain creased their faces. Cháofēng reared up and the two men followed, their bodies suspended in air. The dragon's voice struck like a bass drum.

"Mine."

My mind refused to process what I was seeing, what was happening to Batuhan and his son as they writhed in the air.

What Cháofēng was doing to them.

The dragon's power wrapped around them like a demented lover. Oily black tendrils crept through their auras. As the dragon's voice rose, the blackness advanced, driving deeper toward the men. Their auras faded as Cháofēng drank down their talents. Beside me, Fiona choked back a sob.

Cold despair gripped my heart. It looked exactly like my talent.

The dragon's body glowed with new light and the remaining wounds on his side healed, flesh knitting together and bright scales emerging. Batuhan's aura had faded to a line of faint color around his body. Cháofēng inhaled deeply and let out a satisfied growl.

"Delicious. You will do nicely."

Batuhan and Ariq fell to the ground with a thump. The dragon stepped forward, his talons gouging deep furrows in the asphalt as easily as if it were soil. He stopped when he was straddled atop Batuhan's unconscious body.

"You thought you would rule. I will show you what it means to rule."

Cháofēng dipped his head down. I swallowed a scream, expecting the dragon to bite the man in half. Instead the dragon's form wavered, the feathers around his head blurring together. The light from his scales dimmed, and the pressure of the dragon's will pulled away from me. An unseen weight lifted from my shoulders and I felt as if I could finally breathe freely.

The dragon continued to blur into a blue-green haze of color and Batuhan's body lifted off the ground. Batuhan's head lolled back and Cháofēng's whiskers reached out and pried open the man's eyes again.

This time the dragon's voice was muted and distant, but still hinted at the same power. **"Mine."**

Cháofēng's mist form surged forward and plunged into Batuhan's eyes. The instant they touched, Batuhan's body jerked like he'd hit a high-tension wire. From across the parking lot I heard his joints crack and strain. Cháofēng flowed in, an endless stream of energy compacting itself into Batuhan's body.

My ears popped as a rush of wind pushed past me, the air filling in the sudden vacuum created by Cháofēng's disappearance. I blinked in the sudden dark, now that the dragon's luminance was gone. In its place, Batuhan floated to the ground and landed lightly on his feet. The pink-gold of his aura was gone, replaced with Cháofēng's glittering aurora.

The big man turned and across the darkened parking lot he made direct eye contact with me. His eyes were orbs of glossy black, flecked with starlight. His smile was wide, stretched over teeth too large for a human mouth, the smile of a predator who knows the end of a successful hunt is nigh. He laughed and the sound rang across the top of the hill. Several trees splintered to pieces and one of the jade towers crumbled to dust.

Cháofēng raised his—Batuhan's—hands, opening and closing his fists. His gaze ran up his arms and down his body. He took a deep breath and let it out.

"Much better. Your kind are better suited to living in this privation."

Freddy was on his feet almost before I realized what was happening. Fiona cried out and I grabbed his arm just in time, keeping him from running toward his Hoard.

Cháofēng flicked a finger and a stream of water shot out from the waterfall. The water hit the ground at our feet like a laser beam, gouging a track ten feet wide in front of us. Steam and dust billowed up from the impact.

Half a heartbeat later and Freddy would have been dead. I hissed as the silver links on my arm tightened, instant retribution for keeping Freddy from reclaiming their Hoard.

The dragon's eyes found us through the haze, a pair of glowing lights that pinned us all in place.

"You have been free of the yoke for generations. I hope this was not a demonstration of your true strength."

Cháofēng swept his arm and a briny wind blew away the mist between us. He twitched his fingers and Ariq floated onto his shoulder as easily as a bag of rice. Under his other hand, the scattered piles of Tran silver vanished. Freddy let out a breath like he'd been punched in the gut.

The dragon pointed an accusing finger at us. **"You arrogant children brought ruin to our world, and shame to the Dragon Father. You will be punished for that."**

Cháofēng placed a hand on his chest.

"But I will be disappointed if this one is truly the strongest among you. And I despise disappointment."

The dragon rose into the air and looked down on us. **"When**

you are ready, come show me your dragon strength. Show me you have not wasted the lives of your ancestors, wallowing in this desert."

Cháofēng turned and floated away. Before he'd gone ten feet, he and Ariq disappeared into the darkness. A moment later, the Borjigin soldiers melted into mist and faded away.

RECOVERY

When Cháofēng vanished, the subtle influence of his will went with him. The three of us dropped to our knees like puppets with cut strings. A wave of exhaustion crashed over me and the only thing that kept me from falling asleep there on the concrete was Fiona's groan of pain. She was curled on her side with her hands clutching at her head.

Freddy looked half dazed himself and crawled to her side. "Fi?"

Fiona said, "Skies, I think I'm going to be sick."

She had a concussion. It had to be that, plus the absence of their Hoard. She and Freddy were going through the wringer right now. Popo could fix them up, though.

I put a hand on Fiona's shoulder. "Let's get—"

Fiona jerked away from me, scrambling on hands and knees. "Don't touch me!"

The shock of it stopped me in my tracks.

After her sudden movement, Fiona's eyes rolled up into her head and Freddy had to catch her before she crashed to the pavement.

Linh melted out of the darkness. Fiona's trusted lieutenant looked like she'd been dragged under a bulldozer but her eyes were clear and she read the situation perfectly. Without a word, Linh pulled Fiona to her feet and put herself between us.

I sat back down as another wave of fatigue rolled over me. It was all too much.

Telegraph Hill was a smoking wreck with some rather nice new jade monuments that were sure to attract the wrong kinds of attention. Mother's Gate pulsed under my city, a time bomb that hadn't quite gone off, but also hadn't stopped ticking. A literal Dragon god was somewhere in my city, eager for us to throw ourselves at him in what would assuredly be a futile effort.

And now, only now, did my friends finally choose to see me as the monster I'd always said I was. I should have stayed in Thailand. "Fiona . . ."

Linh drew the two blades from her shoulder holster. "Stay where you are, Sentinel."

I'd done this to myself, let myself think that I'd somehow put my past behind me. But my past was crafty, like me, and it had simply been lying in wait, ready to strike from the darkness when I was least expecting it. And it knew how to hit really, really hard, because even Freddy couldn't meet my eyes.

All the pain and alienation I'd felt after Pearl Market, all the hurt I'd buried years ago, burst through my emotional scar tissue. The sting of fear and loneliness crept up the back of my throat. "Well, Freddy? Do you still think I'm not a danger to you?"

Freddy's gaze moved to Fiona, then back to the rocky ground somewhere between us. That was answer enough.

Fiona finally stopped wobbling. "Linh, get everyone up and moving. We'll regroup at the secondary safe house." She snapped her fingers. "Freddy, let's go."

That pulled him out of his daze and a trace of his regular good nature ghosted across his face. "Emi, do you want to join—"

Fiona and Linh both cut him off with a glare. His shoulders drooped and he trudged away. Fiona was holding it together, but it looked like she was hanging on by the skin of her teeth. Before Linh stepped away to rouse the rest of her soldiers, she put one of her blades in Fiona's hands. Linh held my gaze for a moment, then faded into the night.

It seemed Fiona and I were back in the awkward phase again. But it was fine, really. It wasn't like I hadn't already survived years like this. I had a Talon Call to fulfill, and a dragon to expel from my city. I had work to do.

Fiona finally spoke up just as I turned to leave. "Thank you, Sentinel, for holding Freddy back. You saved his life."

Her tone hurt, but I nodded. "It was nothing."

Fiona gave me a stiff wai. "My brother's life is not nothing. We are grateful."

I couldn't blame her for this stilted formality. If my talent could do anything like what Cháofēng had done to Batuhan, then it was even more monstrous than I had originally thought. Fiona was smart. You didn't ignore a bomb, but you did have to handle it very carefully. Maybe this was just how things would be now. The only way we could make it work.

It hurt a lot more than I expected.

I returned the bow. "Good night."

"Good night, Sentinel."

I turned and headed for the south side of the parking lot. A walking path cut down the hill from there and gave me the straightest path to my home. I was both too tired and too keyed up. A walk home would steady my nerves, and calm my qì.

I set out across my city, filled with millions of my people sleeping through the night, and I felt as alone as I'd ever felt in my life.

The increasing density of crows as I neared my house had never felt so reassuring. As if the city sensed my needs, the birds gathered when my energy dipped about a mile from home. Some flapped lazily above me while others perched on trees and buildings, cawing encouragement. By the time I made the last turn before my house, the sidewalk was nearly covered in crows except for a neat path that led to my door.

One of the them fluttered in close and landed on my shoulder. Too exhausted for anything other than my bed, I didn't fight it, and humored the bird as I walked the last hundred yards. The crow leaned in close to my face, bringing one beady eye close to mine.

A thrill of cold fear ran down my spine when I turned and found a dirty seagull perched on my shoulder. The gull's eye glittered, and an oily sheen of magic passed over it like a mirage.

I cycled my qì and reached for the city. My connection with San Francisco stuttered once, like a cold engine on a foggy morning, before syncing up smoothly. The cool reassurance of my city ran through my limbs and shook me to wakefulness. My sleepy street lit up in my eyes. In the middle of the block, my house was a beacon of welcoming light. All around me, the crows were a shifting field of stars.

The bird on my shoulder was a greasy patch of darkness.

Several things happened at once.

The gull lunged forward, its sharp beak plunging toward my eye.

I jerked my head back and dropped into a roll.

The scent of fresh-cut grass blossomed around me and a streak of orange flashed through my peripheral vision.

My concentration shattered. Maybe it was the fatigue. Maybe it was the shock of seeing Kamon here in San Francisco. When I came up from my roll my foot slipped out from under me and I was forced to turn the momentum into another backward roll.

A large, striped shadow bounded over me, smelling of primordial jungles, predator musk, and fresh-cut grass. Kamon landed on light paws, six hundred pounds of supple tiger muscle propelling razor fangs and claws. He sniffed at the air, his shining eyes locked on the seagull that had just tried to spike my eye out. Kamon gave a growl like a great coughing sound and a ripple of air pressure rolled over me. The wave pushed the gull back another ten feet.

I got to my feet and held Shokaku at high guard. The bird

flapped lazily overhead. Gray clouds drifted behind the gull and gave the fleeting impression of an undulating, snakelike body. I inched forward until my leg rested against Kamon's flank. Reassuring warmth and the vibrations of his growl spread up my thigh from where we touched.

A tiny ember of anger glowed hot in my chest. I pointed my sword at the gull. "You want to test me? Let's do it."

The rotten little bird gave a croak that sounded suspiciously like laughter before it wheeled and flew off into the night. I sheathed my sword and slumped. The little ember of rage winked out. I should take it as a good sign that the crows were still around. My connection with the city felt uneven, as if Cháofēng's arrival was pushing the city away from me. What usually felt like a vast pool was down to a sluggish trickle of energy. With that, I was barely on my feet. The best thing I could do right now was get in my house, behind my protective wards.

Kamon turned to me and butted his head against my side. His ear twitched.

Funny how that one small catlike movement infused me with guilt. The fumes I'd been running on finally gave out and I sat down on the pavement. "I was going to call you, but . . ." I waved a hand in the direction of the fleeing bird. "I've been a little busy."

His fur rippled down his back, making his stripes dance.

I threw up my hands. There was nothing in my arsenal for this. "You came all this way to deliver an 'I told you so'? Fine, I need help. Are you happy now?!"

My voice rose and cracked, and echoed off the buildings. The sound of my desperation bounced down the empty street. Kamon leaned in and his rasping tongue brushed away the tears rolling down my cheek. My arms were suddenly full of tiger, my hands buried deep in Kamon's orange-and-gold fur. I hid my face in his shoulder and let the heat of his body burn away the aching cold of the loneliness inside me.

"Thank you for coming," I whispered.

His purr in response set my arms tingling.

In an odd reversal of host and guest, I collapsed into my lounge chair while Kamon, no longer in tiger form, bustled around my little home. He informed me that he'd arrived with a score of his cousins, all of whom were grateful to me for bringing Prem back to sanity. Tears of gratitude dried salty on my face and neck. My body ached everywhere but less than it had an hour ago. My Pearl radiated cool energy that slowly eased my injuries from the battle at Coit Tower. Unfortunately it did nothing for the thoughts running panicked circles in my head.

Skies, my life was in ruins. Batuhan had been right. At worst, our ancestors were thieves who'd stolen priceless treasure from our Dragon gods. And an actual dragon had come to my city, through my portal, to exact his vengeance.

I hoped Leanna and Lucy were recovering now. At least I had done that much, getting them back to Uncle Jimmy. Every time I tried to clear my mind to rest, Cháofēng's pitiless black eyes intruded. How was the dragon inhabiting Batuhan's body? Maybe this was the true reason Jiārén were descended from the dragons—they could shift at will and worse, puppet us. My talent wasn't an accident—it was a legacy. I closed my eyes in despair.

And Coit Tower had been destroyed. What were the Wàirén in that area thinking happened? I could only imagine their confusion at the sudden intense storms in the thick of summer, the downing of powerlines and cellular networks and the inexplicable failure of drones and helicopters to penetrate the nexus of all the chaos. Were Tessa and Andie trying to make sense of the disjointed news reports? I had left their texts unread, too miserable and overwhelmed to try to explain. Honoring the First Law seemed impossible now, which begged the question of why I should even bother. Everything I believed about our Jiārén past was false. Dragons were terrifying and I could no longer worship these false gods.

I wanted to curl into a ball and just ignore everything around me. But I couldn't do that, not as the Sentinel. My people needed me to do better. I wanted to do better for all of them, especially for the tiger in my kitchen.

Kamon brewed oolong with osmanthus for us and whistled softly as he cleaned my swords. He never used swords himself, but he'd picked up an appreciation for them from me. As he cleaned Shokaku my mind went to Kaida, and my mother. Was Batuhan right? Was there a version of history where Kaida and my mother would be revered for their talent?

Unbidden tears came again and I pressed my hands into my eyes. I needed to focus on the present, not some alternate reality that didn't exist. I had a dragon in my city, and a Talon Call to answer.

How was I going to take the Tran Hoard back from a dragon? I set my shoulders and reached for my phone.

"Are you okay?" Kamon asked.

"No. I have to call my father."

Kamon raised his eyebrows. He knew how that usually went.

"Fiona made the Talon Call. I need Father's help."

His eyes landed on the silver on my arm. It felt like the chains twitched a little under Kamon's gaze.

"You want to tell me about that?"

Why were so many of my conversations with Kamon precipitated by Talon Calls? I scrubbed my face with my hands. "It's Fiona's insurance policy."

We were right back in it, where we always were. Somehow Kamon and I couldn't be together unless something terrible was happening at the same time.

With a sigh, Kamon went back to rummaging around in my

tiny kitchen. After a moment his unerring nose found my hidden drawer with my backup supply of matcha Kit Kats.

Way better than extra clothes.

He tossed the bag to me. "You might want to fortify yourself first."

For the first time in hours, I smiled.

By the time I dialed my father, the fragrant tea was gone, and the Kit Kats had been reduced to a mound of empty wrappers on my table. Father didn't pick up.

I texted Tatsuya.

The Trans cashed in their Talon.

My fingers tightened around my phone as the bubbles on the screen indicated my brother was typing.

After what felt like a century, he responded.

Father has readied the Iron Fists. We're on our way.

I closed my eyes with relief and leaned back against my chair.

My family was coming. It was at once an incredible relief, as well as anticlimactic. Even after keeping myself apart from them for years, they had stood by me in Tokyo. There was no telling when they would get here, but I knew they were moving heaven and earth right now to get to me. It would have to be enough for now. The knot of tension I'd been holding in my chest unwound so fast that my head swam and pins and needles danced down my arms.

Kamon scooted closer. "Good news?"

I tried to nod, but the ability to control my body was rapidly fading. Without the stress of trying to stay alive, my system reasserted itself, demanding rest. My eyelids drooped, and even a bagful of Kit Kats wasn't going to keep me awake. Kamon stepped away on quiet feet and returned with a blanket that he draped over my shoulders.

He pulled up a chair and sat. “Get some rest. I’ll stay up.”

There was a dragon loose in my city, but I was home and safe behind my wards. And Kamon was here. Within that cocoon of security, I finally let the last of my tension go and I relaxed into the lounge chair.

RIOT

I awoke to midmorning light and the ringing of my phone. Sometime during the night Kamon had carried me into the guest bedroom of the front house. Instead of trying to tuck me in, he'd covered me with my spare kakebuton, the pale silk embroidered with an enormous fenghuang in flight. I kicked my way out of the covers and scrambled for my phone, panic rising in my chest. What had Cháofēng done? Which of my people had he hurt?

The panic ebbed a little when I found my phone and swiped across Adam's face. He was probably upset about how I'd disappeared on him at the museum.

"Adam, I'm sorry—"

Adam's voice was as hard as stone. "You're sorry? You gave me your word, Emiko. I thought that meant something to you."

My sleep-addled mind stumbled as I tried to catch up. "What are—"

"I brought Kenji to you because you're the only one who can help him, and this is what you do?"

Kamon walked into the room, a silent question on his face. I waved him off and tried to tamp down my frustration.

"Wait, wait. I left Kenji at the museum. What's happened?"

"You know damn well—"

I copied one of my father's tricks, infusing my voice with command. "Adam! Tell me what happened."

That finally got through to him, and I heard the panic behind his anger. "Kenji's unconscious. I can't wake him. You and your cursed dragon laws. I was an idiot to believe that you'd—"

I pitched my voice over whatever Adam was going to say next.

"Adam, if I had obeyed the First Law last night, you and Kenji would already be dead."

That got him to stop talking. My mind raced. Was Kenji's condition a product of Cháofēng's influence?

I softened my tone. "I know you don't like how I operate, but even you have to know that whatever happened to Kenji isn't my style."

Adam's voice broke. "I promised his mother he'd be safe."

"I gave you my word, Adam, so I'll help you keep your word. I'll do whatever I can do to keep Kenji safe. I swear it."

Adam was quiet for so long I thought the call had dropped. "How?"

It was a fair question. I'd already burned him once. But I was trying to be better, and now I had a way to convince him to trust me. "I promised you I would help Kenji and I will. He will wake soon, and he will learn about his Jiārén heritage. He will be trained to control his talent. I swear it on my power."

Adam sucked in a breath. As part of my clan, and sworn to our Hoard, he'd felt the conviction of my words.

He needed to finish the exchange. "Say 'witness.'"

Adam's voice was a little unsteady. "Witness."

Behind me, Kamon chimed in. "So witnessed."

Adam found his footing and his voice evened out. "What do we do next?"

They had to get away from Cháofēng's reach. "Take Kenji far outside this city. Somewhere away from Jiārén. Hunker down until I call for you."

"Okay. Okay. I can do that."

The uncertainty in his voice was jarring. Maybe Adam was finally getting a taste of just how deep these waters were. Waters he and Kenji were never getting out of.

"Emiko . . . thank you."

I hung up. Keeping Kenji safe would at least keep Adam occupied. It wasn't the greatest plan, but I knew Adam would do it.

The world swayed as the floor seemed to shift under my feet. Kamon grabbed my hand before I toppled, a look of concern on his face. I wasn't the type to trip over my feet.

Kamon ducked his head to catch my eye. "Emi?"

I held up a hand. The city felt suffocatingly close, and the floor of my house had a strange, porous quality. San Francisco's magic pushed up from below like an updraft. Like a train roaring through a tunnel, forcing a column of air in front of it.

A half a second before it happened, I clamped down on Kamon's wrist. The city barreled up through my house and swamped my perceptions. Like the night before, something kept the city away from me for a heartbeat, just long enough to notice. The sensations swirled around me for a moment before catching hold.

Disjointed images of the city flashed across my mind and a confusing mix of voices crowded through my head, each one shouting to be heard. I was dimly aware of my body collapsing and landing in Kamon's arms.

People screamed and ran, a blur of faces and colors. A massive weight seemed to loom in the sky above them, like a plane about to crash.

On a crowded street, dragon talents burst into the open. Scattered through the undulating wave of people, pendants of blood jade winked in the morning sun, an army of unblinking, singular, bloody eyes.

The facade of a building cracked, raining shattered brick and plaster down onto the sidewalk. A voice boomed and people fell to their knees, hands clutching at their ears.

A singular thread ran through the images. I couldn't see it, but I felt it as surely as I knew my own hands. It was a river of blazing red. It twisted through every scene, was part of every word, and drove through the heart of my people. It coursed through my city and straight into my own chest.

It was fear, and it left a prickling trail of sour bile down the back of my mouth. The trail ended in my gut where my insides twisted into knots and made me want to scream in pain.

My people were afraid. Worse, my city was afraid. Terrified.

As quickly as it had appeared, San Francisco's presence vanished, leaving me heaving for breath on my kitchen floor, feeling hollowed out like a gourd. Kamon knelt at my side, his aura huge and bright, his eyes bracketed with worry lines.

"What happened?"

My heart thundered in my chest. I wiped at my eyes and my hand came away wet. "I'm not sure, but—"

It was faint, but impossible to miss. Dragonsong drifted across my city and through my windows. The song wasn't a melody like before, just a low hum that made my teeth vibrate. It didn't have the magnetic pull like before, but if I could hear it then . . .

"It's Cháofēng, he's here, he's—"

The ringtone on my phone broke the tension and I jabbed at the screen with trembling fingers. "What?"

Baby Ricky was always so cheerful. The sheer terror laced through his voice wrenched my heart. "Emi—Sentinel, everything's—and Sally, she—"

I was already running for the front room with Kamon close behind. "I'm on my way."

Kamon snatched Shokaku and Hachi off the wall. I grabbed my gear bag and we bolted out the door.

When we stepped on my porch, I was surprised to see a massive black Mercedes SUV in the driveway and Colin doing something idly on his phone as he leaned against the driver's-side door. I rekeyed my wards and then dashed over to Colin.

"What are you doing here?" I asked.

He stood up straight and bowed. "Sentinel. I'm your driver, remember?"

"I told you to get behind your wards." Couldn't I keep even one person safe?

Colin's mouth flattened. "I'm not going to hide while you're fighting. I won't sit this one out."

This was the young man who shielded his friend when an assassin came at them with a katana. It couldn't have been easy, watching his friends run the Tourney without him, while being saddled with the weight of his family's disappointment. I knew exactly how that could crush you.

I clapped him on the shoulder. "Great, get us to the Sun Emporium."

Kamon tilted his head, clearly amused that I now had a driver. But we hopped in, and Colin navigated the roads to Lotus Lane. Above us the sky darkened, a river of atmospheric turmoil that seemed centered directly over our destination.

Cháofēng. Truly a god of weather, and we were going to be canoeing soon if this rain kept up.

On any given day, Lotus Lane was the epicenter of Jiārén activity in San Francisco. All major business was conducted on these two blocks, and the majority of Hoard wealth that flowed through the city stopped on these two blocks at some point. That meant a lot of people and activity that had to be screened from curious Wàirén to keep our people hidden.

As we approached the entrance to Lotus Lane, strange noises and lights echoed between the buildings. We hunkered down in a doorway on California Street and peered down the alley. From this distance, it was a narrow, nondescript alley between two apartment buildings. If I squinted hard, I could just make out the barrier of subtle persuasion laid over the entrance. But whatever was happening inside was straining the capabilities of the no-look spells.

Lotus Lane was boiling over.

Kamon felt it, too. A low, rumbling growl had started in his chest, a sure sign that his hackles were up. He nodded toward Lotus Lane. "Can you sense anything?"

I dropped my eyes and cycled, reaching for the Pearl in my chest. After a moment I made the connection, but got nothing more than a few dim images of people yelling and flashing auras. "No, nothing useful."

Kamon grimaced. "So we're going in blind."

"We know Cháofēng is in there."

It had to be him. The Dragonsong had been growing steadily stronger as we got closer, and now felt like a vibration in my jaw. "So, we're not totally blind."

Kamon gave me a look that I chose to ignore.

I checked the straps on my swords, and tightened my belt. "It wouldn't be our first time."

The grimace turned into a rueful smile. "Hohhot. I had sand in my fur for weeks."

My fingers roamed over my armor, extra blades, and my canned magic, triple-checking everything. "I still had sand in my gear a month later. Took me days to get it out of my scabbard."

All those blood jade pendants had to be the Borjigin. If Cháofēng was still wearing Batuhan like a cheap suit, then he probably had control of the man's army, too.

Kamon stretched his neck from side to side. "This will be a bit more difficult than a Mongolian death worm."

A death worm was a walk in the park compared to this. And I also had two solid blocks of merchants and civilians who were counting on their Sentinel to protect them from a threat they could never have imagined.

"He's wormlike."

"Emiko." Kamon's eyes were stern. Behind him, Colin's usual bravado had evaporated and the poor kid looked like he might throw up.

I drew Shokaku and clamped my hands to her grip to stop my fingers. "Sorry, nerves. We slip in, find the Sun kids, and get out. Quick and easy."

"Nothing we have done together has ever been quick or easy."

I nodded. My heart hammered in my chest. "Fair point. Ready?"

He cracked his knuckles. "Of course."

Kamon grabbed Colin's arm and pulled him close. "Stay in my shadow and keep up."

Colin swallowed visibly and nodded.

We loped across the street. I took point with Shokaku leading the way. If we ran into something I couldn't handle with my qì or my sword, Kamon would bring the tiger out. It was a good system, and we slipped back into our roles like old, comfortable shoes.

I hit the barrier of persuasion at a full run and hoped there wasn't anyone on the other side. My qì was already cycling, humming through my meridians like an electric field, and it cut through the barrier as easily as my sword. In the space of a heartbeat, we passed from a gray San Francisco morning, and landed in a riot.

Lotus Lane was usually a festive place, with colorfully painted buildings and lanterns strung across the street. It always smelled like a dozen different kinds of food, starting with roasted pork and duck, and ending with dried herbs and teas.

Today the colors were the auras of Jiārén, out in the open and fighting for their lives. The stink of combat hung over the street, the intermingled scents of dragon talents clashing back and forth. Over all of it, Dragonsong droned like the buzzing of hundreds of bees, filling the space between each breath and thought.

My foot hit the pavement inside the protective barrier and I dove into a forward roll to avoid a blast of frozen air from an ice talent. I felt more than saw Kamon dodge to the side behind me. I came up to my feet and kept sprinting forward. In the corner of my vision, Kamon kept pace with me, ten feet to my left.

Kinetic strikes lanced back and forth across the crowd. The fighting was punctuated with shouting and curses, and with bursts of more powerful talents. Batuhan's soldiers seemed to be everywhere, wading through the crowd and fighting everyone in sight. A trio of Borjigin smashed through the front doors of an Herbalist's shop. After a brief fight, two of them ran back out, arms laden with glass jars filled with dried herbs.

I almost angled to intercept them. But we couldn't afford to get bogged down in this fight before we knew what was going on. We had to get to the Suns first. Besides, it wasn't like the inhabitants of Lotus Lane were helpless.

The merchants were out in force to defend their businesses, some with improvised weapons, and enough with heirloom swords and spears that their numbers made things harder for the Borjigin. Here and there, small squads of Louies and Trans helped the merchants hold the Borjigin at bay.

Under it all, the glowing red streak of fear ran through the hearts of my people. Fear for their loved ones, and their livelihoods. San Francisco also trembled with fear.

The Sun Emporium was up ahead on the left. I bobbed and weaved between a half-dozen separate fights. Holding Shokaku in front of me had the pleasant effect of clearing my path. No one wanted to be on the wrong end of a sword.

I jabbed with my left hand, taking opportunistic dim mak strikes where I could. One satisfying strike took out a man's legs. He collapsed like a handful of wet noodles and a squad of aunties descended on him, beating him with woks and broomsticks. Kamon used his speed and size, bumping soldiers off-balance and sending them into their attackers.

Less than a hundred yards to my target and it looked like a hive of activity. A thick cluster of bodies formed an arc around the doors to the Sun Emporium and soldiers threw rapid-fire bursts of red and blue dragon talents. My heart sank. We were too late. An assault like that would reduce the building to rubble in less than a minute.

Wait, no.

I slowed up and squinted. From the second story a pair of dark gun barrels protruded from the windows and spit blue and red dragon flames down on the Borjigin soldiers. The front line of soldiers barely kept up, throwing up kinetic bursts to break up the dragon flame.

Well, I wasn't going to pass up the opportunity. I stowed Shokaku, brought out Hachi for the close-up dirty work, and waded into them from behind. Dim mak strikes took down the first two. Hachi flashed out, severing hamstrings on my left and right. Kamon barreled into them from my left, giving me another second to deliver two more nerve strikes. Every two steps into the fray I dropped another tile on the ground. By the time the soldiers realized we were behind them, we'd taken half of them out.

I was pulling Hachi out of someone's thigh when instinct jerked my head to the side. A streak of color whizzed past my eyes and exploded on the street. A half sphere of blue light bloomed on the asphalt, pinning down my prior victim by encasing his arm in ice. My gaze whipped up to the second story where I found a pair of very round eyes staring at me from the darkness beyond the window.

"Ricky!" I yelled.

The gun barrel retracted and Kamon, Colin, and I pushed through the last line of Borjigin to make for the double doors.

Kamon put his back to mine when we met at the doors. "They'll swarm us when he opens the doors." At our knees, Colin crouched and tried to make himself as small as possible. He looked decidedly pale.

Hachi flicked out and caught a soldier who'd drifted too close.

He fell back, hands at his neck and gurgling blood. Kamon was right, we couldn't defend and try to relock the door. Luckily I'd been cheating the whole time.

When the bolts on the door clicked I squeezed the Might of the Mountain tile I'd kept in my hand. I shot a burst of my qì into the tile and snapped it in half. The tiles I'd dropped on our way in triggered in response and gravity multiplied in a fifty-foot radius around the doors to the shop. Dozens of Borjigin soldiers went to their knees in a wave. Men cried out in pain as bones snapped and they fell on top of their injured mates.

The door creaked open. Kamon grabbed me and Colin and pulled us in. Ricky slammed the door closed and threw the bolt. "How long will that hold them?"

I shook my head. "Ten minutes, maybe. We need to go out the back way. Where's Sally?"

Baby Ricky trembled with unspent adrenaline. His long black hair was plastered to his broad forehead and the neck of his gray hoodie was soaked with sweat. A paint gun was strapped across his back. He hustled past us toward the stairs. "Everyone's upstairs, we haven't been able to move her."

Big Ricky and Mama Sun were perched at the upstairs windows, both armed with the same kind of paint gun Baby Ricky had. From here we had an unobstructed view of the entire street in both directions, and the chaotic fighting that ebbed and flowed across it. The zone of increased gravity was holding for now, and the elder Suns were taking advantage of the reprieve to pick off soldiers at the boundary.

The Suns weren't a powerful family, but they had sensible, practical talents, and good control of their qì. They used their talents to build a respectable life and a business that was thriving. Now they used their talents to feed a little bit of qì into the paint guns before each shot, which then spewed from the end of the guns as dragon flame.

I was impressed and mildly horrified to see the normally congenial Mama Sun gunning down men like a guerrilla fighter. "You loaded paint balls with dragon crystals?"

Baby Ricky nodded. "It was an idea I'd had and we just started experimenting with it last week. Lucky us." He made a face.

Mama Sun squeezed off a flurry of shots that pushed the soldiers back to the far side of the street. "Yes, lucky us or those terrible men would have overrun us already. Emiko, please tell me you can do something for Sally."

The Sun's younger daughter was laid out in the back of the room on an air mattress. She looked like she was asleep, although even a casual glance told me her aura was guttering dangerously low.

I knelt and placed two fingers on her neck. Her pulse was there, but faint. "When did this happen?"

Big Ricky sat back from his window and mopped the sweat from his forehead. "Right about the time all the buzzing started."

I squeezed my fist so hard my knuckles cracked. It had to be related to Cháofēng's Dragonsong. Maybe if we could get her farther away from it . . .

Colin swayed next me, his face graying. He tilted against the wall and then slid down into a heap. I barely had time to prevent his head from knocking against a beam. "Colin!"

What was happening? Adam's words from earlier echoed through my ears. Had Kenji fallen to the same effect?

Kamon put two fingers on Colin's wrist. "It's weak. Must be some effect of the Dragonsong."

My heart sank. I knew so little of Dragonsong, beyond the fragments Father had tried to teach us just before Tatsuya's Tourney.

Mama Sun spoke up from the window, her voice a breathless gasp. "Emiko! Does this mean we're winning?"

I crept up behind her. The fighting had shifted. I'd felt it before, the moment when you know the tide has reversed, and the time has come for the defenders to go on the offensive. There were noticeably fewer Borjigin soldiers and those who were left slowly retreated to the far end of Lotus Lane. A few of the merchants let loose with triumphant shouts and traded high fives with the Tran and Louie soldiers. Despite what it looked like, every fiber of my being said the fight was only getting started.

I put a hand on Mama Sun's shoulder. "No, it's not over yet."

At the upper end of the block, the doors to the Central Road Bank burst open with a sound like a gunshot. Mama Sun gasped as Batuhan walked out the doors and onto the street. It wasn't every day you saw someone with an aura that reached the sky.

Baby Ricky crowded in behind me and whistled. "The Borjigin are making a move? Here?"

If only we were still in the realm of simple clan war. I would certainly have a better chance of protecting my people. "That's not Batuhan. That's Cháofēng, a Son of the Dragon King."

That statement brought looks of profound disbelief and confusion from the Suns. I wished I was telling them anything but the truth. "We have to get out of here."

Batuhan stalked up the street, fury radiating off his shoulders like smoke from a fire. Most of the retreating Borjigin gave the man a wide berth, but one unlucky soul didn't notice he was in Batuhan's path until too late. Batuhan grabbed the man by the neck and lifted him bodily into the air. Cháofēng's voice erupted from Batuhan's throat like a clap of thunder, dripping with contempt.

The Suns moved in unconscious sync, each of them ducking their heads in deference as the dragon's voice struck that essential resonance in their cores. We'd been apart from the dragons for so long, but we were still wired for them to control us.

As Cháofēng spoke he shook the man like a rag doll and swept his other arm toward the bank. **"This hill of turnips is your treasure? Your Hoard? Coins and baubles? Pathetic. Barely worth my effort."**

The Borjigin soldier had both hands on Cháofēng's wrist and struggled to breathe. "My lord . . . the Louies . . . they are . . ."

Cháofēng squeezed his fingers and the man's face purpled as his throat was crushed. The dragon growled through his teeth. **"The Louies are nothing. They are no more, because all they have, however a pittance, is now mine."**

A wave of power pulsed out from the dragon and blew everyone back like a stiff wind. It rattled the windows of the Suns' building, and then everyone in the room doubled over in pain. A spike of agony drove through my chest as the dragon claimed the Central Road Bank and all the treasure within.

No. Cháofēng had the Hoards of two families behind him now. Who could stand up to that kind of power?

The dead man dangled from Cháofēng's hand as he turned slowly in place. As his gaze swept over the Borjigin soldiers and the remaining merchants, heads bowed and knees bent. The dragon's face lifted, and even though I stood back from the window, I knew he'd seen me. His eyes sparkled with recognition. He smiled and turned back to the bowing masses.

"Subdue them. Bring me the strongest. Find the dark walkers. Can none of you follow simple commands?"

The ground trembled as his words rolled down the street. The dragon tossed the dead man aside and the body landed in a heap of limbs, blood trickling from eyes and ears.

Cháofēng raised his arms. **"Lóng Jiārén! Your true lord is here! Come out and pay your respects!"**

In the dead silence following that pronouncement, a ticking, syncopated beat came from the building across from the bank. Tick step, tick step, tick step.

I couldn't help it. I moved to the window to see better.

She emerged from the shadows under an awning. The first thing I saw were the ends of her titanium crutches and the glossy expanse of her lavender dupioni slacks. The low, rumbling anger in my belly rose in pitch and volume as Byun A-Yeong stepped out into the street. The aged matriarch of the Byun Clan made her way slowly over the ruptured asphalt with her forearm crutches. If she'd experienced the same pain when Cháofēng had claimed the bank, it didn't show in the regal lines of her ageless face, the flowing waves of her steel-gray hair, or the immaculate cut of her pantsuit. Across a street filled with kowtowing Jiārén, she walked with her head high and her spine straight. Maybe her knuckles were a touch whiter than normal on her crutch grips, it was hard to tell from a distance.

A-Yeong stopped about ten feet from Cháofēng. She turned slowly, taking in all the bowed backs, and her lip curled in a disdainful sneer. Her milky-white eye followed Cháofēng's look and found me. A-Yeong's jaw clenched and worked as she stared daggers at me through her so-called blind eye.

The stinging citrus scent of her empathic talent was there, even at this distance, trying to get a read on me. She had some gall, coming to my city after she and Batuhan had conspired to kill my brother. There was no need to make it hard for her. I held my ground and stared my own blades right back at her.

Cháofēng laughed as he watched our interplay. **"Your talent burns bright, little one. You may speak."**

It looked like she stiffened a touch as she turned back to the dragon, but A-Yeong hadn't risen to power by not being adaptable. She didn't bat an eye at the diminutive, or at the strangeness of hearing Cháofēng's voice from Batuhan's mouth. The iron-fisted Byun matriarch bowed as low as I'd ever seen and kept her voice honey sweet.

"Praise to you, Great Dragon. This humble one is delighted to stand in your august presence. I am Byun A-Yeong, head of the Byun family, Heart Seer, and Truth Speaker. I have brought you a gift."

The hateful woman came up from her bow, her face wreathed in a beatific smile. She swept her arm behind her. As she turned her gaze found me again and her smile turned hard and cruel.

My belly went cold.

From beneath the awning, footsteps and the unmistakable sound of a body being dragged over the ground. A tall young man emerged from the darkness, and my jaw dropped open.

Minjae Byun was one of Tatsuya's best friends from Lóng Kǒu. Rather, they'd been friends before they'd been tested to their limits during the Tourney. I wasn't sure where they stood now, but in the few weeks since I'd last seen him, Minjae had clearly been through a lot.

His once ridiculously luxurious hair had been hacked down to a brutally short fade that exposed a mesh of fresh pink scar tissue behind his right ear. Minjae's pained eyes sat in dark hollows above stark cheekbones. He'd been tall and lanky during Lóng Yá, but now he was verging on skeletal. The deep purple leather trench coat that hung off his shoulders did nothing to hide his slender limbs or his ragged T-shirt and jeans.

Despite his starved appearance, he moved with obvious strength. His right hand glittered with thick silver rings set with rough-cut amethysts. That hand dragged a much smaller person by the collar of a canvas straitjacket. With a casual movement, Minjae wrenched the smaller person off the ground. They flew through the air, long, dirty hair splaying out in oily hanks, and landed on their back.

I bit back a cry as the figure got up. Kaida rolled to her knees and hissed at Minjae, her voice as ragged as broken glass. Her eyes blazed with fury. The skin of her neck was an angry field of broken blisters and boils. Kaida got one foot on the ground and launched herself at Minjae with a scream.

Minjae opened his mouth and a solid wave of sonic energy slammed into Kaida. She should have dodged. She had the skills, and even in the gray, overcast light, she had a healthy amount of shadow beneath her. Kaida had pulled the same trick on me more than once, dark-walking into her own shadow to evade a strike.

Instead, the force of Minjae's shriek flattened Kaida to the ground. Her head hit the concrete with a crack and her eyes rolled up. All the ground-floor windows of the bank shattered out of their frames and one of the great double doors cracked in half.

A-Yeong stepped over Kaida's senseless form and approached her grandson. He stood with his head bowed and said nothing. His hands were clenched hard enough to whiten his knuckles, and his shoulders trembled. Minjae's grandmother leaned on one cane, then raised her hand and cupped his cheek. A-Yeong's voice was low, but the street was deadly silent. "Such a good boy. So strong. So handsome. Such a good dragon."

He only flinched a little at her touch.

An inferno of rage burned in my belly. I still owed A-Yeong a lesson in retribution for the injuries she'd dealt to my family and friends.

A-Yeong turned back to Cháofēng. "One of the dark walkers, my lord, as you commanded."

I sucked in a breath. It wasn't enough for her to manipulate my cousin, now she was offering Kaida up as some kind of sacrifice to the dragon?

Cháofēng knelt and inspected Kaida like a bug on his shoe. **"What have you done? Her talent is crippled."**

The force of the dragon's voice knocked A-Yeong back a step. To her credit, she clung to her crutches like her life depended on it, and managed to keep upright. "Apologies, my lord. She was held in our prison, and her talent was suppressed as part of her punishment."

Batuhan's face split into an inhuman grin and his voice dripped with disdain. **"Tell me, Truth Speaker, how clever you were to damage my dark walker."**

A-Yeong's face paled. "My lord, it wasn't me! The Soong Clan imprisoned her! My grandson rescued her for you, at great cost to himself."

The dragon's eyes looked out from Batuhan's face, going from A-Yeong to Minjae and back. **"So . . . perhaps the least foolish of all the fools in this world."**

A-Yeong visibly choked back her response and plastered her smile on. "My lord is too kind."

My arms tingled with unspent anger. One scenario after another played through my head. I ran along Lotus Lane with my swords out and singing through the air. Droplets of blood hung in the air, suspended in time as my blades carved a deadly arc through the street until I rescued my cousin. I would savor the shock in A-Yeong's eyes as Shokaku carved out the hateful woman's heart.

The familiar weight of Kamon's hand landed on my shoulder. When had my hands clenched into fists? My arms and legs nearly vibrated with tension. The warmth of Kamon's presence brought me back to reality. I forced my limbs to relax, and my hands to open. In the space of a few breaths, my qì and my mind settled. I gave Kamon a grateful look and covered his hand with mine.

The Suns were all giving me wide-eyed looks. I guessed I'd really been that close to flying off the handle. Which just reminded me again of why I was here. I needed to get these people out of here. A-Yeong needed a visit from my blades, but that could wait for another day. My people and my city needed me, and now, my cousin needed me as well.

I pointed to Sally and Colin. "Kamon, let's get them downstairs. We need to be ready to go when the time is right."

He nodded and bent to scoop up Sally, then Colin, one on each shoulder. I took half a moment to marvel at how well we worked together, and the depth of our implicit trust in each other. I'd been seconds away from diving out the window and doing something stupid, and Kamon had brought me back to my senses with only a touch. And now it was behind us, and we were moving again, trusting each other to keep fighting toward our goal.

Big Ricky looked dubiously out the window. "When's that going to happen?"

I'd been making regular visits to the Sun Emporium for the entirety of my two years here in San Francisco. I'd done business with them and I probably knew their inventory well enough to work for them. In fact, many of their staples were stocked because I had asked for them. As I went over the items I knew they would have on hand, the beginnings of a plan formed in my head.

I nodded to Big Ricky. "We're going to make it happen. Can I do a little shopping?"

Baby Ricky flipped a set of hidden switches and the interior of the Sun Emporium transformed. Kitschy souvenirs and tourist T-shirts vanished behind sliding panels. Brightly lit glass counters slid into place from beneath the floor, and tiny LED lights sparkled off brilliant jewels and polished steel.

Normally I would have spent at least an hour poring over all of their wonderful inventions. Father and son, the Suns had a unique ability to compress and store other people's talents. Their craft had given me a much-needed leg up during my years as the Blade, and I was a huge fan of their work. Today, however, I had a very specific shopping list in mind.

Baby Ricky, ever sensible, saw my mood and he simply unlocked the main display case before hustling out of my way. As I started pulling out the things I needed, Kamon stepped up behind me.

"What are you doing?"

"We're getting the Suns out of here."

I stretched to reach a bowl of brilliant ruby crystals in the far corner of the display. With two Might of the Mountain tiles, the red crystal made a neat sandwich of compressed magic.

Kamon grunted. "You say 'we' but I get the feeling you're planning to stay behind."

I riffled behind the register until I found a roll of packing tape in a battered shoebox. A few loose tiles carved with the outline of an insect rattled at the bottom of the box. I pocketed those as well. You couldn't be too prepared.

With the packing tape, I secured my new creation. Maybe a dozen of these would do it. I laid out all the pieces and started making the rest of them. "The Suns would never make it. Not with Sally and Colin. They're going to slow you down, too. I'll keep Cháofēng distracted and buy you time."

Kamon grabbed my arms and turned me to face him. He stood very close, more than close enough for my talent to stir and growl at the scent of his tiger magic. I concentrated on my breathing until the growl subsided. Kamon searched my face, his eyes intent.

I put my hand on his cheek. His skin was fiery hot. "Hey. I'm not doing anything stupid. That dragon is a nuclear bomb. I'm not planning to fight him."

Kamon closed his eyes. "No stupid heroics. Not now, when—"

The years we'd spent apart stretched between us like a vast canyon, with only the barest thread connecting us across that gulf. He opened his eyes and nodded once.

Baby Ricky cleared his throat. "Uh, we're ready whenever you say so, Sentinel."

They had to get out of here, now. But where could they go? Where could I send them where they could be safe, and among our people? I knew the answer, I just didn't know what it was going to cost me.

I took off my pendant and handed it to Kamon. His eyebrows climbed up but he didn't question me. "Take the Suns to Japantown. The Nakamotos have a funeral parlor there. Show them my pendant and they should let you stay there until I catch up."

Kamon put Bāo's pendant around his own neck. More than

anyone else, Kamon understood how important the pendant was to me. I had no doubt he would bring Bāo back to me even if the world was ending.

I threw my canned magic into a bag and slung it over my shoulder. As I headed for the front door Kamon drew me close, his lips brushing against my cheek. His breath tickled my ear.

"Swear you'll meet me there."

I slid my hand up the side of his neck and felt an electric thrill that was only partly due to my talent. My fingers curled around the back of his head and I pressed his forehead to mine. "I will. Wait for the signal, then get going and don't look back."

Before he could say anything else I pulled away and ran back up to the second floor.

DIVERSION

Whatever Cháofēng and A-Yeong had been discussing while I was making my plans, it hadn't made the dragon happy. The Borjigin hadn't moved, to a man they all remained in their bowed positions. Worse, Kaida was gone. Cháofēng was right in A-Yeong's face, and even in Batuhan's body, he loomed over her like a tree. A-Yeong stood her ground, but she'd protectively moved Minjae behind her.

The weather had been calm and gray only a few minutes ago. Now the winds had picked up and dark clouds swirled above the dragon. Low thunder rumbled overhead and a biting wind barreled across Lotus Lane, bringing sheets of rain. Minjae had seemed sullen before, but now his eyes were wide and terrified.

It wasn't every day that a dragon pulled down a storm right before your eyes.

I had to move fast. Fiona's silver chain tightened a little on my arm as I considered the best way to put my plan into action. I tried to ignore it. Fiona's Hoard would mean nothing to any of us if Cháofēng subjugated my people. What would happen if he went past Lotus Lane? There was no reason for the dragon to care about our boundaries. I shuddered when I considered what might happen if Wàirén authorities decided they needed to involve themselves.

I double-checked the contents of my bag. Yes, this would work. If I could keep the dragon busy, more people could get away, instead of just the Suns. I just needed to give Cháofēng something else to focus on, quickly.

I moved to the other side of the room and slipped out one of the back windows. A blast of wind and rain soaked me to the bone in seconds. My cycling qì warmed me from within and San Francisco pumped fresh energy into my limbs. The Pearl in my chest glowed white hot in my vision and the distance between me and my city shrank to the thin membrane saving my sanity.

I'd pulled back last time, but the luxury of hesitation was gone now.

The winds howled in what seemed like every direction at once. When I cleared the window I was blasted back and forth like a Ping-Pong ball. I reached out for the city again, but this time, I cast off my doubts and reservations. San Francisco welcomed me with open arms and my consciousness began to blend with the city.

I stood on the windowsill and reached up. My hands met the side of the Sun Emporium building and instead of hard stucco, my fingers found a soft, pliable surface. I dug in and the wall firmed up as I flexed. I leaned back a little, testing the holds.

It was secure as a ladder. I pulled myself up, and my boots found the wall to be just as accessible as my hands. I scaled the wall in seconds and crested the roof of the building.

From here I commanded a view that stretched the whole length of Lotus Lane. In the center of the street, Cháofēng continued to rage. I placed the first of my canned magic tricks on the edge of the building and aimed it at the dragon. With a little help from the city, my creation sunk into the concrete tile, as secure as if it had been welded in place.

The next step was a bit of a guess. I'd done it at the Labyrinth. At least, I thought I'd done it. I'd entered the city in one place, and exited in another, moving myself through the magic underbelly of the city. A pretty handy skill if I could harness it.

The barrier between me and San Francisco was as thin as I'd

ever known it to be. A sea of minds and emotions roiled just beyond the scope of my consciousness. Diving into that, willingly, was one of the hardest things I'd ever done.

I needed to be on the other side of the street. The grocer's roof was flat and wide and a perfect placement for two more of my traps. I focused on it, keeping the image of the rooftop firmly in my mind.

It was stupid, but I held my breath.

I dove into the city. The maelstrom of minds hit me again, striking me hard enough to drive the wind from my lungs. Images of the city swirled around me, faces smearing into a blur as they spun around me.

But the image of the rooftop remained crystal clear.

I let out my breath.

And I tumbled onto the flat expanse of the other building. I looked around and my senses rebelled at the sudden shift in perspective. The winds also buffeted me from the other direction. I fell to my knees and dry heaved, but there was no time to be pretty about this. On my hands and knees I scrambled to the edge of the roof and placed the next two of my traps, spitting bile from my mouth as I did it.

On the street below, A-Yeong argued with the dragon. Gutsy. I couldn't hear her over the rising winds, but the dragon's words came through loud and clear.

"Your complete loyalty is my only requirement."

When I had my traps aimed properly, I clenched my teeth and fell into the city again. Another half-dozen times, I dove into the ethereal plane of San Francisco's magic and emerged at different points on Lotus Lane. The transitions became easier with practice, as did my landings. It wasn't too different from the nausea I got when Freddy transported me through one of his funnels, so the dry heaves backed off after the third or fourth jump.

I caught the rest of the exchange between A-Yeong and Cháofēng in bits and pieces. Two of her minions appeared, each carrying a heavy chest bound with iron bands. Cháofēng ripped one of the chests open with a flick of his hand. Sparkling jewels spilled across the street like rice.

The dragon's derision landed on Lotus Lane like a fog bank. **"Do not attempt to bargain with me. I am your lord. Your petty clans mean nothing to me."**

The world finally stopped spinning after my last jump. When I placed the last trap, the sour taste of bile coated my whole mouth and my throat was raw, but I was ready. I made one more jump and came out at street level, about halfway between the Sun Emporium and the entrance to Lotus Lane.

A-Yeong's men lay in motionless, bloody heaps at her feet. Minjae huddled behind his grandmother, but A-Yeong stood tall in the driving rain. Her blind eye tracked the dragon as he advanced on her, menace radiating off him like heat from a bonfire.

Blue-green mist coalesced around Batuhan, trailing after him like a long tail. His neck arched and he stared straight up, wide-eyed, his throat working convulsively. Minjae bit down on a knuckle and whimpered. Tears streamed from Batuhan's eyes, more and more, until fluid slicked his cheeks. He gave a long, rattling exhalation and his eyes bulged. Batuhan pitched forward, landing on his hands and knees. He retched and blood-flecked spittle spewed from his mouth.

His neck strained back again, bending to an inhuman angle. His face flamed red, his eyes burning bright, and the cords of his neck stood out like bowstrings. **"Bow before your dragon lord!"**

Cháofēng's cry rang out along Lotus Lane like a temple bell, resonating with the core of every Jiārén present. My hand froze in my pocket, inches away from my trigger. I wanted to act, but the pull to obey was too strong. Even A-Yeong, that stiff-necked crone, bent at the waist, her clear eye blazing with fury as she bowed. San

Francisco's power surged through my legs and I managed to fall against the wall instead of going to my knees.

The water Batuhan had spit up pooled on the ground and ran together. It lifted up, a little floating bubble of water that spun like a top. His blood smeared against a background of whirling blues and greens.

Batuhan let out a primal scream of pain as more water ejected from his body, from his eyes, ears, and mouth. A-Yeong backed up, pushing Minjae along. Her grandson was beside himself, whimpering like a trapped animal. A sphere of water floated in front of Batuhan and formed into an elongated head with growing antlers and whiskers. It joined up with the tail of mist. Batuhan collapsed and his head cracked against the pavement. Cháofēng crystallized out of the mist, his shining coat of blue-green scales winking brightly in the morning light. The dragon's sudden weight crushed a trench into the street.

Cháofēng slammed a foot down and dug in with his talons, raking up huge chunks of the street. He grabbed one of A-Yeong's chests and hurled it all the way to the next block. The dragon roared, a sound like the world splitting open. Merchants scattered like ants as the chest smashed into a building and caved in the storefront.

"This paltry showing is the respect you give your gods?"

Cháofēng rose into the air, his aura swirling around him like a storm. **"You have forgotten who you are, little rabbits. It is time for a lesson!"**

Up and down Lotus Lane, people screamed and covered their heads as the wind picked up to howling speeds, shattering windows and filling the air with rocks and debris. Not even the Borjigin soldiers were immune to Cháofēng's wrath as flying debris slammed into everyone.

Enough of the city's power permeated my core and allowed

me to shake off Cháofēng's control. I watched the horror unfold through a haze as my mind settled back into place.

Black clouds crowded overhead and a peal of thunder echoed between the buildings. The dragon lifted his head to the darkening skies and sang a ululating melody of Dragonsong.

Lightning ripped out of the clouds, a jagged bolt of electricity that hammered into the middle of the street and split the road in half. A fissure rippled open and propagated up and down both blocks. People on all sides screamed as the ground bucked underneath them. In the far corners of my mind, San Francisco cried out in pain.

A geyser of water burst through the crack in the street. Thunder ripped across the sky and a deluge of rain drenched all of Lotus Lane in an eyeblink. One moment I could see the other side of the street, and the next, even the dragon himself was obscured behind a heavy curtain of slate-gray rain.

Knee-deep water ran down Lotus Lane in a torrent. People, my people, who had been too slow to get to cover were swept away by the current. The water tore at the sidewalks and washed away chunks of concrete. Rain flooded in through shattered windows and flushed merchandise and furniture out into the newborn river.

My city was afraid, but that fear was slowly changing into anger. I grabbed onto that anger and let it fuel me. There was no way to fight a dragon, but I could give my people a chance to get to safety. I had one last Might of the Mountain tile in my pocket. With my qì free now, I charged up the tile until it was nearly glowing. When it was too hot to hold I snapped it in half.

Just like when we'd cleared the way into the Sun Emporium, the tile I triggered connected with those I'd set on the rooftops along Lotus Lane. Only this time, I'd faced them inward with dragon crystals sandwiched between them. The increased gravity focused on a pinpoint in the heart of the crystals and ruptured them like a gāo-class talent had set them off.

Fountains of blue-red flame poured off the rooftops and covered the Dragon god in liquid fire. Cháofēng roared as flames licked at his feathers and horns. The next sequence was dragon ice. Spears of ancient ice flew through the air and smashed into him. There was no hope of piercing his tough dragon scales, but hundreds of pounds of ice moving at freeway speeds was not lightly ignored. One spear the size of a telephone pole caught the dragon on the jaw and sent his head whipping back.

As my traps hammered the dragon, the monsoonal rains lessened. I ran out and began picking up merchants and hurrying them off the street. More flames, emerald green this time, blasted Cháofēng. He snarled, his head whipping back and forth as he searched for his attackers.

With the dragon's concentration split, more people rose from their knees and ran for their lives. As I ran from door to door I spotted Kamon leading the Suns away from Lotus Lane like a ragged line of panicking ducks. Kamon had Sally and Colin hoisted over his shoulders and while he kept the elder Suns in front of him, he was also leading away another family. Our eyes met for a split second, and then he was gone.

The next round of traps went off with a high, keening whistle. Wind blades that would make Fiona proud scythed through the air. Again, they weren't strong enough to cut through the dragon's hide, but they were enough to batter him back and forth. He roared again and his serpentine form twisted in the air.

"Enough!"

Cháofēng's energy blasted across the street like a cleansing wave. Everything stopped in that instant. My little traps disintegrated. The wind blades petered out, and the next sequence failed to ignite. My connection with the city dimmed, and even the rain and wind simply vanished. A thudding pulse of energy radiated out from the dragon and purged the water from the street. People who had been leaning against the wind and water toppled over. In the sudden calm my ears ached from the silence.

At least we weren't fighting the weather anymore. I yanked the last few merchants to their feet and ran at their backs like I was hunting them down. "Go! Go!"

I felt it when the dragon's eyes landed on me. The last of my people made it out of sight, but I was caught out in the open. I bolted for the nearest alleyway but a thundering boom and a wall of steam slammed into my face, throwing me back into the street. I tucked into a roll and came up on my knees.

Cháofēng had somehow appeared before me, his enormous body destroying the alleyway I'd been aiming for. The dragon leaned in and speared me with his dead, black eyes.

His mouth widened into a wolfish grin. **"Ah, the rabbit returns."**

FALL

The dragon's power ebbed as he loomed over me. San Francisco rushed into the space he left behind and the city's power pushed me to my feet. Lotus Lane was empty except for me and the dragon. At least I'd done that much right. Now if I could just get away from the all-powerful Dragon god, I'd call today a win.

Cháofēng's serpentine body slid over the wrecked buildings, collapsing one of them as his massive weight pulverized a wall. His eyes remained fixed on me all the while. He inhaled sharply, and a breeze rushed past me. The dragon's nostrils flared, and electricity crackled between his antlers.

"Not a dark walker, but the spawn of one. Who are you?"

I'd faced off with a dragon exactly one other time. That time I'd leaned on decorum to buy myself some time. Maybe it would work again. Talking with a dragon was far superior to fighting one.

I drew and raised Shokaku, her jewel steel winking as the sun reappeared through the clouds. Nothing said I had to let the dragon know I was terrified. "I am Emiko Soong, daughter of Soong Zhènmíng and Sara Hiroto."

Cháofēng's black eyes sparkled. **"Finally. Someone with claws."**

He gave me no warning. Cháofēng lunged at me and several tons of dragon hurtled toward me like a runaway freight train. Battle-honed instincts saved me, and I rolled away at the first glimmer of movement. The city gave me a push as well, the asphalt surging under my feet to move me out of the dragon's path. I rolled to my feet with Shokaku up, but my katana could have been a toothpick for all the good it did. The edge of my sword skipped harmlessly off the dragon's immaculate coat of scales.

I backed away, making some space between us. The thing about gods was that they got their way most of the time by doing the same thing I did: cheating. Squaring off against Cháofēng went directly against many of my basic tenets of battle. Namely, that I was standing at the end of said battle. I wasn't ready to stand against Cháofēng until I had a way to cheat better than he could.

The dragon took a step toward me, his forefoot landing on an overturned car and crushing it to scrap. **"Quick little rabbit. Show me your strength!"**

I continued walking backward, and as the distance between us grew, so did San Francisco's presence within me. If I could merge with San Francisco again, maybe I could jump away from the dragon. I tapped my Pearl and reached for the city. In my mind, my arms and legs faded, merging with the city. My body began to feel light and insubstantial, and I could almost feel the winds blowing through me.

This time, when Cháofēng launched himself forward, I felt the movement before it happened. Where the dragon touched the ground, I felt his weight shift. As he moved his head, I felt the air move. Before Cháofēng made even the slightest motion, I knew where he was headed.

I kept Shokaku at low guard and stepped calmly out of the way as the dragon barreled past me. Bringing my katana to bear against the dragon's hide would just be disrespectful to her. Cháofēng slammed into the tea shop on the opposite side of the street. Glass jars and delicate ceramics shattered under the dragon's impact. I winced.

Cháofēng crawled out from under the wreckage, shaking shards of pottery from his head. His nostrils flared again, scenting the air. **"Very quick, little rabbit. What are you?"**

"I was the Blade of Soong, I am the Sentinel of San Francisco, and I am no rabbit."

Cháofēng grinned. **"Arrogant as a dragon. Do you think you will bleed gold when I gut you?"**

The dragon came at me again, and again, the city showed me his path. This time as he careened past me, I swept my hand out. The city moved with me, like another limb, and a venerable oak tree at the corner bent over and smacked the dragon across the face. Cháofēng roared at the insult and he grabbed the tree in his jaws. With a heave of his powerful neck he ripped the tree out by its roots, tearing up a chunk of the sidewalk as well. The dragon's maw slammed shut and sheared the tree in half.

He chewed the remaining bit of tree in his mouth and eyed me. **"Impertinent. But the time for games is over."**

My convergence with San Francisco was greater than ever before and nearly complete. At the edges of my vision, hazy, iridescent shapes appeared, giving me the briefest impression of wings. With my next breath, my heart soared, and the land beneath me surged with power. "I will—"

San Francisco cried out in fear and the raw emotion shook me to my core.

Cháofēng didn't move. He was simply not there, and then he was there. The dragon appeared next to me, materializing out of thin air. His whiskers grabbed me by the arms and they were bands of solid iron. My communion with the city stuttered and I fell back into my body. I thrashed, reaching again for San Francisco, but all I got from the city was prickling, panicky terror.

The dragon wrapped my arms close to my body and brought me next to his eye. **"I must know what you are."**

Smaller whiskers played over my face and flicked into my eyelids, peeling them open.

Oh. Gods, no.

I bucked and kicked, but I was fighting against an ocean, a

mountain. How do you resist the force of worlds? Cháofēng loomed close and his form began to dissolve.

My heart hammered in my chest. I tried to squeeze my eyes shut. I clamped my lips together, tried to stop breathing. It was useless. The dragon's will crushed mine like a bug.

Batuhan still lay unmoving on the street like a discarded suit of clothes. What would Cháofēng do once he was in control of me? I had faced untold terrors as Blade, but nothing like this. Nothing that would subvert my will so completely.

The dragon's shape continued to blur. His voice was a thundering croon. **"Don't fight. This is what your kind were made for."**

Cháofēng's head disappeared completely, until all that was left was an amorphous cloud of blue mist with two darkly glowing sparks floating within. If I wasn't faced with one of our gods, I would have sent a prayer to the Dragon Father. Who could I plead to for help now that I was fighting one of our very gods? My connection with my city frayed to a final, tenuous thread of light.

The dragon plunged into me. My world twisted, becoming black-blue lightning, brine-soaked winds, crashing salt waves, and horizons lined with storm clouds. My body elongated, sheathed in scales, and talons erupted from my fingers.

And still the shining thread of light remained. My humanity returned and my mind settled back into place.

San Francisco and Cháofēng pushed back and forth, with me whipsawing in the middle like a buoy adrift in the ocean. However hard the dragon pushed to take over, my city only ebbed away to flow back with greater force to reject his efforts.

The dragon pulled back. His head reformed out of the mist. If he was disturbed by his inability to subdue me, it did not show in the broad expanse of fangs he showed me. **"You are an interesting challenge, little rabbit. Very well, I will grant you an example of my true power."**

And then Cháofēng began to sing.

The fragment of Dragonsong I knew was nothing in comparison to Cháofēng's. His Dragonsong struck a foundational vibration in my core and started a resonance that I felt through my soul. San Francisco cried out to me as the last thread of our connection fell to shreds, but I couldn't be bothered as I reveled in Cháofēng's glory. The majesty of his power cowed and awed me. There was no greater service than to kneel at his feet and hope for his grace.

The dragon's aura expanded even farther in my vision until the vibrant colors seemed to bend toward me. At the edges of my sight, Cháofēng's aura morphed into black tendrils that twisted their way into my talent. A vast feeling of emptiness pulled at me, lulling me to sleep.

In the distant corners of my mind, San Francisco wailed in despair. The pain started slowly, insidiously, like a creeping cancer. As Cháofēng took more of me, agony spiked through my center, a white-hot lance that pierced my core.

In huge, slavering bites, the dragon ate my connection to San Francisco, my true power. He ripped away essential chunks of me, tearing them off like meat from a bone. Trapped inside my own head, I howled in agony.

Skies. Is this what Prem had felt? Kaida?

Gods, I'd done this to Freddy? To Father?

The pain continued for what might have been seconds or minutes, but felt like endless years. What would happen when Cháofēng drained my core completely? What would be left of me? The pain began to fade.

Fiona would know I was gone, our link through the Talon would let her know. The task would fall to Father and Tatsuya. Would they answer the call? Would they harbor hopes of avenging me? Could they even hope to match the dragon's strength? Cháofēng was powerful beyond our imagination. I hoped Freddy didn't do something brave and stupid.

I hoped Leanna could find it in her heart to understand.

I wished I'd had another moment with Kamon.

As my core dwindled to a singular, dim spark, Cháofēng released me. His song ended, and even as the pain stopped, I craved its beauty. I fell to the street and landed in a boneless heap. Just keeping my eyes open was a monumental task. The dragon's prehensile tongue played over his fangs.

"Most exquisite. A bit of dragon, and something else as well. The first unique talent I've tasted in ages. As a reward for your service to me, I have chosen not to kill you, so that you may yet serve me again."

My vision darkened, and my eyes drifted closed. Fatigue dragged me down into the abyss.

Cháofēng grabbed me again and jolted me with a shot of qì. The cobwebs in my mind burned away to ash. My eyes flew open and the scent of ozone filled my nose. Agonizing pins and needles danced over my body. The dragon shook me roughly.

"No. You must witness this revitalization."

He dropped me again to the street and pinned me under one claw. Cháofēng lifted his head to the sky and only then did I notice the vast streaks of buttery gold running through his aura. I cycled what little qì I had left and reached for my city.

Too late.

Cháofēng's Dragonsong blasted out from him and wrapped its muscular coils around San Francisco's neck. The city's voice, already distant in my head, blinked out of existence. As Cháofēng made his own connection with the city, his aura surged again, the gold overtaking the rainbow hues. He rose into the air, leaving me gasping on the pavement.

Waves of energy pulsed out from him. As each one passed through me, they hit me in the chest like a fastball. Exactly like when I drove over the Bay Bridge and left San Francisco.

Cháofēng was remaking the city right under me.

The Central Road Bank seemed to melt, the walls sagging like soft clay. Once square and upright, the entire building morphed, the walls reshaping into twisted, organic shapes. The buildings on either side of the bank began to shift as well, leaning into the bank and merging with it.

A pattern of dragon scales appeared on the walls at the bottom of the building and extended up. The building stretched, reforming the blocky bank into a towering structure with slender spires that reached to the sky. Translucent arches of glass stretched between the towers. Gems and gold appeared and encrusted the tops of the spires.

Seawater gushed from the storm drains and began to fill the street. A spire of translucent jade erupted from under the concrete. Serpentine statues emerged from the sidewalks and twisted their way through the buildings. Above, the color of the sky shifted to purple.

A familiar, almost electric sensation passed over me. In the violet sky, yellow stars winked into existence.

Oh, gods. He was turning my city into the Realm.

Cháofēng swam through the air, his booming song carrying to the horizon. He twisted through the clouds and exulted as his aura spread out in a wave. His voice echoed across my city and inside my head.

He landed on top of the bank. Only, it wasn't a bank anymore. It was a towering palace with spires sheathed in translucent jade dragon scales. Glittering jewels trimmed the roofs and windows. Carved figures of fantastic creatures stood guard at the cornices, as finely wrought as any of my father's creations.

The only entrance at the base of the dragon's fortress lay at the end of an arching bridge that spanned a small lake. This lake occupied much of the center of Lotus Lane. Flower petals danced on invisible air currents across the mirror surface of the water.

In the center of the castle, spires and arches came together, supporting a broad platform the dragon now rested on. In this fragment of the Realm that he had somehow sung into existence, Cháofēng truly became the Dragon god of our stories. He grew in size until he seemed to fill the world. His scales shone with mirror brightness. His feathers were the downy, pristine white of new clouds. Twisting runners of lightning danced along his flanks. His fangs and talons gleamed like polished ivory. His aura was the sky, and it spoke of beauty, madness, and destruction.

He arched his neck high and his song rang out to the corners of existence. Cháofēng's song called to me, and at the core of my being, I knew that every Jiārén in the world could hear him. Every Jiārén was being called home by our former lord.

Maybe it was my last connection to the city, or the jarring dissonance of Cháofēng's qì in my system, but I shook myself to my feet and stumbled to the end of the street.

When I reached the end of Lotus Lane, I found the persuasion charm torn to shreds. Crowds of curious Wàirén were gathered at the mouth of the alley. Several people jumped back from me when they saw my swords.

All I focused on was San Francisco's return to my senses when I crossed the intersection. As surely as a curtain being drawn, I left Cháofeng's zone of influence and emerged in my city. Calming waves of San Francisco's power flooded me with sweet relief that brought tears to my eyes.

I didn't think, I just acted on instinct, tapping into my Pearl. It was as easy as falling down a flight of stairs. Someone nearby gasped as I fell over. I finally let the exhaustion and despair draw over me like a smothering blanket. Cháofēng was stealing my city out from under me. Where could I go? My world dissolved into the city and my last conscious thought was to focus on somewhere safe, somewhere hidden. I vanished.

JAPANTOWN

Again, the smells came back first.

Tobacco. Wood shavings. Smoke.

I opened my eyes and found Gu Ma looking down on me from point-blank range. The cigarette in her lips bobbed up and down as she spoke.

"What did I tell you about dropping in unannounced?"

My eyes adjusted to the dim light and I found myself in the rough-cut tunnel leading to my door to the Archive. Interesting that my Sentinel powers hadn't taken me into the Archive itself. Maybe my authority didn't extend that far? Gu Ma sat in a little folding lawn chair next to her battered walker, her book of sudoku puzzles open on her lap.

I groaned but it was mostly out of habit because I didn't hurt as much as I thought I should. Cháofēng had turned me inside out, but I felt relatively good, considering. In fact, I didn't feel much worse than a normal night's sleep on my hardwood floors. I took in a breath and San Francisco's power coursed through my lungs. I was deep in the bones of the city, down past the bedrock. The magic of my city was thick here, and it seemed to have done me a lot of good.

Gu Ma backed off to let me have a little space as I got up—slowly—and tried to keep my head from spinning. "I didn't exactly have time to call you first."

She huffed, blowing out a cloud of smoke. "Been busy up there, yes?"

I narrowed my eyes at her. Whoever Gu Ma really was, I would do better by treating her like my father, assume she knew nearly everything, and get to the point.

"Cháofēng stole my Sentinel powers."

Gu Ma stared at me, deathly silent. I'd never seen her angry, exactly, but I had a feeling I was treading dangerously close. Maybe this wasn't the best place to escape Cháofēng. When she finally spoke, her voice was a low whisper that still managed to cut right through my chest. "That was unwise."

I buried my face in my hands. "The poem was right. Cháofēng is even more powerful now. The flood has already come. It's just a matter of time now."

The old lawn chair creaked and Gu Ma leaned in close. I had the sudden insight that the heat washing over my face had nothing to do with her cigarette. I went very still.

Once, Gu Ma had threatened to kill me. Only it hadn't been a threat. Gods didn't threaten, they simply told you what they planned to do. What was I supposed to do, in the face of such powerful beings?

At the very least, I could hold my head up. I faced Gu Ma and held her gaze. Her dark eyes were bottomless, like wells of blackest ink. What secrets were lost in those depths? If my time was ending, I might as well try for some answers.

"You knew the truth of the Cataclysm."

"You mean the lie of your legends."

"And the prophecy?"

"What of it?"

"I opened the door for Cháofēng. My mother was right. I've been heading for this doom my whole life."

Gu Ma's black eyes sparkled. "Well, you've formed quite an opinion of yourself."

I blinked. "The dragon—"

Gu Ma huffed. "I know about your dragon problem. You're like a noisy neighbor who won't keep quiet. And now you've let your party spill out of your house."

She raised an arm to the roof of the tunnel, where I could just make out a dim pattern of dragon scales etched into the rock. The pattern crept down the walls, toward the Archive.

"What's happening?"

Gu Ma jabbed me in the forehead with a finger. "You're the Sentinel. Your city. You tell me."

She was right. I closed my eyes and reached for San Francisco. Here in the depths below the Library, the city was right at my fingertips. Just like on the surface, the connection was tenuous at first. Just like at One Bayhill, I floated up as the sensations of the city began pouring into me. Gu Ma looked right at me, not where my body knelt on the ground.

"What are you waiting for?" She waved her hand and I shot upward like she'd slapped me.

When I came to a stop I hovered above the San Francisco Public Library, but something was wrong. I rose until I got a bird's-eye view of my city and saw the extent of Cháofēng's influence. The dragon's power hung over my city like a sticky layer of dark mist. The darkest section nearly obscured Lotus Lane from view, and it dissipated from there. As I tracked east, the darkness cut off like it had hit a wall. I climbed higher, looking for the reason, when Gu Ma's voice rang in my ear.

"All right, that's enough. Get back here."

Gravity reasserted itself and my stomach traded places with my throat. I bit back a scream as I plunged through the Library and landed back in my body. Gu Ma was leaning into me again.

"Well?"

I'd gotten a pretty good look just before I'd been yanked back, and I hoped it meant my hunch had been right. "The dragon's power is spreading. But it doesn't seem to be spreading into Japantown."

The cigarette bobbed in her mouth. "Curious."

I waited a moment but Gu Ma seemed unwilling to say anything else. Why wouldn't anyone simply give me a straightforward answer? Irritation made my movements stiff. I got to my feet.

"I guess I'll be going."

That got me a glare.

"And I'll call, next time I plan on stopping by."

Gu Ma nodded and returned to the puzzle book in her lap. "See that you do that."

She looked small in her rickety lawn chair, almost frail. Maybe the dragon's influence was beating her down too given her deep connection to the Archive. My irritation vanished. I'd gotten what I needed and Gu Ma was counting on me, too.

I reached for the city and fell into the darkness.

I never called Oliver Nakamoto unless it was totally necessary. The head of the Nakamoto Clan and I didn't really get along very well. Honestly, all I ever did was bring business to his crematorium. In the dark of night. You'd think I was putting him out or something. So by mutual consent, in a city that was only seven miles by seven miles, and within a microscopic hidden community of Jiārén, Oliver and I somehow managed to keep from scraping up against each other.

After three rings, I was sure he was sending me to voicemail. To my surprise, Oliver picked up on the fourth ring.

"Sentinel, to what do I owe the pleasure of this call?" His Oxford education made him sound like he regularly had tea with the Queen of England. Given that he had spent his formative years in California, I found it pretentious.

To be perverse, I responded in Japanese, which I knew he was much less fluent in. "I sent my friends to you for protection."

If possible, his English accent grew more posh. "One would

think that as Sentinel, you would have the resources to protect them."

"Oliver, how is Japantown resisting the dragon's influence?"

A deep sigh. "You can see that?"

"Yes, Oliver. As Sentinel, I can see that."

"What do you want, Sentinel?"

I heard the change in his tone. We were getting to what this would cost me. "My duties are to you, yours, and everyone else here right now. Two of those I sent to you need help. Is there something you can do?"

"You already know there is. Meet me at the Pagoda." With a click, Oliver hung up on me.

Peace Pagoda marked a part of the city that had been around since the 1850s, established just after the Gold Rush. Many had fled from Japan after the Meiji Restoration, and as a result, a few Japanese enclaves had sprung up around the United States. Even though the internment had decimated the families here, many had returned. The colorful window displays of the boutiques reminded me of walking past shops in Ginza. It also made me realize why I rarely came here. I'd kept my shopping limited to Lotus Lane because it didn't remind me so much of Tokyo.

Peace Pagoda was a hundred feet tall, its five concrete tiers a tasteful fusion of classic architectural design and modern aesthetic. Sadly, the cherry blossoms were long gone. The courtyard was bare, and the only motion came from the pond, and the colorful koi making lazy ripples on the water.

Oliver was waiting for me at the base of the Pagoda.

Even at a time like this, he was dressed as if he had stepped off Savile Row. His only concession to California living was the pale blue of his bespoke suit. Never mind the upheaval and chaos of the last several hours, his subtle floral-patterned pocket square was perfectly tucked, and his polished wingtips and Patek Philippe watch made him look like he'd taken a wrong turn from the financial district. I marveled at his fastidious manner of dress, which concealed his barrel chest and bulky muscles strong enough to lift a higuma bear carcass.

The contrast between us was stark. Rain had drenched my hair, which was now plastered against my forehead and neck. My clothes dripped as I walked and only my combat boots had remained blissfully dry after Cháofēng's antics. Oliver's hair was swept up in a smooth pompadour and had the slight sheen of pomade. I eyed Oliver's pristine appearance with annoyance and debated wiping my face off on his pocket square.

He spoke first. "Sentinel."

"Oliver. Thank you for seeing me."

I bowed deeply to him, knowing he was going to do me a great service, whether he wanted to or not. He returned my bow, just correct enough to an outside observer, but shallow enough to carry an edge of insolence.

His aura was the hazy orange of a píng-level fire talent. The faint scent of baked bread clung to his superfine-wool suit. Perhaps I'd interrupted him while he was working a shift at the crematorium. He wore a wide platinum wedding band on his left hand. No telltale red sheen of Hoard jewelry. It struck me as oddly mundane for him to wear such a simple wedding band, especially when he was otherwise so showy.

His tone was peevish when he responded and he folded his hands together primly. "Your . . . friends are waiting in the foyer of the funeral parlor. I thought it best we talk first before you join them."

I lifted a brow. He wanted to haggle with me out of earshot of everyone. Fine, that meant I didn't have to be particularly deferential, either.

I pressed my original question. "Why is this area resistant to the Dragonsong?"

"Our clan has never forgotten our origins. For millennia we have safeguarded the art of resisting Dragonsong." Oliver sounded proud and for once, I couldn't begrudge him this bit of preening.

"Can it help others? Those who aren't your clan?"

Oliver unclasped his hands. "I'm sure I don't know the answer to that. And that would be a considerable drain on our resources."

This was exactly why I gave him such a wide berth. "I don't think I'm asking for that much, Oliver. I'm trying to protect my family. Like we all are."

"That's admirable of you. However, we would still need assurances that we will be adequately made whole for the expenditure."

What was he angling for? "What do you believe would be an adequate assurance?"

"As you have observed, we plan for the long term, which is why our protections are in place. That means we are looking for a long-term relationship that will favor our clan."

So no amount of Hoard would suffice. He wanted something that they could hold. Like a favor. Or the ultimate favor—a Talon.

Pretending not to understand him, I said, "The Sentinel is a lifetime position. Therefore, by its very nature, any understanding with the Sentinel is long-term."

Oliver sneered. "Provided the Sentinel lives long enough."

"What do you want, Oliver? Just spit it out."

Oliver cleared his throat, clearly irritated that I had interrupted his long-winded posturing. "My husband, Manny, is our matchmaker."

Hearing the word *matchmaker,* alarm bells went off in my head. I had no intention of pairing off with anybody. I glared at him. "No."

He held up a hand. "Hear me out, Sentinel. We know that your brother is the heir to the Soong Clan and that eventually, he will become head. Surely it would be better for your clan if he had a capable partner to share the burden."

I had a horrible flashback to dinner in Golden Gai, where my father and Old Li had casually bartered for their children's future dynasties and alliances. That night hadn't ended well. I could still feel the stinging sensation of Old Li's blood spraying across my arm and the aquarium glass cutting into my skin as the leader of the Koh Clan had died over the platters of sliced jellyfish and vegetarian goose.

"Like I said earlier, no."

"Don't be so hasty. You need us."

Cold fury rose up my spine, stiffening my resolve. "My brother will make his own choices. You can keep your matchmaker away from us."

But even as the words left my mouth, I thought about Sally's prone form sprawled against the tile floor of the Sun Emporium. Her skin had been colorless, her pulse thready. What if she never woke? What if the secrets of the Nakamoto Clan were the only way to keep her alive?

I would have to find another way. I wasn't in charge of Tatsuya's life, and I wasn't going to bargain away his future. I wasn't going to lie about it, either.

I had tried to play along with Oliver's opening gambit, but now it was time for my own. I let my aura flare tall and wide, glowing gold. Oliver's eyes widened. I inhaled the mist of my city, clean and unsullied here in this one spot, and I let myself draw it all inward, taking along with it the curling tendrils of the city's power so that it could cycle along my meridians and fill me.

Pressing a finger onto Hachi, I let my qì infuse the short blade, watching with satisfaction as the phoenix blood jade glowed crimson red in its pommel.

Oliver took a step back.

He didn't need to worry. I wasn't going to attack him. I was going to give a demonstration.

Faster than the eye could see, I drew Hachi and slid the edge across my palm. Blood welled, fat red drops rising over my skin, defying gravity a moment before inevitably falling to the sidewalk.

My voice was low, from deep in my belly. "Oliver Nakamoto, if your clan refuses aid to me, know that you have lost the Sentinel's goodwill. I vow this on my blood. I vow this on the city's might, and if you take one step against me in my efforts to remove the dragon from my city, I will cry feud with you—not from my clan but from my Hall."

Oliver started, his lips gaping like that of a dead fish. It gave me an unreasonable amount of satisfaction to have his full attention. Before I could seal my vow by placing my bleeding palm on my forehead, a grinding noise rang out from the inside of the Pagoda.

The center of the Pagoda shuddered, a previously invisible seam opening in the ground. The slate tiles slid apart, parting like an oculus as a stone cradle rose out of the earth. I watched in amazement as it emerged behind Oliver, as tall as a Mercedes van, and slid perfectly into the hollow interior of the Pagoda.

A pair of doors slid open and three people stepped out of the stone elevator.

One of them I recognized as Ito-san, an elder who still considered me the Blade of Soong Clan and who had often asked me to handle various retrieval duties here in the city.

Ito-san's salt-and-pepper hair was shaggy and unkempt, as if he'd been running his hands through it on the verge of yanking it out. To his left was a wiry, lean man just about my height but with a featherweight wrestler's physique. His hair was shiny as a crow's wing, and his skin a deep brown. He flashed a quick bright smile at Oliver, who flushed. Manny the matchmaker?

To Ito-san's right was a statuesque woman with silver-white hair, bundled up in a cream cashmere wrap and camel slacks that looked warm and expensive, perfectly tapered over Italian calfskin boots the color of aged cedar. She rolled slowly forward, bent slightly over her walker. I studied her jawline—she had to be Oliver's mother or aunt.

They must have been listening inside the Pagoda this whole time.

Ito-san waved a hand in a careless gesture to my bleeding palm. "You don't have to do that, Emi-chan. Put that away. We'll take care of your friends."

He clucked like a mother hen, continuing to make sounds of disapproval.

The adrenaline that had surged in me ebbed, leaving me oddly deflated and yet relieved. They were going to help me, to help us. Thank the skies.

The younger man stepped forward then, took the pocket square out of Oliver's jacket with an easy familiarity, and pressed it over my palm. "I think it's time for proper introductions, don't you, Oliver?"

Oliver cleared his throat, clearly thrown off balance. "This is my husband, Manny Reyes."

Manny dimpled. "Actually, it's Reyes-Nakamoto."

I smiled back, not immune to Manny's effortless charm. I wondered what he saw in the humorless man he'd married. Maybe Oliver was different with him. Or maybe there was something to that notion that opposites attract. As Uncle Lau said, there's a shoe for every foot.

I took inordinate pleasure wrapping Oliver's dainty floral pocket square into a makeshift bandage over my bleeding palm. The fabric was finely woven, crisp navy with delicate blossoms in pink, yellow, and orange, reminding me of fabrics from Liberty of London. Oliver blanched when he saw the bloody ruin I was making of his pocket square, but he composed himself and made a wide sweep of his arm toward the woman standing before us.

"My mother, Jane Nakamoto, head of the Nakamoto Clan."

I bowed deeply to her, which gave me some cover to mask my

surprise. I had never heard of her, and though my dossiers weren't the most up to date, she'd likely been the head of their clan for some time. Why did everyone think it was Oliver?

She stepped forward, her eyes shrewd. "It's so nice to finally meet our new Sentinel."

Her voice was deep and charismatic. What a waste it had been that I always called Oliver when I could have spoken with his much more pleasant mother, the actual head of the clan.

"Nakamoto-san, it's a great honor to meet you. I wasn't aware of your position, or I would have visited much sooner." That was as close to a reprimand as I could give.

Her lips curved into a small, secret smile. "Yes, I don't go out much. Now if you'll follow with us down to the tunnels, we can get you back to your friends."

Tunnels?

SHISA

The elevator ride to the depths below Japantown, which I didn't even know existed, was mercifully short. While Ito-san chattered away on my right side, I kept sneaking glances at Manny flirting with Oliver. To my shock, Oliver looked perfectly fond. Clearly most everything I knew about Oliver was a facade—this was the real Oliver, happy and a newlywed. What else had I missed about Japantown? Their whole secret underground was classic for Jiārén—always a front house and then the real house. This was the same strategy on a larger scale.

When the doors opened, I wasn't prepared for the sight before me. Jane stepped out, rolling her walker inches at a time. Unlike the dark cavern I had imagined, this level was completely finished with red lanterns hanging every few meters, giving a cheery glow to painted green columns. This place smelled cool and fresh, hinting at efficient ventilation to the surface. Between the crisp air and the soft lighting, it felt like sunset in autumn.

We were in some kind of vast community room filled with dozens of low tables set on tatami mats. Each table was surrounded by an array of colorful zabuton cushions. Thick red columns supported the roof, each column carved with a swirling motif of small lion dogs, painted in black and red. Their eyes seemed to follow our movements as we entered.

I unzipped my boots and thanked the skies my socks were dry. Manny offered me a hanger and I gingerly draped my wet haori on it. A teen with an undershave and sleek long bangs took my wet clothes from me. They wore a denim apron with the Nakamoto azalea stitched in hot pink over a black turtleneck, paired with flowing black hakama trousers and Doc Martens. The teen's aura had none of the orange hue of Oliver's talent. Instead, it hinted at an earth mender talent, with soft streaks of forest green.

They gave me a small bow and winked.

Manny chuckled. "Sentinel, this is Yui, Oliver's youngest sibling. They are one of our potters."

I studied their hands and forearms, rippling with colorful tattoos. They must be responsible for the beautiful raku cremation urns that the Nakamoto parlor offered. I bowed in return and Yui opened a closet door to hang my jacket.

Another set of elevator doors was set into the far wall. The doors opened and my friends appeared. My heart stuttered and I ran to them when I saw Colin and Sally slumped over in wheelchairs.

I nearly bowled into Kamon. He caught me and answered before I could ask.

"They're still unconscious. It doesn't seem to be getting any worse."

Jane caught up to me and laid a hand on Sally's head while Ito-san knelt and checked Colin's eyes. Mama Sun wrung her hands and buried her face in Big Ricky's shoulder. Ito-san stood and nodded to his matriarch. Jane waved some people over and addressed us all.

"Friends of our Sentinel, you are welcome here. You can rest as we care for your young ones."

She gestured over to the west hallway, where a stream of young people came in carrying trays with pots of tea and assorted small plates. I wasn't ready to relax, but my stomach rumbled when I smelled the warm toasted barley and brown rice of genmaicha.

I spotted trays of onigiri and fresh fruits—segments of glistening satsuma wedges and sliced Asian pear with little toothpicks sticking out of the slices. That must have taken some time to prepare. Jane had been telling the truth when she said they were planning to help us. Which again made me wonder why Oliver tried to haggle with me upstairs, bargaining for Tatsuya's hand in marriage. Clearly he wasn't in charge here.

Ito-san gestured that we should all sit on the floor cushions. A team of quietly efficient people rolled Sally and Colin to a quiet corner and got them settled on thick futons. I tore my eyes from them and chose a seat where I could watch most of the room. Kamon sat next to me and put Bāo's pendant in my hand. My fingers closed over the familiar comfort of the jade.

As everyone settled in, a crowd of young people clustered around Oliver, smacking him on the back, high-fiving him, and giving him knuckle bumps. He loosened up considerably and shrugged off his jacket. Oliver rolled up his sleeves, and all of a sudden, he was a completely different person, one of the boys instead of their boss.

Jane clearly commanded the room; I saw the way everyone deferred to her. Maybe she had instructed Oliver to test my willingness to bargain. I wouldn't put it past her—she'd already managed to pull the wool over my eyes, letting everybody think that Oliver spoke for the clan when all along she was the matriarch in hiding.

We went through all the polite rituals, and when I finished my tea, Manny immediately appeared to refill my cup. Baby Ricky seemed as bewildered as I was. He had spent his whole life on Lotus Lane and while I knew that some Jiārén preferred to live in or near Japantown, this underground community was clearly a surprise to him as well.

I touched Ito-san's hand. "We appreciate the hospitality, but is there anything we can do for—"

He patted my hand. "Help is coming."

Ito-san gestured to the east wall. The expanse was decorated with a full-length mural of small, doglike creatures that resembled Bāo in miniature form, minus his wild mane and flowing red-and-gold locks. Shisa dogs. They were white and gold with flatter foreheads and smaller ears. On the right side of the mural, they appeared to be howling, their jaws open wide. On the other side, those that faced them had closed muzzles, as if there were mice clamped inside that they didn't want to let out.

I heard a faint scrabbling on the bamboo flooring, reminding me of the way Sugi's wooden claws would clack on the tiles at home as she followed Father around. A pair of small Shisa dogs scampered into the room, yipping and leaping, reaching no higher than my knee. The little dogs cavorted around the room, drawing cheers from every table, and generally acting in a way Bāo would have viewed as completely undignified.

Ito-san sat down next to me and gave a short whistle. The Shisa came running. Up close I marveled at their red and gold coloring and the way their eyes glistened like polished emeralds. Ito-san took a couple slices of persimmon off his plate and tossed them to the pair. They reared up, balanced precariously on stubby legs, and snatched up the fruit, their jaws working rapidly. I couldn't help but smile as orange pulp dotted their little beards after.

Ito-san handed me his plate. "Now you try it. They love persimmon." I took the heart-shaped fuyu persimmon, the ripe sweet fruit bursting apart in my fingers as I tossed it to the Shisa. I patted the closest one, giving it a scratch behind one ear. Their fur was short and fine, almost like suede.

Ito-san scratched the other behind its ears and he began whistling again, a low, droning note. The Shisa leaned into his hand and purred. The sound was a rumbling hum that seemed to vibrate through my chest. Ito-san smiled and tossed a whole persimmon across the room where it landed next to Sally. The Shisa leapt away and pounced, continuing to hum as it ravaged the fruit.

He leaned over and pointed at Sally. "Watch."

While the Shisa devoured the persimmon, Sally gave a sleepy moan and rolled onto her side. From her table, Mama Sun gave a yelp and was at her daughter's side in an instant.

"This is our secret," Ito-san said. "When the Shisa hum, it counteracts the Dragonsong."

Now the murals made sense, and I understood the architectural significance of seeing pairs of Shisa on so many rooflines when I was in Okinawa.

"How many do you keep?"

Ito-san gestured to the wall murals and the red columns carved with continuous spirals of Shisa pairs.

"When we gather, we can sing them down."

Incredible.

These fierce guardian protectors were meant for a higher purpose, and maybe—just maybe—it meant we had a chance, however small, to send the menace back through the veil where he belonged.

Kamon tilted his head at me. "I know that look," he said.

"What look?" I asked.

He lifted his eyebrows. "It's the same look you had that time you shot flaming arrows off the bow of our fishing boat, and that time you said 'duck' when the penanggalan was attacking us."

Oh. That look.

It had worked out with the pennaggalan though. After all, Kamon had those fast tiger reflexes.

"I need to get rid of Cháofēng. But I need a distraction."

Kamon frowned. "To do what?"

"To get his attention away from the bank, so I can get in."

He set down his teacup. "You can't take on a dragon, Emiko."

"I know that."

"Do you?"

I bristled at his tone. "You think I want to fight him with my bare hands."

Kamon leaned close. The gold flecks of his eyes were flames under the red lantern lights. I wanted to cup his face and smooth out the lines that bracketed his lips. The lines that said he was worried about me. I hated that I put them there. Again. But also I resented how quick he was to assume I was going to go in without a plan. I was making a plan.

"Emiko, I didn't mean that."

"Really? Because next you're going to tell me I shouldn't go."

He flinched and I instantly wished to take the words back, the opening refrain of an argument we'd had too many times before.

"I know better than to do that . . . now."

His voice went softer at the end and I wondered why this time was different. Was it because he thought I was stronger now with my repaired meridians and as the city's Sentinel? Somehow I didn't think so. I wondered if it was because he was different now, after our time apart. And after his time with Fiona.

My shoulders sagged. I was different now, too, and maybe he didn't know that. "I have to do something and I know I need help."

"What did you have in mind?"

I blew out a breath. "It's just . . . I feel like with the young ones safe here, I have a better shot at dealing with Cháofēng. If we can magnify the effect of the Shisas' humming, maybe it's enough to give me an edge against the dragon."

Kamon chewed thoughtfully on a mochi square. "Maybe Bāo can do it."

I gave my own whistle and my foo lion appeared next to me. His sudden appearance started the Shisa dogs, who immediately started jumping and yipping. Bāo pointedly ignored them.

Ito-san pulled some dried squid off the platters as he coaxed Bāo to mimic the sounds the Shisa dogs made. Ito-san pressed two fingers to Bāo's massive chest, coaxing the low vibration that could counteract the Dragonsong. I wanted to laugh as I watched

Bāo drop his disdain for these little Shisa, as he allowed himself to be bribed with pieces of dried squid.

The young men around Manny and Oliver let up a cheer as Manny pulled out a gigantic clear glass jug with a pit viper inside, floating in rice wine. Habushu.

"The cure for all that ails you!" Oliver poured shots around, and my eyes widened when his mother, Jane, downed a shot before rolling off on her walker to the rear alcove.

By the time the jug made it to me, people had decided to forego the glasses altogether. Yui lifted the bottle with one strong hand, their tattooed fingers splayed across the base of it. When Yui handed it to Kamon, I stared at the pit viper in rice wine. It was frozen in a rictus of death, right about to strike. Apparently, it became less venomous the longer it stayed in the jug. I was skeptical.

"I don't drink," I said.

Ito-san scoffed. "This is not a drink. This is medicine."

Kamon laughed, a low rumble of amusement. "Well, if it's for medicinal purposes, then sure."

Around me, the young men and Oliver chanted, "Habushu! Habushu! Habushu!" as they passed the jug around. I steeled myself and took a swig, wincing as the alcohol burned its way down my throat. My belly lit with fire, and I hoped it was the rice wine itself and not the venom.

A cry jerked my head around, but it was only Mama Sun, this time weeping openly as she hugged a very confused-looking Sally. Sally who was awake now, and patting her mom on her back. On the other futon, Colin rolled over, rubbing at his eyes.

For a moment, I let myself forget about the predator hovering over Lotus Lane and just slowed time down so that I could be here, watching the Nakamoto Clan share their hospitality. As they tended to our wounds, I drank in the clean scent of the tiger next to me.

Somehow, despite the worst of threats looming over us, we

were laughing and drinking together. Hope bubbled up and a plan began to take shape. We didn't need to use the Shisa to overwhelm the dragon, just to buy me enough time to tap into the city's own wellspring of power.

I leaned over to Ito-san. "So how long would it take to sing down all of the Shisa on the columns?"

FAMILY

Yui tapped me on the shoulder just as Ito-san was getting to the good part. "My mother would like you to take tea with her somewhere quieter."

The Habushu was still burning a hole in my stomach lining, so tea sounded perfect, but I was reluctant to let Jane separate me from the others. That never boded well. I looked up into Yui's deep brown eyes, and they were clear and steady. Reassuring almost.

"Of course." I excused myself from Kamon and Ito-san. Kamon watched Yui, studying their hands. I had done the same seconds earlier. The anticipation of violence causes an adrenaline surge. It can be difficult to mask, especially when your body thrums with the need to act. It had taken me years of training to manage those tells.

Yui had the strong hands of a potter, and they were steady, betraying no tension.

We walked to a small area tucked away from the main room, screened off by black noren panels. Yui pulled aside a panel and gave me a smile and a wink, transforming their countenance into one of mischief. "Mother says it's getting too tough on her hip to manage the cushions."

Jane Nakamoto sat at a small round table, the top a polished surface of mottled koa wood. A small Seiji teapot and two cups sat at the center, the celadon glaze interspersed with thin lightning strikes of gold. The gold gave off the red hue of Hoard gold. Stunning. I had no doubt this kintsugi was Yui's handiwork, a mingling of classic vintage ceramic strengthened and fired with Hoard gold.

Jane stood slowly and bowed. I returned it, the depth showing true respect for her station as head of her clan. Behind me, Yui slid the screen closed, muting the sounds of the other clan members.

We sat in silence as she poured and beyond the curtains the plucking of shamisen lent us our soundtrack. My mind ran through the various ways this meeting could go. In the end, I needed her more than she needed me.

After the ritual of pouring, we both drank.

The tea was deceptively strong for its appearance, very much, I suspected, like the woman serving me. Nakamoto-san poured again for the two of us, her form both precise and elegant, like the delicate teapot in her hands.

We drank tea and nibbled on lightly sweet, buttery cookies in silence. The subtle bitterness of the tea was a fine pairing with the richness of the cookies. Between the warmth of the tea, the blessed quiet, and the rice wine, I fought to stay alert. Nakamoto-san appeared to be a hospitable grandmother, but I had no illusions that this graceful tearoom was anything but her killing field, the heart of her power. She hadn't brought me here for tea. This was business.

Father always advised negotiating from a position of strength but I didn't have much going for me right now. Leaning into Nakamoto-san's goodwill seemed like a good place to start. "Thank you, Nakamoto-san, for agreeing to shield our young."

She smiled. "I think, as heads of our clans, we can dispense with the formalities. It will make everything go faster, wouldn't you agree?"

I blinked. "I'm not a head."

Jane gave me an arch look over the lip of her teacup. "You sounded quite like a head when you were dressing down my Oliver."

"What? Oh, no, my apologies but—"

"Shh. First lesson. Heads never apologize."

I shook my head. "No, my father is head of the Soong Clan. I can't speak for him."

"Who said we were talking about the Soong Clan?"

Somehow this conversation was only getting more confusing as it progressed. Jane seemed to take pity on me and relented.

"Let's table that for now and get back to why you're here."

I grabbed for the change of subject like a lifeline in pitching seas. "Nakamo—"

She gave me a glare.

"Jane, I need your people to protect our children . . ." I paused, the idea still only half formed in my mind.

"And?"

"And I need you to sing down your Shisa dogs so that I may use them to rout Cháofēng."

"There, so much easier, right? Yes, my clan will protect your young. They are our future, and must be ever guarded. Of course, this is a significant drain on our resources. And angering the dragon, well, that is quite a risk."

She wasn't talking about money. Oh no, Oliver had already made their lofty ambitions known. "Maybe you don't understand the gravity of the situation, but—"

Jane leaned forward, her eyes intent. "Believe me, between the two of us, I am the more well versed in just how precarious our situation is."

Touché. They were the ones who had kept their safeguards against our Dragon gods in place for generations. "Then why are we bargaining? If Cháofēng has his way, none of this will even matter."

Her hands toyed with the rim of her empty teacup. After a moment she spoke in a quiet voice, as if reciting a story. "Like the Borjigin, my family never forgot our true story. When the other families chose to forget, we isolated ourselves, so our children would not be subject to your lies. So that we could better protect ourselves against this very future.

"All this is to say that we . . . I am always looking to the future. To do so I have studied our story, our histories. I have read our books, our scrolls, our . . . poetry."

A chill went down my spine. Jane met my eyes, her gaze blazing with the kind of intensity I associated with my father.

"You are the Sentinel of our fair city. And possibly the subject of a very old and dangerous prophecy. In you, I see a number of interesting futures that do not include our subjugation. So with that in mind, I continue to plan for those futures."

The slight buzz from the rice wine vanished under Jane's assault. I drained the dregs of my tea and wished I had a handful of Kit Kats. Jane was certainly nicer to deal with than Oliver's topside persona, but it seemed she was going to be just as inflexible on her demands.

"I can't speak for my brother. I won't push him to do this."

"Admirable, but as head you will learn that at times you must use your influence."

I didn't know what to say to that, so I poured more tea into our cups to cover the silence. A light tap sounded on the noren panel and it slid aside with a whisper. Yui stepped in and gracefully knelt at Jane's side. They leaned in and whispered.

Jane's calm expression didn't change, but she did stop moving for half a heartbeat as Yui relayed the message. Yui reached into their coat and pulled out a sparkling silver hairpin encrusted with lustrous black pearls. Jane sucked in a breath when she saw it. Her eyes misted over with nostalgia as she took the piece in her hands and turned it over in the lamplight.

What on earth was going on?

At a whispered order from Jane, Yui bowed and left the room, sliding the door shut. Jane remained fixated on the hairpin, tracing her fingers over the pearls.

With a visible effort she stowed the pin in her pocket, stood, and composed her expression. Jane reached for her walker and pulled it to her. I knew better than to offer to help. With her walker in place she stood straight and tall and brushed the wrinkles from her slacks. It was like watching her put on armor.

Jane smiled. "Let's go meet our guests."

I was once again in a dim elevator with a powerful, aged woman using a walker. While my experience with Gu Ma was certainly singular, this instance didn't feel too different. Jane had insisted on more familiar forms of address, but I wasn't about to get chummy with her. I intended to treat her as if she was just as dangerous as me.

If not more so.

As the ancient elevator lumbered to the surface my resolve cracked and I broke the silence. "Who exactly are we meeting?"

Jane gave me a small, knowing smile. "An old friend."

The question that had been burning in me since the alcohol fled my system jumped out of my mouth. "What makes you think I can fix all of this?"

She chuckled. "Oh, I didn't say you would fix all of it."

"Fine. It's just that, I have no idea—"

Jane turned to me and now I really did flash back to my elevator ride with Gu Ma. The head of the Nakamoto Clan let her aura go big, a hazy corona of silvery blue that nearly filled the elevator. I backed up a step as Jane's eyes unfocused and the rich, leather scent of her talent pummeled me.

Skies, her talent was Dragon Sight. And not the light touch of it like Colin had, but a rare gāo talent. What else were the Nakamotos hiding from everyone?

Jane's hands clenched down and the plastic of her walker grips creaked in protest. Her eyes unfocused, staring through me and down an infinite hallway of possibilities. When she spoke, her voice dropped an octave, rumbling from somewhere deep in her chest.

"Little Phoenix, even from afar, I have seen your futures, so great are the waves you will cause. There is violence and destruction in your path, but enough outcomes that include banishing the dragon and protecting your city. Enough for me to wager the lives of my people on you. Because I know you will put your own life on the line for your people, for all Jiārén. This is what I see."

Her eyes refocused and she straightened. It took me a moment to find my voice.

"The poem . . ."

Jane's voice returned to normal. She waved a hand dismissively. "Uzai. A piece of advice. Do not waste your time trying to decipher prophecies. We are dragons. We do not *suffer* our fates."

Reckless hope surged behind my ribs. "We can change it, then?"

She grimaced. "*Change* is a strong word. Shape, perhaps."

The hope faded but didn't disappear. It wasn't a terrible answer, at least. The elevator dinged and rattled to a rickety stop. My jaw dropped as the doors creaked open.

The Japantown underground garage was packed with ranks of soldiers standing at rigid attention. Swords and spears bristled in neat rows that stretched into the distance. Everywhere I looked, pearls glimmered in the dull lighting, studded into armor, worn at necks, wrists, and ears.

My Uncle Lau stood at the head of this field of soldiers. He carried someone over his shoulders like a sack of rice. His usual gourd of industrial-strength rice wine hung off his belt, but the ceremonial battle cloak on his shoulders clashed with his easy manner. Our eyes met and he gave me a wink, but it lacked his usual good humor. His head tipped ever so slightly to his left.

At the other corner of the formation, I found my father.

Father believed in appropriateness. If a gift was sent to another family, he considered our relative strengths, wealth, and prior gift exchanges. When he'd selected the restaurant for his deal with Sabine Koh, he'd chosen an older venue to appeal to Old Li, as well as to not bring the ensuing chaos to a newer establishment.

And when he dressed, he always dressed for the occasion.

My father wore a Tangzhuang of blackest silk, the frog buttons neatly secured up to his neck. A fenghuang stitched in fine, pearlescent embroidery flew up his right arm and ended on his chest, where the phoenix's flashing eyes and open mouth made a clear statement of defiance. His suits were custom made to his blocky frame, but this one hung at strange angles, hinting at protective layers worn underneath.

Sugi, Father's wooden Hokkaido wolf, sat at my father's feet, her eyes laser focused on an acorn in my father's hand. As she tracked the movement, the interlocking tiles of her construction made a soft clicking noise, the music that followed my father everywhere. The wolf was his oldest continuous animate, a wedding gift from my mother, and the only animate to leave clanhome with him.

Until today.

A jade hawk perched on his right shoulder, and his jade monkey sat on his left shoulder. The eyes of both animates glittered and followed me as I exited the elevator. Father's personal guard stood behind him, carrying more jade statues. A pair of badgers, a fox, another hawk. More soldiers stood guard around Father's prized bull, which was secured to a sturdy wheeled cart that groaned under the weight of all that jade.

Soong Clan had come to San Francisco, and they'd come for war.

Father's square face was as impassive as a stone monument. The only hint to his thoughts was the acorn that danced across the knuckles of his right hand. When I met Father's gaze, he dropped the nut. Sugi snapped it out of the air in one precise movement.

I held the door open for Jane as she shuffled out, leaning on her walker. When my father saw Jane the corner of his mouth curled up.

Jane stopped in front of my father and pulled the hairpin from her pocket. She clasped the pin between her hands and gave my father a shallow wai. "Thank you, for returning it."

Father inclined his head. "It was time for it to return. I trust the negotiations for the children have been concluded?"

Of course he not only knew where to find me, but also what I was doing, without even asking a question. Anything less would have been out of character.

Jane nodded and her gaze slid over to me. "Nearly. We were just discussing the particulars."

My father waved and Uncle Lau came forward to gently set down his load. "I have one more provision to add."

Tatsuya rolled off Uncle Lau's shoulder and lay unconscious on the ground.

PLANS

I rushed to my brother's side and rolled him onto his back. His pulse was steady but weak. Tacchan's skin was pale and clammy, his breathing shallow. I looked up at Uncle Lau. My brother had looked almost as bad at the end of his Tourney. "Who did this?"

Father appeared at my side. "The dragon has done this."

I stood. "Why Tacchan?"

Father shook his head. "It's not just him, is it?"

No, of course not. Always with the lessons. Sally was also affected. And the Nakamotos knew they needed their Shisa lions to protect their home. "It's all the younger Jiārén. All the clans."

I knew better than to ask my father another question. Instead, I took a moment to think through the ramifications. "Cháofēng knows some of the families won't come back to him willingly."

Father nodded. "He is using Dragonsong to hold our children hostage. The Emerald Pagoda was thick with travelers. All on their way here to bargain for their children."

Jane stopped next to my father. "Not just our children. Our very futures."

I turned to the Nakamoto matriarch. "Will you protect my brother as well?"

Before Jane could answer, my father cut in. "I have a few stipulations. As you said, these children are the future of our clans. I must insist on certain arrangements for my son's care."

Jane narrowed her eyes. "Go on . . ."

"I would simply feel more comfortable if I knew my son was receiving more attentive care. Perhaps you could have one of your grandchildren watch over him for me. That way, someone will be with him when he awakes."

Jane's expression slipped for a microsecond, then her eyes darted back to me before going to my father. A small smile curled her lips. ". . . Yes, I can arrange that."

My fatigued brain, laden down first with snake wine, then with tea and cookies, finally caught up. Comprehension spurred anger. I turned to face Father. "A word, please."

"Certainly, Mimi."

Fury rolled off of me and threatened to steam off my skin. Father waved a hand and a soldier stepped forward and bowed, his aura rippling with blue as a bubble enclosed us. The echoing sounds of the parking garage disappeared.

My voice sounded strangely hollow in the wind bubble. "How can you do this again? Was marrying off Tacchan to the Kohs not enough for you?"

I had never spoken to my father like this. A small part of my primitive mind recoiled from this rebellion. But the betrayal that burned through me seared away any filial reserve that usually tempered my speech.

Maybe it was because I was in my city and strong and whole in a way that I had never been before. Or maybe because I hadn't forgotten how Father had guided my hand to Old Li's death.

Father folded his hands together. "Mimi, maybe if it had been you, I wouldn't look to forging a close alliance with another strong clan. But your path is different, and with Tatsuya I must consider the future of the clan."

I closed my eyes as his words landed a one-two punch to my gut. Trust my father in one masterful statement to remind me that I was the failed heir and that I had abandoned the clan. Soong clanhome was no longer my home. A hot mix of elation and shame closed my throat. My sword arm was no longer guided by another's will, but the loss of my ties to the clan still left me raw. I was free from the yoke, but I no longer solely served one clan—now I served an entire city.

Tatsuya was softer than I was but I considered that a boon, not a liability. The clan loved him and he would lead with that love rather than the stern duty that guided my father and me.

Unbidden, Tatsuya's image rose in my mind, crumpled on the ground at his Tourney, his features twisted in pain from Minjae's sonic blast. My brother had been more powerful—he could have pulled out all the stops to neutralize his opponent. I would have.

And what was better for the clan? A leader who wouldn't survive a skirmish to win the war or one who ruthlessly crushed opposition before it could become a war?

I had been ready to punish Oliver, threatening vengeance to get aid.

I opened my eyes, taking in the warriors behind us in their full fighting regalia. My brother was right. I was more like our father than I had ever admitted to myself.

Maybe Tatsuya just needed more time. He was so young.

But you were young, too . . . a voice inside me whispered. And my parents had dropped me off at Jōkōryūkai with no regard for my tender age. To better forge a blade, start when the metal is soft. But my brother could be made into something else.

"Tatsuya will make his own choices," I said firmly.

"Of course. And he is young, he can use this time to expand his social circle. Meet Jiārén outside the confines of Lóng Kǒu."

Like the Nakamotos, a secretive family with powerful talents and Shisa dogs, probably not on most families' radar. A political windfall for my father to strengthen our position. I bowed my head at Father's victory.

Father unclasped his hands and gave my shoulder a squeeze. "I feel better knowing Tacchan has you here, teaching him."

Wait, what?

"Won't Tacchan be with you?"

Father spread his arms wide. "Look at all you have accomplished. You are a Sentinel. Cháofēng's arrival signals a great change. Regardless of the outcome of the next few days, our world is changing. If our clan is to move forward in the new world, we must see beyond our limited borders. Tacchan will learn those lessons from you."

I didn't know what to say. He sounded proud of me. Like I wasn't a failure thrice over, a repeated oath breaker, and no longer welcome in my clan home.

My throat tightened with emotion. It took a concerted effort to make my voice work again. "But I . . ."

I couldn't make myself say the words. To repeat my failures.

The hard lines around Father's eyes relented a little. "Growth does not occur without challenges, and you have led a challenging life. Yet you have always grown to overcome your challenges and my expectations. This is what makes you precious to . . . your clan."

He hadn't said the words, but he'd left enough space between his words to make his meaning clear. I dipped into a low bow, lest the tears stinging my eyes mar the moment. A thick knot of emotion closed my throat, and I stayed down until I was sure I had composed myself.

When I straightened, Father had returned to business. Our eyes met for a moment, and then he waved a hand and the wind bubble popped. The world returned to normal.

He nodded to Jane. "We have an accord."

Jane gave a shallow bow. "Excellent. I took the liberty of having your son taken to our sanctuary. He will be well cared for."

Father turned to me. "I trust you have a plan to remove the dragon from your city?"

I did have a plan. Most of a plan, even. "Yes, Cháofēng must be sent back to the Realm. We have to rescue Kaida first to ensure he can't use her to dark-walk and return."

For once, my mother not being here was something of a help. The fewer dark walkers at risk, the better. I brought out the dragon tooth Madam Yao had given me, and sketched out the rest of my plan in broad strokes. There was no sense in going into detail. I had so little information about Cháofēng's fortress that much of what would occur would be decided on the spot. The lives of thousands would hinge on some snap decisions. My snap decisions.

I suppressed my surprise as neither my father nor Jane objected to any of it. Jane simply nodded in agreement. Other than asking some clarifying questions, Father said nothing counter to my choices. He treated me as an equal, which felt good and strange at the same time. I tried to focus on the good.

Jane frowned and looked out over the Pearl Guard. "With the other families arriving to beg for their children's lives, the dragon will have many powerful talents at his disposal. These men are not enough to assault his fortress."

Father nodded. "Agreed. It is fortunate then, that the Sentinel has so many allies."

I did?

My father snapped his fingers and one of the Iron Fists stepped forward with a polished cherrywood box in her arms. "Put your plan into motion. Find your cousin. I will gather additional allies and meet you at the dragon's fortress. We will await your signal."

The guard handed the box to my father, who took it and turned back to me. "Until then, I thought it best to bring these to you."

He opened the box and spun it around. "It seems I am giving up more than just Jane's hairpin today."

My heart stuttered. The box was lined with pale pink silk and held several Hoard pieces. Sweat slicked my palms as I looked over the contents. Two strands of pale pearls, a set of pearl earrings, and a set of silver bangles encrusted with seed pearls. The pale red light from the pearls made the interior of the box glow like banked embers. Mother and Father had gifted these to me over the years. Each one had been a knife to my gut when presented to me, like my parents had been mocking my lack of talent.

Now I held my hand over them and my qì responded, sending a tingling rush of power up my arm. I tried not to react when I noticed the wide blood jade bracelet in the rear of the box. A carved phoenix wrapped around the bracelet, one of the pair Tacchan and I had worn during our dinner in Golden Gai.

Father offered the box to me. "These are yours, Mimi. I have kept them safe against the day you could use them. Today is that day. I suspect we will all need whatever power we can grasp. And as you establish your own house, it is right that you hold all of your Hoard in one place to cement your power. You are past due to have these in your possession."

He really had never given up on me. I traced a finger over the blood jade, enjoying the little thrill of power that tickled my palm. "My house? My Hoard?"

Father gave me his look. The one that said he didn't enjoy repeating himself. "Are you not building your own house, here in San Francisco? Have you not already collected a Hoard?"

Why was his ability to see me so clearly always such a surprise? In the past, this had always made me angry, as if even from afar, he was still orchestrating my life and taking my decisions from me.

My last trip to Tokyo had given me a different perspective, though. One that I needed to use more if I were to ever be at peace with him. My father was a master of strategy and behavior. He played our games of power ten moves into the future. The fact that he knew what I was up to wasn't a sign of his manipulation, it was a sign of his high regard for me.

Not that that wouldn't take some getting used to.

Some of what Jane had said to me made more sense now, as I

allowed myself to consider what my life would be like in San Francisco, assuming we repelled the dragon. What I dared to make of my life, if I had the power to make it happen.

I nodded once to my father, a quick, decisive motion. Like him. He returned the nod and gave me his trademark grunt of approval. High praise. He pulled the two strands of pearls from the box and handed the box back to the Iron Fist.

"If I may?"

I stepped closer to him so he could affix the clasp of the necklace. The cool pearls contrasted on my skin with the electric flow of energy. Lights and sounds sharpened a little more, and little details around us jumped out at me now.

He spoke low, just for my ears. "I have always felt these looked best on you."

The Iron Fist handed the closed box back to my father, who handed it to me. "Your blood jade may be required as well. I trust you to know when to use it."

His gaze dropped to my arm, and the tight loops of Tran silver. "A final piece of advice. You have always excelled when presented with singular goals, but our lives are rarely so simple. I have always believed that multiple goals will present unique solutions that had otherwise been hidden. Keep your mind open to the unseen opportunity."

Father stepped back and looked me up and down. "It has been difficult to watch you grow into your own, even knowing that I have prepared you as well as I could. Yet your performance has always exceeded my expectations. I anticipate nothing less from you in the future."

There was a time when I would have quailed at this tall order, had my resolve shaken by the idea that Father held me to some unreachable standard. Now I knew he simply trusted me to do what he knew I was capable of doing. I gave him a deep wai and closed my eyes to steady myself.

When I rose, Uncle Lau barked an order, and the Pearl Guard smoothly turned as a single unit. Father's eyes lingered on me for just a moment longer before he pivoted on his heel as well. Sugi click-clacked after him as he strode away. My father did not look back.

With the precision of a finely tuned watch, the Pearl Guard followed my father out of the parking garage. Never one for sentimentality, Uncle Lau simply tipped me a small bow as he marched out with his troops. He took a swig from his gourd before returning to calling out the marching cadence to his soldiers. Even though they were going out to meet a dragon, for him it was just another day on the job.

His life was so simple. Father gave him orders, and he followed them. His world was a simple construct, and he was happy. I'd had that, too, once, but it had chafed. I'd thrown it away in search of freedom.

No one told you that freedom was so much harder, so much more complicated. Or that you had to fight to safeguard it, or it would be slowly eroded in a series of decisions where you gave a bit of it up each time without even realizing.

Jane had gone down to see to the Shisa, so I was alone in the parking lot, which felt right. I took the dragon tooth out of my pocket. It was about as long as the width of my palm and curved sharply to a fine point. There was a chip in the wider part of the tooth, but I had not found anything capable of breaking the tooth's surface.

I'd asked Oda to take a look at it as well. Unfortunately, other than confirming that it was a powerful artifact, he was unable to read the glyphs carved upon its length. Gu Ma had growled at me when I'd asked her about it, and refused to talk to me for days afterward.

In the end, I supposed it didn't matter. These were details that didn't change what the tooth allowed me to do. I gripped the tooth in my hand and hummed a little tune that had been sung to me only once before. I'd practiced it in my head many times since, somewhat terrified of what would happen if I did it out loud.

The tooth glowed blue, the light moving slowly through the glyphs. I cycled my qì and fed some into the tooth. A low thrum of Dragonsong poured out of the tooth, filling the parking garage with the warmth of a sunny summer afternoon.

I closed my eyes and luxuriated in the sensation, letting it refresh and revitalize me. Even the strongest matcha wasn't this good. Was this how Dragonsong felt, when it wasn't being used against us? How had our lives diverged so far from our stories?

When the Dragonsong felt like it had peaked, I called her name. "Most Exalted, Ever Luminous, Heavenly Madam Yao."

In the space between heartbeats, they appeared. I felt their presence, even without opening my eyes. There was no fanfare, no display of power. One moment, I was alone in the garage, and then two demi-gods stood before me.

Madam Yao was a full head shorter than me, with the kind of ageless beauty I only saw on the very young, or the very, very old. She more than made up for her stature with her power, which radiated off of her like a furnace. Her russet hair was swept back and plaited into two braids that fell in front of her shoulders, exposing her pointed, tufted ears.

I still had to look up at her though, as her petite frame sat calmly astride a massive snowy white qílín, ten feet tall at the shoulders, and able to reach fifteen feet by the end of the twisted golden horns on its forehead. The qílín stamped its hooves, the sound echoing through the garage, gouging into the concrete like it was soft clay. The fine white feathers around its fetlocks danced as the qílín moved.

What did a godlike huli jing do in her spare time? Maybe I'd caught her in the middle of a picturesque ride by a lake? Because today she wore a casual, lightweight yukata in pale peach with a bright floral pattern. A wide obi in sky blue cinched across her middle, tied in an intricate knot at her back. Like the last time I'd seen her, the hem of her yukata did not hide the wide fan of tails by her feet.

She looked around, taking in our drab surroundings. "The flattery was appreciated, but not necessary, Emiko. Although, I had not expected you to call on me so soon. Are we having a girls' night out?"

"Um . . ." A sudden spike of terror shot through me. Had I misunderstood the significance of the dragon tooth?

"And in such an . . . interesting location."

The qílín snorted. Madam Yao hopped down nimbly and made a show of looking around, her ears swiveling back and forth. "Oh, I know! There must be an entrance to a secret sake bar hidden here!"

"Madam Yao—"

The fox spirit's ink-pool eyes crinkled with delight. She covered her mouth and laughed, a high yipping sound. "You should see your face."

Heat flushed my cheeks. I gave Madam Yao a deep wai. "Apologies, but time is of the essence and—"

Madam Yao sobered. "It only is for those with such short lifespans. One day, when you approach your five hundredth year, you will understand."

"What?"

"I think it's like reverse time dilation. The older you get, time feels slower for you, even as the world seems to age in a blink. Soon you start wondering why everyone is rushing around all the time. It can be quite tiring."

She'd done this last time, started spouting something about physics, or electricity, and totally thrown me off. She put her small hand on mine. "It's okay, dear. You'll get used to it eventually."

Something about her touch cleared my head, and I wondered

what had been so confusing in the first place. But Madam Yao was here, so my plan at least had a shot. I told her my plan.

Like with my father and Jane, she simply nodded at the right places and asked a few questions. Otherwise she did not seem surprised at my request, and in fact, she seemed to expect it. Being treated as an equal by my elders was surreal.

“So you’ll do it?”

Madam Yao patted my hand and smiled, showing her sharp, white teeth. “My dear, I have been looking forward to this moment for hundreds of years. I wouldn’t miss it for the world.”

INFILTRATION

You couldn't kill a dragon. At least, I couldn't.

Good thing I didn't need to kill one—just uproot it from its jade fortress and then shove it back through an unstable portal to send it back to the Realm. Much easier.

Possibly even easier than dealing with the Wàirén chaos unfurling before us. Kamon stood at my back, close enough that I could feel his agitation. His Zen demeanor frayed when faced with a street jam-packed with police and fire vehicles, all with their lights and sirens blaring.

The first responders formed a barricade in front of the entrance to Lotus Lane. A crowd of gawking civilians had gathered and gave collective gasps as distant bursts of dragon talent sent arcs of energy into the pale blue sky.

Whatever had happened to Lotus Lane's protective persuasion barrier had only partially crippled it. Police and firemen took turns running toward the entrance with clear intentions, only to be turned back at the last second. This resulted in a thick band of very confused people.

My people. Frustration burned in me. I didn't want these people hurt, and at the same time I didn't have the time or the resources to help them. This close to Lotus Lane, Cháofēng's power was stronger, already bleeding past our self-imposed borders. The city was a distant melody I could barely hear.

Kamon squeezed my shoulder. "The best way to help them is to deal with the dragon. Stick to the plan."

Right. I nodded and whistled up Bāo. In a burst of white pepper my loyal foo lion emerged from my pendant. A few people around us screamed at Bāo's sudden appearance but there was nothing to be done for it. We had to keep pressing ahead. At least everyone was backing away from us, which gave me more room to work.

I dug my hands into Bāo's mane. "Okay, boy, just like you practiced."

Bāo's mane rippled in a statement that was simultaneously supreme disdain and pained resignation. I understood. No one liked being shown up. The hum started low in Bāo's chest, a dissonant sound like great rocks grinding together. Power built like a massive engine spinning up. He opened his mouth, baring dual rows of wickedly curved fangs, and sound exploded from him, blasting my hair back and pushing me into Kamon's arms.

Around us, civilians continued to scream in terror. Whatever let them usually believe that Bāo was a harmless dog, clearly wasn't working right now. Undeterred, Bāo continued to hum, the sound building in intensity. As his power built, the effects of the dragon began to recede. San Francisco drew close, close enough for me to reach out for it. There was something new this time, a faint, discordant melody that teased at the edges of my perception. Before I could focus on it, the music slipped away, leaving me only with the feeling of bracing, salt winds.

My city flowed into me with a feeling of triumph and relief. San Francisco's cool and calming power coursed through my meridians and lit up my senses. The landscape of my city opened to my eyes again, even if it dimmed as I looked toward Lotus Lane.

First I had to get these people to safety.

With the mantle of my Sentinel power glowing about me, I

approached a cluster of policemen who were engrossed in a quiet argument about what to do. The city's consciousness, which was also mine, flitted through their minds, sampling their emotions and desires. I picked the older gentleman to my right and reached up to put my hand on his shoulder.

When I made contact his eyes widened and he turned to me. His colleagues startled and reached for their weapons but he raised his hand to hold them off. I let the power of the city infuse my voice so that when I spoke, I gave him the barest taste of my power as the Sentinel.

"Sergeant Davies, I know you want to protect these people. I also need to protect them, because they are my responsibility. You are also my responsibility. Do you understand me?"

The sergeant's eyes unfocused, looking through me. Jiārén hid in plain sight. I didn't know what he was seeing, how his mind tried to reconcile what I was, with how he understood the world. Was he seeing someone from the government?

He was a good man, and had served many years with the police, but this was beyond anything he'd ever encountered. The day's confusion threatened to break the last of his resolve. His mind was a fragile globe of glass. All of his colleagues, in fact, were on the brink.

For now, though, he was listening to me, as the city's power made my voice as familiar as the surf hitting the shore at Ocean Beach. "What's happening beyond this intersection is not for you or your men to deal with. I am the Sentinel of San Francisco, and it is my duty, and mine alone. You will instruct your men to push the civilians back, and clear an area of two blocks around Chinatown. Is that clear?"

Davies seemed to wrestle himself back to his version of reality. "I don't know who a Sentinel is and I don't care. You need to step back."

I had to show him. It went against everything I knew, against the First Law, but there was no other way. Were he here, Father would probably find a very quick and expedient solution. Wàirén lives were so fragile, so transient. My father wouldn't bat an eye at eliminating so many of them. But I was trying to be different. I had friends, well, long acquaintances, amongst the Wàirén. How could I face them if I didn't try to protect all the residents of my city? I wasn't the Sentinel of the Jiārén. I was the Sentinel of San Francisco, and this man was under my protection.

"You know nothing about the forces awaiting you in there. Let me show you."

My Sentinel senses gave me a wide, almost omniscient view of the city. When I was connected with San Francisco, my citizens shared bits of their lives with me as images, and flashes of emotion. It stood to figure that I could share with them as well.

I opened my mind, not just to the city, but to the man in front of me. San Francisco plunged into the space I'd made, and before I could react, all of Davies's subordinates had been included as well. My vision of the city spread out around us, the landscape illuminated with golden light, and the dragon looming huge over an area of darkness. Cháofēng sat atop his castle, built on the remains of the Central Road Bank.

A high, whistling sound came from Davies's throat. "Is that . . . ?"

"A dragon. Yes."

I had never used my Sentinel powers like this before, but doing anything to help my citizens felt right. The city sensed my need, and pulled away, releasing the policemen. Some of them went to their knees and I winced in sympathy as their stomachs evacuated.

Davies gave me a look, and turned to squint at the persuasion barrier. Could he see something of the truth now? I hoped he did. I didn't want to resort to my usual methods. He gave me another look that was equal parts hope and mistrust. Thankfully, the hope won out, and he began barking instructions to his men. In another minute the police had dispersed and the civilians were pushed back.

Kamon appeared by my side. "Nicely done, but I wonder how Bā Tóu would feel about what you did."

I shrugged. Between this and the full-blown battle at Coit Tower, Jiārén secrets were going to take a beating. "I don't think we have that luxury right now, and I won't have any of these people cleaned. It's not our place to alter their minds. My father was right, whatever happens, things are going to change. Best if we're the ones doing the changing."

The echo of my father's teachings faded to the strength of my own voice. I moved the pieces on the board now, and I accepted the cost of winning our peace.

With the civilians gone I could set the stage for later. I didn't know what I was going to face inside Lotus Lane, but I believed in planning for success. Bāo's humming had built to a high buzzing sound that made my ears itch. It was time.

I reached for the city again and dove through the tenuous barrier that separated our minds. This time, instead of fleeing the storm of power and taking refuge in the calm at the center, I stayed midway in both. I wanted to access that center space, while not actually traveling through it.

It was one of the stranger sensations I'd experienced in my life, an extreme dichotomy of roiling chaos on one hand, and utter quiet and peace on the other. I held on to the chaos, and reached through the quiet until I found the parking garage over the Japantown enclave. With my mind so close to the city, our desires aligned, and a ragged portal opened into Japantown.

Jane and Yui jumped back a little, clearly startled by the appearance of a portal in front of them. Behind them, what looked like two dozen Shisa sat obediently in neat rows. Jane recovered first, bending down over her walker to peer into the portal. "Emiko?"

This definitely wasn't something the city was used to doing. I clenched my teeth as I struggled to keep both sides of the portal open. It was hard to talk and do this at the same time. "Nggg!"

Thank goodness Jane was so practically minded. She moved away from the portal and began waving her hand. "This is it! Go, go!"

I nearly screamed as seventy-seven Shisa dogs barreled straight for me and plowed through my chest. The next strangest sensation of my life was the Shisa dogs moving through my now insubstantial body. My arms ignited with feathers of pale blue light and traced a path through the calm of the city's center. The Shisa followed the path like a beacon, and they burst through my portal into Chinatown.

My lungs burned, and my arms ached, even though I hadn't been running, or actually physically lifting anything. I was back at the entrance to Lotus Lane and once again on all fours, hurling my guts onto the pavement. So silly of me to think I'd left this kind of behavior behind me.

Kamon pulled me to my feet and held me steady as I found my bearings. His gaze was locked above us and I followed it up.

From a spot above us, Shisa dogs appeared, one after another. Each one announced itself with a roar and then immediately began humming, adding its counteracting music to the existing song. In an unbroken line of brilliant silver and gold, the dogs soared into the sky and circled Lotus Lane.

In perfect synchronicity they descended, landing on trees and apartment buildings. They raised their snouts to the sky and began humming in earnest now. The sound battered Cháofēng's influence, beating it back into the confines of Lotus Lane. As the pressure of the dragon's power disappeared, Bāo stopped humming and slumped to the ground, his eyes drooping closed.

I ruffled his mane. "Not as easy as it looks, is it, boy?"

All he gave me was a disdainful shrug of his shoulder. Even if you took everything away from a cat, he still had his pride.

The tattered remnants of Lotus Lane's persuasion charm hung in the air before us. Crossing it would be like leaving my city again, separating myself from this power that made me feel whole for the first time in my life. Yet there was no other way to do this. I knew I had exactly who I needed with me to do this.

I grabbed Kamon's hand and our fingers interlaced, fitting together as snugly as my hand over the knots on my sword grips.

Kamon nodded to me. "We get in, we find Kaida, we get out. Easy."

I gave him a smile. "When has anything ever been easy?"

He squeezed my hand. "Remember the part of the plan where you come back."

I squeezed his hand back and the three of us plunged through the persuasion barrier, and into the domain of the dragon Cháofēng.

The dragon had put in some work while I'd been away. Sheets of translucent jade in a rainbow of colors now covered what remained of the shops along Lotus Lane. On the left side of the street, a delicate pattern of dragon scales was etched into the jade. Opposite this, the jade was worked with a design of ornate feathers. Statuary that hinted at dragons encased in stone was prevalent through the ruined buildings. Graceful arcs of polished granite and marble dove in and out of the rubble, like some impossibly long dragon soaring through the earth.

And none of that compared to the weather. When we crossed the border, the rain was a slap to the face. Driven by howling winds, the rain hit us like a thousand frozen needles. We ducked our heads and leaned into the gale.

Kamon leaned close. "Like Hohhot, but cold and wet, instead of dry and gritty."

I grumbled. "Not helping."

At my knee, Bāo growled, expressing generations of genetic cat displeasure at being soaking wet.

The three of us stumbled to the nearest toppled building and found shelter in the lee of a wrecked wall. Kamon slicked the water out of his eyes. "The city?"

I shook my head. "It's gone. Cháofēng's power is too strong here."

"But your talent . . ."

As if the hunger at the center of my being could ever be sated and put away. Just at the thought, my talent growled and uncurled like a beast seeking prey. Kamon took my moment of silence the right way and let me have a moment to control my talent.

When I had a firm grip on it with my mind, I let the smallest wisp of it out. This was the part of my talent I'd used my whole life, without understanding what it was. The ability to discern other talents by their scent wasn't something I'd heard of any other Jiārén possessing. It was really only the first part of my talent, selecting the choicest morsels from the buffet.

Standing next to Kamon and Bāo, my talent homed in on their power and their scents nearly overwhelmed me. Starved of attention for a day, my talent bucked against my control. I cycled my qì until it quieted, and then I sent it down the street, hunting for the distinct ginger scent of a dark walker.

Unsurprisingly, the trail led us directly to Cháofēng's fortress. We ducked into the wreckage of the Sun Emporium's storefront to assess our approach.

The dragon's palace was built over the remains of the Louie bank, not that you could tell anymore. Luminous sheets of unbroken jade shot up from the ground and covered the original bones of the building. Even the old redwoods at the entrance had changed, their bark morphed into something like tortoiseshell, branches bowed down with thick clusters of strange yellow fruits.

Central Road Bank had originally stood three stories high, with a stone roof supported by thick columns. Cháofēng's fortress stood at least twice as high and thick fog obscured the spires that rose even higher. Here and there, marble arches connected the spires together. While the bank had occupied about a third of the block, the dragon palace had cannibalized all the surrounding buildings. A moat of clear, blue-green water surrounded the castle, easily the width of the road. It didn't look very deep, but ominous shadows slithered through it, just under the surface.

The real threat was the dozen or so Jiārén who stood with their chins tucked down and their shoulders hunched, trying to fend off the rain. They had clearly been ordered to stand guard at the entrance to the palace, maybe to receive those who came to plead their case to the dragon.

Even poor Byun A-Yeong had been reduced to hostess duties, although she managed to hold her head high as she crutched back and forth across the walkway that crossed the moat. I pitied the lackey who trailed alongside her with a golf umbrella.

My talent snaked through the guards, silent and unnoticed, sampling lightly of each of their talents, just enough to let me know what we faced if we approached the Gate. At least ten gāo-level talents, every one of them wearing Hoard jewelry. "There's no way we're going in the front door."

Kamon squinted at the moat. "Well, there's no way we're going swimming, either, and I'm not saying that because I'm a cat."

I sent my talent farther into the palace and let the hungry beast sniff around, tracking down the elusive scent of ginger. When I found it, I realized I'd already guessed where Kaida would be held.

The building was, after all, a bank. The underground vault hadn't changed. Why change a perfectly good prison?

I turned to Kamon. "Sorry, we're not going swimming, but we are going down."

RETURN TO THE VAULT

We went back the way we came, making our way to the edge of Cháofēng's power, where the dragon and the city vied for dominance. When the power of San Francisco tickled my senses again, I stopped and turned my attention down.

My visit to Gu Ma had proved it. The farther down I went, the more powerful the city was, and the more strongly it resisted the dragon. I found the city's power and pulled open the earth like wet clay, pushing aside concrete and asphalt with a wave of my hand. A nearby tree leaned over, shielding my tunnel entrance from the rain. When the hole was a few feet deep I jumped in and felt an immediate uptick in the city's power as I landed in the mud and water.

I looked up at Kamon and Bāo. "It's working, come on down."

To their credit, they only hesitated a beat before joining me in the bottom of the hole. Kamon made a face as the mud nearly sucked off one of his shoes.

"Dry and gritty is already sounding better."

"Tell you what, after this is over, we'll take a vacation in the desert. My treat."

The words were off the cuff, but once they were out, I couldn't deny the spark of warmth in my chest at the idea of going on vacation with Kamon. Our eyes met for half a breath before we both decided that there was more important work to do first.

I bent my will to widening the tunnel and carving a path forward. Around us, tree roots extended through the walls, keeping the roof from caving in. The three of us marched down into the cold, damp earth, toward the dragon's lair.

I'd been a guest of the vault before. Last time my Sentinel powers had been new, and I'd ripped my way out of my prison on instinct. In the aftermath, Uncle Jimmy had repaired the bank and rebuilt the vault to be even stronger. He'd made quite the show about it in the community.

I took savage pleasure in tearing my way into it. This far below the surface, my connection with San Francisco reignited. I stood in the beating heart of the city, as physically close as I could be. The roots of northern redwoods were tenacious. Add a boost of the city's power and even enchanted steel couldn't withstand the onslaught.

Where heavy steel met earth and bedrock, the roots found tiny seams and wormed their way in then swelled until they were fat with power. Metal groaned, screeched, bent, and buckled. A flash of heat washed over my face as the steel door gave way to the roots of the ancient tree.

I climbed down my makeshift path and emerged in the plush confines of the Louies' vault. The interior gleamed with gold on nearly every surface and reeked of the scent of Hoard treasure.

The Tran Hoard was here. Fiona's chain squeezed my arm, pulling me deeper into the vault. I had pledged to recover the Tran Hoard, but I couldn't exactly waltz out of here unnoticed with that much Hoard. Not unless I had an instantaneous escape route. Standing inside Cháofēng's seat of power, my connection to San Francisco dimmed again. Luckily, an answer to my problem sat in front of me, draped lazily over one of the richly upholstered wingback chairs the Louies favored.

Kaida was the only occupant in the vault. Up close her aura fluctuated in strength, hazy at times, a bolt of color at others. Mohe had drained her and even now that the circlet was off, she didn't seem to have control over her talent. The faint scent of ginger told me she'd tried though. No wonder the Byuns and Cháofēng left her unattended. She couldn't dark-walk like this. Hopefully I could take enough of her talent to get the Hoard out of here.

She scowled at me as the noise and dust from our entrance died down. "Crashing my party again? I'm not really set up for entertaining company." Her voice lacked its usual venom, as if she only snapped at me out of habit. She flicked a glance at Kamon and proceeded to ignore him.

"Oh right, that's your signature move, right? Dropping in unannounced." I watched her warily but she didn't get up from the plush chair.

"Why are you here?"

I gestured to the giant hole I'd torn in the wall. "Thought you could use an exit strategy."

She arched an eyebrow. "And what's it going to cost me?"

"A few things."

Though her expression remained indifferent, her posture shifted. She was listening.

I held up a finger. "You leave Tatsuya alone." I paused and watched her closely. Her eyes had narrowed as she heard my omission. I did not include my mother, father, or myself in this vow—we could fend for ourselves.

I held up a second finger. "Two, you let me take some of your talent."

She sneered. "You think a petty thief like you can learn to dark-walk just like that?"

I tilted my head. "You think you're good enough to show me?"

"Why should I?"

I spread my arms wide. "Aren't you tired of always doing

someone else's dirty work? Are you just waiting here at their beck and call?"

Her eyes lit with black fire. Good. Some of the fighter I'd dueled in Tokyo was still in there. The one I knew was better than I was. Truly she was more my mother's blood than I was.

When she stood, I felt Kamon tense beside me but he needn't have worried. Kaida wouldn't be satisfied with fighting me to a standstill or merely trouncing me. She'd wait until she was at full strength then make sure she got the full measure of besting me. Nothing less would satisfy her pride and that was where we were different. I couldn't afford pride. I didn't care so much how I got things done, and in my view faster was better.

Kaida's eyes flicked to the daishō at my waist. Shokaku's pommel sat comfortably next to Hachi. She'd carried Shokaku longer than I had. She was a little taller than me, with the reach to match. I'd seen her in action with the katana, a master weapon wielded by a master swordsman. A Hiroto legacy. At last she tore her gaze away, although her eyes still blazed with hunger. "What else do you want?"

I wasn't too proud to ask for help. "Help me open the Gate again."

"You mean you want me to do your dirty work for you."

"This is different. When we send Cháofēng back you'll be free."

Kaida narrowed her eyes, suspicious. "You'd just let me go? After I tried to kill your brother?"

Kamon growled and I held up a hand to keep him back. I wouldn't trust me, either. But Kaida had suffered enough at the hands of my family. If I had to be the one to stop it, then so be it. "Yes, just like that. You shouldn't have paid for my failures at Jōkō. I know this doesn't make it right, but I'm willing to start here."

She gestured to her thin frame. "I'm in no shape to help you with anything."

Kamon relaxed. Now she was bargaining.

I laughed, genuine amusement bubbling up in my chest, the frothy feeling at odds with our situation. “Don’t be modest, cousin.”

She scowled. “Fine.”

“And my first condition?”

“I’ll give you six months.”

“Two years.”

“One year.”

“Done.” A year was plenty of time for me to work with Tac-chan.

I drew Hachi and nicked my palm, then handed the wakizashi to her hilt-first. She could stab me or she could make the deal. Kaida took the blade from me, her fingers awkward on the grip.

She ran a fingertip over the blood jade on the pommel, lighting it up. Hachi had always been mine, just as Shokaku had always been hers. Until now, neither of us had wielded the full set.

When Kaida drew the blade lightly against her own palm, I exhaled.

“Witness,” I said softly.

Kamon stepped forward. “So witnessed.” He held out his hand for Hachi. Though Kaida seemed reluctant to part with it, she gave it back.

Hachi sheathed, I tilted my head to Kaida. “Shall we?”

The silver links on my arm pulsed in anticipation.

I held out my hand. “Hold out your palm.”

Kaida did so and I said, “I won’t take much.” Almost to myself as much as to her. Then I let my talent rise to the fore, striking like the pit viper in the jug of snake wine.

My eyes flew open and I met the bottomless dark of Kaida’s eyes. Mother’s eyes.

Kaida’s power surged in fits and starts, the familiar scent washing over me. Mohe had crippled my cousin, reducing her qì flow to erratic jolts of energy. My talent struggled to pull her power to me, but it was like dancing with a partner out of step. First, too slow and then, too fast. The sensation threatened to drown me, a tide of blackness and chaos. Then a flash of memory, and Kaida's qì smoothed out.

Sara taps the crane pin on her soft pink yukata. "Never forget your anchor, Kaida."

My voice replies, "May I have the same one as you, Aunt Sara?"

The garden at clanhome, chasing after Tacchan as he swirls two fat pears above my reach, giggles erupting as I, no, *as* Kaida, *dark-walks to get behind him.*

With a start, I dropped Kaida's hand. I inhaled, taking in the rich loamy scent of the soil, the cool bite of the air, heavy with the oil of crushed redwood.

I'd felt her do it, the way she'd had line of sight before immersing in shadow. The way she'd held the target firm in her mind and her fingertips on her anchor.

Kaida screamed and slapped me. I let it come, didn't dodge. The bright flush of anger tightening her fine features made her look even more like my mother. "Those are mine!"

She was right. That's why I let her have one free hit.

I'd told her I'd take some of her talent but not that I'd share some of her deepest memories, too, in doing so. In this, I was my father's daughter when driving a bargain. "That was the deal."

She let out a cry of rage and ginger bloomed around her. She vanished, only to reappear behind me, reaching for Shokaku. I twisted my palm in a flaring motion and tree roots burst from the tunnel and yanked her back.

Her aura was a bright halo of power now and pungent ginger swirled around us. Whatever Mohe had done to her, my talent had apparently resolved. Even so, she struggled against the roots and branches, her breath coming in shallow, panicked gasps. My heart twisted when she began to sob. How much pain would my family force her to endure?

Kamon snarled. "Oath breaker."

I flinched. If anyone here was the oath breaker, it was me. I placed a hand on his arm. "Don't."

"You can't trust her."

I shook my head. "It's the other way around. She doesn't trust me."

I couldn't expect her to. All of us had abandoned her when she'd needed us. I wouldn't do that again. Trust couldn't be demanded, only nurtured.

I unstrapped the sheath from my hip. Shokaku was one of the few things I'd received from my mother. A delicate crane was worked into the sheath, etched artfully into the wood. But maybe she was never meant to be mine. After all, I wasn't my mother's true heir. The crane was the Hiroto symbol. I sent a whisper of thought to the trees and the woody cage unraveled. Kaida landed heavily, her arms shaking with tension.

"Your anchor." I tossed Shokaku to my cousin. She caught it on reflex and cradled it to her chest, fingers tight enough to whiten her knuckles.

A roar filled the vault for half a breath before the entrance to my tunnel exploded in a wall of dirty water. Three stories below the surface, Cháofēng brought a thunderstorm down on our heads. The dragon's voice slammed into us like a physical blow.

"Dark Walker! I smell you!"

Through the downpour I barely registered Kaida's grip on my wrist until the sharp ginger scent of her talent cut through the water and darkness washed everything out.

I reappeared on my knees, coughing water out of my lungs. Kamon landed neatly on his feet and helped me up. To add insult to injury, the silver chain on my arm tightened as it sensed me moving away from the Tran Hoard. My right hand tingled and throbbed with my heartbeat.

We were on one of the lower walkways of Cháofēng's palace, a sturdy archway of polished jade. Kaida's ginger scent was swept away by the wind. I whirled and found my cousin standing behind me, a smug smile on her face.

Cháofēng roared again, the sound coming from far below us. I eyed Kaida. "Your talent is line of sight."

She hadn't released her death grip on Shokaku. "We all have secrets, Emiko."

The palace trembled as the ground beneath us exploded.

I shoved Kamon toward Kaida. "Go! Take Kamon!"

Kamon roared. "No!" He leapt to avoid her grasp and rippled into his tiger form. Inky darkness blossomed around Kaida's feet like my own questing vines. They reached out for Kamon but in tiger form he was too fast. In an eyeblink he was gone.

Kaida gave me a little shrug and sank into the shadows, darkwalking to her freedom.

Gods, what had I done?

"Look what we have here. A lost little dragonet."

Batuhan appeared at the far end of the archway. His skin was pale and hung off his cheekbones like melted wax. He looked like he hadn't eaten in a week. Only yesterday he'd been tall and barrel-chested. Now he was shrinking into himself, as if he were being eaten alive.

The only parts of him that looked alive were his featureless, black eyes. The eyes of Cháofēng. Batuhan opened his mouth and Dragonsong filled the sky. The city's magic withered around me.

I was caught. I was the Sentinel, but no longer with a Sentinel's power.

CHÁOFĒNG

I prayed Kamon would stay away. If Cháofēng could cancel out the city's magic with his Dragonsong, who knew what he could do to a tiger shifter? The dragon advanced on me, his limbs moving oddly, like his joints weren't working properly anymore.

"You cost me my dark walker, but I'll take you in trade."

Time to pivot.

I ran. There was no rhyme or reason to it. I had no idea how the fortress was built, if I was heading to a door, or a dead end. But the palpable atmosphere of anger, like thick humidity closing in on me, turned on something in my primitive brain that made my legs move. Prey instincts were strong, and when a predator chased you, the only thought was to run.

Cháofēng came after me, his voice a bellow of rage that shook the walls. I bounced through narrow corridors and across the archways that connected the jade towers. There were no handrails, no safety nets. I stepped lightly across bridges no wider than my two hands with barely a thought other than to get away.

The next tower was milky-green jade, the interior staircase a tight spiral that went up three stories. I took the steps three at a time. As I went up the jade faded until it became translucent, like running on stairs made of glass.

Cháofēng slammed through the door and ran up the staircase as easily as water flowing downhill. As he ran his Dragonsong continued, the power pushing a column of air past me like a windstorm.

Ahead of me, the open door melted like taffy, the shape shrinking down as Dragonsong changed reality before my eyes.

I launched myself into a dive and tucked through the hole just before it slammed shut. When I got to my feet I bolted for the other side of the bridge, and the next tower. A crash came from behind me. I looked back and found Cháofēng blasting through the door he'd just closed. In another moment he would clear the rubble he'd created.

Instinct took over and I jumped off the bridge. I felt the rush of air blow by as Cháofēng blinked into the space I'd just occupied. He'd missed me by a hair.

This scenario was not optimal, but staying ahead of a dragon was a losing battle. I had to change the rules. My guts changed places with my stomach as gravity vanished for a split second before reasserting itself. Forcefully.

The bridge below accelerated toward me with nightmare speed. I threw my qì out as hard as I could at the last moment in a broad kinetic strike at the walkway below me. The force slowed my fall down just enough for me to grab for the edge of the bridge as I slammed into it hard enough to lose my breath. Stars exploded across my vision as I slid down the bridge, angling to the other side. I slapped my hands on the smooth stone, desperate now. Gravity clutched at me again as my hips slipped over the edge. The stone bit deep into my gut and cracked against my lower ribs as I spread my arms wide and finally caught enough purchase on the stone to stop my fall.

Cháofēng had already spotted me though, so I let go and dropped straight down, landing on the next walkway below me. The impact shot up my legs and rattled my teeth. I rolled to bleed off the momentum and came up at a run to the far door.

The dragon landed on the bridge in front of me, shaking the structure enough to throw me to my knees. Impossibly, the delicate arch of the walkway held up under the assault.

Cháofēng drew himself up to his full height. I blinked. Batuhan looked like he was inches from death, but the dragon was stronger than ever. The power that surrounded him seared my eyes. I ducked my head to blunt the impact. He chuckled, the sound low and ominous.

"Yes, quick little dragonet. Know your place. Bow before your lord."

With a lazy flick, the dragon snapped his fingers and the bridge behind me simply vanished, the stone cleaved off just behind my heels. Thick towers of jade surrounded me on all sides, blocking my view of the street. I had nowhere to go but up or down, and down was a fifty-foot plunge onto jagged concrete. And I wasn't high enough yet for the next part of my plan.

The dragon focused his will on me and his strength became a physical weight that pressed my shoulders down, threatening to compress my bones. I gritted my teeth and locked my knees but he was too strong. I fought him down to a half crouch and kept my eye on Cháofēng. He crooned as I went down.

"There. That's better, isn't it?"

Inside my pocket I traced the carved lines of the grasshopper on the tile I'd taken from the Sun Emporium. How hard could it be? Uncle Lau made it look easy, but it would take a lot of juice to get past the dragon. I fed my qì into the tile until it was burning hot.

Cháofēng stared me down, but I was busy looking past him. There, beyond his head, I spotted a wide, translucent bridge, three stories above him. I snapped the tile and a rush of spiky energy filled my legs.

I met the dragon's eyes and spit the words past my clenched teeth. "No, it's not."

I jumped. I really jumped.

Power exploded through my legs, enough to rattle the bridge as much as when the dragon had landed. The whipping wind ripped tears from my eyes as I rocketed past the dragon. I'd been aiming for the third bridge up but I shot past that one in the first two seconds. The peak of my grasshopper-legs-fueled jump carried me over a walkway so clear it might have been made of glass. I landed on the delicate stone with a wobble and finally took a breath. I was over ten stories up and while my view of the ground was obscured by fog, I could see clear to the north, and Coit Tower.

Perfect.

Cháofēng shot past me then came down and landed in a crouch. His weight slammed into the bridge, knocking me off-balance. My guts jumped into my throat as the sky and ground switched places in rapid succession. I fell for the space of a heartbeat before a massive hand wrapped around my wrist like a steel band. I jerked to a stop, my shoulder screaming in pain as I dangled over the edge. Something snapped and my guts heaved again as I dropped another foot.

The dragon made a sound of disgust and threw me onto the walkway. I landed on all fours and backed away. Cháofēng looked down at his arm, where the elbow had snapped backward, shards of glistening white bone protruding through his skin. **"This shell is so weak. How do you tolerate this?"**

Batuhan fell to his knees as golden fluid flowed from his mouth and down the front of his tunic. He gagged and retched as the dragon re-formed himself outside of Batuhan's body.

As Cháofēng coalesced back into his dragon form, Batuhan collapsed to the stone bridge, gasping for breath. He rolled onto his back, clutching at his ruined arm. The tears streamed down his cheeks had nothing to do with the dragon. His eyes were cloudy and unfocused as he searched for me.

"Emiko."

I barely heard him. He was human again. His voice had none of the dragon's weight. Between us, Cháofēng had nearly completed his transformation.

"Emiko . . . Tell Ariq . . ."

Batuhan coughed and the spasms shook his whole body. Thick blood sprayed from his mouth. Whatever the dragon had done to him was finishing the job right before my eyes.

"Tell Ariq . . . only . . . wanted him . . . be . . . strong . . ."

He continued to shrink, as if Cháofēng was draining him of everything in order to transform. Maybe that's what was happening. Batuhan's head hit the bridge like a stone and his eyes stared sightlessly into the violet sky.

Cháofēng reared up, scales gleaming, feathers full and lush, the talons on his forelegs tapping on the stone. Was he even bigger than I remembered? He gave me a knowing smirk. **"Much better."**

A smear of brilliant orange and black flashed across my vision. Kamon's roar shook the air. A tiger was no match for a dragon, but then again, Kamon was no ordinary tiger. I'd seen him in the open ocean, clawing at the back of a nure-onna, a sea serpent ten times his size.

Kamon leapt past me, claws and talons bared. He slammed into the dragon at full speed, enough force to cave in a truck or batter down a brick wall.

Cháofēng didn't move an inch. Kamon's claws skittered uselessly across the dragon's scales as he slid to the walkway. He came up in a crouch, a rumbling growl in his chest, standing squarely between me and the dragon. Cháofēng smiled, showing all his fangs.

"Are all of you so impertinent?"

The dragon whistled one clear, piercing note of Dragonsong and Kamon collapsed. My heart leapt into my throat as the orange and black fur melted away, leaving Kamon, in human form, gasping for breath on his hands and knees. With a negligent wave of his hand, Cháofēng sent Kamon plunging off the edge of the walkway.

"No!" The scream ripped out of me as I lunged after him.

The dragon blurred and stars burst across my vision. Thick

bars like iron clamped around me, crushing my ribs, pinning my right arm against my body. Faster than I could see, Cháofēng had grabbed me. My head swam as the dragon crushed the air from my lungs. Kamon disappeared into the fog below. I caught the barest flash of orange before he vanished.

I screamed again and pounded on the dragon's claws, but I could have been beating on concrete columns for all the good I did. Kamon had shifted back to his tiger form. I had to believe that.

Cháofēng launched into the sky, so maybe breaking free from his grip wasn't the best idea. The dragon carried me past the top of the fog bank, where the violet sky of the Realm opened above us, complete with winking yellow stars. Up here, the voice of my city was less than a whisper across a crowded restaurant.

Cháofēng came to a stop and floated with easy grace. He curled down until we were nose to muzzle.

"Just where did you think you were going?"

I pushed Kamon out of my mind. Worrying about him wasn't going to get me out of this. Unfortunately my next trick was trapped in my right hand, inside the dragon's claws. I twisted in his grip, making a little space for myself in the creases of his knuckles.

"This isn't your world. I'm sending you back to the Realm."

The dragon grinned, baring a wide row of impressive fangs. **"I think not. You have given me a gift. Power unlike any I've tasted before. For that, I will allow you to live as my most honored servant."**

My elbow wiggled free with a little pop that sent a shiver of pain through my fingers. I gasped at the pain. Between the claws and Fiona's chain, my arm was getting torn to shreds. "No deal."

"Your kind were always meant to serve us. Our Great Father molded you for this. This is your purpose."

He brought me closer, until it seemed I would drown in the endless black of his eye. In his true form, the scent of his effortless power was like nothing I'd ever encountered before. The thing that was my talent awakened, as if tasting the air. For once, there was no hunger to consume this power source. As if my talent knew better. **"You feel it, do you not? Your place in this world? It is what you are."**

I pulled a little more of my arm out and lost most of the skin off my knuckles with my hand clenched around the tiles. My head swam, between the hot and cold flashing pain in my arm and the force of the dragon's will pressing down on me.

"In due time, you will learn to appreciate your station."

With one last yank I extracted my arm from the dragon's grip. A white star of pain exploded in my elbow and my vision clouded at the edges.

Cháofēng sniffed. **"Your struggle is futile. You are mine."**

My hand was a haze of scattered sensations, hot and prickly, cold and wet. The tiles were still inside my closed fingers, I could just barely feel the corners digging into my skin. I cycled and pushed my qì down my arm, igniting the tiles I'd taped together. The tile flashed with sun-bright heat. Was it bad that I couldn't feel it?

The dragon leaned close. **"Very well. Try me."**

I raised my arm. Gods, it weighed so much. My muscles and joints cried out in agony. I centered my will on my hand, willing the tortured muscles to work, to open my fingers. Light bled out around my knuckles as my hand slowly opened.

Cháofēng roared. **"Do it!"**

I released the tiles. One side was Dragon speed. It gave the barest blink of pale green light and shot out of my hand. It carried itself and the other tile past the dragon's head like a bullet, parting the feathers over one eye.

The dragon chuckled. **"So close."**

It was hard to talk around the pain. "Are all dragons so chatty?"

Somewhere above us, the second tile, Light of Heaven, exploded with the force of a small warhead. A rush of expanding air rocked my head back and managed to ruffle the dragon's feathers. The flash of light bleached this side of San Francisco in cleansing white light. Cháofēng turned to look. When the flash faded, a tiny new star hung low in the sky, casting light and shadows even through the dragon's rainstorm. My miniature sun burned away the fog below us, revealing the expanse of Lotus Lane and the armies my father had brought to repel the dragon.

Ranks upon ranks of soldiers filled the streets leading to Lotus Lane from all directions. At the center of the dragon's domain, the Byun and Borjigin armies formed a barricade around Cháofēng's palace.

From the rooftops, seventy-seven Shisa dogs took up a chorus. In the light of the new sun, their silver and gold fur shone like polished coins. As one they raised their voices and a wall of dissonant music crashed into the barrier of Cháofēng's Dragonsong. Even ten stories up Cháofēng and I both felt it, like a seismic event shaking the dragon's core.

The dragon roared. **"Impudent insects!"**

Gravity swerved as the dragon dove down. I screamed as my injured arm flailed from the sudden movement.

Cháofēng growled. **"I will teach all your kind a lesson today. You have been too long without your—"**

His words cut off as a blur of green streaked by, grazing the dragon's eye. Cháofēng screamed in rage, twisting in the air. He didn't look hurt until I looked up and spotted one of father's jade hawks wheeling through the sky, sunlight glinting off its rain-slicked stone wings. In its beak, it carried a massive, downy white feather.

The dragon opened his mouth and lightning crackled between his fangs. A bolt of electricity as thick as my leg launched from his mouth. The sudden heat flash fried my skin like an instant sunburn and blinded me. When my vision returned the hawk swooped in for another strike, and took another feather before the dragon could turn to blast it.

On the street a rallying cry rose from Father's armies as our forces marched into Lotus Lane. Even from up here I spotted Uncle Lau at the head of his troops, riding tall on the back of Father's bull. Hope surged in my chest, seeing the citizens of my city standing up to the dragon.

More of my father's animates appeared in the air. The hawks he'd brought with him, and a half-dozen wooden kites painted with soaring cranes. The kites didn't attack the dragon but their movements told me they were definitely controlled by my father.

Another streak of green flew by; this time the hawk didn't come as close but it dropped something that landed on the dragon's tail. Father's jade monkey clung to Cháofēng's scales as easily as climbing a ladder. The monkey had a little pouch tied to its back and it dropped tiles as it clambered nimbly up the dragon's body.

Tiles? Was Father stealing plays from my book?

Cháofēng twisted, bringing his jaws around to snap at the monkey. The monkey jumped off, narrowly avoiding the closing jaws and Father's hawk swept by and smoothly plucked the monkey out of midair.

One by one, the tiles burst and thick crusts of ice formed over the dragon's body, weighing him down one section at a time. Cháofēng whipped his body back and forth, breaking the ice off in huge chunks. My head spun from getting thrown around. The dragon was so wrapped up in removing the ice, he didn't notice the kites drifting closer, and the dark shadows they held underneath.

A burst of sharp, fresh ginger snapped my gaze up. The dragon's eyes widened. **"Dark walker!"**

Mother melted out of the shadows under one of Father's kites. She dropped like a stone, her haori jacket flaring open in the wind, giving the crane on her back the impression of flight. Even dropping out of midair, my mother was unflappable, with three slender kunai held between her knuckles. Her blazing eyes focused on the dragon as she fell and she shoved the kunai into the darkness inside her jacket.

Ginger bloomed.

Cháofēng's head snapped back as the blades appeared in his head, piercing through his snout from the inside. Another of Father's kites swept by underneath, and when her shadow appeared on it, Mother tucked her arms in and disappeared into the shadow.

But before she disappeared, Mother sent something to me as well, tucked into the darkness inside Cháofēng's claws. I reached inside and found a stack of Might of the Mountain tiles, already tingling and prickly, overflowing with quivering potential. I looked up. The timing had to be right. The kites moved closer and Cháofēng repositioned himself, waiting for my mother to appear again. One of the kites dipped a little.

I fed more qì into the tiles, and snapped all of them at once.

My breath exploded from me as the weight of the world landed on my chest. It also landed in the dragon's grip, dragging us down sharply. Cháofēng screamed, trying to right himself while also holding onto me. The dragon's claws slowly opened.

Ginger bloomed again.

The dragon roared. **"Mine!"**

He opened his claws and the tiles scattered to the wind. Gravity righted itself and I hung in midair for a split second. Mother appeared under the nearest kite and plummeted toward me. Her eyes were fixed on mine. I stretched my hand toward her.

With lightning reflexes, the dragon caught me, his claws wrapping around my right arm and trapping it to the elbow. I screamed in pain as he clamped down, crushing Fiona's chains into my tortured flesh.

Cháofēng dragged me close. **"You're not getting away."**

The dragon clenched down and my vision darkened from the

agonizing pressure, narrowing to the silver chains crushed into my flesh. *Unique solutions . . .*

My life had been a series of impossible choices. Why would today be any different?

With my left hand I reached over and smeared more of my blood across the chains on my upper arm. The glyphs flashed with ominous light. I prayed Fiona and Freddy would forgive me.

"I reject the Talon Call."

The chains cinched shut, chewing through muscle and tendon, cracking my bone to splinters. A bright ring of wretched agony encircled my arm. Blood sprayed, hot and sticky.

My voice wobbled with pain. "Witness."

Fiona's chains crushed down like ancestral disappointment. The pulling sensation started in the center of my chest, and traveled down my arm, a too-tight string. And then the last sinew gave way and I was falling, Cháofēng staring stupidly at me as I dropped away from him in an expanding fountain of blood.

Mother's weight slammed into me and her arms locked tight around my chest, her face hot against my neck. Her breath tickled my ear as roaring winds whistled past.

"Fall back, Emi-chan. I've got you."

Ginger bloomed and darkness swallowed us.

PHOENIX

Scents and sounds came at me in the darkness. Deep, aching pain throbbed at the center of my world like some auxiliary heart that existed solely to torment me. Muffled voices shouted in the distance as hands pulled me back and forth. Someone was crying, a raw sound of agony.

The pain pulsed again and the voices grew more distant. I wrapped the growing silence around me like a protective cloak. If I hid myself well enough, the pain wouldn't find me. Maybe then, I could get some rest.

My world shrank to a tiny bubble. I pushed everything else out and curled into myself.

The smell of tobacco tickled my nose.

"She's done. What a waste."

"She is not. And you know it."

More smoke. "It won't work."

"I must try. I owe it to her. And we need her. We all do."

Why wouldn't the voices go away? I curled in tighter.

Something came through my bubble. I pushed back, frantic, but I was powerless. Whatever it was, the force passed through my defenses like they didn't even exist. Huge hands, or the impression of hands, grabbed me, moved me, gently.

The voice moved closer, closer, until the voice was inside my head.

"This will feel a bit strange."

My bubble was obliterated and the world returned in an instant. Rain poured down around me, but not on me. In the distance, voices screamed and weapons clashed. The scent of a dozen blazing talents clogged my senses. My clothes were soaking wet, and biting cold crept up my limbs toward my core.

The huge man looming over me had a pleasant smile on his face and a polished naginata over his shoulder. His eyes twinkled with kindness as he placed a finger on my chest and exploded my world.

Silence again, but this time it was familiar. I opened my eyes and found myself in the heart of San Francisco, the eye at the center of my city's power. Only, I had never been here with someone else before.

I looked down at myself. Despite the beating I'd taken, I felt good. I looked good. Both my arms were here. I flexed my right hand and marveled at the absence of pain. What had happened?

Oda Tanaka walked around the space, staring out into the swirling currents of power. He wore better armor than when I'd last seen him, and all the pieces matched. While his trusted naginata rode high on his back, he still carried Crimson Cloud Splitter on his hip, the scarlet scabbard as elegant as a stroke of calligraphy.

He studied my city's energy like he was reading it. "This is fascinating."

"You don't have this back home?"

Oda turned to me. "The city is shaped by the Sentinel. Whatever you need to understand your city, it conforms to you."

His gaze crossed the expanse of the city's eye. "Your mind clearly works very . . . differently from mine."

I chose to be the bigger person and let that slide. "What are you doing here?"

He made a face. "You should have seen Gu Ma. Angry as I've

ever seen her. Complaining that the Archive isn't a train station. Do you know how upset she must be to get her to leave the Library?"

I choked. "She's here?"

"Well, not here. But she's standing over your body. Refused to let your father's medics touch you. Said she wouldn't trust them to put bandages on a limping ox. But it's fine, I sealed your wound with a lightning strike from Crimson Cloud Splitter." He sounded proud of himself.

That took a moment to sink in. "Am I dying?"

His eyes dropped to my arm. "Do you remember what happened?"

A cloud of disappointment settled on me. "I'm guessing this isn't really my arm?"

He shook his head. "Just like this isn't really your body. We're metaphysically in your city right now. Our bodies are on Lotus Lane. And when you freed yourself from Cháofēng, you left him with a significant quantity of your blood."

Oda turned and pointed beyond the wall of the eye. In the midst of the swirling energy patterns, little turbulent whorls disrupted the flow. When I concentrated on the turbulence, the dissonant music I'd heard before returned. Dragonsong. "As we speak, Cháofēng is using your blood to exert his control over your city."

The old dragon had been worming his way into my city from the moment he got here. And I just made it a lot easier for him.

"Is that why Gu Ma is here?"

He nodded. "She is the check against the Sentinels. This is her duty."

"What will she do?"

Oda frowned. "Gu Ma will not allow Cháofēng to obtain the power of a Sentinel. She will destroy you before that happens. But . . ."

Again, a statement, not a threat.

"I'm not going to make it, am I?"

He gave me a pained expression. "Your wound is grave. Even with the city supporting you, you will not last long. Gu Ma is here simply to ensure that . . ."

"What happens to my city?"

The big man's eyes turned sad. "The Sentinel and the city are one. When you are gone, San Francisco's power goes with you. There will be nothing for Cháofēng to take."

"So what, you're here to hold my hand while Gu Ma ends me?"

Oda rubbed his chin. "It's actually very hard to kill a Sentinel. Especially in their city, with a mature Pearl."

I put a hand on my chest, over the scar next to my sternum. "My Pearl isn't mature. You told me that. The way you said it, it's not going to happen anytime soon."

"You can mature it faster. But it's dangerous."

"More dangerous than a dragon in my city?"

Oda smiled. "Touché."

In the whirling energies outside this space, Cháofēng's Dragonsong grew in strength. As I watched, the dragon's power spread through my city, my people. San Francisco fought back, but now that the dragon had my blood, even I could see the inevitable. My city would fight to the bitter end. Could I do anything else?

"How do I mature my Pearl faster?"

"You may lose yourself."

"This is my duty. To my city."

Oda's eyes flashed. "Open yourself to your city. Truly open yourself. Become one with it, in all its glory."

I was the Sentinel. The Butcher. The Blade of Soong. The Broken Tooth. Lóng Jiārén. My life had been filled with risk and danger, but I always protected my family. Now the city was my family, and I would go to any length to protect it. I nodded to the old Sentinel. "I'm ready."

Oda smiled grimly. "Good. Take us back."

I took Oda's hand and the eye vanished.

My eyes opened to rainwater dripping down on me from the brim of Gu Ma's knitted cap. One of her eyes was hidden behind the glowing ember of her cigarette. She sucked on the cigarette and blew out a cloud of blue-gray smoke. "Do not disappoint me, girl."

Oda appeared at Gu Ma's side with a large umbrella. She squinted up at him. "And you should be getting back to your city where you belong."

The big man ducked his head in a bow. "Yes, Gu Ma. Of course." His eyes smiled, but his manner was respectful.

When Gu Ma shuffled off with her walker, Oda gripped my shoulder. "The city is you. And you are the city. Remember that."

As they moved away my mother rushed in and helped me sit. A wave of dizziness passed through me and I made the mistake of looking at my arm. The mangled mass of flesh was a jarring dissonance with the fact that I could still feel my hand.

Mother cupped my cheek and turned me away from my arm. "Emi-chan, how . . . ?"

I clutched at her with my left hand. "I'll explain later. Help me up."

She was right. I should have been dead just from shock and blood loss. But the thumping double beat in my chest kept me alive. My city was keeping me alive. For now.

My father's men had put me in a side alley off Lotus Lane. Just a block away the fighting was intense, with swords clashing and talents flying back and forth.

I was looking at just the right spot when Freddy popped out of one of his signature tunnels and landed on the backs of a couple Borjigin soldiers who had been bearing down on a group of Louie enforcers. Before the Borjigin could get up he opened another tunnel and flung the soldiers across the street, where they crashed into a knot of Byun soldiers. He waved to the Louies and turned to open another exit tunnel for himself. I gasped at the bloody ruin of his left eye. Then he ducked into the tunnel and vanished.

Mother pulled me close and shifted my gaze up.

Cháofēng was enormous. I'd never heard of dragons this big. His body was as thick as the Louie bank. His shadow left all of Lotus Lane in dim twilight. As I looked across my city, I felt his power growing, and the changes he'd made to Lotus Lane expanding beyond its borders. The Shisa dogs were still humming, but their song had grown weaker. Any minute now, and Cháofēng would burst through and claim my city.

My father had done the impossible. He'd brought the Trans and Louies together to do their duty for the city and our people. Could I do any less?

I looked to Mother. "Did Father . . . ?"

She picked up the cherrywood box at her feet. "Your father is ever prepared."

I traced my finger over the smooth lacquer. Yes, his plans surrounded us and guided us to success. The only question was whether I was strong enough. The box's presence indicated my father's opinion on that. I would need every advantage at my disposal.

I opened the box and pulled out the blood jade bracelet. Mother affixed it around my wrist and fresh energy surged through me. She put the rest of the jewelry on me, and by the time she was done my teeth were nearly vibrating.

I wasn't too close to the dragon here. San Francisco's song was faint, but present. When I called to my city it answered and strengthened my legs. Mother felt my stance firm up and she let me go. I clasped her hand awkwardly with mine. It felt strangely appropriate.

"Thank you for saving me. I've got it from here."

She nodded and her eyes gleamed. "I know."

Like Mother had said before, it was all about trust. Did you trust your power? Did you trust your resolve? Did you trust yourself?

I did.

I closed my eyes and fell back into my city.

Cháofēng was a rot on my city, a black stain spreading out from Lotus Lane. He ate up San Francisco's power and it swelled him like a bloated worm.

But Cháofēng was just a dragon. He wasn't a Sentinel. He saw the wellspring of power below the city like a Hoard to be taken. Like a dragon, he ignored the people.

I opened my mind and my heart to my city and let the power flow into me, full force, and I shunted it into my Pearl. My chest swelled until it felt like my ribs would shatter. San Francisco's power coursed through me and swirled into my Pearl. It pulsed and writhed like a living thing. The thin membrane that kept my mind my own dissolved away in the face of that power. I had always been afraid of losing myself to the hundreds of thousands of minds in my city. But there was strength in numbers as well.

The knot in my chest grew hot and tingly with the influx of so much power. It beat with a rhythm that interwove with my own heartbeat. As more of the city rolled in, the beat quickened, until my chest was a vibrating thrum of energy.

Instead of just taking on the city's power, I reached for my people as well. Like I'd done with the police sergeant, but this time I cast my net wide until it covered the city. Thousands of souls called out in response, a ringing chorus of power that hummed through me.

I opened my eyes and found myself floating a foot off the ground. My qì flew through my meridians and filled me to bursting, but I knew this still wasn't enough. Mother hadn't moved. I reached into my pocket and gave her the dragon tooth. "Tell Madam Yao to be ready. It's time. Tell her I said thank you."

Mother gave me a quick nod and dropped into her shadow.

I rose above the buildings and called out to the city again. Again, a new chorus of voices joined their strength with mine. I raised our voices and they boomed across the sky. **"Cháofēng, the Sentinel of San Francisco is here!"**

The dragon turned, his black eyes huge and incredulous. **"The rabbit."**

He opened his mouth and Dragonsong burst forth, a titanic wave of sound and power. It was the dragon's willpower made real, the resolve of a god pressing down on me. On the street, the fighting came to a standstill as every Jiārén within hearing froze in place. Cháofēng's Dragonsong slammed into me and shoved me back.

Behind me, the city pushed back. It had been faint before, but with my people singing with me, the song of San Francisco rose in volume. My Pearl swelled again, and the extra heartbeat in my chest strengthened. I took up the melody and like the Shisas' harmonics, it struck a chord that I felt in my core. I opened my mouth and the citysong came out, a counterpoint to the dragon's power. The wave smashed the dragon in the face and sent him reeling.

The dragon crashed into his fortress and caved in the wall. Shards of crystalline jade rained down on him. Cháofēng shook himself off, his eyes wary now. He sniffed, and turned back to the remains of the bank.

I smelled it, too. A fortune in Hoard. The Louies, the Trans, and whoever stored pieces at the bank. It was nearly every piece of Hoard in the entire city. Cháofēng laughed with glee and dove into the bank.

Oh, no. I chased after him, a moment too late.

Cháofēng burst out of the bank with a river of glittering gold and silver trailing behind him. Far more treasure than my mother had used to create her Gate. The dragon rose into the sky, crowing in triumph. Hoard gold swirled into a tight orbit in front of the dragon. He sang his Dragonsong and the formation closed, tighter and tighter, until the pieces began to meld together into a massive sphere of gold and jewels.

Sharp, prickling panic rose up from the city. I had to protect the Hoard. At any cost. My Pearl swelled again, and pain arced across my chest as my ribs cracked.

A thousand lights rose up from the city, each one a small piece of one of San Francisco's residents, Jiārén and Wàirén alike. Another thousand, and another. More and more, until a river of lights flowed to me from the skyline. Power draped over me, one layer at a time. The lights blanketed over my shoulders like a glittering cloak of stars. Light and color shifted and flowed through the mass as the shape of the cloak stretched behind me, and out along my arms. I flexed my missing right arm and felt the lights extend, completing this form.

At my back, the stars tinted red and fanned out into a tail of feathers stretching twice the length of my body. Down both arms the colors became green and yellow, extending out to graceful wings. My Pearl felt like it filled my chest to bursting. Around my head the stars went black and formed a hooked beak, open wide in a defiant shriek.

My voice shook the city. **"Not a rabbit. A phoenix."**

With the strength of the city behind me I reached out and pulled the Hoard away from the dragon. He met my force with his own, and the globe of treasure stopped between us. The Pearl in my chest thumped like a drum and fresh energy surged through me. I pulled the Hoard closer.

Cháofēng screamed with rage and sent his Dragonsong at me like a spear. I spread my wings and my citysong tore his magic apart again.

White legs with powerful talons formed below me. I surged forward and rammed into the dragon. The force of our impact exploded across the sky. The blast wave flattened everyone on Lotus

Lane and blew windows out of buildings for blocks in every direction. The Hoard wobbled in the air and I wrapped the city's power around it, cradling it tight. Heat baked off the molten surface.

Cháofēng flew toward me, eyes blazing. **"Mine!"**

His willpower crashed around me like a wave breaking on the rocks. I blocked out the pain and kept my grip on the Hoard, pulling it closer to me.

Again and again, Cháofēng pummeled me. San Francisco wrapped me in protective layers, drawing me and the Hoard to the ground. And then I knew what the city wanted.

I waited until Cháofēng charged me. This time I let the dragon slam into me and the force drove us both into the street. Our massive bodies tore up the asphalt for an entire block. I twisted and got the Hoard in contact with the bare earth.

San Francisco's melody rang out in triumph. The pain of my wounds faded for only a glorious instant as cool mist washed over me. The dragon roared and clawed at the gold but with each second the city devoured the treasure, pulling it into itself. A murder of crows circled us, their caws a rising soundtrack to the city's absorption of a fortune in Jiārén power-drenched gems. I put my hand over the scar on my chest, my heart thudding in my ears. As the massive Hoard disappeared I saw it pulse in time with the Pearl in my chest.

The earth closed, accepting my offering, and something opened in the back of my mind. The rest of San Francisco's power came to me.

A storm of power swept me up like a leaf in a hurricane. Wind and water swirled around me. Before, when I had come close to the city, I had let fear drive me. Fear of losing myself to the storm, because I viewed the mantle of the Sentinel as another set of chains to hold me down. Fear of losing my identity, as the millions of minds in San Francisco crowded around mine.

But I had been wrong.

Losing myself to the city was impossible, for I was the city. The city was me.

The power had limits, and responsibilities, but here in the heart of my city, they certainly were not chains.

The storm calmed as my mind merged with the city, and I floated weightless in a sea of quiet power. Before, I had felt the need to fight the city, to make my place within it. That fell away now, as the city took its place in me.

More lights flowed up to me, growing my wingspan, thickening my legs. The strength of countless minds stood behind me, pushing me up. Their memories flowed over and through me. Instead of fighting it, I rode the wave with effortless grace and let it carry me forward. Faces, names, and emotions flitted across my mind, each person willing to give a little of themselves to protect the city. To protect me.

Cháofēng swelled in size and struck again. He kept growing in size, his strength limning his torso with a perilous blue fire. I took the blow on one wing and it sent me spinning. When I stopped, Madam Yao and my mother hovered in front of me on the back of the qílín.

The petite fox spirit was inordinately happy. "Emiko! This is just what I was hoping for!"

I tried to say something, but words were hard now. Cities didn't speak, not like people. Cities existed, they sheltered, they protected.

Madam Yao seemed to sense my difficulty. "We've brought the Gate. It's at the top of the fortress."

Her words slid off me like rain, but something of the meaning came through. I had to get rid of the dragon. My wings flapped and a fog bank rose to blanket the city. I raised my head and called out, and a peal of thunder was my voice. I burst through the fog and found Cháofēng waiting for me.

The dragon opened his mouth and lightning ignited between his horns. He came at me again, his face twisted with fury. Thick bolts of lightning rained down from the heavens, cracking the sky open. I wove between them and let the dragon chase me back to his fortress. Cháofēng probably thought the jade palace was his seat of power. But the entire city was my seat of power.

I soared to the top of the castle, following the jade towers as they rose into the sky. Cháofēng followed, throwing more lightning after me.

Mother stood on the highest arch, between the qílín and the huli jing. Above them, a fortune in Hoard gold and jewels hovered in the sky. The damaged Gate leaked power around the edges that lit up the sky with showers of sparks.

When she spotted me she raised her arms and the ginger scent of her talent filled the world. Sara Hiroto, the most powerful dark walker in generations, ripped open the Gate. Above her head, the gold and jewels flowed like jelly, pulling away to reveal a gaping hole in the sky.

Sara was important. Without her, the dragon would remain here. She was not a citizen of my city, but she was helping. With her help the Gate of gold and jewels disappeared into nothingness and the portal to the Realm stood open.

Cháofēng spotted the Gate a second too late. He tried to veer off but I folded my wings and fell onto him like a stone. My claws wrapped around his serpentine body. I tried to crush him like a worm, but his scales were too strong, too tightly fitted. He writhed in my grip, spitting runners of electricity that crawled up my legs. I spread my wings and flew up to the open Gate.

Sara held her arms out, sweat beading on her forehead. Behind her, the huli jing and the qílín braced her back, lending their power to her. It was time to send the dragon back where he came from. Away from my city.

I rose up until I was over the Gate. The searing energies of the Void blasted out of the open portal, but these were nothing I worried about. Cháofēng screamed in rage as I lowered him into the Gate.

At the edge of the portal, the dragon reached out with his claws and hooked them into the edges. With a surge of power, Cháofēng grabbed hold of reality itself and stopped himself from falling into the Realm. I pushed, leaning the weight of my city on the dragon, but he didn't move. We were at a stalemate. He was trapped, but I couldn't leave. I pushed again.

And again.

And again.

The huli jing's voice was quiet and musical. "You're sure, Sara?"

"Yes. Take me to her first, please."

The qílín floated before me, with Sara and the huli jing again on its back. They drifted closer until they entered the cloak of stars that surrounded me. I didn't know why, but I felt I could trust them with this much. The qílín came close enough for Sara to trace her hand along my jaw. I couldn't look at her, not as I tried to force the dragon through the portal. Sparks and flares of light spewed from the edges where the dragon had dug in his talons.

Sara moved away, changing something, before coming back to me. Something settled around my shoulders. It was warm, and smelled familiar. She came close and put herself in my line of sight, her eyes searching mine. Then she wrapped her arms around my neck and put her lips to my cheek.

"I know you're in there. Know that I have always been proud of you, and I will find a way back to you."

The huli jing handed Sara a naginata with a blade made of chipped, polished black stone. Sara took another look at me and jumped off the qílín's back. She plummeted to the open portal and landed on the dragon's belly, right between my claws.

Sara reversed her naginata and slid the blade between the dragon's scales, slipping it deep into his flesh. With the blade to anchor her, she raised her other arm. Her dark walker powers surged again, another burst of ginger scent, and the portal began to close.

Cháofēng screamed but I held him down, pushing him farther in as the opening narrowed. Inch by inch the portal closed over him. Sara held one arm up, drawing reality shut over her head. Her eyes stayed on me as the rift between our worlds shrunk to a pinpoint.

At the last moment, my mind found words again and my heart, my real heart, clenched into a tight ball of agony. "Mother!"

My mother gave me a smile as the portal closed with a pop. The dragon's scream cut out. The only thing that remained was one talon, sheared off with as clean a cut as I'd ever seen. Madam Yao caught it before it could fall.

The fox spirit tucked the talon away in her pocket and drew close to me. "Emiko, are you there?"

Words were still hard, but I held onto the sharp blade of pain twisting in my heart. Something wet ran down my cheek. "Mother . . ."

"Come back to us. It's what your mother wanted."

"Mother . . ."

Madam Yao touched my forehead and a calming energy spread from that spot. It felt like springtime. "You are the Sentinel, not the city. You are Emiko Soong, daughter of Sara Hiroto. Come back, Emiko."

Hearing Mother's name did something. The door in the back of my mind slowly swung closed, blocking out the city. As the power drained from me, I broke. Color washed out of my cloak of stars and the image of the phoenix dissolved into a shifting sea of lights. The lights wheeled like a flock of birds and spread out beneath me, returning to my people.

I slumped and the qílín caught me neatly on its back. Madam Yao snuggled up behind me, her arms sure and strong around my waist.

My mind returned to me. Finally just me again, and the tears came. I clutched at the haori Mother had draped over my shoulders. The one with the majestic crane in flight across the back. Her anchor. I took a huge, hitching breath, and the scent of her filled me with exquisite pain.

Madam Yao sniffled. "It was the only way."

"She said she would come back."

The fox spirit rubbed her face against my back. "Without her anchor . . ."

I finished the sentence. ". . . the dragons can't force her to open a portal to come back."

The qílín blew a melancholy note through its horns.

Madam Yao laughed, the sound tinged with tears. "True, but now Emiko can be our friend."

That got a clearer note from the qílín. I didn't know what they were talking about, and I was too tired to ask.

Madam Yao snuggled against my back. "I don't know about you, but I'm tired. I could sleep for an age now. I hope we don't have to get up early tomorrow."

The qílín began a slow descent and blew a questioning note. Madam Yao mumbled something sleepy and patted her pocket, where she'd put Cháofēng's talon.

"Of course I have it. And I did tell you it would all work out."

I didn't know if she was talking to me or the qílín. Then sleep pulled me under, and I didn't care.

SENTINEL

Battle was chaos, even in the aftermath. Possibly more so.

My spirits, already dangerously in flux from banishing the dragon and my mother in one stroke, threatened to crash and burn as I walked through the ruins of Lotus Lane. The flood waters were nearly gone, but the damage was done. And little had been built that could withstand the destructive power of gāo-level talents, much less dozens of those talents at once.

Lotus Lane, the heart of San Francisco's Jiārén community . . . the heart of my community, was gutted. Rubble clogged the street for as far as I could see. Storefronts lay in ruin, generations of labor reduced to shards and splinters. Only one of the iconic pillars in front of the Sun Emporium remained intact, but it was nearly unrecognizable, the once-vivid paint covered in thick layers of dust and mud.

And as painful as it was to see Lotus Lane covered in dust and soaked in seawater, the twisting knife was the merchants themselves. With Cháofēng's Dragonsong only an echo in our minds, the residents of Lotus Lane had begun to trickle back in to survey the damage. Many simply collapsed to their knees in tears at the sight of the destruction. Rebuilding would take years. To my Sentinel senses, the entire stretch of Lotus Lane felt like a fresh wound, the edges raw and bloody.

Every time I took a step, even that little impact jarred my right arm enough to ignite a star of pain that shot through my shoulder.

That pain set off spasms that started in my nonexistent elbow that ran down to my nonexistent fingers. I gritted my teeth and kept to the shadows, my arm clamped tight to my chest. These people didn't need me bothering them, but I felt like I needed to be here. How could I wallow in my pain, and not witness theirs? As their Sentinel, I was responsible for this. The least I could do was to not hide from it.

Moving quietly was hard with all the shattered concrete and glass. Losing my arm had also done a number on my balance. Across the street from Golden Dragon Potstickers, my heel slipped on a scree of loose rock and my leg shot out from under me. Agonizing visions of landing on my arm flashed through my head and I twisted like a fish out of water. I ended up in a tangle of limbs and even though I'd wrenched my right arm out of the way it didn't stop a fresh avalanche of pain from whiting out my vision.

Color slowly leached back into my world as the throbbing in my shoulder calmed to a mere taiko drum. I must have cried out because my world darkened again as several people approached. My feet scraped against the broken concrete as I shoved myself back, suddenly afraid.

I'd failed them. Lotus Lane was in ruins because of me. My heart pounded against my battered ribs and each beat sent a fresh wave of agony blooming out from my arm.

My vision swirled again as a large figure squatted in front of me. It took a moment for my eyes to refocus and bring Chef Kelly's stern features out of the shadows. A deep frown line creased her brow, and her chef jacket, usually crisp and white, was loose and torn, covered in soot and stains.

Kelly's eyes were dark and unreadable. They traveled over and above me, and down to the ruined stump of my arm. She extended one calloused hand to me.

"Come, Sentinel. Let's get you on your feet."

When our hands touched a pulse of San Francisco's power

spread up from the contact. The cooling energy soothed my nerves and dulled the pain in my arm. Kelly's strong fingers wrapped around mine and pulled me up. Voices whispered my name and spread through the crowd. More merchants rushed up to support me and help me walk to the center of the street.

I didn't want to be here. Not like this, not while everyone had to deal with this disaster. Not when there were so many more important things to do. But Kelly's hand would not let go, and the hands at my back propelled me forward. Pushing me toward my judgment.

Once I was in the street, dozens of eyes locked on me, an endless parade of the people of my city. All of them were weary from fear. Like trees bowing before the storm, they hunched under the stress of the destruction of their livelihoods. One more strong gust, and they might break. What could I do for them?

I opened my mouth, but how could I possibly apologize for the magnitude of their loss?

Kelly waved an arm at the gathering crowd. "What are you staring at? Have you never seen our Sentinel before? You're making her uncomfortable!"

Tears stung my eyes and I squeezed down on Kelly's hand.

After Kelly's proclamation some people went about their business, but many more approached. They stopped a good ten feet from me and bowed deeply. Most of them carried small children in their arms. Children who were awake, and clearly wondering what had happened while they were asleep. The adults all said the same thing as they bowed.

"Blessings for our Sentinel."

Kelly leaned in and whispered, "My nephew just woke up as well. Thank you, Sentinel."

I turned to her but she cut me off before I could speak.

"Still just one order per week."

I squeezed her hand again. "Thank you, Kelly."

Chef Kelly stood with me for another hour as more people came up to offer thanks.

The last time I'd seen Freddy, he'd clearly taken some hard hits. I went to the medical tents to see if I could find him. Instead, I found several of my father's soldiers wrestling with a thin young man who lay on the sidewalk next to a wrecked wheelchair.

Ariq's aura wasn't quite what it had been under Cháofēng's influence, but it was quite a sight to see. No wonder my father's soldiers were concerned. Ariq seemed like a bomb in the midst of detonating.

I waded into the men and pulled out one of them at random. He whirled on me and immediately bowed his head when he saw who I was.

The soldier spoke without looking at me. "Emiko-san! I mean, Sentinel, or . . ."

I sighed. "Either is fine. Call your men back. Let me handle this."

"Are you . . . ?"

I was really tired, so my death stare was probably at half strength at best. Still, it was enough to back the man off and he quickly pulled the others off Ariq, leaving the young man struggling to get back into his wheelchair. Unfortunately, the dustup had attracted a lot of eyeballs, and once again I was the center of attention.

Ariq moaned, the sound thick with the kind of nuanced pain that I was an unfortunate expert in. I didn't have the luxury of waiting for privacy. As if sensing my need, the city's power flowed up beneath me, filling my meridians with cool, salt-tinged power.

The border between myself and the city was still there, a tenuous border, but now that I had crossed it and returned, it wasn't so . . . final. Like a friendly neighbor, I knew I could traverse that line and still remain myself. I knelt at Ariq's side and placed a hand on his brow. His skin was fever hot and clammy with sweat. He barely noticed my touch as his eyes rolled and his jaw clenched.

Ariq's convulsions slowed as his talent devoured his qì. With my Sentinel eyes, it was easy to see that Father's estimation had been correct. Ariq's Hoard gift was self-destructive, and startlingly similar to mine. Why was it turned in on himself? Could he be trained to direct it outward, and spare himself? Would Jiārén suffer the existence of another talent like mine?

This was the fate Batuhan had been trying to save his son from. Given the choice between self-destruction or exile, he'd tried to navigate a third path for his son.

I'd found an alternate path for myself. How could I not do the same for Ariq?

I dipped into San Francisco's power, a vast lake of quiet stillness. At the same time, I released the tightness I held in my gut, the chains I held over my talent. Freddy had been right. It wasn't a separate thing inside me. It had only ever been me, and I was done holding myself back. My power leapt out of me with easy, feline grace, and plunged into Ariq.

Memories poured into me. Riding on horseback across the steppes. A chorus of a thousand voices raised in triumph.

Joy.

Pride.

Pain.

Shame.

Ariq's memories were a song I knew all too well. And this time, with the might of the city beside me, I rode the wave of his emotions without being overwhelmed. My Pearl was larger now, and it helped, acting as a buffer, blunting the surge of power rushing into me.

I wasn't sure what it looked like, but I caught gasps of surprise, possibly horror, at the edges of my perception. None of them mattered and I refocused my concentration on Ariq.

The black tendrils of my talent carved into the kaleidoscope of Ariq's aura, blotting it out like an eclipse. I swallowed huge chunks of his talent and cycled his power away, shunting it off to my Pearl and my city. Slowly, the pained arch of Ariq's back relaxed and he settled to the ground. As my talent reduced Ariq's to manageable levels, the lines of agony etched around his eyes faded.

When his aura was down to a faint line, he drew a shuddering breath and looked at me. It took a while for recognition to dawn in his eyes. When it did, some of the lines around his eyes returned as he drew the obvious conclusions. His gaze went to where my arm used to be and I resisted the urge to hide it.

"Is . . . ?"

I shook my head.

Ariq closed his eyes for a long moment. "It wasn't supposed to be like this."

If there was one thing I could do for him, it was to not blame him for his father's actions. "I know. He only wanted you to be strong."

Ariq sat up and buried his face in his hands. Only then did he notice that he wasn't in pain. "How . . . ?"

I explained to him what I'd done. Tears overflowed his eyes.

It was maybe the first time someone hadn't recoiled in horror, learning what my talent did. It was certainly the first time someone seemed grateful for it. His tears weren't all sad, as little hiccups of laughter broke through here and there. I knew then that I would open my city to him, let him stay in San Francisco and live as normal a life as possible. He didn't have to rely on blood jade to live here. If Colin and Tatsuya were going to be here, why not Ariq as well? If I wanted to change how we did things, I'd have to start with myself. It was up to me to set the example.

PROMISES

I was exhausted. Heartsore. Beaten bloody. And missing an arm.

It was all making it very hard to deal with my father. In the aftermath of the battle, he had applied his masterful administrator skills to triaging the wounded, detaining the Borjigin and Byun soldiers, and claiming any Hoard jewels from defeated combatants. He was very good at his job and for some reason, it angered me.

He had set up a wide table under a field tent in the center of Lotus Lane, at the very spot where I'd placed my Pearl of Hoard gold into the city, I noticed. There was no need to wonder if he'd chosen this spot by accident, but I couldn't see his angle. Unspoken between us was how I had failed to fulfill the Tran talon, which was a Soong obligation. Certainly I had saved all of us, so my father's silence on this matter was his de facto acceptance of my actions.

A line of Iron Fists waited patiently, their hands and arms laden with jewelry won in battle. As each soldier approached, Father made a notation in his journal and the valuables were evenly loaded into two large cases on the table. His eyes flicked over to acknowledge me, but he did not stop his writing. His gaze did not linger on the spot where my arm used to be.

"The soldiers aren't keeping the spoils?"

Father shook his head. "Everything we collect will be inventoried. We will send a portion to Jimmy and Fiona. Seed Hoards to get their houses back on their feet."

"Charity?"

He raised an eyebrow. "Do you really think so little of me?"

No, of course not. This move cost him nothing. Our soldiers did not want for Hoard gems, or weapons; my father and Uncle Lau saw to that. For the cost of some time and tabulating, he could have two houses in San Francisco beholden to him for their recovery. Very efficient.

Within a few years, Father could move his businesses into San Francisco, his road paved with Tran and Louie favors. Except, this was my city, and if the last few days had taught me anything, it was that we needed to do better.

"It occurs to me that this battle was fought in my city."

Father's pen stopped moving. He didn't look up at me, just froze in place for a moment. The Iron Fists took the hint and they backed up until they were well out of hearing range. My father set his pen down and fixed me with his calm gaze.

That look used to paralyze me. It wasn't exactly comfortable, but I found I could tolerate it now. He wasn't being malicious, he simply wanted to extract the most from everything, including me. I forced my hands—my hand—to relax.

His silence was an invitation for me to make my argument. "You brought the Soong Clan to my city to fight on behalf of my house, and my Hoard. You said so yourself."

Did the lines around his eyes tighten a little? His poker face was masterful. "My soldiers bled and died on behalf of your house and your Hoard."

"The disposition of those spoils goes to the leader of the house that claims the territory. That's me."

"It occurs to me that your house has yet to be recognized as such. And to claim an entire city as your territory would seem to stretch credulity."

I put my fist down on the table and reached for the city. With the Pearl below my feet it was as easy as reaching down and grabbing a handful of dirt. I let a sliver of my Sentinel authority into my voice.

"This. Is. **My** city."

A shiver went through the air and ruffled the flaps of the tent. Father's journal pages rippled in the wind. He looked down to his book, but before he did, I swore I saw a smile grace his lips. When he looked back up he'd schooled his expression.

"Very well. What are your wishes for the disposition of the spoils?"

Could Father hear how fast my heart was beating right now? "Half each to the Louies and the Trans. You'll tell them it's from me. No strings."

The lines around his eyes softened. "Mimi. Just saying there are no strings attached does not mean there are no strings attached."

"It does if I say it. You also said it. Things are changing. We need to change how we do things, how we treat each other. I'm starting here."

Father waved his hands at the two chests. The amount of Hoard gems inside each was paltry, less even than the Winner's Pot at Tatsuya's Tourney. "The Trans and the Louies were nearly crushed today, their Hoards stolen, their strength crippled. What you hope to do . . . They will not see this as the act of a friend."

He was right, of course. Our lives did not allow for these kinds of things. Power was not something given. It was taken. But when I thought of Leanna, Freddy, and Fiona, I knew I had to at least try. "They may not see it that way, but I know what it is."

He took a long moment, simply taking me in, before he gave me his customary short nod of approval. Father raised his hand to wave the Iron Fists forward, but I waved them back. My little victory gave me the nerve to ask, so I wasn't going to let the moment pass.

"How can you do this?" My voice broke a little at the end.

He seemed genuinely confused. “Do what?”

I wanted to explode, but I wouldn’t do it in front of the Iron Fists. I waved my arm at all the cleanup going on, the utter mundanity of it all. Like we were tidying up after a particularly bad party. “All this! You put up a good front, but I know you loved Mother.”

I couldn’t hold it all back and tears streamed down my cheeks. I thought I’d been fine, spending most of my life without her. The last few weeks had shown me just how much I really needed her. The ache in my heart was a hole I could never fill. If I tested the boundaries of it too closely, I would fall in and never come out. “How can you sit there when Mother is gone?! What are we going to tell Tacchan?”

Father’s expression didn’t change. “I will tell him what I always tell both of you. Your mother is away, but she will return when she can.”

Before I could really explode, he raised a hand. “In the years we have been together, your mother has never shied from a challenge. She has performed the kinds of feats that are written of our heroes. What was the last thing she said to you?”

I felt myself tipping toward the hole, but I made myself say the words. “She said she would find a way back to me.”

“There. That is all I need. She said she will return. I have complete faith in her. To act any differently is a disrespect to her.”

“But—”

“Do you really think the Walker of the Void will be hampered simply because she doesn’t have her anchor? Do you think so little of her as well?”

“Wait, what? What do you know?”

Father waved the Iron Fists forward and returned to tabulating. “You can ask your mother yourself when she returns.”

I stepped away and let him get back to business, his words spinning through my head like a storm. Trying to hold the thoughts down was like trying to catch leaves on the wind. How was he so good at throwing me off-balance? His every statement was precise and measured, designed to hit with maximum effect. What effect?

What effect was he trying to produce in me? What shift in perspective?

Father's mind was a web of possibilities stretching into the unknown dark. Except maybe it wasn't all dark. He discarded unlikely scenarios, turning his energy to those with higher probabilities.

I didn't doubt that he knew more about Mother's dark-walking than anyone else alive, with Mother herself as the only exception. He knew her history, her training, her capabilities.

Of course Father had foreseen this outcome.

Of course Mother was alive, she'd found the Realm before and returned.

Of course Father had predicted this, and he would have formulated plans, with plans within those plans, because that's what he did. He left nothing to chance.

And so he focused on the utterly mundane task of leading our clan, tabulating jewelry, because he'd already planned for this. Mother was on the other side of the Void, fighting for her life in the Realm, evading Cháofēng, possibly other dragons, and plotting her return to our world. Just another day at work for the Walker of the Void.

I had trusted Mother enough to free myself from Cháofēng's grasp when we were over ten stories in the air. Father had brought the warring clans of my city together. Trusting them to find Mother a way back from the Realm was no effort at all.

When the soldier before Father turned away I stepped into the gap, bringing the line to a halt. I gave my father a bow.

"Thank you, Father, for the lesson. Again."

He inclined his head. "You have been . . . an exceptional student."

Something bloomed deep within me. It was warm, comfortable, sharp, and painful. It felt like a start and an ending.

Father's gaze went to the ruined buildings around us. "Don't you have work you should be doing?"

I smiled. The reward for work well done was more work. I had a lot of work to put my city, and my people, back together.

My thoughts turned again to Mother as I left Father to his work. The more I considered, the more I started to feel bad for the dragons.

HEALING

My healing was going well enough, according to the doctors. The bandages had come off my arm last week, and physical therapy had been ordered. I still had bouts of pain that brought me to my knees, and there were times when the phantom sensation of my right hand made me want to cry. I mourned the loss, but what that loss had bought for my city was priceless.

And who knew? Maybe without my sword arm, people would finally stop calling me the Butcher. If nothing else, I knew people would appreciate the grisly poetic justice. For now, I simply pinned up the sleeve of my nicest haori and hoped for the best.

Kamon drove me to Hayes Valley. For someone who had survived a ten-story fall, he was in remarkably good shape. When I'd asked him about the fall, he'd only smiled and reminded me that cats always landed on their feet.

He waited in the Jeep as I stood on the porch of Tessa and Andie's lovely Victorian home. The neighborhood was a few miles away from Lotus Lane, but they had still been subject to an onslaught of rain during Cháofēng's occupation. Things were muddled for most Jiārén, but it was clear to me that First Law no longer applied. It was past time I came clean with Tessa.

I pressed the button of their door camera and watched the blue light swirl in a circle before steps approached the door. Andie opened the door in her characteristic running gear, strong and slender as a willow. Her eyes widened at the sight of me and she gasped when she saw the pinned sleeve where my right arm used to be. "Emiko!"

She rushed onto the porch and gathered me into a quick hug. She smelled like herbs from her garden, fresh and earthy. "Hi, Andie."

She released me and pressed her hands to my face, her palms cool as she gently tilted my chin. "Girl, what happened?"

Inexplicably my eyes filled with tears. I didn't even know where to start. "Is Tessa here? It'll be easier if I tell you both at once."

Andie let go of my face and frowned. Her eyes flicked to the open door and then back to me. I knew Tessa was inside.

"Emiko, we saw you on the news . . ." She shook her head.

I'd created a miniature sun to dispel Cháofēng's fog. My father's army had stormed Lotus Lane. An army of Shisa dogs' howls had echoed through the night air. I could only imagine what other incredible sights Wàirén technology had captured.

"That's what I was coming to talk to you about . . ." I licked my lips, my mouth suddenly dry. "About my family and why I've been gone a lot lately."

Andie gestured to my pinned sleeve. "And what happened to you?"

I nodded, my throat tight as I realized that Tessa wasn't coming out to the porch to talk to me now. Maybe not ever.

Andie's lips firmed and her eyebrows drew down as if she'd come to a decision. "Look, I'll tell Tessa you came by. We want to hear all of it. Really." She looked back into the house and her voice lowered. "She just needs a little time to process."

More like she needed time to understand how she could be partners with me for years and never know anything about my family, my abilities, and just how I was able to procure all those finds for our small artifact business.

I gave Andie a tight nod. "I understand."

Her eyes were sympathetic as she shut the door.

In the Jeep I let the tears come. Kamon offered me a handkerchief and I mopped my face as we drove to Lotus Lane in silence. I told myself that Tessa and I had time, and that I wouldn't give up. I tucked the hankie in my pocket and ran my fingers over the familiar ridges of Bao's pendant for comfort.

The cleanup of Lotus Lane was nearly done, but there were still plenty of big projects to tackle. I tapped Adam to act as liaison between the Lotus Lane Merchant Association and the San Francisco city government. All his prickliness from the night of the opening had vanished once Kenji woke up. Adam's new position would afford us a lot of interesting opportunities, and I knew his instincts were good. Certainly I'd been on the other end of his negotiation tactics before and was glad we'd be on the same side going forward.

There was plenty of work to go around, and like my father, Adam was excellent at getting the sticky wheels of bureaucracy to turn. A few people in city hall had been made a little more aware of just what kind of business happened on Lotus Lane. On Adam's advice, we were moving slower on that front than I would have liked, but his approach seemed to be working, so I let him run with it.

With today's event in mind, we'd arranged for the road in front of my "temple" to be moved to the top of the list for repairs. Even with the entire width of the road repaired, we still managed to fill all the folding chairs. The overflow of spectators made do with standing on the opposite sidewalk, and off to the side in the construction zones. Kamon and I picked out a spot far to the back, where fewer people might bump into me. Or see me.

I looked up at what was now dubbed Phoenix Hall. Cháofēng's changes to my former Sentinel's Hall had oddly made it only more majestic, the previously graceful slopes of the roofline now luminous with some kind of tile that was as dark and mysterious as the deepest parts of the ocean.

A small stage had been erected on the steps leading to the front door. The festivities were scheduled to start soon, so the little entourage cutting through the crowd caused a bit of a stir. Instead of heading for the reserved seats at the front, the movement came our way.

Kamon's eyes narrowed and he moved to put himself slightly ahead of me, protecting my right side. The group broke through the crowd, a circle of Louie enforcers with Uncle Jimmy and Leanna at the center.

My breath caught. Leanna's hair was cut to a severe bob and she was dressed in white—mourning for her father. She walked just ahead of her uncle. I put my hand on Kamon's arm and moved around him. If Leanna had stepped into her role, I owed it to her to face her on my own.

Leanna gave me a shallow wai. "Sentinel."

Once, she had called me Sifu. I knelt, so we could see eye to eye. "Leanna."

Her head tipped ever so slightly to her uncle before she fixed back on me. "Thank you, Sentinel, for opening this school, and for accepting my application to attend."

With their Hoard crippled, the Louies had no standing at Lóng Kǒu anymore.

"Leanna—"

"Thank you for your generous Hoard donation. My family will use it to rebuild, and I promise we will return the Jiārén community, and the city, to its former prosperity."

So, it was going to be like this. "I was happy to provide it, with no expectation of reciprocity. You are my Jiārén."

This time Leanna did hesitate and look to her uncle for guidance. Uncle Jimmy gave her a brisk nod. She'd done her job. Leanna gave me another wai and turned to leave. I tried to catch her eye again but she was gone. It was more than I expected, but less than I had hoped for. Jimmy held my gaze for a moment longer before he turned, putting a protective arm over Leanna's shoulders as they walked away.

I stood up and the crowd filled in around us.

Kamon tracked the Louie entourage as they left. "I don't trust him."

I shook my head. "I usually don't either, but I trust him to do right by Leanna."

"I don't like it."

"It's okay. They're too weak to make a move now. And my father was right. Just because I said it, doesn't mean there were no strings to my Hoard donation. Their clan strength can grow now because of me. He wouldn't dare move on me."

"That won't last forever."

I shrugged. "They need to focus on rebuilding. By the time they've recovered, Leanna will come into her own. I can't change Jimmy, but I believe in her."

"The same way you believe in Kaida? Is that why you told everyone she died?"

Hearing my cousin's name squeezed my heart. "She lost control over her life because of my mistakes. I can't measure my debt to her."

"She tried to kill you."

Kaida had walked the path meant for me. "She endured years at Jōkōryūkai. I know what that can do to your mind. And Batuhan put her under the influence of blood jade. Kaida needs a fresh start, and I can give it to her. After all she's lived through, because of me, it's the least I can do. I have to believe that she'll take it."

Kamon tilted his head, considering. After the silence stretched out between us, he relented. "I understand."

A final band of tension around my heart broke loose and I savored the warmth and gratitude spreading through my chest. I could always unburden myself to Kamon's gentle compassion. No one else would have agreed with me, let alone understood. Not the way he did. I lifted my head and caught a last glimpse of Leanna's white dress before she vanished into the crowd. "The school is a new start. For everyone."

Kamon heard the way I said it, and gave my forearm a gentle squeeze.

Up at the stage, the speakers filed out and took their seats. To slightly raucous applause, Freddy took the stage and made his way to the microphone.

Freddy cut an interesting figure, standing behind the lectern. The suit said powerful CEO. The long, ragged haircut said let's skive off work and catch some waves. The scar on his face and the patch over his eye said . . . pirate? He wore suits a lot more now. I missed seeing him carefree in board shorts.

Despite the confused imagery, he worked the crowd well, peppering his speech with enough funny anecdotes to keep the audience engaged and awake. After the talking was over, there was only the ribbon to cut.

Ever the gentleman, Freddy invited Fiona to the stage and asked her to do the honors. She wore a somber gray sleeveless dress, perfectly tailored to her slim form, and patent leather black ballet flats. I wasn't used to seeing her in anything so staid. Fiona tilted her head in a demure smile, deferring the honor to the new headmaster. Freddy blushed and cut the ribbon, officially opening the first Phoenix Hall School. Everyone applauded and lined up to tour the new facility.

Kamon and I hung back, avoiding the tight press of bodies approaching the doors. The crowd actually gave us quite a bit of space. The steady low growl from Kamon might have been the reason. I wasn't in a hurry to get inside anyway. Freddy finally finished shaking hands and posing for photos. He spotted us over the crowd and made a beeline for us.

I wiped my suddenly sweaty palm on my jacket. Kamon put a steadying hand at my back. Freddy wove through the crowd and when he made it to our little island of calm he pulled up short, his eye going to my pinned-up sleeve. I forced my left hand to hang at my side, resisting the urge to cover my missing arm.

So of course my gaze went right to the patch over Freddy's left eye.

In that moment we both realized what we'd done and the tension broke. Freddy's face eased into his trademark sunny smile and he rushed up to me, his arms wide. "How do I do this without hurting you?"

I hooked my hand around his neck and pulled him in for a hug. His arms closed around me. It hurt but I didn't care. Freddy tried to pull back when I flinched but I held him close. "I'm good." And I realized it was true.

When we broke apart I lifted my hand to his face, tracing the backs of my fingers along the scar that ran up his cheek and under the patch. I chuckled through the tears. "Very dashing."

"I know! Fi wants me to get it fixed but I think I want to try out this new vibe."

Fiona's voice cut in from behind Freddy. "That pirate patch is not dashing, it's horrid."

She stepped into our little bubble, smiled quickly at Kamon and then her expression grew stiff as her eyes moved to me. Fiona dropped her head as she gave me a formal wai. The bow felt wrong between us. Where were her ridiculous air kisses? Not that I missed them, but I understood them. But like Leanna, Fiona seemed bent on keeping things formal. Maybe it was for the best. I'd failed to fulfill the Talon Call, and to make things more awkward, her ex who was also my ex was standing beside me now.

I spoke up before Fiona could. I kept my eyes rigidly on her. "I tried, Fi. I really did."

A shadow of anguish passed over her eyes. "I know."

My shoulders loosened a bit. She believed me. Fiona took a moment and visibly recalibrated. "I underestimated you, right from the beginning, and I apologize for that. Is there anything the Trans can do for you, Sentinel?"

My brain stuttered as I tried to process not merely her words, but what was underneath them. Even Freddy looked perplexed.

Did she think she owed me something? Father had been right, after all. Saving Fiona's family had only made her feel beholden to me. Or at least to the Sentinel. I didn't want this power dynamic with her. Not after losing Leanna. And Tessa. And Adam.

Funny, a few months ago I'd been trying so hard to avoid everyone, and now I was desperately trying to hang on to as many friends as possible.

I stepped closer to Fiona. "You can take a seat on the board of the Phoenix Hall School."

Freddy laughed. "Yeah, that would make you my boss, Fi."

Both Kamon and I grinned, and finally Fiona saw the humor in it. "As if you would ever do anything I suggested." She sniffed.

Freddy pointed finger guns at me. "Monday morning, bright and early."

I groaned. "Hope you have a coffee station in the teacher's lounge."

"I got you covered, fam." He leaned in and wrapped my shoulders in a quick squeeze. I smiled at him and looked uncertainly at Fiona. Were we going to be okay?

She reached up on her tippy toes and bussed my cheek. "Mimi, you're going to need a tailor for your jackets. I'll send mine over."

The familiar scent of her perfume was almost a benediction, and I smiled as she blew an air kiss at Kamon before turning to Freddy. He tugged on Fiona's arm and the two of them waved and turned back to the school. There were more hands to shake and people to impress. They would do fine, much better than I would have, in fact. Freddy had come quite a ways from being my assistant. The last few days had carved him into a powerful man, like an artist finding the soul within a block of marble. The students were lucky to have him. As lucky as having Madam Yao and the qílín as official visiting instructors.

"Emiko, everything is so much more entertaining around you! I think I'll stay a century or so here in your city." She'd tittered and then leapt on the qílín after making that pronouncement.

I shivered in the morning chill. The crowd had mostly dispersed, and Kamon and I had the sidewalk to ourselves. Even though my clothes were dry, my body was as cool as if I'd taken a dip in the Pacific. Earlier we'd walked a couple doors down and gotten coffee the way it was meant to be enjoyed, with plenty of cream and cinnamon.

It was awkward trying to drink with my left hand. A lot of things were feeling awkward these days. The place where the city had marked me lay quiet, its power thready, but it was there. Like all of us, I wanted it to heal faster but all I could do was wait and rest. Maybe I had finally earned the right to lay down my weapons. I looked at my right side, the phantom wisp of sensation that wanted to reach for Hachi. On my left, the empty space at my hip.

No more. That version of me was in the past. I had to focus on the future, and not just mine—those who had charged me to guide them.

What was next for me lay inside—a new kind of school. One that didn't worship the old Dragon gods and sacrifice our young.

"Are you done admiring your new Hall?" Kamon teased.

"It's not my Hall anymore." Thank the stars. It was for the students now, which was infinitely better.

He arched a brow. "So is there a reason we aren't going inside?"

How did he always see me so clearly? I didn't want to go in and I was dawdling. I had faced a dragon and lived, but I was too scared to step inside this building. It was absurd. I knew it but it didn't change the fact that my legs were like leaden weights anchored to the sidewalk.

"I . . . don't want people to stare at my arm." My arm that wasn't there, but sometimes itched.

He reached over and squeezed my shoulder. "Maybe they need to look. Maybe they should see what you did to save this city."

"I'm not some kind of hero," I whispered.

"Saving people is pretty heroic," he replied firmly.

I hadn't thought about it that way. Like maybe you didn't have to be a hero to be heroic—that taking action to save people was the metric that mattered.

"Is that the only reason you don't want to go in there?" he asked.

I ducked my head. "It might require talking. I don't want to talk to anyone."

His eyebrows furrowed and I thought maybe he would agree. Then his face brightened. "You won't have to talk. I'll direct all inquiries to Freddy."

I laughed. "Why do you think I hired him?"

He crooked his elbow, inviting me to put my left arm through. I did and we strolled in through the curved double doors of Phoenix Hall.

The last time I'd been inside, it had the look and feel of a corporate office, with charcoal carpets and sterile gray walls adorned with splashy modern art. Cháofēng's tenure had transformed it, the graceful high ceilings now supported by laminated bamboo columns. The gray brick outer walls held the patina of a forgotten era. The remaining surfaces glowed a soft white, much warmer than the corporate gray. Golden wood gave way gently under our steps and I marveled at the transformation to this welcoming space.

Scrolls inked with columns of calligraphy were mounted on the columns, the soft paper rustling against the smooth bamboo. Thankfully, they appeared to be Tang dynasty poems.

Freddy had made changes as well. The hallway funneled into classrooms on the left and right, separated by tall frosted glass walls. Etched in the glass of the west wall was the graphic of a phoenix in flight, soaring above a cityscape. My throat tightened as I realized that was me. Or at least, my city through me. Sometimes just before I woke, I had the sensation of cool air beneath me, a ruffle through my hair and the spray of salt on my cheeks like I was gliding over the waves. I didn't know if I would ever truly fly again.

Behind a moon gate were two doors, one with a discreet sign that said FACULTY ROOM, and another that said HEAD OF SCHOOL.

I had a feeling that Freddy's office would be nothing like the snooty headmaster's office at Lóng Kǒu and I was glad for it.

Classes started tomorrow so for now, students and teachers milled around in the classrooms and out in the courtyard. Kamon was right, I didn't have to talk to anyone. Everyone seemed to be mingling just fine on their own. We walked out onto the tiled floor of the spacious courtyard. The edges were lined with tall fruit trees, peach, persimmon, and cherry. A giant fountain splashed over rough-hewn boulders, and fat white koi swam about within. Wisps of smoke rose up from a beaten copper bowl lit with joss sticks.

I closed my eyes and let the scent conjure memories of temple visits and ancestor celebrations. This was a celebration, too, and I leaned against Kamon as I took it all in.

"Can we stay out here a while?" I asked.

Kamon smiled. "Why not?"

Popo was holding court on the east wall, pouring a selection of fragrant teas for the students and their families. Dried blossoms and herbs lay in small dishes, a long row of them that people oohed and ahhed over.

Sally Sun picked up a tiny cup of tea, held it up to me in a salute, and gave me a shy smile. Her free hand fussed with the new student binder balanced across her knees. Even though she routinely dealt with Louie enforcers in their store, she looked nervous as she sipped her tea. I doubted attending academy had ever been on her radar, but I had insisted. Phoenix Hall was going to be an opportunity for those who weren't born into Hoard Guardian families. Baby Ricky had urged his sister to go. "Bring back good stuff for the Emporium!" he'd exclaimed.

I returned Sally's salute with a nod and motioned for her to give Popo her attention. It was bad form to ignore your instructors.

"Nee-san!"

I whirled and my brother ran through the courtyard like he was five, his arms outstretched for a hug. Tacchan. His arms wrapped around me, only jostling my right side a little. I breathed in the familiar pepper scent and squeezed him tight with my left arm.

When we pulled back to look at each other, I couldn't help but beam at him. He looked radiant, his fair skin holding healthy undertones of pink. A far cry from the pallor of Cháofēng's trance. His eyes twinkled at me, and I wanted to pat his cheeks but he wasn't a child anymore. Also, he wouldn't like it if I mussed his meticulous makeup.

"Are you sure you want to stay?" I asked.

"This was my idea."

Maybe. Or Father was merely letting Tatsuya think that. I couldn't help but see the parallels to my self-exile, and how I had healed here in this city, letting it curl around me like a tabby cat. I had thought it was my idea, but Father always played the long game.

Tacchan spread his arms wide, a sweeping gesture. "I wish Mother could see this."

I did, too.

Our eyes met, and all the conversations we'd had while I recovered washed over me. Was Father right? Would she make it back to us without her anchor? I blinked tears away and gave him a watery smile. "Knowing her, she'd show up just in time for the persimmon harvest this fall."

He grinned back at me and in that instant, we were back at clanhome, the two of us running through the orchards.

"I need to find Colin, Freddy called a meeting." He rolled his eyes.

"You two can't be late to that, Tacchan."

I was surprised to find I was going to miss having a personal driver, but I couldn't let Colin waste his talent like that.

My brother grinned. "It's Professor Soong to you."

I snorted as he rushed back to the hall.

Just before the doors, a familiar head of wavy peach curls emerged from the crowd. Colin and my brother traded high fives. A young girl with a pixie haircut, and dressed in a sleek plum sweater dress over black tights and black Converse high-tops bounced impatiently behind Colin, looking like she wanted to be anywhere but next to her brother.

Colin urged her forward to meet Tatsuya. She grinned when Tacchan gestured toward her Chucks. Fellow sneakerheads, I guess.

A moment later Freddy stepped out, rolling a gong. With great relish, he swung the mallet and struck the gong. The sound rolled through the courtyard. Clearly Freddy was a natural as headmaster.

"Friends, please return to the meeting rooms. You will be welcome to continue touring the school this afternoon." With that, he bowed and headed inside. The crowds in the courtyard rushed to comply.

I tugged on Kamon's sleeve. "Let's not go in just yet."

We let the people go by, and then it was just the two of us the in the courtyard, the sound of the fountain serenading us.

"At least this part of Lotus Lane wasn't flooded." Kamon's nose wrinkled and I could almost see his whiskers twitch.

"Don't be silly. You love swimming." He'd always been a strong swimmer.

"Not in these clothes, I don't."

I grinned. Not even a war with a Dragon god could diminish his fashion sense. He always looked like he'd stepped off fashion week in Milan and this morning was no different. With Oliver, it annoyed me because he wore it like a costume. Kamon did it because it was who he was, and it enhanced his elegance. His creamy Burberry trench was perfect for the city fog that hadn't burned off yet. It lay open, draped over a pale blue cotton dress shirt that fit him the way only a bespoke shirt tailored in Rome could. The shirt set off the deep brown skin of his throat and for an indulgent moment I let my gaze wander up his neck and over the chiseled bones of his handsome face.

Kamon was beautiful by any measure but for me, it was the fiery depths of his warm brown eyes that always drew me in. His generous heart lay open in his gaze and these past days had pulled us closer and closer. I realized I was holding my breath because I couldn't bear the thought of not seeing him, not standing this close, not breathing in that cut-grass scent that cleared away all the bad thoughts and feelings that threatened to pull me under.

If only it could always be this way, the two of us, side by side.

Did he feel the same?

"Kamon . . ." I held out my left hand, hoping he would take it. Even now, after all I'd done to protect us, most Jiārén didn't like me to stand too close, let alone bear my touch, lest I steal their talent.

But Kamon had never shied away, had always trusted me, no matter how unworthy I'd felt at times. He trusted me more than I trusted myself.

"What is it?" He grasped my hand with both of his, and pulled me a step closer to him. Heat poured off of his body in delicious waves and enveloped my hand.

My pulse jumped. I had to ask now or else be angry at myself forever for being a coward.

I searched his eyes, desperately wishing I had the right words. But all I could do was tell him what was in my heart. "I've missed you."

His response was soft. "I'm right here."

"No, I mean I've always missed you. Missed us."

He didn't say anything but his hand squeezed mine.

My blood thundered in my ears, a roar of the waves. I was flailing but I wouldn't drown. Not with the cool sensation of the city keeping me afloat. I licked my lips, as if it would ease the words out. But nothing could do that. They were all difficult.

"Would you . . . could we . . ." I closed my eyes in embarrassment.

The moment of silence pulsed between us as he waited and my cheeks burned hot.

He pulled our joined hands to his chest, then spread my palm over his heart. It beat steady and strong and I wanted to lay my head there, too.

"Ask me, Emiko."

I swallowed hard, the bubble of hope in my chest lifting me above the waves, over rough waters.

"Could we try again?"

He placed a gentle hand under my chin, tilting it up. "Why?"

I bit my lip, trying to hold back the words that threatened to tumble out. Words I couldn't take back. But what did I have to lose? I already had nothing but the gnawing ache reminding me of what I'd given up. I'd been afraid for so long. Afraid I wasn't powerful enough to be a Soong, wasn't dutiful enough to be a good daughter. I had almost lost myself fighting a dragon.

But I had found the strength to survive it all. I had faced my fears, and fought side by side with my family. I had vanquished the enemy at the gate. How hard could it be to overcome the small foes that lurked within me?

Maybe this was why I was brave enough now to open my heart

to him, to share all the dark spaces that I had tried to run away from. Whole enough to trust him not to turn away when he saw who I truly was.

"Because you'll always be the one I long for, the one I want standing with me." The waves crashed over me, smashing everything in their wake, but when they passed I was still there.

I exhaled. "The one I have always loved, even when I was afraid to." The sea within me calmed and I was washed clean. I was empty now that I had finally admitted my feelings. Full, too, because I was still whole and strong, even as I confessed how much my heart had longed for him.

His eyes closed, and when they opened again, they blazed hot with emotion. "I let you go once."

He let go of my chin and wrapped his arms around me, pulling me close. "I won't do it again." His voice was raspy with emotion and my heart soared, a bird above the sea, wings spreading wide.

Under my feet, the magic of San Francisco surged like a king tide. That feeling of joy and rightness swelled within me until I thought it would burst. The force nudged me onto my toes and I bridged the small distance between us, pressing my lips to his, telling him without words that this time it would be different. I wouldn't hide who I was, and I wouldn't run away again.

This was a promise to him, and a promise to myself I knew I would keep. Forever.

ACKNOWLEDGMENTS

November 2024

When we were younger, we had no fantasy books where the protagonist and the cast of the story looked like us. Seeing Emiko's story across bookshelves everywhere, and in the hands of readers around the world, has been a dream realized.

Ebony Gate didn't start as a statement about Asian American culture. We wanted to write something fun, with big fights, big monsters, and big family drama. We wanted something that paid homage to the myths and stories our parents told us. By the end of that book, we had learned a lot from the writing process, and with every subsequent book, we've learned a little more about ourselves and about our readers. For *Pearl City*, we wanted to answer the question of whether redemption was possible for Emiko.

Pearl City was a particularly challenging book to write. We wanted to deliver a powerful finish that was worthy of Emiko and company. Like Emiko, we didn't do this alone. We are indebted to our editor, Claire Eddy, and the team at Tor for their tremendous work in publishing this trilogy. Sanaa Ali-Virani, Julia Bergen, Laura Etzkorn, Rafal Gibek, Eli Goldman, Julianna Kim, Jacqueline Huber-Rodriguez, Jessica Katz, and Jess Kiley.

Thank you to our narrator, Natalie Naudus, and producer, Katy Robitzski, for bringing Emiko and the world of the Phoenix Hoard to life in this audiobook. We really couldn't have asked for a better team.

Our agent, Laurie McLean, and the team at Fuse Literary have been a bedrock of support and encouragement. Thank you always, and in particular, Laurie, thanks for deciding to stay up late the night you read our first manuscript.

Thank you to the booksellers who have championed this story, showcasing it on their shelves, writing shelf talkers, passing around ARCs, and hand-selling it to unsuspecting readers. We have loved meeting you, talking shop with you, reading your encouraging messages, and hearing that you've been hand-selling our dragon magic books!

We have thanked our friends and family with every book and this one is no different. Thank you and we love you.

Special thanks to Andrea Stewart who passed on the legendary trilogy diagram!

Ebony Gate was written during 2020 in the early days of the pandemic and lockdown. It was our escape from the fires, orange skies, and the fear that marked that year. Five years later, the trilogy is complete. We hope this story continues to resonate with readers, and we look forward to bringing new adventures to the page.

With love and gratitude,
Julia & Ken

ABOUT THE AUTHORS

Nicole Gee Photography

JULIA VEE likes stories about monsters, money, and good food. Vee was born in Macao and grew up in Northern California, where she studied at UC Berkeley and majored in Asian Studies. She is a graduate of the Viable Paradise workshop.

juliavee.com

Twitter: @valleygrrl

Ann Dang

KEN BEBELLE turned his childhood love for reading sci-fi and fantasy into a career in prosthetics. After twenty years, he came